TAMED
BY A
LAIRD

AMANDA SCOTT

TAMED BY A LAIRD

FOREVER

NEW YORK   BOSTON

Cover design by Claire Brown

Forever
Hachette Book Group
237 Park Avenue
New York, NY 10017

Forever is an imprint of Grand Central Publishing. The Forever name and logo is a trademark of Hachette Book Group, Inc.

Printed in the United States of America

ISBN-13: 978-1-61523-193-5

To Donal Sean,
who provided the bones of this trilogy,
in the hope that he will be pleased with the result, and
To Bonnie Jenny,
who is not—and could not be—tamed by anyone

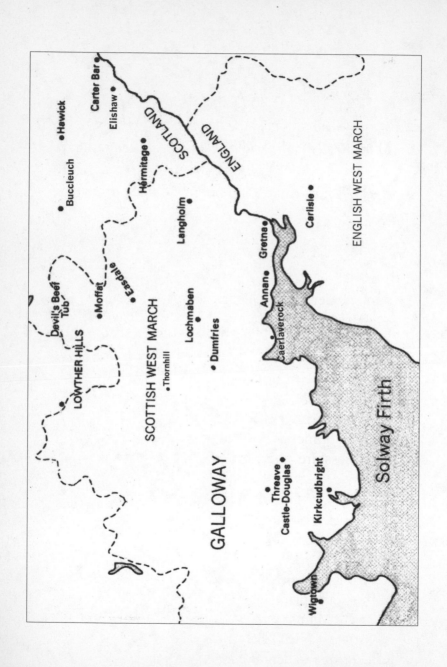

Author's Note _____

For the reader's convenience, the author offers the following aids to pronunciation and comprehension:

"Himself" = in this instance, Sir Archibald Douglas, Lord of Galloway

Caerlaverock = Car LAV rock

Castle Mains = (now Castledyke on an Ordinance Survey map) the primary seat of the Lords of Galloway from their earliest times. See "Mains" below.

Dumfriesshire = (west to east) Nithsdale, Annandale, and Eskdale

Easdale = EASE dale, Jenny's estate

First-head privilege = with no delay, like family, a right granted trusted visitors

Forbye = besides

Kirkcudbright = Kirk COO bree

Mains = the primary seat of a lord (from "demesne"), as in Castle Mains

Nithsdale = NEETHS dale

Snickering = a demand made without proper warrant

Snickets and ginnels = Yorkshire terms for narrow passageways between fences or buildings, used mostly by locals to avoid crowded streets (called "gates")

Tocher = Scottish term for dowry

Prologue

Galloway, Scotland, December 1367

Minstrels had been playing music in the minstrel gallery from the time the first guests of the new laird had entered the ancient castle hall to take dinner with him. Since then, a juggler had juggled, dancers had danced, and now a harpist was plucking merry tunes from his wee harp.

As the harpist performed in a cleared space below the dais, men swiftly set up trestles behind him and laid stout planks across them, an indication that the best of the entertainment was about to begin.

The harpist took his bows, and a man and woman stepped to the edge of the clearing. As he plucked out a tune on his lute, she began to sing:

> *From the East the Ass has come,*
> *Beautiful in truth and strong as a gale,*
> *So leap to the boards now, Sir Ass,*
> *And bray for us your tale!*

Drumming of tabors from the minstrel gallery and applause from the guests accompanied a long-limbed fool in a belled and ass-eared cap, whiteface, and the colorful patchwork garb called motley that all fools wore, as he turned flips and tumbled his way to the stout trestle stage. He leapt wildly onto it, only to sprawl in a heap on its boards. When laughter erupted, he looked around in confusion, then slowly raised himself to a handstand and flipped to his feet. Narrowing his eyes, he shifted his gaze to the high table and began to recite in a sing-song voice:

> *There once was a wee bit buffoon,*
> *Who dwelt in a gey grand hall . . .*

What followed was at first clever, even humorous. But it soon developed into a strange farce about a ruthless invader with an army of foreigners determined to subjugate a defiant land and its freedom-loving people. As the speaker neared the end of his tale, he made a sweeping gesture from the audience to the dais, saying,

> *Such is that wee bit buffoon,*
> *That laird in his gey grand hall.*
> *That he hath declared the king's peace on the land,*
> *A Grim peace for one and all!*

The crowded hall remained silent when his recitation ended, leaving only the sound of the tinkling bells on the fool's ass-eared cap as he made his bow.

The tinkling continued through the silence as he straightened. He looked bewildered, absurdly so, thanks to exaggerated features on the chalky whiteface that he, like most of his sort, wore. Apparently, he had expected applause if not laughter.

Instead, eyes throughout the hall shifted focus from his white face to the dark-faced, dark-haired man in the central chair at the high table.

"By God," his lordship growled. "What I've heard be true, then. Though you call yourself a wit and a poet, fool, you have composed only claptrap mocking my character and his grace's royal command that I impose peace on Galloway. Having prated that claptrap to the delight of mine enemies, you now dare to prattle it to me. Worse, you do nowt to make me laugh. Send him on his way, lads!"

Three men-at-arms stepped forward to carry out the order.

"My lord, ha' mercy!" the fool cried. "'Twas all done in jest, and it be blowing a blizzard outside. Sakes, but I do claim hospitality!"

"Faugh, that be a Highland notion and none of mine," his lordship snarled. "Afore ye speak ill of men with the power of pit and gallows, you should learn to cloak your words in at least a thin coat of wit. I *am* showing you mercy. We'll see if God thinks you deserve more from Him. Get him out of my sight, lads!"

Two of the three men-at-arms grabbed the fool, one by each arm. They hustled him the length of the hall, down a step, and across a landing of the stairway spiraling in the thickness of the wall. Pulling open the great door, they forced him outside, where thickly blowing snow covered the outer stairs and the courtyard.

As they marched him diagonally across the yard to the

main gate, his feet crunched on gravel beneath that snowy blanket.

The third man-at-arms motioned to the gatekeeper, and the gate swung slowly open, scraping ruts in the snow as it did. The fool's escort dragged him outside to a wooden walkway that he vaguely recalled led ahead to a river wharf and east toward a nearby town. Just outside the gateway, they gave him a heave.

Stumbling, slipping, he crashed onto the walk, where they left him.

He heard the gate swing shut, but the snow swirled so heavily around him that he could not see the castle wall or the edges of the walkway.

He could see nothing, anywhere, but thickly swirling snow.

Fear crept in then and grabbed him by the throat.

Chapter 1 ─────────

Annandale, Scotland, March 1374

Seventeen-year-old Janet, Baroness Easdale of that Ilk—but Jenny Easdale to her friends and family—tried to ignore the hamlike hand on her right thigh belonging to the man to whom, hours earlier, she had pledged her troth. To that end, she intently studied the five jugglers performing in the space before the dais in Annan House's great hall, trying to decide which might be her maidservant's older brother.

Since Jenny's betrothed was drunk and she had no information about Peg's brother other than that he was a juggler in the company of minstrels and players entertaining the guests at her betrothal feast, her efforts so far had proven futile.

All five jugglers wore the short cote-hardies and vari-colored hose favored by minstrels of many sorts and not one had a mop of red curls like Peg's. Jenny could find little to choose between them.

Reid Douglas squeezed her thigh, making it harder to ignore him.

Two fools in whiteface—one tall, one as short as a child and bearded—chased each other, creating havoc among the jugglers, who nonetheless deftly kept their colored balls in the air.

"Give me a kiss," Reid muttered much too close to Jenny's right ear, slurring his words. "'Tis my right now, lass, and I've had none o' ye yet."

She glanced at him, fighting to hide her revulsion and disdain. He was four years older than she was and handsome, she supposed, with his strong-looking body, softly curling brown hair, and chiseled Douglas features. And doubtless all men got drunk occasionally. But she had not chosen Reid and did not want him.

However, Lord Dunwythie and his lady wife, Phaeline, had made it plain that Jenny's opinion did not matter in the selection of her husband. Dunwythie, her uncle by marriage, was also her guardian. Had her father still been alive . . .

"Come now, Jenny, kiss me," Reid said more forcefully, leaning so near that she feared he might topple over and knock her right off her back-stool. His breath stank of ale and the spicy foods he had eaten.

She stiffened, bracing herself.

"What's this?" he demanded, frowning. "Now ye're too good for me, are ye? Faith, but I'll welcome the schooling of ye after we've wed."

Meeting his gaze, she put her hand atop the one on her thigh, wrapped her fingers around his middle one, and bent it sharply upward. "Pray, sir," she said politely as he winced and snatched his hand away, "have the goodness to wait until after the wedding to make yourself so free of my person. I like it not."

"By my faith, ye'll pay for such behavior then," he snapped, putting his face too close to hers again. "Just a month, Jenny lass, three Sundays for the banns, then six days more, and I become Baron Easdale of Easdale. Think well on that."

"You are mistaken," she said. "Although others may address you then as 'my lord,' I will remain Easdale of Easdale. My father explained long ago that once I became Baroness Easdale in my own right, my husband would take but a pretender's styling until he and I produced an heir to the barony. You will *not* become Easdale of Easdale unless I will it so. And I've seen naught in you to suggest that that is likely."

"We'll see about that," he said. "But a betrothed man has rights, too, and ye'll soon be finding out what they are, I promise ye."

"Here now, lad," Lord Dunwythie said from Reid's other side as he put a hand on the younger man's shoulder and visibly exerted pressure there.

Dunwythie was a quarter of a century older than Reid was, with dark hair beginning to show gray. His forbears had been seneschals of Annandale in the days of the Bruce overlords, so his lordship commanded great respect in any company.

"Lower your voice, Reid," he said sternly. "Ye've had too much to drink, lad, which can surprise nae one, but—"

"A man's entitled to drink to his own betrothal, is he not?" Reid interjected, shrugging his shoulder free and shifting his heavy frown toward Dunwythie.

"Aye, sure," the older man replied. "But he should not treat his intended wife unkindly. Nor should his actions distract his guests from the entertainment—which, I'd remind ye, I have provided at great expense."

Realizing that their discussion had drawn the attention of the powerfully built, dark-haired man on Dunwythie's right, and unexpectedly meeting that gentleman's enigmatic gaze, Jenny raised her chin and returned her attention to the jugglers.

Sir Hugh Douglas had sharp ears. Despite a desultory conversation with his host that now and again required dutiful attention, his younger brother Reid's gruff muttering to his betrothed had drawn Hugh's notice before drawing Dunwythie's.

Hugh was observant enough to note a spark in Janet Easdale's eyes that he easily identified as anger. Having seen Reid snatch his hand out from under the table, he guessed that the lad had taken an unwanted liberty.

Reid was inebriated, but it looked as if her ladyship could manage him. Hugh had noticed little else about her other than a pair of speaking eyes and deep dimples that appeared now on either side of her mouth as she hastily looked away. In any event, Reid's behavior was of small concern to him.

He liked the lad well enough, although he had seen little of him for years. Reid had been their sister Phaeline's favorite brother from his birth, some seven years before her marriage. He was ten when their mother died, and Phaeline had insisted then that he would do better to move in with her at Annan House than to remain with their father at Thornhill, the family's estate in nearby Nithsdale.

Their father had not objected, nor had Hugh. At the time of their mother's death, he was serving as squire to his cousin Sir Archibald Douglas. After winning his spurs on the field of battle two years later, he had continued to follow Archie.

He had done so, in fact, until his father died. Hugh had married six months before then, and he and his beloved Ella had been expecting their first child.

Ella and their newborn daughter died three months after Hugh's father did, and the grief-stricken Hugh had left Reid with Phaeline so he could devote his own energy to his Thornhill estates. Having had the chance to observe Reid for the past two days, he could see that Phaeline's up-bringing had done his brother little good, but Hugh found it hard to care. In truth, he had found it hard since the deaths of his wife and tiny daughter to care much about anyone or anything except Thornhill.

He noticed a gillie heading their way with a jug of claret. Dunwythie saw the lad, too, and motioned him away. Then he turned to Hugh and said quietly, "Mayhap if ye were to invite the lad to stroll about some with ye, sir, his head might—"

"Sakes, don't talk about me as if I were not here," Reid said in a tone more suited to a sulky child than to a man soon to marry. "I see a chap I want to talk to, and I don't need Hugh to look after me." Turning to his betrothed, he said curtly, "Don't wander off before I return, lass. I'll escort you to your chamber myself."

Her dimples had vanished, and Hugh saw that the curt command annoyed her. But she said calmly, "I never wander. Prithee, take time to enjoy your talk."

As Reid ambled off, she glanced again at Hugh.

He noted that her beautifully shaped, heavily lashed eyes were an unusual shade of soft golden-brown, almost the color of walnut shells. Her caul and veil covered her hair, so he could not tell what color it was, but her rosy cheeks glowed.

She wore a green silk gown with a snug-fitting bodice under a surcoat of pale gold silk. As his gaze drifted over her softly shaped breasts, she shifted position slightly. A glance upward revealed that her dimples were showing again.

Dunwythie's voice jarred him as the older man said, "I've been meaning to ask if ye ken the reason for this new tax that Sheriff Maxwell of Dumfries has demanded, Hugh. He is trying to impose it even on us here in Annandale, although the man must know that we have never recognized his authority over us."

"As you know, Thornhill lies well within his jurisdiction, so I must recognize his authority," Hugh said. "But his demands have increased notably, so I suspect the Maxwells need money to rebuild Caerlaverock."

"Aye, sure, and with Archie Douglas now building *his* new castle, we'll likely have them both trying to snatch gelt from our purses. I'm willing to support the Douglases because they can keep the English at bay. But the Maxwells have twice lost Caerlaverock to England, so I've told the sheriff I'll pay nowt . . ."

He went on, but Hugh listened only enough to respond suitably. He could scarcely advise Dunwythie. Maxwells or no Maxwells, Hugh's loyalty remained with Archie Douglas—now known to all as Archibald "the Grim," Lord of Galloway—the most powerful man in southwestern Scotland.

In the clearing below the dais, a tall juggler in a long scarlet robe joined the others, juggling six balls and manipulating them with deft skill. In whiteface like the fools but with a turned-down mouth and tears drawn below each eye, he looked older than the others, Jenny thought, too old to be Peg's brother.

Plucking a long dirk apparently from thin air, the man flung it high to join the balls. As his audience emitted a collective gasp, a second dirk joined the first. A red ball and a yellow one flew from his agile hands toward the high table, the red one to the ladies' end, the yellow to the men's.

The younger of Jenny's two Dunwythie cousins, fourteen-year-old Lady Fiona, leapt up and captured the red ball with a triumphant cry that on any other occasion would surely have drawn censure from her lady mother. At the other end of the table, a nobleman put up a hand almost casually to catch the yellow one.

By the time Jenny looked again at the jugglers, the older one was alone with six daggers in the air. She had no idea where they had come from or what had become of the four balls he'd still had when she looked away. Others had performed sleight of hand, making a pin or feather plume disappear from clothing of an audience member only to have it reappear on someone else. But this man was much more skillful.

Musicians had played from the minstrels' gallery throughout the afternoon and into the evening. But now, as the dirks flew ever higher, each one threatening to slice the juggler's hands when it descended, the music slowly faded. Soon the hall was so quiet that one could hear the great fire crackling on the hooded hearth.

Clearly oblivious of the juggler and the increasing tension his skill produced in his audience, Phaeline, Lady Dunwythie, fingered the long rope of pearls she wore as she said, "Our Reid is much taken with you, is he not, Janet, dear?"

Concealing irritation as she turned to her uncle's round-faced, eyebrowless, richly attired second wife, Jenny said bluntly, "Reid is ape-drunk, madam."

"He is, aye," Phaeline agreed.

"Such coarse behavior does naught to improve my opinion of him."

"You are young, my dear. So is he. But he will soon teach you how to please him, and I cannot doubt that you two will ultimately deal quite well together."

"I fear the only thing about me that pleases Reid, madam, is my inheritance."

"Doubtless that is true, although clearly he is not blind to your attractions," Phaeline said without a blink. "One must be practical, however, and although my lord husband would have preferred that my brother Hugh marry you, because 'tis he who is Laird of Thornhill and thus equal to you in rank—"

"Sir Hugh may be more suitable, but I'd not want him, either."

"Nor he you," Phaeline retorted.

"Faith, did you ask him?"

"I had no need to ask," Phaeline said. "Hugh declared two years ago, when his wife, Ella, and their bairn died, that he would not marry again. And when Hugh makes a decision, let me tell you, no one can turn him from it."

Resisting an impulse to look again at the dark-eyed gentleman at Dunwythie's right, Jenny said, "Surely, *you* can be most persuasive."

"Not persuasive enough to compel Hugh to do aught he has decided he will not do. However, you must not think that Reid is *wholly* unsuitable for you, my dear. Thanks to our inheritance laws, if Hugh dies without a son of his own, as he is likely to do, Reid will inherit Thornhill."

"In faith, madam, I should think Sir Hugh may well outlive Reid. He cannot be much older than Reid is."

"Just five years, and that was the difficulty until I realized that Reid should marry you. You see, Hugh refuses even to provide an adequate allowance for him. He is ever impatient with poor Reid, saying he would do better to win his spurs and perhaps even an estate of his own. But Reid has no great opinion of taking up arms unless a man must, and one cannot blame him for that—certainly not now, when we enjoy a truce of sorts with England. But had Hugh fallen in battle—"

"Surely, you did not hope for such a thing!"

"I am not heartless, Janet," Phaeline said stiffly. "But knights often do fall in battle, and our Reid must have an income. However," she added with a sigh, "devising a way to provide him with a proper one did vex me until—"

"Until eight months ago when your lord husband assumed guardianship of me and my estates," Jenny said.

"Aye," Phaeline admitted. "Easdale being such a fine and wealthy barony, one might say that Reid's betrothal to you simply arranged itself."

"You are very frank, madam!"

"'Twas providential, though, as even your uncle was quick to see."

Jenny did not bother to point out that it had proven other than providential for her. She knew she would be wasting her breath, just as she had wasted it in trying to avoid having her eyebrows and forehead plucked as bare as Phaeline's.

Phaeline had said that one must follow fashion, so Jenny's face was now a hairless oval framed by the expensive beaded white caul that concealed her tresses.

Applying to her uncle to support her against Phaeline would likewise prove useless. Lord Dunwythie exerted himself to please his wife, because he still hoped for an heir. At three-and-thirty, Phaeline was thirteen years younger than he was, but although they had been married for fifteen years and she had several times been with child, she had produced only their daughter Fiona.

Dunwythie's first wife, Elsbeth, had been Jenny's maternal aunt and had died in childbed just as Jenny's mother had. Elsbeth's daughter, eighteen-year-old lady Mairi Dunwythie, sat at Phaeline's left with Fiona just beyond her.

Should Phaeline fail to produce a son, Mairi would eventually inherit the ancient Dunwythie estates. Such occurrences were not rare at a time when men went frequently to battle, but most men hoped nonetheless for a son to inherit. And Phaeline had declared just the previous month that she was pregnant again.

Leaning nearer, Phaeline said, "Reid was wrong, you know."

Jenny looked at her. "Wrong?"

"Aye, for today is Friday, so your first banns will be read just two days from now, on Sunday. Thus, your wedding is but three weeks hence . . ."

". . . and two days," Jenny said, stifling a sigh of frustration.

But Phaeline was no longer listening. Looking past Jenny, she said to her husband, "Prithee, my lord, I would take leave of you now. In my condition, I need much rest. You need not escort me, though," she added graciously as she stood. "Pray, continue to enjoy this fine entertainment with our guests."

Dunwythie stood then, too, as did everyone else at the table. Those below the dais were watching a troupe of players run into the central space and paid no heed.

Summoning a gillie, Dunwythie told him to see his lady to her chamber. When they had gone, everyone sat and his lordship resumed his conversation with Sir Hugh.

Mairi immediately changed her seat to the one beside Jenny; whereupon, Fiona—doubtless fearing as usual that she might miss something—moved to Mairi's.

"Art reconciled yet to this marriage they've arranged for you?" Mairi asked Jenny as the players took their places to begin the play.

"Resigned, I expect, but scarcely reconciled," Jenny said. "'Tis of no use to repine, though. The betrothal is done, and Phaeline is most determined."

"I think Uncle Reid is handsome," Fiona said, her light blue eyes gleaming. She had inherited her father's eyes, but she looked more like Phaeline. Her pink gown plunged lower at the bosom than was proper for her age, and her flimsy veil failed to conceal the pair of thick, dark plaits looped beneath it. "You are lucky, Jenny," she added. "I just hope I can find someone like him one day."

"You are welcome to *him* if you want him," Jenny said.

"Sakes, I cannot marry my own uncle," Fiona said with a giggle. "But I do think you will come to like him in time, don't you?"

Mairi said, "Don't tease her, Fee. You know how much she dislikes him."

"But I don't understand *why* she does," Fiona said.

"We can talk about that later," Mairi said. "For now, if you wish to stay with us, you must keep silent. Otherwise, I shall tell Father it is time you were in bed."

"You would not be so mean," Fiona said.

When Mairi only looked at her, she grimaced but subsided.

Jenny had returned her attention to the players and was wondering what sort of lives they led when Mairi said, "That tall juggler was astonishing, was he not?"

"Aye, he was," Jenny agreed. "You know, my maid-servant Peg's brother is a juggler in this company. Don't you wonder what it must be like to travel about as they do and see all the fine places and important people they must see?"

When silence greeted her question, she looked at Mairi and saw that she had cocked her head and that her gray eyes had taken on a vague, thoughtful look. She said at last, "In troth, Jenny, I do not know how they bear it. No bed of one's own, only pallets on a stranger's floor, and traveling, traveling, all the time."

"But the only traveling I have done is to move here from Easdale, whilst you have traveled with your father and Phaeline," Jenny said. "You enjoyed that."

"Aye, sure, for we went to Glasgow and stayed with kinsmen everywhere we stopped. That was fun, because they were all eager to show us how well they could feed and house us, and provide entertainment for us. But minstrels must *be* the entertainment wherever they go, and if they displease the one who is to pay them, they go unpaid. They may even face harsh punishment if they offend a powerful lord. It cannot be a comfortable life, Jenny. I prefer my own."

"Aye, well, *you* don't have to marry your odious uncle," Jenny said.

"I am thankful to say that Reid is *not* my uncle," Mairi reminded her.

"He is as much your uncle by marriage as Fiona is my cousin," Jenny said. "Reid is gey eager to marry me and clearly expects to become master of Easdale. Sithee, *that* will create difficulty, because he knows naught about managing a large estate, whereas my father trained me to do so. Such a marriage cannot prosper."

Fiona said, "It is better than if they had betrothed you to Sir Hugh, Jenny, which is what everyone knows Father would have preferred. Think what that would be like! Hugh *is* accustomed to managing estates and would not care a whit that you can manage yours. Why, for all that Mam claims he was a mischievous child who liked to ape other folks' movements and voices till he'd get himself smacked, he is so stern and proper now that she says one could light a fire between his toes and he would just wonder if one had built it to burn as it should."

Jenny laughed but took care not to look at him again. Fiona's portrayal was apt, for Sir Hugh Douglas was unlike any man Jenny had met.

He did not flirt with her or tease. Nor did he laugh or make jest with his friends. And Phaeline had said that once he made up his mind, he never changed it. He would fold his arms across his chest, she'd said, and pretend to listen. But one's arguments would have no more effect on him than drops of water on a stone.

"I don't want Sir Hugh, either," Jenny said firmly. "I should infinitely prefer to choose my own husband."

"But you don't know any other eligible men," Mairi said. "Had Father taken you to Glasgow, or to Edinburgh or Stirling, I warrant many men more suitable than Reid is would have paid court to you, for you are beautiful, wealthy, and—"

"Prithee, have mercy!" Jenny interjected, striving to keep her voice from carrying to anyone else. "I do not count my worth low, Mairi, but my looks are *not* what fashion decrees for beauty. At least, so Phaeline has told me. And she, you know, takes good care always to be well informed about matters of fashion."

"That is true, Mairi," Fiona said. "Mam does know what people like. Indeed, she fears that one reason you have not yet contracted a marriage is that men consider your extreme fairness unfashionable."

Mairi smiled. "If Phaeline fails to give our father a son, leaving me to inherit the Dunwythie barony, dearling, men won't care a whit about my coloring. Jenny is already a baroness in her own right, and her estates are fine ones. Had your mam not decided to wed her to Reid before any more eligible noblemen clapped eyes on her, Jenny would have many suitors eager to admire her."

To change the subject, Jenny said, "Reid will return shortly, and I do *not* want him near my bedchamber. I think I will retire now, before he gets back."

"Sakes, Jenny, you cannot leave your own betrothal feast!" Fiona protested.

"I am feeling decisive tonight," Jenny said. "I want to go, so I will."

"Then we should go, too," Mairi said. Before Fiona could protest, she raised her voice and said to Lord Dunwythie, "Forgive me, sir, but Jenny would like to retire now. I think Fiona and I should go, too, if you will excuse us all."

Jenny glanced toward the lower end of the hall, half fearing to see Reid Douglas lurching drunkenly toward her between the trestles. She did not see him, but when she shifted her gaze to her uncle, she realized he had been watching her.

"D'ye want to seek your chamber now, lassie?" he asked.

"Aye, sir, I do."

He nodded and scanned the hall before meeting her gaze again. "I'll see that ye're no disturbed then."

"Thank you, my lord," she said with sincerity as she made her curtsy.

Hurrying from the hall with Mairi and Fiona, she cast one more wistful glance at the minstrels and wondered again what it would be like to be one.

⌒

Hugh was bored, so when the play ended, he lost no time in bidding his host goodnight. He did not want to spend the next hour exchanging polite phrases with other guests, most of whom would be eager to be away if they lived near enough to go home, or longing to seek the quiet of their bedchambers if they did not.

The hour was still early, and he was not ready to

retire, especially as he was sharing his brother's chamber. Deciding to seek fresh air, he went outside, taking care to avoid the forecourt, where others would be taking their leave.

The air was crisp, the waxing crescent moon high, and he heard the surf in the distance, for Annan House sat atop a hill overlooking Solway Firth. By walking a short way, he obtained a moonlit view of the water. The tide was surging in.

Annan Hill also commanded a view of the dark vale stretching northward and the golden lights of Annan town beside the wide, gleaming silver ribbon that was the river Annan. Dark woods and rolling hills rose to the east, while to the southwest he could see the gentle hills separating Annandale from Nithsdale, gray now in the moonlight. Southward lay the sandy shore of the Firth, its glittering water, and in the distance, the long English coast backed by tall, dark, distant mountains.

After two days spent in company, the solitude was pleasant. He had not been conscious of tension, but he felt himself relax as he watched the moonlight creating paths of silver on the waters below. The sight reminded him of Ella and the only time he had brought her to Annan House, to meet his sister.

He had thought it his duty to present Ella, because Phaeline had been unable to attend their wedding. It had been a small one, because Ella had been shy and Hugh disliked the pomp and circumstance his father would have demanded for the marriage of his heir, despite his lordship's disapproval of Hugh's chosen bride.

The only thing about Ella that had pleased the late laird was her portion. As the only daughter of a wealthy Lothian baron, her tocher had added significantly to Thorn-hill's coffers. Even so, the laird had thought her nobbut a wee dab of a lass.

But Hugh had loved Ella dearly. She had been sweet and quiet, and believed he could do no wrong. Although shy with others, she had never been shy with him.

She had been a gentle lass who never thought ill of anyone, and when she died, it seemed to him that most of what was soft and gentle in him had died with her. The rest had died with her wee bairn a sennight later.

He had stopped feeling any strong emotions then and doubted that he would ever feel such things again. Now, watching the moonlight on the water, he felt only linger-ing sorrow and the familiar, ever-present sense of loss.

Although Mairi and Fiona had offered to go with Jenny to her room, she had disclaimed any need for their protec-tion. "Faith, Mairi," she said on the first landing. "Even if Reid were sober enough to find my chamber, my door has a strong bolt."

"I thought you might like some company," Mairi said, unpinning and pulling off her caul to reveal a long tumble of silky, sand-colored hair.

"Forbye, it will be easier to send him away if we are all there," Fiona said.

"Right now, all I want is my bed," Jenny told them. "Goodnight now, both of you. I'll see you in the morning."

Turning away, she hurried upstairs, trying to ignore the gloomy mood that threatened to overcome her. She had known from childhood that she would marry one day, but it had never occurred to her that anyone could make her marry a man for whom she had no respect or liking. Her father had talked to her of marriage, but he had envisioned a comfortable and loving union such as he had enjoyed. He had certainly never imagined a man like Reid Douglas as his only child's husband.

Entering her chamber, she found her maidservant laying out her night things.

"Och, mistress, 'tis glad I am to see ye," Peg said, trying without success to straighten her cap over her untamed riot of red curls. "If ye dinna mind, I'm hoping to walk a short way wi' me brother Bryan and them, so I can talk wi' him."

"You mean to leave Annan House with the minstrels?" Jenny raised her eyebrows. "Will the lady Phaeline allow such a thing?"

"I dinna mean to ask her," Peg said. "'Tis more than a year since I've seen our Bryan, and I saw nowt o' him today long enough for speaking."

"Then you *should* go," Jenny said. "What's more, if you'll help me change out of this gown into a plain one, I will go with you."

"Nay, then, ye mustna do any such thing!" Peg exclaimed. "'Tisna fitting for a lady to be traipsing about wi' a lot o' such common folk!"

"I've been longing for an adventure before I must wed, even a wee one," Jenny said. "If I take off my caul and veil and don my old blue kirtle and a cloak, people will just think I am another maid bearing you company whilst you meet with Bryan. And if anyone does catch us, I will bear the blame," she added. "My lord and my lady will assume that I succumbed to impulse and you went along to look after me."

Peg hesitated, visibly moved by the latter argument.

"Hurry," Jenny said, feeling a surge of excitement that she had not felt since childhood. "Oh, Peg, this will be fun!"

Peg looked askance at Jenny's stout walking boots. "Them boots be too fine to belong to any maidservant."

"Well, there is still snow on the ground, and I haven't any others," Jenny said. "If anyone asks about them, just tell them I'm a waiting woman to her ladyship and she often gives me her castoff clothing."

"We'll ha' to hope that nae one o' them kens what big feet she has, then," Peg said dryly. "Will ye be having me tell any more lies for ye?"

"Aye, if necessary," Jenny said with a grin as she pulled off her caul and veil and began to unpin the long, thick golden-brown plaits thus revealed. "I'm no good at telling lies myself, so if we've any to tell, you must do it."

"What about Bryan? Must I lie to me own brother?"

"Only if he cannot hold his tongue," Jenny said. "But for this one night, I want to be just a common Border lass, Peg. That way, my going with you and the minstrels will not stir any talk or upset." As she spoke, she took a fresh shift from one of the kists, rolled it up, and stuffed it into a covered basket along with a hairbrush, a long scarf, and an extra pair of stockings. Then, snatching up her oldest hooded riding cloak and a pair of warm gloves, she announced herself ready.

"What be ye taking all them things for?" Peg asked suspiciously.

"In case I need them," Jenny said. "Hurry now, or they'll be gone."

⁓

Hugh continued to watch the churning, moonlit tidal surge, letting his thoughts roam as and where they would until he grew chilly.

Then, reluctantly, he went inside and up to his brother's room. Finding it still empty, he went to bed, expecting Reid to disturb him on his return.

Instead, he slept until a clamorous pounding on the door woke him.

Chapter 2

Learning from Peg as they hurried down the stairs that the minstrels meant to travel only five miles before camping for the night on their way to Dumfries, Jenny assured her that they could walk with them for as long as she liked.

"But ye'll no be wanting to walk five miles, me lady," Peg protested.

"Don't talk so loud," Jenny said. "And do not address me so when we are with them, Peg. I think I should be your cousin—and gey common, remember?"

"Aye, me la—" Clapping a hand to her mouth, Peg fell guiltily silent.

They found the minstrels milling in the stableyard, chattering and laughing as they piled things in carts or lashed them to loudly braying mules while Dunwythie men-at-arms tried to see what they were doing and what they meant to carry away.

"Do you see your brother?" Jenny asked, raising her voice so Peg would hear it above the din. She wished she had not done so when she saw the itinerant knacker, Parland Dow, passing by.

A tradesman of many skills, Dow had butchered beef and lambs for the feast. He served many noble families in Dumfriesshire and Galloway, and had first-head privileges with most of them, meaning he could come and go as he pleased. One reason for his great popularity was that he cheerfully shared gossip with everyone he met. He knew Jenny well, and she did not want him to see her with the minstrels.

When he rode past her, leading his laden pony toward the gate, she was sure he had not recognized her. In her old clothes, with her hood up and her hair in plaits, she doubted that anyone could who did not look her right in the face.

Peg, still eagerly scanning the scene, was quiet a little longer before she pointed and said, "There he is, near the bell tower. Bryan!" Shouting, she waved.

As the knacker passed through the gate, one of several young men standing nearby waved back to Peg and hurried to meet her.

"I'm glad ye came," he said, giving Peg a hug. "I ha' scarcely seen ye!"

"Aye, so we were thinking we'd walk with ye for a time," Peg told him. "Ye dinna all ride them mules, do ye?"

"Sakes, no, we'll walk ahead and they'll follow us— the carts, too," he said, chuckling but casting a curious glance at Jenny. "Who's your friend, lass?"

Peg gaped but recovered herself when her gaze met Jenny's. "I'll tell ye true, Bryan," she said. "But only an ye promise ye'll tell nae one else."

"Why should her name be a secret?" he demanded, frowning.

"Because I will it so," Jenny said quietly but with a mischievous smile. "If you cannot agree that whilst I stay with you, I am your cousin Jenny, then Peg must tell you no more."

Bryan looked at his sister, then back at Jenny.

"I dinna ken who ye be, mistress, but I ken fine that ye be nae kin o' mine."

"Will you not accept me so, just for a short time?"

"Dinna be mean, Bryan," Peg begged. "Let her come."

He shook his head. "These be my friends, lass. I canna tell them lies."

"I shan't ask you to *tell* them anything but only to accept what I tell them myself," Jenny said. "Many of my own people call me Jenny, and if we tell the minstrels who I really am, I fear they may not let me go with you. But, indeed," she added earnestly, "I mean them no harm."

"Who are ye then?" Bryan asked. "I warrant I should call ye 'me lady.' "

Meeting Peg's anxious gaze, Jenny nodded.

"She's me lady Janet," Peg said. "She just wants to ken more about the minstrels and them that she saw tonight, and mayhap enjoy a wee adventure."

Bryan stared at Jenny, his eyes wide with astonishment.

"Sakes, my lady, was it no *your* betrothal feast where we performed?"

"Aye, sadly," Jenny said. " 'Tis why I yearn for adventure now. Sithee, I'll have no time for it when I'm married, and that will happen in three weeks' time!"

"But what o' your betrothed man? What will *he* say about this?"

"He can say naught," Jenny said firmly. "He is not yet my husband."

Bryan hesitated, clearly reluctant.

Peg said, "What harm can it do? We want only to walk wi' ye for a bit."

Jenny kept silent, fixing Bryan with a somber but hopeful look.

He sighed. "Come along then," he said. "But mind, ye'll both ha' to turn back afore we reach Castle Moss."

"Castle Moss?" Jenny said. "'Tis an odd name, surely."

He chuckled. "'Tis named for the Water o' Moss on which it sits. They say the castle's walls be fourteen feet thick, but I dinna ken if that be right, 'cause we camp in the laird's woods. But tomorrow night, at Lochmaben, they'll let us sleep inside *their* wall. I warrant they dinna trust us in their woods, minstrels or no, nobbut what their castle be surrounded mostly by water."

"Lochmaben!" Jenny exclaimed. "But the English hold Lochmaben Castle. They have held it all my life. Do they not still occupy it?"

"Aye, sure, for all the good it does them," Bryan said with a shrug. "The Annandale folk keep them pent up inside and sell them their food and supplies. So they welcome us to entertain them every year when we come by."

Peg nodded. "'Tis true, me lady. Minstrels, fools, and players can go almost anywhere, even places other folks cannot."

"But you said only that this company was going to Dumfries, Peg," Jenny reminded her. "You never mentioned Lochmaben."

Peg shrugged. "I didna ken they'd go there, but it be

nae great surprise. Even Englishmen like to laugh and hear music now and now."

"Faith, but I'd like to see that castle," Jenny said wistfully. "Lochmaben was the Bruce's own seat, was it not?"

"Aye," Bryan said, his attention clearly wandering back to his friends.

Peg eyed Jenny with mistrust visible even in the dim light provided by the high crescent moon and the stable-yard torches. "Ye're no thinking we should—"

"Not another word, Peg," Jenny said with a laugh. "I think the others are ready to go now. Are they not, Bryan?"

"Aye, mistress, although them guards do still be a-searching yon carts."

"Cousin Jenny," she reminded him gently.

"Aye, cousin," he said with a resigned smile.

He made no further objection and apparently saw no need to discuss his two companions with any of the others, most of whom engaged in conversation and merrymaking as they went. Despite their long performance, they did not seem to be at all tired. Strung out along the narrow track, with carts and sumpters lumbering behind, the minstrels seemed to number at least a score if not many more.

Some sang, and Jenny heard much laughter, turning their procession into an adventure by itself, because she had never traveled in such rag-tag company before. Nor had she ever walked outside at night before for such a distance as five miles.

The moon and stars lit their way, and the air was clear and crisp. The track they followed descended toward the river from Annan House until they could no longer see the sparkling water of the Solway Firth.

They forded the river south of town. The crossing took time, because the water, although shallow there, was still too icy to ford on foot.

The mules and high-wheeled carts transported the company's baggage, while those afoot used a footbridge purposely made too narrow for horses and too wobbly for more than two or three people to cross safely at a time. On the west bank of the river, they followed another, hillier track toward the northwest.

Soon, the castle and town of Annan had vanished behind them, and the moon lit only the narrow track and the tree-laden hills flanking the long, flat expanse of Annandale that lay to the north of them. Moonlight reflected from the many silvery streams that tumbled down the hills to join the wider, twisting ribbon of the river.

Whenever the road crossed such a stream lacking a footbridge, as most of them did, men laid boards for a makeshift one so those on foot could cross. Jenny knew that one rarely found any bridges in the Scottish Borders, because Borderers viewed them as open invitations to English raiders and invaders.

Ever conscious of Peg's frequent glances but enjoying the minstrels' antics, Jenny watched them and listened to their songs as she tried to think how she might contrive to stay with them long enough to see Lochmaben.

She had hoped to retain her freedom just long enough to feel that she had enjoyed one small adventure. But to see Lochmaben, the chief seat of the Bruces, would be a special treat. The Bruces had been lords of Annandale for nearly two centuries before Robert the Bruce became King of Scots.

The English had occupied Lochmaben now for nearly ninety years, with only one brief interruption. Therefore, few Scots living in the dale had ever been inside the castle. For one seeking adventure, to learn that the minstrels could enter was simply too great an opportunity to ignore.

They soon came to a wider road that Bryan explained was one of many ancient Roman roads in the area. It was more heavily wooded there than the east bank of the river, and less populated, but they had not gone far when they saw that folks ahead of them had stopped to gather around something in the road.

A saddled horse and a pack pony stood nearby. Some distance ahead, a man sat on a white horse in the middle of the road and watched as other members of the company, some with torches, scattered into the woods on either side of it.

Jenny saw then that two of the men who had stopped were helping another man to his feet. Although he held a hand to his head, she easily recognized him.

"What's happened here?" Bryan asked.

"'Tis the knacker from Annan House," the tall, thin fool—still in whiteface—told him. "Someone clouted him when he dismounted to take a piss, he said, though he never saw who it was. The scoundrels must ha' been hiding in the woods."

Jenny glanced at the sumpter pony as Bryan said, "His packs dinna look as if they'd been disturbed."

As the knacker walked unsteadily to his pony, Jenny

avoided his gaze but watched nonetheless closely as he checked his packs and lashing.

He looked bewildered when he'd finished. "I dinna think they took nowt," he said. "I ken fine that I lost me senses for a wee while, but I heard you lot laughing and singing behind me before then, so the villains must ha' run off straightaway."

"Likely they heard us, too," Bryan said.

"Aye, sure," murmured the tall fool. But he was not looking at Bryan.

Following his gaze, Jenny saw two men she recognized as members of the company step out of the woods. As they strode toward the others, their colorful cote-hardies showed beneath the long dark cloaks they wore over them.

"Did ye see anyone, Cuddy?" the fool shouted.

"Neither man nor beast," the smaller of the two searchers shouted back.

"Any tracks?"

"Nay, the ground be all mucky from snow melt," Cuddy shouted back.

"They'd be gone now, in any event," the fool said.

The knacker agreed, but he traveled with them a half hour longer, until they came to a side road leading to a farm where he said the owner expected him.

The air had grown colder by then, and Jenny knew the hour was late. When the road headed uphill again, Bryan said, "Ye'd best be turning back now, the pair o' ye. As it is, ye'll be gey late by the time ye reach Annan House."

"Much too late," Jenny agreed. "The moon is sure to set soon, and I do not know the way back well enough to find it in the dark."

"Well, I warrant our Peg kens how to—"

"Nay, I do not!" Peg exclaimed. "Hoots, but I never meant to walk beyond sight of Annan House!"

"That was my fault," Jenny said. "However, I am sure, Bryan, that if we go on to Castle Moss with you and stay the night, we can easily find our way back by daylight. Mayhap the laird of Castle Moss will even be kind enough then to—"

"Mistress, ye canna stay overnight wi' the likes of us," Bryan protested. "What would your people—especially your man—think o' that?"

"Only that you were kind enough to look after me," Jenny said glibly. "Unless you'd like to ask two lads from your company to guide us back to Annan House . . ."

"I knew it," Peg said with a sigh. "Ye *want* to stay, and that be the truth of it, me lady. Be that not so?"

"Aye, sure," Jenny said. "I'm having more fun tonight than I have had for a very long time. You cannot bc so cruel as to make me abandon my adventure now." With a beseeching look at Bryan, she added, "Just listen to them singing up ahead!"

Bryan shot a look at his sister that Jenny feared boded ill for Peg, but he said only, "I canna make that decision myself. I must ask the Joculator."

Having no idea what a joculator might be, Jenny thought it wise to keep quiet. She doubted that any reasonable person would send her back to Annan House with only Peg to escort her, or send any of his own people all the way back with them. She would at least, she hoped, get to see Castle Moss.

Well aware that Bryan would make a poor advocate for her, she took care to stay with him and kept Peg at her side as he led them to the front of the company. There, singing in a pleasant tenor voice with the others, was the man on the white horse she had seen earlier. Although he had removed his whiteface, she recognized him as the juggler who had astonished everyone with his ability to juggle daggers.

Gaining his attention, Bryan said, "Sir, with your permission, my sister and . . . and her friend would stay the night with our company. They meant only to walk a short way with us, but what wi' talking and all, the time sped by. Now, they fear they'll miss their way back in the darkness and crave permission to stay—"

"Stay the night with us, aye; ye said that," the rider said, casting a swift glance over Jenny and Peg. "Ye were foolish to come so far," he said to them sternly. "Did ye hope to join my company as a pair of fools?"

"Nay, sir," Jenny said hastily before Peg could speak—if she had meant to. "Being a fool, as we ha' seen, takes more wit than we ha' shown tonight."

His stern expression relaxed into a peculiarly sweet smile. "Ye show some sense now, at all events. What be your name, lassie?"

"Jenny, sir," she said, smiling back.

"A bonnie name for a bonnie lass . . . And your friend be Bryan's sister?"

"Aye, sir, she's Peg. We're cousins of a sort, though Bryan didna own to that, being gey wroth with us for our foolishness and doubtless fearing, too, that ye'd think less o' him for being kin to such a pair. But 'tis my fault and none o' theirs that we be here. I'd fain learn more about minstrels and how they do live."

"Ye'll stay the night with us, for I'll no send two such

lassies alone all the way back to Annan House. 'Twould be nobbut what ye deserve, mind. But his lordship will doubtless punish ye both for this foolishness, so I need do nowt."

Jenny had not considered what Dunwythie might do. She had thought only briefly about Phaeline's likely reaction and had dismissed Reid's altogether. In any event, she decided, she would do all she could to extend her absence.

She was tired of not being able to make her own decisions anymore. Whether they punished her or not, she would first make the most of her adventure.

Sir Hugh had time only to open his eyes before Lord Dunwythie burst into his bedchamber, saying abruptly, "Jenny's gone, and your brother still lies in a stupor in the hall where he passed out last night. Not that I'd send him after her even if he were sober," he added with a grimace. "That lad lacks discretion."

Sitting up, annoyed and feeling even less interest in Reid than in Reid's betrothed, Hugh said, "Where did she go?"

"Heaven kens," Dunwythie said. "Nae one saw her leave."

"Then why do you come to me?"

"Sakes, lad, I canna go after her without creating the devil of a stir, and your brother would create a worse one. Nor can I send my men. Ye'll have to go."

"The lass is no concern of mine," Hugh said.

Dunwythie glowered at him. "'Tis nobbut your plain

duty to attend to this," he said. "I'll agree with ye that the lass ought no to have run off alone as she did, but we canna leave her to her fate. Worse, this start of hers will likely put my lady wife in a taking, which canna be good for *her* in her present condition. Forbye, Phaeline's your own sister. Ye canna want her in a lather any more than I do."

"Phaeline has been with child many times and seems none the worse for it."

"Aye, well, that may be true, but ye forget that the wee bairns have no fared so well. God kens, I want a son, so I'll no have this upsetting Phaeline. Bless us, but I canna think why Jenny ran away. I thought she had been happy here."

"I've seen gey little of her, sir, but I'd guess that she does not want to marry my brother. From what little I've seen of him these past few days, one could scarcely blame her if that is so."

"If it *is* so, she should have said she did not want him," Dunwythie said.

Hugh gave him a direct look. "Did you ask her?"

Dunwythie grimaced. "I canna say I did, for their betrothal was Phaeline's doing. But she told me Jenny would do as we bade her, and so she has till now. Still, if the lass didna want Reid, she could have told me."

"Could she?" Hugh frowned. "Unless my sister has altered considerably, I should think it would be hard for such a young lass to stand against her. In the old days, when Phaeline wanted something, she rarely let anything deter her."

"Aye, well, the question can be of nae concern now that they're betrothed. The wedding is set for three weeks hence, as ye ken fine. They'll be reading the banns on Sunday, and on the next two Sundays as well, so ye must find her, Hugh, and bring her back straightaway. I dinna want any scandal over this."

"If you don't know where she went, how can you be sure she has not sought shelter with kinsmen who will oppose the marriage?"

"Bless her, she has nae kinsmen of note, save ourselves. As to where she has gone, Phaeline thinks the maidservant we set to look after her must ken summat o' the business. After Phaeline breaks her fast, she means to question Peg herself."

"If you want me to find your missing baroness, you'd best let me talk to this Peg," Hugh said. "Phaeline may force her to speak, but as I recall my sister's grasp of geography, her interpretation of what the lass tells her may prove faulty."

His host chuckled. "'Tis true, that. When we went to Glasgow two years ago, she was certain we must reach Edinburgh first and kept saying she did not want to miss seeing the castle. As if one could be in Edinburgh *without* seeing the castle! I couldna persuade her, though, that Edinburgh's lying to the northeast o' here and Glasgow to the northwest meant we'd not pass through the one to reach the other. Sakes, but I think she believes there is only one passable road in all of Scotland."

"Just so," Hugh said. "Therefore, I will speak with this Peg, if you please."

"That would doubtless be wiser," Dunwythie agreed. "Then, whether Peg kens aught of our Jenny's whereabouts or no, ye'll be off after her. The longer she's gone, sithee, the more likely it is she'll come to grief."

Hugh agreed. He realized, too that he could not in good conscience go on saying that her disappearance was no concern of his. He did owe some duty to his family, and from what he had seen of Reid, that young gentleman would only make a bad situation worse. He realized, too, that he had no reason, other than the selfish one of wanting to go home, to refuse even to try to restore the lass to her guardian.

Even so, he could not help wishing that he had ordered his horse saddled the night before and taken his leave then of Annan House and everyone in the place.

With the last thought echoing in his mind, he said with a sigh, "Pray, send for my man, sir. If your Peg can provide a direction, I'll do what I can."

After attending to his morning ablutions and dressing, he joined Dunwythie and his family at the high table only to learn that Peg was also missing.

～

"Ye're no a fool, Peg," Bryan said angrily. "Dinna tell me ye didna ken what your dearling ladyship were about when ye brought her with ye. What did ye think were in that basket o' hers that she'd need for just a short walk in the moonlight?"

Jenny, having awakened that morning to find Peg gone from the tent Bryan had set up for them the night before, had hurried outside to find her only to stop short on the path when she heard Bryan's voice. Shielded by the dim light of an overcast morning and the dense woodland where the company had set up their encampment, she felt sorry for Peg and remorseful but nonetheless determined to keep Bryan from sending them back to Annan House.

That Peg kept silent did not surprise Jenny. The maid-servant would not want to tell Bryan she had known ex-actly what her mistress had put in the basket.

"Dinna be wroth wi' me, Bry," Peg said at last with a sob. "I ha' served her since she came to Annan House, looking more like a half-drowned kitten than a grand bar-oness. It had been pelting rain all day, and they had no let her bring even her own woman wi' her. And, too, she has been gey kind to me."

Wanting to hear no more reminders of how she had looked and felt on her arrival at Annan House, Jenny stepped forward. "Don't blame Peg," she said quietly to Bryan. "Had she refused to bring me, I'd have followed on my own."

"But why did ye want to run off, mistress?" he asked.

"Prithee, call me Jenny. I prefer it so, particularly whilst we remain here where so many others might hear us. Mayhap you will understand if I tell you I have lived at Annan House since my father died nearly eight months ago. For all that time, I have felt as a captured bird must feel if denied the right to fly free. Even hawks and falcons do escape the falconer's leash sometimes."

"But noble ladies do not fly from their protectors," Bryan said. "Nor do they deceive the people who admire and look after them."

"She did not really deceive me," Peg admitted in a small voice. "I watched whilst she put the things in her basket."

"Still, right is right, and wrong is wrong," Bryan

declared. "People at Annan House must be gey worried about both o' ye by now."

Jenny bit her lip. "I should not have brought Peg so far," she said. "I did promise to see that she does not suffer for aiding me, though, and I will."

"'Twill be harder to keep that promise now," he pointed out.

"All you say is true," Jenny said. "But, if I do not seize this chance, I may never know such freedom again. The man I am to marry has made it plain that he expects me to seek permission from him for aught that I do."

"Aye, sure, as any woman should," Bryan said.

Jenny sighed. "I cannot agree, but I know I have not explained myself well. Sithee, until I moved to Annan House, I lived with my father and our people. My mother died in childbed when I was a bairn, so I scarcely remember her."

"Your da should ha' got ye a new mam," Bryan said, frowning. "Most men o' property would ha' married again."

"Aye," Peg said. "Just as Lord Dunwythie did after the lady Mairi's mam died a-birthing her. The lady Phaeline be the only mam she kens."

"Doubtless many urged my father to remarry," Jenny said, seeing no reason to tell them she did not envy Mairi's having Phaeline as a stepmother. "But my father was a shy man and sought no second wife. Instead, he trained me to take his place at Easdale. I expect he raised me more as a son than a daughter. As a result, I had little by way of a normal childhood, because I spent most of my time with him."

"Did ye ha' nae friends or playmates, then?" Peg asked, frowning.

"I knew other children, of course, but they were all common and trained to treat me with great respect, because of my rank. Their parents and the others who worked on our estates or looked to us for protection did likewise."

Bryan still eyed her with disapproval. "At Annan House, did ye no find the ladies Mairi and Fiona friendly and kind t' ye?" he asked.

"They are my cousins," Jenny said with a smile. "I love them as kin, but we were raised so differently that I find it hard to feel close to them or confide in them. Since my father died, I find it well nigh impossible to confide in anyone."

"Aye, well, losing one's da must be gey hard," Bryan said.

Peg nodded, her expressive face revealing strong sympathy.

Jenny nodded, too, saying, "I used to ride out whenever I chose, go wherever I pleased, and attend to any matter needing attention without asking permission first. My father trusted me as he would have trusted a son, whereas I am a sad disappointment to the lady Phaeline, because she believes I lack all feminine accomplishments other than my music. She does like to hear me sing and play, but she frequently deplores my lack of skill with needle or scissors." Unable with propriety to share any deeper feelings about her life at Annan House, she fell silent.

Bryan said casually, "Ye can sing and play, can ye?"

"Well enough to please her ladyship and amuse our people, at all events."

"What instrument?"

"I can play a lute, of course, the gittern, and the French *vielle*—I think you might more likely call it an *organistrum*."

"'Tis an ancient instrument, that."

"My father had one," Jenny said. "He taught me to play it with him."

"Ye didna bring any instruments in yon wee basket o' yours."

"Nay, for I had only my lute at Annan House and did not think of it."

"I'm recalling that the Joculator has a *vielle*, but I dinna think anyone here kens how to play it. We ha' been asked by the laird o' Castle Moss to entertain him and his men in the courtyard today, though, afore we go on to Lochmaben."

Jenny kept silent, but a thoughtful note in Bryan's voice stirred a ray of hope.

Peg, too, was silent.

"Wash your faces and ha' summat to eat," Bryan said abruptly. "I ha' to think on this, but mayhap . . ." With similar abruptness, he turned and walked away.

"Well, of all—" Peg began, but Jenny quickly hushed her.

"I think he has thought of a way to let us stay longer," she said. "If so, I shall bless him, but I scarcely ate last night, and I'm starving. I hope there is food left."

Because it was no part of the minstrels' plans to burn their benefactor's woods down, they had built their two small cook fires with care in a tiny clearing.

Jenny could appreciate their care, although she thought it unnecessary at such a damp time of year. The surrounding shrubbery fairly dripped with dew, and what little sky showed through the canopy of leaves overhead was gray and dismal. The air retained an icy crispness and smelled of rain if not snow in the offing.

Her hooded cloak of moss-green wool was fur-lined and warm, her boots and gloves likewise. Like most Borderers—indeed, most Scots—she was used to inclement weather and paid it little heed. But had Mairi been there to ask how comfortably she had slept, she'd have found it hard to do aught but agree with that young lady's condemnation of the conditions under which minstrels traveled.

A mug of hot cider warmed her, and oatcakes hot from a griddle over the fire and spread with bramble jam sated her appetite. Peg introduced her to some of Bryan's friends in the company as a distant cousin, and she soon found herself chatting amiably with a number of people, including two women, a mother and daughter named Cath and Gerda, who identified themselves as gleemaidens.

Jenny learned that although there were but a dozen minstrels in the company, including three women, many other folks accompanied them, some as apprentices but most being family members or others simply wanting to travel with them. They earned their keep by providing services for the company such as cooking, mending, hunting, and fishing, or helping to care for their animals.

By the time Bryan returned, Jenny and Peg were comfortably chatting with the others. However, Jenny viewed his approach with some trepidation, gathering her wits so she might counter any further objection he might make to her staying.

"The Joculator wants to talk wi' ye," Bryan said. "If ye

follow yon deer trail through the shrubbery, ye'll find him in a green tent after ye cross the rill."

"I'll go with ye," Peg said.

"Nay, lass," Bryan said, catching her by an arm. "He wants to see her alone."

Chapter 3————————

Annan House

When Sir Hugh learned at the high table that morning that the maidservant who attended young Baroness Easdale had likewise gone missing, he said dryly, "Do your people make it a habit to run away from Annan House, my lord?"

"Dinna fash yourself, lad," Dunwythie said. "My lady wife has sent for her own maidservant. She's a friend o' Peg's, and will likely ken where she has gone."

"I'd think Peg must be with her mistress," Hugh said, nodding to a gillie to fill his mug from the jug of ale the lad held.

"You are mistaken if you think Peg is Janet's servant," Phaeline said. "She is ours and answers to me . . . or to my lord," she added with a coy look at Dunwythie that stirred in Hugh only a wish that her husband would occasionally slap her.

Repressing the thought, he said mildly, "It would hardly be unusual if Peg's loyalty has shifted to the young woman she serves."

"I should be most displeased if that were so," Phaeline said. Frowning, she added, "*You* would please me more, brother, had you taken the trouble to dress properly before joining us at this table. To present yourself in riding dress—"

"Dinna scold him, my love," Dunwythie interjected. "I have persuaded him to go after the lass. He'll leave as soon as we learn which direction he should go."

Fiona said, "I think—"

"Hush, Fiona," Phaeline said.

Hugh saw Mairi touch Fiona's hand in clear warning as Phaeline went on: "Mercy, but it must be plain to the simplest mind that one must ride north to go anywhere from Annan House but into the sea. I expect Jenny grew homesick and is foolishly trying to return to Easdale. That *is* north of here, is it not?"

"Aye, it is," Dunwythie said, patting her hand. "But she may not ken that as clearly as ye do, my love. She may have thought that she could more easily elude pursuit by crossing the river straightaway."

"Such speculation is useless without facts on which to base it," Hugh said, helping himself to some rare sliced beef. "It is true that her most likely direction is north, but the lass—indeed, both of them—may have gone anywhere and must be some distance away by now. We would be wise to learn as much as we can before I set out after them. I can go in only one direction at a time, after all."

Phaeline said with edged calm, "I still fail to see why her departure should interest *you*, sir. Our brother is quite capable of retrieving his own betrothed wife."

Taking a manchet loaf from the basket, Hugh took a bite without replying. He was hungry and had no interest in discussing his decision or Dunwythie's with Phaeline. As he chewed, he put down the roll and applied his knife to his meat.

Dunwythie said then, "As I told ye, my love, I *asked* Hugh to see to the matter. Sithee, I want no scandal, and thanks to his years of service with Archie Douglas, he has more experience with such delicate matters than Reid does."

"But this is Reid's business, not Hugh's," Phaeline said. "He should at least go with Hugh if Hugh is to find Janet."

Hugh continued to eat, but his jaw tightened at the thought of having to deal with his brother on such a mission. It was enough that Dunwythie expected him to run after their baroness and drag her back without saddling him with Reid, too.

Apparently Dunwythie agreed, for he said in the mild tone he seemed always to use with Phaeline, "I fear ye'll find Reid in no shape this morning to ride out for anything, my love. He never made it to bed but slept here in the hall with the men. I had two of them carry him to an empty bedchamber before I went to wake Hugh."

"Why did you not have them carry Reid to his own bed?" she asked.

"Because I did not think the sight of him would aid me in persuading Hugh to see to this matter for me," Dunwythie said with more bluntness than usual.

When she bristled at his tone, he added soothingly, "Nay, my love, dinna fidget yourself trying to defend Reid. I will own that he is young and deserved to enjoy his betrothal feast. But, believe me, he would no thank ye for rousing him now to ride after Jenny. Only think what his reaction to her disappearance will be, and ask yourself if ye want him tearing off in such a state to find her."

"It would serve her right if he did," Phaeline said. "She wants beating."

"One surely cannot blame him if he is angry with her," Fiona said. "It was wrong to leave without permission. But surely he does not have the right yet to—"

"It was indeed wrong of her, Fiona," Phaeline interposed. "But, prithee, do not interrupt us again. You know better than to do that."

"She spoke nowt but the truth, my love," Dunwythie said. "However, until we talk to Jenny, we canna tell what drove her to leave. Ye must admit that such behavior is most unlike her." After a pause, he added, "Hugh suggested that perhaps she doesna want to marry Reid."

Shifting position enough to see how Phaeline would react to that statement, Hugh saw that Mairi, sitting between Phaeline and Fiona, had apparently done likewise to see Dunwythie.

As their gazes collided, Phaeline said testily, "Do not fidget so, Mairi. If you have finished breaking your fast, you may go upstairs and see to your duties. You, too, may be excused, Fiona."

Fiona, standing, looked as if she might protest, but Mairi turned as she stood up, and gave her sister a gentle push. Making their curtsies, they left the hall.

Phaeline, still irritable, said, "How did you come to think that Janet does not want to marry Reid, Hugh? You must agree that 'tis an excellent match. After all, you made it plain these two years past that you will not marry again. So if Thornhill is to remain in the family, Reid must produce an heir to succeed, himself."

"Did you ask Mairi and Fiona if Lady Easdale had con-
fided her plans to them?" Hugh asked, wanting to avoid
discussion of his position and seeing naught to gain from
pointing out that any benefit from the match between Reid
and Janet Easdale would clearly be Reid's. "I'd think she
might have talked to them."

"Of course, I asked them," Phaeline said. "I was not
surprised, though, to learn that Janet had said naught to
them of her intention to leave. She does not seem to converse easily with anyone, and therefore has had much to
learn since she came to us. I am sure her father meant
well by her, but he was only a man, after all, and scarcely
equipped to teach any daughter how to get on in life."

Dunwythie said, "I find Jenny sweet and charming, but
she did have an unusual upbringing. Still, she is a gey
competent lass, so I warrant she will manage to look after
herself until ye find her, Hugh."

Looking toward the lower hall, Phaeline said, "Whatever can be keeping that girl? Oh, there she is," she added
as a plump young woman hurried into the hall. "Sadie,
come and tell us what you know of Lady Easdale's
whereabouts."

The maidservant hurried forward, pushing stray dark
curls back up under her cap as she did. Without stepping
onto the dais, she curtsied, saying, "I ken nowt o' her ladyship, me lady. Be she not in the house?"

Sensing Phaeline's impatience even from two seats
away, Hugh looked at Dunwythie, but his lordship had
already put a calming hand on his lady's.

He said, "Sadie, lass, we depend on ye to aid us. Peg
doesna seem to be in the house this morning. D'ye ken
where else she may be?"

Color flooded Sadie's cheeks, and her eyes widened, but she remained mute.

Dunwythie said, "Come now, if ye ken aught, ye must tell us."

Biting her lower lip, Sadie glanced at Phaeline.

"It becomes clear, Sadie, that you feel some mistaken notion of loyalty to Peg," her ladyship said. "Let me remind you—"

"My love," Dunwythie said gently, "this morning has been a most unrestful one for ye, and I'd have ye consider our wee son's well-being. I'm thinking we should let Hugh talk with Sadie whilst I see ye laid down on your bed. Come now, and I'll take ye up m'self," he added with a speaking glance at Hugh.

To Hugh's surprise, Phaeline made no objection to her husband's decision but rose at once and let him take her from the hall.

Alone with a nervous Sadie, Hugh said, "I must order my horse saddled, lass. Stay a bit whilst I finish this fine beef, and then you may walk with me to the stable."

If it occurred to her that he could easily shout for someone to take his order to the stable, Sadie did not say so. She just nodded and waited patiently until he had finished his meal. He did so without haste, as usual, and tried to decide how much he should tell her. When he stood at last, he noted with satisfaction that she looked less fearful albeit much less patient as well.

"You'll do, lass," he said approvingly. "I suspect we'll get on well. So, as we walk, I want you to tell me all you know or suspect about where your friend Peg may have gone. I vow you'll not suffer for the telling. Whatever the tale may be, I'll make all right for you with his lordship before I leave Annan House."

She glanced up at him as he touched her shoulder, urging her toward the stairway to the courtyard. "We'll go this way," he said. "If my man comes looking for me, I want to be sure someone tells him where I've gone."

Motioning a gillie over, he gave his order, then turned back to Sadie. "Now then, tell me what you know," he said, gesturing for her to precede him.

"Aye, sir," she said. "I canna tell ye much, except Peg canna ha' meant to be gone for long. Certes, but she never said nowt about going away overnight."

"But she *was* going somewhere, I think."

"Aye, for her brother Bryan be one o' the jugglers wi' the minstrel company that performed here yestereve. Peg had been busy all day and had nae time to talk wi' him, she said. So she meant to walk a wee while wi' them after they left."

"I expect she saw no reason to seek permission for this walk," Hugh said, glancing down at her as she stepped aside to let him go ahead of her into the yard.

Her color rose again at his words, telling him she was still nervous.

"Well?" he said when she did not reply.

"She didna mean to beg leave," Sadie said. " 'Tis why I ken fine that she didna mean to be away overnight. She'd lose her place did she do that a-purpose."

"I cannot speak for what his lordship will do about Peg, but I will do what *I* can to protect her. I *can* tell you that he is most interested in finding her."

Sadie was silent until they reached the stable, where

she paused to look up at him. "The lady Phaeline did speak earlier o' Lady Jenn . . . Lady Easdale."

"Aye, for it looks as if she went with Peg, or Peg with her," Hugh said.

"I dinna ken, sir, but I do mind one other thing Peg said about the minstrels."

"What was that?"

"That they be bound for the town o' Dumfries."

Hugh frowned. "If that were so, would they not follow the Roman road that fords the river a mile or so north of Annan and goes straight on to Dumfries?"

"I expect so," Sadie said. "But Peg didna say that. The only other thing I can recall be summat she told me a time ago. I doubt it would help ye now."

"Tell me," Hugh said.

"She said the company be going to entertain the Laird o' Galloway a few weeks hence, when his great new castle on the river Dee be finished."

"I hope that information will *not* prove helpful to me," Hugh said with a grimace. "I want to find her long before then."

"Aye, sure, sir, but I warrant she'll be back soon now. She'll no want to lose her place, I can tell ye. Forbye, I doubt she would ha' taken Lady Easdale with her, or that her ladyship would ha' consented to go in such company."

Hugh doubted it, too. He tried to conjure up an image of the elegant young noblewoman he had seen, traveling with assorted minstrels and players, some in patchwork motley and all easily recognizable as common folk.

He dismissed Sadie, certain that he had learned all she could tell him and uncertain whether it helped him. Dunwythie and Phaeline both assumed that Peg's disappearing at the same time Janet Easdale had meant the two had gone together.

The assumption was logical, but he put no faith in Lady Easdale's doing what was logical. His experience with the fair sex was limited, but those he knew tended to put feelings ahead of logic when it came to taking action. He thought it was just as likely that Peg, finding her mistress gone, had gone in search of her.

Returning his attention to the present, he entered the stable to find that his man, Lucas Horne, had already set things in motion there. Their horses, saddled, waited with another horse for her ladyship and a sumpter pony with its two baskets already laden and tied in place. Lucas was not there.

When Hugh's bay whickered softly, he moved to stroke the animal's soft muzzle and murmur nonsense to it. Hearing a sound behind him, he turned to find the lady Mairi Dunwythie eyeing him uncertainly.

"May I be of some aid to you, your ladyship?" he asked.

"I'm thinking I may be of aid to you, sir," she said. "I was coming to find you in any event when I met Sadie going in. She told me what she said to you."

"If you know something more that will help me find your cousin before she falls into a scrape, it is nobbut your duty to tell me."

"I ken my duty fine, but I do *not* want to betray Jenny if she is truly trying to get home again. She does not say much, but one can easily tell that she has not been happy here. And she does *not*—"

Stopping abruptly, she looked rueful, as if she had said more than she had meant to say.

"If you believe she does not want to marry my brother, you need not keep it to yourself, lass. I suspected as much myself when I saw them at their feast."

"I did think you looked like a sensible man."

"What possessed her to accept him?"

"Phaeline, of course. I'd best tell you the rest now, sir. Sithee, Jenny took great interest in the minstrels. She wondered how they lived, and tried to imagine traveling about as they do. I told her I thought it must be a horrid way to live, but I don't think she agreed. And now, Sadie tells me that Peg meant to walk just a short way with her brother. So I'm thinking . . ."

". . . that your unhappy cousin went with them," Hugh said when Mairi paused. "If she did, one can only think that Peg and her ladyship have no notion what such a life is like, or into what sort of company they are likely to fall."

"I don't know about that," Mairi said. "But I am sure Peg did not mean to be gone long. And we must find her, sir, because before I came looking for you, I learned that some of our guests are missing valuable jewelry."

~

Following the trail through dense shrubbery, Jenny paused at an icy-looking rill. Still seeing no sign of the Joculator's tent, she tried to collect her thoughts.

The man clearly led the minstrels, and what she had seen of his juggling skill indicated a person worthy of respect. Although his extraordinary dexterity offered no clue to how astute he was, she knew she would be wise to tread lightly.

The other tents all stood near the cook fires. That his stood at such a distance from them suggested he had a particular fondness for privacy.

The woods were silent, the shrubbery muffling the murmur of conversation from people near the fires. The narrow rill chuckled low as it tumbled downhill to join the river Annan. A low-pitched voice, although speaking quietly from shrubbery on the other side of the water, was loud enough to startle her.

"They do say the King may be at Threave to see us," a man said.

"I dinna want to talk about Castle Threave or the King o' Scots," a second, female voice retorted. "Not after being in such a fidget all through the night, me lad, wondering where ye might ha' run off to this time. I expect ye were wi' that—"

"Now then, Cath—"

Jenny cleared her throat loudly, hoping to prevent further such comments in what sounded like the beginning of a lovers' spat, comments she knew would likely embarrass all three of them.

The man stopped speaking at once. She had not heard any other sound of their approach, over that of the chuckling water, before he'd spoken. But clearly, they were nearly upon her, so catching up her skirts, she jumped across the rill.

Despite her subtle warning, her appearance on the path clearly unsettled them, so she sought to put them at ease. Recognizing the gleewoman Cath, Jenny wished her a cheerful good morning. "'Tis a chilly one, though, is it not?" she added.

Plump Cath smiled then and agreed that it was very chilly. "But just now, any day without snow be a good one," she added. "Ha' ye missed your way to our encampment, lass?"

"Nay, for I'm to see the Joculator," Jenny said. "I hope I'm on the right path."

"Aye, sure, ye are," the man said. He was smaller than Cath, in every way. With a gesture, he added, "His tent be off the path near that tall beech tree yonder."

"I thank ye, sir," Jenny said with a polite nod.

"This be my man, Cuddy," Cath said. "Ye'll be Jenny, if I remember right."

"Aye," Jenny said, wondering a little nervously if anyone in the company might yet remember, or recognize, her as Janet Easdale.

She had not worried about that the night before, in darkness, when she'd had her hood up against the chill. But morning light was more revealing, although she wore no headdress, had plaited her hair so soft wings drooped from its center part and nearly hid her high, shaved forehead, and although Peg had drawn eyebrows on her.

Nevertheless, it remained possible that by daylight the Joculator or someone else might recognize her. Cuddy did give her a searching look but then nodded and grinned when she smiled. She remembered hearing his name the night before and recognized him as one of the searchers she had seen after the attack on the knacker.

Bidding them both a good day, she went on. But as the Joculator's green tent came into view, its very isolation suggested that Cuddy's quizzical look might simply have been a reaction to learning her destination.

When Lord Dunwythie had agreed to Reid's suggestion and Phaeline's insistence that they hire minstrels for the betrothal feast, he had commented that, of all the folks who traveled to make their living—tradesmen, craftsmen, even beggars and such—only minstrels had developed a reputation for honesty. Nevertheless, Dunwythie had said, when one hired them, it was sensible to watch the men in their troupe, if only to preserve the dignity and virtue of one's maidservants.

He had told his people, therefore, to stay vigilant. But he had treated the minstrels with the respect he showed tradesmen he trusted, such as the knacker Parland Dow, who enjoyed first-head privileges at Annan House and at Dunwythie Hall, the much larger Dunwythie estate to the north. Dow came and went as he pleased, especially when it was time to turn Dunwythie cattle into Dunwythie beef.

As Jenny neared the green tent, her uncle's warning echoed in her mind, making her hope the Joculator would not insist that they talk alone inside. Her steps slowed, and she was contemplating the wisdom of shouting to him when the tent flap opened and he stepped outside, ducking considerably to do so.

He wore a long red-and-black striped robe that made him look even taller than he had looked the night before. His soft, flattened black cap tilted rakishly over one eye, and the shoulder-length hair that had looked golden by the light of the hall cressets, and silver-gray in the darkness afterward, was pale flaxen by daylight.

As he straightened, his gaze swept over her, piercing and shrewd. "So ye wish to stay with us, do ye?" he said.

"I do not ask to stay long, sir, but I'd not refuse an invitation to bide with your company for a few days," she said, relieved to detect no indication that he recognized her as the young woman whose betrothal he had helped celebrate.

"Ye speak uncommon well for a maidservant, if so ye do be," he said. "How does our Bryan come by a cousin wha' speaks like a lady?"

Feeling heat flood her cheeks, Jenny said, "If it offends ye, I'll keep to me old ways, sir, but ye should ken that I ha' served the lady Mairi Dunwythie for many months past, and I do try to speak as she does."

"I've nae objection, lass. I've made my fortune by learning to speak as my betters do whenever it will serve me, in this country and in others. Bryan tells me ye claim to play several instruments. That, I own, does interest me. Did he speak truly?"

"Aye," Jenny said. "But I warrant ye'll want to judge for yourself."

He smiled then, the sweet smile she remembered from the night before. "I will, lass. I certainly will. Let me just fetch out my lute."

He dove back into the tent and emerged seconds later with two lutes, one of which he handed to her. Moving to a rocky outcropping, he used the skirt of his robe to whisk off dirt and pebbles, then indicated that she should sit.

"Play whatever ye like and sing, too, if ye can," he said. "I want to judge your skill, but ye needna try anything difficult. 'Tis not the nimbleness o' your plucking that will impress me but your ability to entertain others."

Nodding, she swiftly reviewed the songs she knew and selected the Border love song she had been playing the first time Phaeline had commented on her skill. As Phaeline rarely said anything kind to her, that moment had impressed Jenny. Moreover, the love song had been one of her father's favorite tunes. But whether the song would impress this man, she could not know.

His lute was a fine one, its strings true of sound. Delighting in the instrument, she soon lost herself in the song. She was used to playing and singing for others, generally those she knew well, so she felt no self-consciousness now.

When she glanced at him and saw that his eyes had shut, an image of her father looking just so made her smile.

Opening his eyes, he looked as if he had detected the smile in her voice. Then, nodding, he reached for the other lute, plucked one string, then another, and soon was playing along with her. When the song ended, he began another one that she knew, and she quickly joined him, thoroughly enjoying herself.

When that song ended, he said, "Ye play well, and ye've a pleasant voice. Ye'll need to learn to flirt with your audience though, if ye would please them."

"Flirt?"

"Aye, sure, for how else do ye think to stir listeners to throw their gelt to ye? We dinna entertain for nowt, lass, and the more ye impress your audience, the more they'll fling. A tithe of all ye earn, by the bye, goes into the company fund to purchase aught we might need. Ye'll keep the rest for yourself."

She had not thought about making money, and the

thought now stirred only discomfort. "Might not some listeners expect other things of me if I flirt enough to make them throw money at me?"

"They may think about such other things, lassie, but nae one here will expect ye to act on their thoughts. One of our gleewomen invites liberties, the others do not. It is all one to me. We'll play only a short while here at Castle Moss before we depart for Lochmaben, so this be a good place for ye to show us your worth."   ·

"What about the hurdy-gurdy? Bryan did say that you have one."

He smiled again, but this time she detected sadness in him. "I do have a *vielle á roué* that belonged to my son, but 'tis an instrument that requires two to play it. We'll see after Castle Moss if ye'll bide with us long enough to try that, or not."

"I want to see Lochmaben," she said. "But I am unsure what I should do about Peg. This was all my fault, but I fear she may lose her place if she returns alone."

"She made a choice, just as ye did. Ye didna force her to come all this way."

Jenny nearly corrected him, knowing that Peg would have refused to go back without her. But she knew she could not explain that without revealing who she was and why Peg would feel obliged to stay. Remorsefully, she realized that she ought to have thought it all through before deciding to accompany the minstrels.

She had acted on impulse, a fault she had thought she'd long outgrown. Her father had been quick to condemn her impulses whenever she had succumbed to them. She could almost hear him scolding her now from the high cloud on which, since the day of his death, she had often imagined him sitting.

"Take that lute with ye, lass, and practice whilst we make ready to go. Choose two songs—one to sing and the second to sing if they like ye."

"How will I know to play the second one?"

"I trow ye'll ken that fine, lassie, just as ye will if they don't."

In the Annan House stable, Hugh looked long at Mairi before he said, "How many of your guests are missing jewelry, my lady?"

"I do not know, sir. I heard our steward telling my father and Phaeline only that Lady Johnstone and her daughter had missed things. It did seem to me, though, as if they had been discussing the subject before I entered the room."

"Surely, neither Dunwythie nor Phaeline would suspect a servant in their household of theft," Hugh said.

"I know not what they suspect, sir. I do know Peg, though, and I am sure she would not steal from us or our guests. My sister, Fiona, was also present then, however, and she has a knack for making mischief even when she does not mean to. She demanded to know if our steward suspected *Jenny* of taking the jewelry."

Although it was clear to Hugh that Mairi thought that unlikely, he did not know Janet Easdale. "Might she have taken it?" he asked her.

"She has no need, sir. Indeed, I should think it more likely that one of the minstrels, or even a servant, took it.

But Lady Johnstone says she is nearly certain she put her necklace away before she went to bed. The minstrels had gone by then."

"Sakes, lass, so had Lady Easdale and your Peg if you are right about them leaving the house with the minstrels."

"I know that," Mairi said. "I am merely repeating what I heard, sir. I do not have any notion what became of the jewelry. Nor do I know how much is missing."

If the two young women were indeed with the minstrels, Hugh had no doubt that he would quickly find their trail, wherever they had gone. It occurred to him, though, that before he left, he should learn more about the missing jewelry.

Mairi might be wrong about when it went missing. But, even so, if anyone raised a hue and cry to find the women or the minstrels, it would considerably impair his chances of resolving anything quietly.

Leaving word with a lad to tell Lucas he would soon return, Hugh escorted Mairi back to the house and went in search of his host. With a gillie's assistance, he found Dunwythie in a small chamber off the hall, looking over his accounts.

Gently raising his eyebrows, Dunwythie said, "Ye still here, lad? I thought ye'd be well away by now."

"I expect to be away shortly, my lord," Hugh said. "I just learned, however, that some jewelry has disappeared."

"By the Rood, I learned that myself only twenty minutes ago. I am coming to believe that rumors fly through the air on their own wings!"

"'Tis only a rumor, then?"

"I wish it were. At least five people have reported missing items, most last night but others this morning, my own wife amongst them."

"Phaeline has lost something?"

"Aye, her pearls, if she didna misplace them," Dunwythie said with an affectionate smile. "She does forget what she's done with her things, as I expect most of us do. But she nearly always has one hand on her pearls and is sure she put them away early this morning. She says she awoke, realized she had not done so, and got up to attend to them. I suppose she might have dreamed all that, but . . ."

"'Twould be a most coincidental dream, and Phaeline is not fanciful."

"Nay, although she does seem more forgetful when she is with child."

"Still, it seems unlikely that the minstrels or your Peg had aught to do with the thefts if things went missing after they left," Hugh said.

"Aye, and minstrels do take care to keep their reputations clean, lest they lose all chance of plying their craft. My lads searched them even so, and I dinna want a fuss. I've told everyone who lost jewelry that I'll investigate the matter, and each has agreed to leave it to me. Only one suggested reporting the thefts to the sheriff."

"I trust you persuaded that person to wait," Hugh said. "It makes no sense for me to act quietly if the Sheriff of Dumfries will be sending his lads out and about to make noises about stolen jewelry, minstrels, and missing maidservants."

"I agree, and I did make it plain that I'll take responsibility for the outcome. We must recover the jewels in any event. Much as I hate to think it, I fear we may have a thief here in the house. My lads wouldna ha' searched one of our own."

"Aye, well, I'll see if I can glean any useful information," Hugh said.

"You find Jenny," Dunwythie said. "That she was unhappy here disturbs me."

"Unhappiness is scarcely sufficient cause to raise such a dust," Hugh said. "I'd say that what that young woman needs—"

"Now ye sound like Phaeline," Dunwythie said. "But I dinna mind telling ye, lad, if this riot and rumpus causes her to lose our bairn, I may well take a strap to both of our missing lasses when ye find them."

Hugh had been hoping for some such declaration, if only because he found it a damned nuisance to be going after them. But when the mental image presented itself—of Dunwythie beating the self-contained young woman who had refused to let Reid intimidate her—an unexpected stirring of sardonic amusement banished it.

As he and Lucas Horne rode away from Annan House, it occurred to Hugh that had anyone asked him to explain that amusement, he could not have done so, except by admitting a growing suspicion that the lass would deal as easily with Dunwythie as she had with Reid.

She would not, however, deal so easily with him.

Chapter 4

Castle Moss, Annandale

Jenny looked around the noisy, crowded courtyard of Castle Moss, more than half expecting to see a familiar face. Reid must, she thought, be on her heels by now with a large party of men. She had been looking over her shoulder all day. But would he know to follow the minstrels or look for their camp?

It was more likely, she told herself for what must be the hundredth time, that Reid assumed she must be returning to Easdale. But would he assume that?

Recalling her conversations with Mairi and Fiona at the high table and on the way to her bedchamber, she feared she had said enough so that Mairi at least would easily deduce what she had done. But even if Mairi had, would she tell Reid?

Reassuring herself that, in any event, he was unlikely to catch up with them before she and the minstrels were safely inside Lochmaben, she began to relax.

Nearly all the residents of Castle Moss had gathered

enthusiastically in the walled courtyard, leaving a large area for the entertainers and an aisle to reach it.

Men-at-arms tried to keep a walkway clear around the perimeter but had little success. Music filled the air. Tumblers, including the two fools, tall Gawkus and wee Gillygacus, were trying to outdo each other with their antics. The festive atmosphere filled Jenny with the same excitement she often felt at a market fair.

Standing to one side of the intersection of the arched entryway to the keep, the perimeter walkway, and the aisle, she had a fine view of the tumblers and was amazed again at how easily they accomplished each acrobatic movement.

As they left the clearing, three jugglers darted past them to take their places there, sending colored balls into the air and to each other as they ran. The music quickened as a trio of dancers followed them, and Jenny suddenly wished the Joculator had asked her to play her lute with the three musicians strolling through the audience. Glancing toward them on the thought, she saw the flute player lean close to a pretty lass and wink, making her laugh. Nearby watchers laughed as well.

Smiling, Jenny shifted her gaze back to the clearing as a burst of applause sounded. The dancers were making their bows, the jugglers still juggling.

She saw the Joculator standing to one side, watching with a critical eye. As the dancers skipped away, he joined the jugglers with balls like theirs, apparently just one more of them, until his first dagger flew high into the air above his head.

She heard the gasps when he caught it and spun it upward again, followed by a second one, and she marveled again at the man's dexterity. Even now, in broad daylight, she could not tell how the balls had vanished as daggers took their places.

It had all happened so swiftly and smoothly that it was as if the daggers had sprung out of the air. The audience became silent until, flinging his arms wide, he seemed to scoop all the daggers from the air at once and then held them high to thunderous applause and shouts for more.

The acrobats returned for another turn, after which the Joculator moved to stand quietly in the center until the cheering and laughter faded to silence again. Then, he gestured to a lad, who ran to him with a stool.

As the lad ran away, the Joculator set the stool down and motioned to Jenny. He held a lute in his hand now, and where it had come from, she did not know.

Drawing a deep breath, she exhaled and went to take the lute from his hand.

The silence continued as he walked away, and she realized that he had so mesmerized the audience with his skill that by the simple act of inviting her into the clearing and leaving her there alone, he had promised them something special.

Her hands shook, but she breathed deeply again and slowly, telling herself it was just as it had been when she had played for her father and their household, or for special occasions when their people had gathered on the estate to celebrate.

Imagining that the folks around her now were her own people, she sat on the stool, settled the beautiful instrument in place, and plucked the first note. Then she looked up, found a smiling face, and began to sing to it, quickly losing herself in the music and words of the song. The song was her father's favorite, the same love song she had sung for the Joculator.

When she finished, the silence continued, surprising her and making her look uncertainly at the Joculator. As she did, the applause began, and the cheering.

When she smiled, the din grew louder.

She was stunned. They liked her! Seeing the Joculator's nod, she looked back at her lute and plucked the first notes of the other song she had practiced. It was a livelier ditty with a number of verses, a song known throughout the Borders. By the time she reached the third verse, the audience was singing with her and the other musicians had joined in her accompaniment.

When they finished, the applause burst forth at once and continued.

"Ye'll do gey fine with us, lass."

Turning, she found the Joculator at her side and beamed at him. "That was wonderful, sir. I never thought . . . when they were so quiet . . ."

"A high compliment," he said. Then he held his hands high, and the audience grew quiet again. Raising his voice, he said, "If ye liked hearing our bonnie Jenny's singing, ye should ken she'll be singing more as we travel on to Dumfries. We'll perform for the English inside Lochmaben Castle next. But after we leave there, any Scots wha' care to enjoy us again will be welcome to seek our encampment Sunday evening near Dumfries and watch whilst we practice, or to come see us on Monday in Dumfries market square. We'll be performing there each evening for a sennight."

The cheering broke out anew. But Jenny, although

enjoying it immensely, wondered if her adventure could possibly last until Monday, let alone any longer.

⌒

"Nae doots, we'll catch up with one or another of them lasses sometime afore midnight," Lucas Horne said bleakly late that afternoon when they still had found no trace of the minstrels. He added with emphasis, "*If* fortune favors us at all by then."

So far, Hugh thought grimly, fortune had shat on them.

Determined though he had been to lay hands on Lady Easdale by nightfall, he had realized some time before that it would likely take longer than that just to find her trail. The main track from Annan House had revealed no evidence that the minstrels had followed it. Nor could he or Lucas tell if they had taken another route. With so many guests departing, hoof tracks had led everywhere and nowhere.

No one at Annan House had paid heed to aught save the fact of the minstrels' departure. One watchman said he thought they had gone down through the town. Another thought they had headed east toward Gretna.

The Borders were at peace for once. The celebratory mood had continued into the night, and minstrels rarely took sides in disputes, anyway. So, aside from searching their carts and packs, no one had thought it necessary to keep an eye on them. Hugh had asked no questions about the search. But the very fact of it made it even more unlikely that the minstrels had any connection to the missing jewelry.

He and Lucas had quickly learned that the company had not passed through Annan town. But no one could say they had not simply walked around it. They might even have stayed east of it until they met the Roman road heading north, or stayed southwest of it and followed the riverbank to the first ford. If the Solway tides had cooperated, they might have crossed the river before reaching the town.

Despite Phaeline's certainty that Jenny would head for Easdale, and the possibility that she might simply have used the minstrels as cover to escape Annan House, Hugh could not bring himself to believe that any sensible young woman—and she had looked sensible—would attempt to travel such a distance alone at night.

After this careful consideration, he had decided that if the minstrels were heading for Dumfries, he and Lucas should do likewise.

Lucas had muttered faint protest, but Hugh paid him no heed. The man had served him for years and had traveled many miles with him. Lucas could always find something to complain about, but he had never let Hugh down.

They kept to the Dumfries road despite passing two roads that branched north. They found no one who had seen the company. As most folks were abed before darkness fell, Hugh kept going then for some time without seeing a soul.

"Nah then, we should 'ave found someone that's seen 'em by now," Lucas said at last. "They be right numerous, so I've me doots they'd be quiet a-travelin'. We've talked to dunamany folks as live along this road, sir, but . . ." He shrugged.

"Aye," Hugh agreed. "Someone ought to have heard

them. Try that cottage yonder, across that wee field. I'll wait with the horses and stop anyone who comes along. But I'm rapidly coming to believe they may have taken another route."

"Aye, I'm for goin' back to one of them branch roads, m'self."

"Try the cottage, Lucas."

With a nod, Lucas handed him the lead for their sumpter pony and urged his own horse to a trot, respectfully keeping to the edge of the field. To Hugh's experienced eye, it looked freshly planted. An optimist, he thought, to believe that winter was over when one could still feel and even smell snow in the air.

Lucas looked brighter when he returned, because fortune had smiled on them at last. "T' woman were up all night with a colicky bairn," he said. "Nae one passed by but silent travelers. However, she has a sister a-visitin' who lives a mile north of 'ere on the Lochmaben road. The sister were complainin' of a racket set up in the night by a great company of travelers—a-singin' and carryin' on, she said."

"Can we reach the Lochmaben road from here without trespassing where we should not, or must we ride all the way back to that last fork?" Hugh asked him. "'Tis all of two miles and more, I'm thinking."

"Aye, and I did think to ask t' woman. She said her sister be 'eading back shortly and will show us the way." Although Lucas rarely showed his feelings, Hugh could tell he was pleased with himself for acquiring such useful information.

The news, welcome as it was, revealed nothing of the two missing young women, and darkness would fall long before he and Lucas could catch up with the minstrels. Lucas's earlier observation that they would catch up with at least one of them by midnight was looking less likely by the minute.

Hugh could not doubt that wherever they had camped the previous night, they would likely have moved on at first light. He also realized now that they were not going directly to Dumfries, so heaven alone knew how many other places they meant to visit first or which direction they would head next.

He was beginning to become seriously annoyed with Janet Easdale. However, his mood lightened when their guide, a brisk young matron who called herself Mistress Moffat, guided them swiftly to the Lochmaben road.

As he thanked her, he said, "I wonder, mistress, if you can suggest a likely place along this road for a company of minstrels to camp."

She considered for only a moment before suggesting Castle Moss. "The laird there does enjoy the players whenever they come this way, sir. Faith, but he nearly always lets any as wants to camp in his woods. I warrant ye'll find them there."

He was just as certain that he would not find them there, but he hoped the laird of Castle Moss could tell him if the young baroness had been with them.

Only when he began to explain that hope to Lucas did he realize he'd have to be careful in his description, so as not to reveal what Dunwythie wanted kept quiet.

Castle Moss stood only a mile up the road, and although he'd have liked to travel on through the night since they would have moonlight, he knew that both he and Lucas would do better for a good night's sleep.

The laird of Castle Moss proved both hospitable and delighted to entertain his guests with an enthusiastic description of the minstrels.

"Most astonishing!" he exclaimed when Hugh asked about them. "One fellow tossed dirks about like clubs. Didna seem to mind which end he caught, and I swear to ye, he had eight o' them going at once. When he stopped, he just gathered them all together like a bouquet o' spring flowers."

"That sounds like just what I'm after, sir," Hugh said. "I'm looking to hire minstrels for our market fair at Thornhill, and I've heard that this lot is exceptional."

"They are, and the jugglers were only the beginning. Why they've a pair o' fools that nigh made me split m' sides laughing, and then there was Bonnie Jenny."

Hugh raised his eyebrows. "A lass? Dancer or a gleemaiden?"

"Ye might call her a gleemaiden, I expect. But the chief juggler put her out before us, all on her ownsome, and I'm telling ye, that lass has a voice like an angel. She sang only two songs, mind ye. And, although we shouted for her to sing more, the man wouldna allow it. Instead, he said they'd be at Lochmaben tonight—and doubtless tomorrow, as well, it being Sunday. Then they'll go on to Dumfries, he said. He kens his business, that 'un. He'll likely draw crowds wherever they set up their encampments, as well as in Dumfries market square."

"You did say they aimed for Lochmaben from here, did you not, sir?"

"Och, aye, but it will do ye nae good to seek them there, ye ken. Sithee, them English louts willna let in any Scotsmen unless they be minstrels or troubadours."

Having learned all he wanted to know, Hugh changed the subject and spent a pleasant evening with his genial host. But the next morning, as he and Lucas were riding away, he said to Lucas, "We'll make haste now that we know where they are. We need only think of a ruse that will get us inside Lochmaben Castle."

"Aye, sure," Lucas said. "Tha think t' lassies we seek be with them, then."

Hugh nodded. "No one with the voice of an angel sang at Annan House," he said. "If they'd had such a singer, can you doubt they'd have produced her? Also, Lady Easdale's given name is Janet, but members of the family call her 'Jenny.'"

"By, sir, ye're no expecting me to believe a young baroness in 'er own right be pretending to be them minstrels' gleemaiden!"

"I don't *know* that," Hugh said. "But I'll wager half your year's pay that the singer is either the lady Janet or the maidservant Peg *calling* herself Jenny in a hope that someone will hear the name and come to collect her mistress."

"Tha canna expect a man to bargain with half his year's pay," Lucas said scornfully. "I'll put up a groat against ten of yours on such a bet, but no more."

"Done," Hugh said. "Easy gelt, that is, and I'll not turn down a silver groat."

"Aye, well, I canna think what will get ye into Lochmaben without ye spin them one of your grand tales of why they should admit ye. 'Tis true that I've heard ye spin dunamany such tales in days gone by. But if ye think ye can spin one, snatch up the lady, and carry 'er off without raising a fearsome dust—"

"I do not think I can do that," Hugh said. Although he would never be such a dunce as that, he did realize that he had not yet thought the whole thing through.

"And just as ye canna snatch her from Lochmaben, ye canna march up to yon minstrels and demand they hand her over to ye neither," Lucas said sagely.

"True," Hugh said. "We'll have to be gey cautious in our approach to them, so let us discuss the matter as we ride."

⁓

"We should ha' gone home when we could, mistress," Peg said as they prepared their sleeping places at Lochmaben Castle. "I dinna like it here."

"But think of what we're seeing, Peg," Jenny urged. "No one we know has seen the inside of this castle other than the people with whom we're traveling, and this is the castle that produced King Robert the Bruce. He was born here, I believe, and it was the seat of Bruce power for years, even centuries."

"Aye, but the Bruce could go outside its walls when he wanted to," Peg said.

"We'll be out again by noon tomorrow—by midafternoon at the latest," Jenny said, correcting herself when she recalled that the commander of the castle had said he would provide their midday meal for them after their performance.

Peg remained noticeably nervous, however, and Jenny had to admit, if only to herself, that she had felt safer in the laird's woods at Castle Moss than she felt inside the walls of Lochmaben Castle. She did not know if the walls were fourteen feet thick, but they were certainly thick enough for two men to lie end to end.

Situated, as it was, on a flat peninsula jutting into Loch Maben, with most of the loch's surrounding land bog-ridden, the castle's famed impregnability seemed most intimidating when one was inside its walls, surrounded by enemies.

Bad enough that four water-filled ditches stretched across the narrow neck of the peninsula, all but the last one boasting temporary, easily removed drawbridges.

Worse was that the last ditch lacked *any* bridge, forcing them to go in boats through a main gate that opened right over the water into a well-guarded forecourt.

After disembarking, as they passed through the equally well-guarded inner gate and under a fanged iron portcullis into the castle's main courtyard, Jenny had looked back to watch the boats depart. That sight made her wonder if she had been dafter than even Peg had thought she was to insist on coming to Lochmaben.

She wondered, too, if she could trust Bryan to keep her full identity secret. He and the others—even the women—behaved as if they had no concern for their safety. But most of the other women, she had noted, had protectors of one sort or another in the company—husbands, other kinsmen, or lovers. She and Peg had only Bryan, who paid little heed to them now that the company was setting up a makeshift camp in one corner of the inner courtyard.

Jenny had expected to share a tent with Peg again. But although the yard was large, its paving stones made pitching the tents impossible. Feeling exposed not only to the chilly weather and dark, menacingly overcast sky but to the castle's roaming men-at-arms, she recalled Mairi's comments on the likely life of a minstrel.

Until now, her adventure had seemed no more than that. But catching one lustful look, then another, and another, she felt an increasing chill of unease.

To be sure, the looks came from the men-at-arms and not, so far, from any of the minstrels. Even so, she doubted that the latter group would leap to defend her virtue against such odds as they faced inside Lochmaben.

"We must take care to stay together with your brother and his friends or with the other women, Peg," she said as they made their way toward Bryan.

"Aye, sure," Peg agreed vaguely, glancing toward the sky. "D'ye think it will snow in the night, m'lady?"

"Sakes, Peg, would you expose my rank to everyone here?" Jenny said. "I depend on you to protect me, and you'll not do it by flinging m'ladys about."

"Ay de mi!" Peg exclaimed. "But 'tis harder than ye ken! Them two words just fly off me tongue when I speak to ye."

"Then think before you speak," Jenny advised, espying the Joculator making his way toward them through the other minstrels, who were swiftly establishing spaces for themselves in the designated sleeping area.

"I've asked the others to provide ye two with extra bedding," the Joculator told them. "However, I came to tell *ye*, Jenny, that although the commander of the castle will reserve our full performance for their midday meal tomorrow, he wants us to provide music for their supper tonight. Apparently, lass, someone who heard you at Castle Moss has whispered in the man's ear."

"Mercy, do you mean he wants to hear *me* sing?" Jenny asked. "Tonight?"

Although Phaeline had complimented her musical abilities, she had never led Jenny to think them extraordinary, and she did not know what to think now. That the English commander wanted to hear her sing was flattering. But for him to have singled her out in such a way was disconcerting—even, she decided, a little frightening.

The Joculator's attractive smile flashed. "I had suggested that our musicians might play from the minstrels' gallery, and he had agreed. But then he insisted that our bonnie Jenny must sing, too, and *not* from the gallery. He commanded that your stool be set just below the dais, lass."

Jenny swallowed hard and cast a glance at Peg. But Peg was staring at her own feet and said not a word until the Joculator had walked away again.

Then she said bluntly, "*Now* will ye agree that we ought to ha' stayed at home?" The words were barely out of her mouth before she clapped a hand to it and stared guiltily at Jenny. "Och, but I ought never to speak to ye so, me—"

"Don't be daft, Peg," Jenny interjected quickly. "We are cousins, are we not? You may say what you like. However, although we may have been daft to come here, here we are and here we'll stay until we leave. So we must make the best of it. Where do you suppose we go to relieve ourselves in this great place?"

Peg did not know but went to ask one of the other women.

As Jenny watched her make her way through the busy

minstrels, a burst of laughter from somewhere in the crowd drew a smile.

When Peg returned, she said with a rueful look, "The men just piss through grating in the forecourt into yon ditch, one o' the gleewomen told me. They ha' put buckets about for the women, but we'd ha' nowt save our skirts for privacy. She said if we could wait till we go in for supper, the castle commander ha' said he'll let the women go two-by-two to use the garderobe tower."

"Then that is what we'll do," Jenny declared, determined to wait if she burst.

As it was, they kept busy arranging their space and watching to see how others arranged theirs. Jenny noted that most members of the company took care to identify their spaces. The two fools had coverlets made of patch-work motley similar to their costumes, which amused her until she learned that they never let any bit of fabric go to waste but used the coverlets as a way to store bits they could add to their costumes as other bits wore through.

They all went in to supper at last, and found men-at-arms setting up a long trestle just for the company. Jenny felt relief just knowing they'd not be scattered all over the stark hall. The walls were bare stone, their only decorations the rows of weapons hanging on them. Every sign of the powerful Bruce family was gone.

Guards stood close to their table as they ate—too close, Jenny thought, careful to keep her eyes on her trencher. Members of the company, other than the musicians playing for their supper, talked quietly together as if the guards did not exist. But Jenny was well aware of them and knew that Peg was, too.

When Jenny finished eating, she murmured, "I must

visit the garderobe before I have to sing, Peg. So, if you have finished—"

"I have and all," Peg muttered back. "'Tis poor food these men eat, I tell ye, although there do seem to be plenty of it."

They excused themselves, and Peg asked one of two nearby, helmeted men-at-arms where they would find the garderobe. He pointed toward an archway at the southeast corner of the hall, which revealed stairs beyond. Leering at Peg, he said, "We'd fain escort ye upstairs, lassies, to see that nae one disturbs ye there."

"Thank you, sir, but we can look after ourselves," Jenny said quietly.

His eyebrows shot upward. "Can ye now? Well, ye're quite the lady, lass! Should I be bending me knee to ye, d'ye think?"

"Nay, sir, though I thank ye kindly for the compliment," she said. "Come along, Peg. We must hurry."

"Ye do that now," the man said, lewdly licking his lips.

Doing her best to conceal her revulsion and hoping the fellow would not follow them, she hurried with Peg to the archway, only to hear footsteps echoing after theirs as they hurried up the stairs.

They found the required chamber easily, and found, too, that it would admit both of them at once. Without compunction they drew the curtain and made use of the facility. But when Peg pushed the curtain aside again, they found that the two men-at-arms were quietly waiting for them.

"Sakes, but ye're a toothsome pair," the spokesman said when Jenny glared at him. "There be a chamber just above that'll take the four of us easily, so if ye'll lead the way, me ladies, I promise ye'll not regret it. We pay well for our pleasures, and 'tis long since we last had any such tasty lasses here in the castle."

Peg's jaw dropped, but Jenny said, "I fear we canna go with ye, sirs, for your commander awaits us below. He has bespoken our presence and will doubtless be wroth an we keep him waiting."

"He canna want more than one o' ye at a time," the second man said, his patience clearly waning. "Which o' ye has the man bespoken?"

"I am to sing for him, and she is to play the lute," Jenny said.

"Aye, well, I expect ye can play your own lute, so we'll just take this lassie along to amuse us till he's finished with ye." As he reached to grasp Peg's arm, a dagger hissed through the air between them, catching the leather sleeve of his baldric and pinning it to a wooden panel set into the wall behind him.

With a cry of astonishment, he stared at his sleeve.

"What the devil!" exclaimed his companion.

Gillygacus, the much smaller of the two fools, tumbled onto the landing, rolled into a ball, and sat upright, chuckling as he said over his shoulder. "Ay de mi, but 'twere a fine throw, Gawkus! Ye nipped his sleeve and pinned it to the board!"

"By God," the other man-at-arms said, reaching for his sword.

"Hold there, sir, if you please," lanky, whitefaced Gawkus said as he came into view with a dagger in each hand. "Ye may well slay us both wi' yon great sword o' yours. But I've two more dirks in hand, so I'm thinking ye'd be safer an ye let our women return to the hall. Your commander gave his word that every member of our company will be safe within these walls. I warrant he'd be gey displeased to hear that ye're making game wi' two of our womenfolk."

"It be nowt, Gawkus," Jenny said, hoping she was right. "These men were just making sure that we could safely use the garderobe. But now that you and Gilly are here, we need trouble them no further." Bobbing a slight curtsy to both Englishmen at once, she said, "We thank ye, sirs, and shall commend your care of us to your commander. 'Twas kind o' ye both to look after us so well."

The spokesman gave her a look, then glanced at his comrade.

As he did, wee Gillygacus reached up on tiptoe, yanked the dagger free of the wood panel, and tossed it back to Gawkus, who caught it handily.

The man whose sleeve had been pinned to the panel lunged to catch the dwarf, but he'd already skipped beyond reach and now cheekily tipped his cap.

Hastily, Jenny said, "We thank ye again, both o' ye, for looking out for us. Mayhap ye'll come down now to hear me sing."

Gawkus said not a word. With daggers still in hand, he gestured silently for Gilly to go down the stairs.

Casting a last glance at the men-at-arms, the little man obeyed.

Jenny said, "Ye go on, too, Gawkus. We'll follow, and our friends can see that we return safely. Ye *will* do that, will ye no?" she said to the spokesman.

"Aye, mistress, we'll see ye come to nae harm," the man said.

She held his gaze for a long moment, then gestured to Peg to precede her, and the two of them hurried back down to the hall without further ado.

Her performance followed soon afterward, and the reaction was as warm as it had been at Castle Moss. At the end of it, when she saw that the men who had accosted them were also cheering, she felt herself relax. Even so, she and Peg stayed close to the other minstrels until they were outside in their allotted space.

The courtyard was a damply chilled and dreary place. But Jenny had no doubt that after such a long and tiring day, she would sleep well.

"We pay well for what we want, and 'tis long since we had such a chance . . . in the castle," Cath's man said.

Jenny glowered at him, shocked that he would speak so to her and wishing she could recall his name. It hovered at the edge of her mind but refused to reveal itself.

Cath, appearing between them, snapped, "So this be where ye've come, then!"

Sounding absurdly as if he spoke to himself, the man said, "There be a more private place yonder, but make nae mistake. Ye'll do all I tell ye to do."

Cath had vanished, so Jenny knew the man was speaking to her. Sakes, he stood right in front of her. She could see him talking, and no one else was there. He was no longer Cath's husband, though. He was an English man-at-arms.

"Gey toothsome," he had called them earlier. "A pair of tasty lasses."

The villain!

"So, I'll just take ye along . . ." he said sourly.

". . . and our friend Archie the Grim won't ken nowt of it till afterward, if he does even then. Nor will Old Bleary."

"Whisst, ye great gowk. Old Bleary, indeed!"

How odd, she thought, that the man talked to himself in such a strange way.

"Is that no what they call him?"

"Aye, but whisst *now*, will ye?"

Waking, feeling almost numb with cold, and uncertain whether the man in her dream or someone nearby had made the last comment, Jenny opened her eyes.

The dim glow of torchlight over the courtyard revealed several pairs of men moving about. Most looked like men-at-arms.

Deciding she had dreamed the whole thing and had wakened because of the cold, she pulled up her blanket, snuggled closer to Peg, and went back to sleep.

Chapter 5

Sunday morning, Hugh and Lucas arrived at Lochmaben just as the sun's first rays peeked through the space between low rose-colored clouds and the hills to the east. They had left Castle Moss well before dawn and had made good time.

An hour later, they were waiting with their two sumpter baskets for a boat to come and take them across the last ditch into the castle. In the intervening time, they had arranged to leave their horses with lads watching the minstrels' animals and Hugh had talked their way past the sentries at each of the three drawbridges.

The air had grown colder overnight, making the gentle breeze icy. Thinking wistfully of the hooded wool cloak in his gear, Hugh drew his long purple silk cape more closely around him and wished his plumed cap came lower over his ears.

The smell of snow in the air was stronger today, and clouds gathered over hills to the east and south as they had each day for a week. But whether they would do more than thicken and threaten as they had before or dissipate again during the night would be important only if Lochmaben denied them entry.

Lucas was muttering, but Hugh ignored him, because the castle gates had begun to swing open. Aside from men manning the drawbridges from secure stone towers on the castle side of each of three previous ditches, he had seen no guards outside the castle wall. They'd had to shout to men on the wall.

Hugh knew that harassment from Scots in the dale had made the precautions necessary. The life of English soldiers occupying a Scottish castle miles from the border must be unpleasant. Yet the English had controlled Lochmaben for decades.

His private opinion was that the Scots could rout them if a strong leader had the stomach for it. David Bruce, the previous King, had not been such a leader. That he could carry his famous father's blood in his veins and refuse to fight for freedom from English occupation had mystified many Scots. But David was dead, succeeded by Robert the Steward, a man reputed to have been a fine warrior.

And so he had been—in his youth.

The third anniversary of the Steward's coronation was nearly upon them, and so far, he had done nothing to justify his warrior reputation. He was in his sixth decade; his eyes were always bloodshot, and men said he seemed only half awake most of the time. Those who knew him best called him Old Bleary.

His sons were no prizes either. But Robert the Bruce had decreed that the King's eldest son must succeed him, thus ending the ancient practice of Scotland's most powerful nobles' choosing the worthiest man among them to be King of Scots. But Bruce's method had clearly weakened the Scottish Crown and, in Hugh's opinion, even threatened Scotland's future as a nation.

A boat now appeared in the open gateway, with two men rowing a third. They did not seem to be in any hurry.

"D'ye honestly think they'll let us in?" Lucas muttered.

"I believe they'll let me in. I'm hoping they'll keep you out."

Lucas's bushy dark eyebrows shot upward. "Ye're hopin'?" He looked toward the sky. "Behear the man! Have I offended ye then by tellin' ye flat that ye be daft as muck to be walkin' into t' English lion's mouth like ye're a-doin'?"

"Nowt o' the sort, and you know it," Hugh said. "We ken fine that the English have spies everywhere, including a number of Scots, may the devil seize them. 'Tis likely that someone from this lot has seen us traveling together."

"Aye, that be true."

"It is, and for that someone to wonder, after I'd got inside, what had become of the dour chap who was with me would be a nuisance. But if they refuse to let you in and you camp nearby, they'll just think you're waiting for me. They won't molest you even if you make friends with the lads tending the minstrels' beasts."

"But won't the English be keepin' their eyes on me?"

"What if they do?" Hugh said. "They'll seek signs to suggest that we might represent a military threat. I don't mean to give them cause for such worry, nor will you. I do want you to learn what you can, however."

"I'm thinkin' we should 'ave waited patiently 'ere for them minstrels to come out again," Lucas muttered.

"But I want to talk to her ladyship without stirring a lot of curiosity. That is much more likely to happen if I can meet her quietly inside than if I have to persuade the minstrels that I have any right to speak to her as they travel. Moreover, we've no idea where they mean to go next from here."

"They'll be a-goin' to Dumfries."

"Aye, in time," Hugh agreed. "But we don't know how soon or where they might go in the meantime. Sithee, I'm just being cautious—as you suggested."

"Och, aye, ye're right cautious, ye are," Lucas said with a snort.

"Hush," Hugh said. "They're near enough now to hear you."

Lucas fell obediently silent as the boat beached nearby.

The three men in it were well armed. Two drew swords as they stepped ashore but stayed by the boat. The third strode forward, content to keep a hand on his sword hilt as he said, "What be ye a-wanting here, ye two?"

Doffing his plumed cap with a flourish as he swept a deep bow that made the purple cape billow, Hugh said, "I am told that your imprisonment in this great castle marches slowly. I've come to provide music and laughter for your entertainment."

The man shrugged. "We've nae need o' ye, though. We've a whole company o' minstrels inside—fools, jugglers, gleewomen—all sorts."

Hugh straightened and looked down his nose at the man. "Good sakes, am I not aware of this company? In sooth, I come to join them, having been detained in Annan town to sing for Lord Dunwythie because of my great talent. 'Twas he who sent me after them, knowing me to be the finest troubadour in all Scotland."

"Aye, well, ye're a pensie, pompous prink withal, and right full o' yourself."

Hugh dismissed the comment with an airy gesture. "I have performed in many countries," he said. "Soon I will perform for the King of Scots on the anniversary of his ascension to the throne. But, in kindness, I deign to perform here at Lochmaben for you English. And I tell you, sirrah, your commander will be gey wroth with you if you cause him to miss hearing the fine songs and epic tales of the great Hugo."

Replacing his plumed cap, Hugh waited, hoping he had said enough and not too much. It was years since he had last pretended to be other than himself. He took care to avoid Lucas's gloomy gaze.

"Ye say ye be with them others inside?" the English leader said.

"Not to say *with* them," Hugh said. "I come to join them. The so powerful Lord Dunwythie said I should do so, because they go on from here to Dumfries and then to the fine new castle of the Lord of Galloway, who is shortly to honor the King of Scots." He spread his hands. "And so, did the matter arrange itself."

"Mayhap it did," the soldier said. "What of this man? Does he sing?"

Hugh winced. "Nay, he possesses an eldritch voice. He is only my servant."

"Then he must remain here," the soldier said. "Ye'll come with us in the boat and wait in the forecourt whilst I speak with our commander."

"Then I shall need to take one of those baskets," Hugh said with a sigh. "The one with my lute, Bouchard."

Lucas gave him a look that told him he recalled from a previous occasion that Bouchard meant "big mouth" in French. But he nodded and handed Hugh the basket.

"If our commander refuses to hear ye sing, he may order ye chained and cast into our dungeon," the leader of the boatmen warned.

Hugh shrugged. "He will not be such a fool."

They put him in the bow of the boat and rowed back to the castle. Hugh saw Lucas dismally shaking his head before the gates swung shut behind them.

He knew that Lucas would stay close and keep an eye out for trouble. What he would do if he spotted any, he did not know. But Lucas was resourceful.

Putting other thoughts aside, Hugh concentrated on looking confident and relaxed. He was neither. It was not the first time he had walked into the English lion's mouth with no weapon other than a dirk shoved into one boot, but it was the first time he had done so while the two countries were supposedly at peace.

He did not think the English would care one way or the other about a Scottish baroness pretending to be a gleemaiden. However, if they discovered they had two noble landowners inside Lochmaben, both pretending to be what they were not, the English commander would be well within his rights to declare them spies and hang them or—and much more likely—hold each of them for a large ransom.

The hall was unnaturally quiet as Jenny walked toward the dais, where the castle commander and his officers sat in state. She stopped by the lone stool below it, reminding herself that they had liked her performance the night before and that it was all part of her adventure. Holding her head high, she strove to look serene.

Her tension had increased despite their obvious anticipation, or perhaps because of their silence. It had not grown so quiet the previous night until she had been singing for several minutes. They seemed to expect more of her now.

At least she need not worry that anyone would recognize her, because she had never met any Englishmen. Therefore, she could easily pretend she was no longer Baroness Easdale but just common Bonnie Jenny with a pleasing voice.

Taking her seat, she positioned her lute and began gently to pluck the notes of her first song. As usual, the sound soothed her and stirred memories of home. She played it once all the way through before she began to sing.

The love song had five verses, and by the third, she had lost herself in the music, unaware of how quiet the hall was until notes from a second lute joined hers. Sure that it must be one of the other minstrels, she hoped he would not miss a note.

Distracted only for that moment and quickly realizing that she could trust the other musician, she concentrated on the song.

A beat before she began the fourth verse, a man began to sing behind her, changing the lyrics to suit a lad singing to his love instead of a lass to hers. His voice was rich and full, his skill with the lute exceptional, so although she kept plucking the tune, she remained silent until the verse ended.

Then she stood and faced him to sing the last verse with him.

He was tall, broad-shouldered, and wore a long purple cape and a matching, white-plumed cap. Although his clothing was that of a troubadour and the rakish plume obscured much of his face, something about the man seemed familiar.

He was not a minstrel with whom she had traveled, which suggested that he must live in the castle. Not until he swept the plumed cap from his head and bowed to her at the end of the song did she recognize Sir Hugh Douglas. But she did so then with such astonishment that she had all she could do to retain her composure.

Hugh knew the moment she recognized him. He had wondered how she would react and felt a stirring of admiration when she just stiffened slightly.

She relaxed at once, smiling, and he knew the thunderous applause and foot stomping from their delighted audience helped her keep her composure.

Doubtless, too, she had not yet realized that he had come for her.

Instead she was probably wondering what *had* brought him. Thanks to his troubadour's garb and performance, perhaps she suspected that he'd come as a spy.

The commander of Lochmaben's garrison raised both hands, and the audience quieted again.

As the lass turned toward the dais, the commander said

in a voice that carried easily to the rear of the hall, "We had heard of Bonnie Jenny but not that she sang with another fine gleeman. Your music pleases us. Prithee, sing us another."

The lass curtsied to him and then turned again to face Hugh.

He bowed, hoping to indicate that he would leave it to her to choose the song. He could play most well-known ballads. For any he did not know, he could still play appropriate accompaniment after listening for a short time.

She was quiet long enough to make him wonder if her nerves had overcome her at last, although she still looked perfectly calm.

Content to watch her, he felt no impatience. Dim gray daylight showed in several very high, very small windows, but the true light in the hall glowed from a multitude of candles and cressets, gilding her shiny hair.

Having seen her before only in a formal caul and veil, with her eyebrows and forehead shaven, he had not imagined what color her hair might be.

Now he saw that her hair and eyes were exactly the same soft golden-brown. Perhaps the candlelight played tricks with her irises.

Gazing straight at him, she plucked a string, then another and another. The tune was that of a century-old ballad most folks called "Fairlie Roads," a tale of the battle of Largs, when King Hakon of Norway, taking advantage of a famine in Scotland, had tried to assert his lordship over the western isles. The ballad derived from old seanachies' tales, and therefore was well known. It was also many, *many* verses long. Hugh devoutly hoped she did not mean to sing them all.

With a smile and a nod, he matched his plucking to hers, moving closer and then standing beside her so she could turn toward the dais again and still see him. He knew the commander was more interested in her than in him, so it would be wiser for her to avoid giving the man her back as she sang.

The ballad was a favorite with Scottish military men, and Hugh knew all the words. By letting her sing the first line of each verse, he learned with relief that she skipped five verses for every one she sang, concentrating on those lauding the Scots.

Thus, they soon came to the climax of the tale, when weather favored the Scots with gale-force winds that forced their Norse attackers to withdraw in defeat.

As the song ended, it occurred to Hugh that she would be wise to avoid more military ballads, especially ones where the English suffered defeat, but she began a love song next. As he sang it with her, he found himself watching her again and was sure that every other man in the hall must be doing so, too.

Her voice was pleasant and natural, and very soothing. But it was not her singing as much as the way she seemed to lose herself in the music that made her so fascinating. She soon turned a little toward the lower hall, so that she seemed to be singing to individuals there as much as to the men on the dais.

When the song ended, they both turned and bowed to the dais. Then she walked to a table at the back where the other minstrels sat. Following her, he braced himself when the man who had led the company at Annan House rose to greet him.

"Ye've a fine voice, troubadour," he said.

"I thank ye, sir," Hugh replied, relaxing. He had wondered if anyone in the company had paid sufficient heed to those sitting at Annan House's high table to recognize him, but if they had not recognized the young baroness, he thought the likelihood was even greater that they would not recognize him.

" 'Twas a good turn," the leader said. "The two o' ye make a fine pair."

As Hugh answered glibly, he saw that one young woman, sitting by herself at the far end of the table, seemed to pay him close heed. When Lady Easdale went to sit beside her, he deduced that she must be the missing maidservant, Peg.

Returning his attention to the leader of the company, who had just asked from whence he had sprung, Hugh decided to spin much the same tale he had spun the soldiers at the gate. "I come from Annan House, sir."

"Indeed, how so?" the man asked.

"Sithee, I am bidden to Threave Castle soon, to sing for the Lord of Galloway and mayhap the King of Scots. My lord Dunwythie did tell me a band of minstrels that had performed for a feast there yestereve were likewise bound for Threave for that same occasion. He suggested I'd be safer did I catch up with ye and travel in your company. If ye be their leader, sir, what say ye?"

"If you can get our Bonnie Jenny to flirt with ye as ye sing, and with the men in the audience, I'll thank ye for it. If ye think they shout for her now, think what they'll do if each man of them believes she sings just for him. Can ye do that?"

Willing to promise nearly anything if the company would accept him as a fellow minstrel long enough for

him to talk with the lass and persuade her to go quietly
back to Annan House with him, Hugh nodded.

"Aye, sure," he said. "I ken fine what ye want her to
do."

"Then ye're welcome to travel with us. We go to
Dumfries from here to perform for a sennight at the sheriff's behest. But ye'll no mind that, for he'll pay us well
and we'll divide the gelt in the usual way."

Hugh had no idea what the usual way was and no wish
to meet the Sheriff of Dumfries in troubadour's guise.
But as certain as he was that he would no longer be with
them when they reached Dumfries, he agreed without
hesitation.

Jenny kept an eye on Sir Hugh, wondering who had come
with him. She had no doubt that he had come to find her.
But surely, neither Phaeline nor Dunwythie would expect
her to travel alone with a man who was not yet any kin to
her, with only Peg to protect her. He had to have brought
someone else with him.

A chill shot up her spine at the thought that he might
have brought Reid.

The men-at-arms and their leaders had begun eating
shortly after everyone gathered in the hall for the midday
meal. The other minstrels performed throughout, eating
as they found time, but Jenny had not felt like eating before her performance.

Now, taking a seat beside Peg, she felt ravenous.

A few others were eating at the far end of the table but
paid no heed to the two young women. Staring past them

at the Joculator and Sir Hugh, who were still talking, Peg muttered, "Sakes, but isna that—"

"Aye, it is," Jenny cut in hastily. "But do not speak his name here. I cannot think how he got in or why he has come for me. I am naught to him, Peg, so he cannot care that I have come away. But he may not have come alone."

"D'ye think he'll tell the Joculator and all them others who ye be?"

Jenny had given the question some thought. "I don't think he will," she said as she helped herself from a platter of sliced lamb.

It seemed odd not to have gillies hovering or scurrying to serve her, but she rather liked knowing she need not wait for anyone.

When she had taken what she wanted, she said, "They won't want any fuss, Peg, because anyone who did not know me well would think I had run away."

"Aye, sure, but ye did," Peg said, crumbling a roll.

"Nay, for I'm going back again soon. Are you going to eat that roll?"

"I've had plenty," Peg said, handing it to her. "I had nowt else to do but eat, for I'm nae performer. But Bryan says I can help wi' the mending. They're always tearing things, he says, especially them as wears motley. Did ye ken they collect scraps o' fabric wherever they go, to patch whatever wears out? Gawkus told me. And ye did so run away," she added flatly.

Jenny shook her head. "I just decided to do something I wanted to do, and I'll go back when I've had my adventure. I admit that I did not think it all through, though, especially consequences that you might face. I seized an opportunity, Peg, knowing well that it might never come again. Sithee, once a woman is married—"

"Aye," Peg said morosely. "I ken fine that your man tells ye what ye should think and how ye should act, and when ye dinna do it, he clouts ye one, or worse."

Jenny smiled. "Is that how it is in your family? I doubt that my father ever clouted my mother, because he never clouted me. In fact, he never raised his voice. Even his displeasure was quiet, but it was no less powerful for being so."

"Aye, well, I'd liefer me own da were the quiet sort. He rages about like a dafty and me mam cowers when he's on a tear. So do we all, come to that. Bryan's no much like him but does as he pleases all the same."

"I just hope I haven't got you into grievous trouble."

"I'll get by, but look out," Peg said, lowering her voice. "He's a-coming."

Although she kept her eyes on her food, Jenny knew Peg was not still talking about Bryan. Prickles shot up her spine, growing stronger with each heartbeat, as if the sensation strengthened with every step Sir Hugh took toward her.

"Good day to ye," he said, taking a seat on the bench opposite them. "Folks do call me Hugo, and your leader has agreed to let me travel with ye to Dumfries."

Although Jenny was not looking directly at Peg, she could see her jaw drop. Afraid Peg might say something that would land them both in the suds, Jenny raised the eyebrows Peg had drawn on her and said softly, "Hugo?"

"Aye," he said with a slight smile, reaching to help himself from the platter of lamb. "Ye've a fine voice, lass. 'Twas a pleasure to sing with ye."

Matching her accent to his, she said, "Thank ye, sir. Your opinion does gratify me, for ye sing much better than I do."

"Nay, our voices differ, but they complement each other well, I think."

Peg wriggled on the bench. "Whatever are ye—?"

"Not now, Peg," Jenny said. "The troubadour must eat. We can talk later."

He said, "I was thinking, mistress, that if we walk together for at time when we leave here, mayhap we could compile a list of songs we both enjoy singing. Your leader will doubtless—"

"We call him the Joculator," Peg interjected.

Sir Hugh shifted his gaze to her, and Jenny nearly spoke up to explain that she had ordered Peg not to use titles or other formal means of address.

But he smiled at Peg and said mildly, "I thank ye for telling me, lass. The man didna say how I should call him."

"As to that," Jenny said. "*I* dinna ken what he prefers. I simply call him 'sir,' as I do most gentlemen."

"Is he a gentleman then?" he asked, turning back to her.

Meeting his gaze, she said, "I dinna ken who he is or where he is from. I ken only that he was kind to us and gave us shelter. And he has a charming smile."

"You ought not to have required shelter," he said quietly, holding her gaze.

"I think ye should let me be the best judge of that," she replied without a blink. "I was grateful for his kindness and feel much in his debt."

Something hardened in his expression that sent the prickles up her spine again, but she did not look away.

~

Hugh forced himself to take a deep breath. He was not temperamental by nature, but when something did arouse his temper, the sensation he felt was sometimes so strong that he had to exert himself considerably to contain it.

Her mild look of inquiry had reawakened the annoyance he'd felt at having to search for her, and something more. The lass clearly had no idea of the danger in which she might have placed herself with her impulsive escapade.

He felt a strong urge to explain it to her in terms she could not ignore.

However, his quiet reproof ought to have produced a look of remorse, even alarm. Instead, she was looking at him as if *she* required an explanation from *him*, rather than the reverse.

Realizing that he could accomplish little until they were beyond the confines of Lochmaben, he applied himself to his food and said no more.

Shortly afterward, one of the minstrels came to say that the Joculator wanted them all to go outside and be sure their things were ready to load into the boats.

They would be leaving, he added, within the next half hour.

Hugh finished hastily and followed Jenny and Peg to the inner courtyard, now alive with activity. Members of the company hoisted bundles to their shoulders as men-at-arms hustled them to the forecourt and into boats, then ferried them across the water.

Because they had had to tether their horses and mules on the far side of all four ditches, in woodland some distance away, they straggled along in a sporadic line until they had collected all the animals and gathered to reload their gear.

Hugh found Lucas Horne and gave his basket into the man's keeping, saying, "I trust you've made a few friends amongst the lads who tend their animals."

"Aye, sure," the man said, eyeing him speculatively. "'T' company be goin' to Dumfries from 'ere, nobbut eight miles or so. Do I owe ye a silver groat, sir?"

Hugh nodded. "You do. I found them both."

"That be that, then. When do we leave?"

"We'll be traveling with them for a while. I've not yet had a chance to speak privately with her ladyship, although I believe she knows why I've come."

"Then ye'll soon sort it out," Lucas said.

Hugh wished he felt as confident of that. Seeing Peg and her ladyship walking ahead, he left Lucas with the horses and hurried to catch up with them.

"I was told that your brother is a member of this company," he said to Peg as he joined them. "Is that so?"

"Aye, sir," she said, eyeing him warily.

"Mayhap you could walk with him for a time, so I may speak privately with your"—looking about, he saw people near enough to hear—"with your companion."

Peg turned to her mistress, but Lady Easdale nodded. "Go along, Peg," she said. "He will not murder me."

The maidservant looked doubtful, but she obeyed.

Hugh hoped that her mistress would likewise be obedient.

"As you must realize, my lady," he said, lowering his voice to keep anyone else from overhearing, "I have come to take you back to Annan House."

"Have you? I cannot think why you should."

Her tone revealed only mild curiosity. Still, it nettled him. "You must know that I have come here only because Lord Dunwythie—your guardian, I would remind you—sent me to escort you back to him."

"I do not question your purpose, sir. I question the need for *you* to come."

"Doubtless you think my brother ought to have come for you," he said.

"I do not think so at all," she said. "I am not answerable to your brother. We shall not marry for some weeks yet."

"Three weeks is not a long time, my lady. You should perhaps—"

"Prithee, do not call me so whilst we are with these people, sir. I warrant that my uncle and his wife would not thank you for revealing my rank to others just now. You will say what you please to me, of course, but I should prefer to stay plain Jenny whilst I am with this company."

"I apologize and will certainly oblige you in that request," he said. "I have been at pains to conceal my own identity, so you are right to remind me. But my position remains the same. We will depart from here as soon as we decently may."

"I think that would be unwise," she said.

"I did not ask for your opinion. Your uncle sent me to

collect you, and he expects me to bring you home. He told me I should act just as he would."

"Did he?"

"Aye," he said, hoping that news would shake her from her calm defiance.

"I see," she said. "But still, you lack his authority, sir. I am not answerable to you, and I suspect that you have no way to prove my uncle sent you. You have already lied to these good people, so to tell them now that you are someone else and have authority to take me with you . . . I think they will aid me to resist, do not you?"

Chapter 6

Jenny saw that her reply had shaken Sir Hugh, but he said only, "We will talk later, mistress, as you suggest. The road from Dumfries to Annan is better than this one at all events. We'll be able to travel faster."

Clearly, he expected her to submit to his authority. But Jenny was just beginning to enjoy her newfound freedom and was not ready yet to give it up.

Quietly, she said, "We should not walk together for long, sir. I'd liefer not stir talk that I am flirting with the new troubadour."

He nodded and strode off to join some of the other men, leaving her feeling strangely bereft. But Peg soon rejoined her and the two chatted amiably about the countryside and other such mundane topics.

As they passed through a small village, the two fools Gawkus and Gillygacus darted onto the common and, by chasing each other and doing their tricks, quickly drew a crowd of children. Musicians played merry tunes as they strolled by.

They did not linger, because they had been later leaving Lochmaben than they had hoped to be, and everyone was eager to make camp before nightfall.

The journey was just eight miles, and except for the Joculator, who rode his white horse as usual, the others took turns riding the extra mules and ponies or driving the three carts. No one had to walk for long unless he or she chose to do so.

Jenny had enjoyed many long walks with her father and, despite several offers to ride, chose to walk with various members of the company, encouraging them to tell her their stories until they were well into Nithsdale. When at last she did accept a mount, the Joculator soon rode up alongside her.

"That young troubadour who joined us this morning seems to have taken a fancy to you, lass," he said without preamble.

Jenny smiled. "He did speak to me, sir. But I had little to say to him."

"You are new to the ways of the road," he said with a twinkle. "I should warn you that troubadours are rarely to be trusted with a pretty lass like you."

Aware that Sir Hugh was unlikely to let the situation continue as it was for long before urging her more strongly to return to Annan House, Jenny realized that he might seek to enlist the Joculator's aid. Therefore, she decided, she would be wise to make that particular course more difficult for him if she could.

"I expect he *was* flirting with me, sir," she said. "I should perhaps tell ye that I have met him before."

"He did say that he came to us from Annan House, just

as Bryan's sister Peg and ye yourself did. Be that where ye met the man?"

"Aye, and he made his interest plain, even offered marriage." That was nearly true, although his brother Reid had been the husband offered her. Hastily, to conceal her discomfort with the fib, she said, "I swear I didna encourage him. I were kind, because I thought he were just being friendly, but I dinna want to encourage *any* man yet. Moreover, I'd liefer a man be more delicate of manner than this Hugo do be."

"He seemed mild enough to me," the Joculator said, looking vaguely upward as if he were trying to recapture an earlier image of Sir Hugh.

"He does appear so," Jenny agreed. "But I ha' been warned that he can be gey stubborn, sir, and set on having his way." That, at least, was perfectly true, although she doubted that Phaeline had intended to warn her *against* Sir Hugh.

"I see," the Joculator said, nodding. "Well, if he thinks to pursue ye, we must see that he doesna become a nuisance. I'll keep a keen eye on the man."

"I thank ye, sir," Jenny said demurely, hoping Sir Hugh would now find it difficult, if not impossible, to make her do anything she did not want to do.

Her conscience stirred again at the unfairness of her method, but she thought that Dunwythie's having sent Sir Hugh after her was even more so. Hugh Douglas was no kith or kin to her and would not be until after she married his odious brother. Despite what Reid had said about *his* rights, Sir Hugh was not Reid. And a betrothal, although binding in its own way, was *not* the same as a wedding.

She had three weeks of relative freedom left. Anyone

angry with her now would doubtless stay angry, but she could not help that. She had run her father's household for nearly six years *before* he had died, and his death had made her mistress not just of that household but of all the Easdale estates. Then her uncle had come to collect her like one of his deceased first wife's mislaid belongings.

Ignoring her grief and her protests, he had carried her off to Annan House. Jenny had been upset, but given no choice, she had obeyed his will.

Having remained docile then for eight months, she had not realized what a strain that submission had exerted on her good nature until the chance had suddenly presented itself to escape Annan House, if only for a night or two.

Despite Sir Hugh's seemingly unbounded confidence that he could force her to do as he willed, he had much less right than Dunwythie did to order such compliance. Sir Hugh's attitude made her want to dig in her heels and retain her freedom for as long as she could . . . if only to see what he would do next.

The last thought came unexpectedly, but she had to admit—to herself, at least—that the man intrigued her. She had enjoyed singing with him and looked forward to doing so again when they reached Dumfries.

But a man's singing voice was not the man, and she did not admire Sir Hugh's habit of commanding her as if he had every right to do so. She could not doubt that he would prevail in the end, especially as he could send for Dunwythie himself to join them. But until then, she resolved that Sir Hugh Douglas's commands would have less effect on her than his singing would.

Hugh kept an eye on Lady Easdale all that afternoon but took care to move about from group to group as they traveled, talking with all and sundry.

At present, his goal was just to make a few friends, so he offered his horse and the one he and Lucas had brought for her ladyship to others who wanted to ride. And he matched his accent to the commonest Border accent among his companions.

So far the minstrels had accepted him as a wandering troubadour. The rub would come if he could not persuade her ladyship to leave the company at Dumfries.

If he had to perform there to maintain his pretense, that pretense might well fall short. The Joculator had said they would be performing at the sheriff's behest, making it likely that the sheriff would attend their performance. And although Sheriff Maxwell might fail to recognize Sir Hugh Douglas, Laird of Thornhill, in the guise of a common troubadour, chances were just as good that he might.

"Beg pardon, sir?"

Hugh turned toward the voice and found one of the younger gleemaidens, a buxom one, walking a little to his left behind his horse. "Aye, mistress?"

"Me name's Gerda, sir, and I wanted to tell ye how much we did enjoy your singing wi' the new lass, Jenny," she said. "Ye've a fine voice withal."

"I thank ye," Hugh said, dismounting to walk with her. "My friends do call me Hugo."

Simpering at him from beneath long eyelashes, she said, "Do they, sir?"

"They do. Have you been walking long, mistress?"

"Me feet do think so," she said. "They ha' begun to complain."

"Then let me put ye up on me lad here for a spell."

"I'd thank ye kindly an ye give me a leg up."

Instead, Hugh caught her at the waist and lifted her to the saddle, retaining his grip on the reins. She chattered happily as he led the horse, and he replied as often as necessary until she said pertly, "I do look forward to singing wi' ye in Dumfries, sir. I've nae doubt we'll make a fine pair."

Catching sight of Lucas, leading his own horse with the lass Peg laughing down at him, Hugh told himself with an inward groan that things were clearly growing more complicated by the minute. The sooner he and Lucas could pack Lady Easdale and Peg back to Annan House, the happier he would be.

~⸻

Spilling down the sides of two undulating hilltops, the town of Dumfries appeared even from a distance to be of fair size. The minstrels reached it in the gloaming with its lights already showing.

When they approached the hilltop, the view was vast. Jenny could see the forested hills of Galloway to the west across the river Nith, frothing white in its rush southward to Solway Firth. She also saw the fine bridge that crossed the Nith to Galloway, one of the few bridges in the Scottish Borders.

Built in the previous century by Devorgilla, mother of John Balliol, the man who had fought Robert the Bruce for the kingdom of Scotland, the bridge was said to be as fine as London Bridge. Although Jenny had never seen

Devorgilla's Bridge before—or London Bridge, for that matter—her father had described the former, and she recognized it by its nine splendid arches.

Dumfries itself fascinated Jenny, because it was the most important town in southwest Scotland and its sheriff one of the region's most powerful men. Only the fact that Sir Hugh had said he wanted to return her quietly to Annan House allowed her to hope that he would not apply to the sheriff for help.

She could not see Sir Hugh now. He had ridden with different people during the afternoon, often dismounting to offer a ride to someone else. In the diminishing light, she could not tell his horse from the others, or tell if he was riding or walking.

When they reached the woodland where they were to camp, beyond the north end of town, Peg excused herself to find Bryan, and Jenny went with the gleewoman Cath and her daughter Gerda to seek privacy to relieve herself.

Jenny liked Cath, but the woman seemed to have been in a bad mood most of the day. "Is aught amiss?" Jenny asked her as they walked away from the camp.

Cath sighed. "'Tis nowt, lass, only that me man has a cousin I dinna like, and I've had me fill o' him these past days."

"Is he another member of the company?"

"Nay, although Drogo does sing with us now and now," Cath said. "Sakes, but I thought he served a fine nobleman. Saw him with the man more than once, we did. Now I learn he does nowt o' the sort."

"Mam," Gerda said quietly.

"Aye, well, it be true," Cath said. "He's nae good, that

Drogo. He were always getting Cuddy into mischief whilst they were bairns."

"We should get back, Mam," Gerda said. "Here be as good a place as any."

Jenny knew that Peg would set their things to rights as soon as she had talked with Bryan. So, sensing that Cath's comments had made Gerda uncomfortable, she tactfully lingered behind when mother and daughter returned to the camp. Darkness was swiftly falling, but a half moon peeked through the clouds and would soon give more light. Jenny shifted her position a little to gain a better view of the moon.

"Who's there?" a man called out. "If that be ye, Cath, d'ye ken if we're to try our new skills on the folks here tonight, or do we wait for the larger crowds?"

"'Tis just me, Jenny," she replied. "Who are ye?"

Two men appeared out of the darkness.

"Me name's Jem," said one of them in a deeper voice, not the one who had called out, thinking she might be Cath. He indicated the other. "This be Gib."

"Since ye seek Cath," she said, smiling, "I warrant ye must be musicians."

"Gib does play the gittern," Jem said. "But I be one o' the jugglers."

Gib said, "I'm telling ye, Jem, he said we're to do nowt that may keep us from going to Threave. And since the sheriff may come to—"

"Whisst, man," Jem said testily, darting a look at Jenny. "The lass be new and canna care *what* we do or dinna do except as it affects her singing."

Curious now, Jenny looked from one man to the other.

"Aye, well, I've said nowt," Gib said with a shrug. "But

Cath were here just a wee while ago, for I heard her voice. I dinna ken where she can ha' vanished to."

Abruptly, Jenny recalled her strange dream at Lochmaben. Cath had vanished from that, too. And someone in it had told someone else to "whisst."

What if it had not been a dream, or perhaps half dream and half real?

Realizing that the two men were waiting for her to speak, she said, "Cath was going back to the encampment. Doubtless she is in her tent or near the cook fire."

"D'ye no want us to see ye back safely?" Jem asked.

"Ye be kind to offer," she said. "But I ken the way and 'tis safe enough here."

She wanted to think.

When they had walked on, she tried to clear her mind of all but her half-remembered dream.

She was certain that someone in her dream . . . if it was a dream . . . had mentioned the King and Archie the Grim. And, now, thinking about it, she was sure someone had mentioned Threave Castle. What else had they said?

Trying to recall the details, she felt a chill that she did not think resulted from the chilly air. There was nothing ominous in talk of Threave, though. Everyone was talking about the Lord of Galloway's fine new castle. And the minstrels would soon perform there, which would be a grand occasion for them. But something about that dream, coupled with the encounter she had just had, disturbed her.

She should, she thought, talk this strange unease over with someone to see if, between them, they could make any sense of it. But in whom should she confide?

Not Peg. Peg might tell Bryan, and Jenny did not feel

as if she knew him or anyone else in the company well enough to trust them with such nebulous thoughts.

A whisper at the back of her mind suggested that she could trust Sir Hugh.

Although she tried to ignore it by telling herself she did not know him well enough either, the thought persisted.

Rustling in the bushes reminded her of the increasing darkness. Deciding she had lingered long enough, she followed the burn back to the campsite and walked straight into Hugh himself, standing like a tree in her path.

"Where have you been?" he demanded. "The others came back an age ago."

"Not as long as that, surely," she said, feeling perfectly safe now and ready to do battle with him. "I just lingered a wee while to enjoy the woodland peace."

"The woods can be dangerous at night," he said, still stern. "There are wolves hereabouts, and wild boars."

"I doubt such creatures venture so near any town as large as Dumfries."

"Wild creatures are not the only dangers, my . . . lass," he said. "You would do better to stay near your woman or one of the others."

"Or you?"

"Aye, sure, but we do not want to cause talk. You were right about that."

"Then you should not take me to task as you just have," she said. "I will agree that I ought not to walk alone in the woods. But, as we *are* talking, I do have a question that I want you to answer honestly."

He frowned, saying curtly, "I am not in the habit of being dishonest."

"No?" She smiled. "You have always been a troubadour

then. Or, nay, that cannot be, for you have persuaded Phaeline that despite a mischievous childhood, you are now most stern and proper and thus—"

"Enough," he said, but she detected amusement in his tone. "You know what I meant, my la—"

"Me name be Jenny," she said, seeing Bryan and Peg coming toward them. "Everyone here calls me so. 'Twould be easier an ye remember to do likewise."

His gaze followed hers as he said quietly, "You can trust me, Jenny, whatever guise I may wear."

"Would ye keep a confidence then?"

He hesitated.

"Nae more then, not now," she said, because the others were upon them.

He gave her a look that, if not quite the one that had once sent prickles up her spine, still made itself felt to her bones. It was as if he tried to read her thoughts.

She decided then that she would not try to explain her odd feeling to him or to anyone else until she could make some sense of it herself.

~

Hugh watched Jenny walk away with Peg, knowing she had been right to rebuke him. He had resisted calling her by her nickname but knew he'd be wise to *think* of her as Jenny or count the cost if he misspoke at the wrong time.

However, thinking of her as Jenny seemed to make his task even more—

"I ken the truth, sir," the lad Bryan said softly beside him.

Hugh, still watching Jenny, had forgotten Bryan and glanced hastily around for possible eavesdroppers. Several people moved about the campsite, but none was near enough to overhear them if they kept their voices low.

Having taken care that afternoon to talk with all and sundry, Hugh was swiftly coming to know who was who, and from all he had heard, Bryan was harmless. Nevertheless, Hugh's experience had taught him to assume nothing about chance-met folk, and the lad's knowing the truth might mean anything.

Accordingly, he murmured, "The truth about what?"

"About ye and . . . and Lady Easdale," Bryan said, lowering his voice so that Hugh had to strain his ears to hear him. "Nae baroness ought to be here wi' the likes of us, sir, but our Peg did say ye've come to take the two o' them home again."

"I trust ye've said nowt to anyone else about this."

"Nay, sir, and I wouldna say nowt. But they did ought to go back even though Peg will likely lose her place for encouraging her ladyship."

"I doubt she encouraged her," Hugh said dryly. "Her ladyship has a mind of her own. I doubt, too, that Lord Dunwythie will hold Peg's loyalty to her mistress against her. But if she *should* lose her place, tell her to apply at Thornhill. Her loyalty to Lady Easdale does her no harm in my eyes."

"I thank ye, sir," Bryan said. "I took the liberty o' speaking to ye only so ye'd ken that ye've a friend here. If there be aught I can do to help ye, I will."

Hugh nodded, but again, experience warned him to wonder what the lad's motives might be and how much he ought to count on such an offer.

It had long since occurred to him that taking Lady Easdale—Jenny—away by force or anything resembling force would prove difficult if not impossible.

Whatever he did, he felt sure that the minstrels would side with their Bonnie Jenny if she continued to resist his efforts. Therefore, he decided, it would behoove him to discover a way of persuading her without making them choose sides.

~

"Bryan says I should make m'self useful tonight to the women what do the mending, mistress," Peg said in a tone low enough that Jenny did not reprove her for the formality. "I think I should, though I want to watch the fools when they practice. It always makes me laugh to see wee Gilly outsmart that great Gawkus."

Jenny smiled. She, too, liked Gilly and Gawkus. The two seemed to have been keeping a protective eye on her, and on Peg, as well.

Sir Hugh's man—for the stranger in their midst, with his own horses and leading a sumpter pony, must be Sir Hugh's man—seemed to be keeping at least one eye on them. She had seen Peg riding one of his horses during the afternoon while he led it and the other one, with the sumpter trailing behind them.

"Have you arranged our sleeping places?" Jenny asked Peg now.

"Aye, yonder," she said, pointing. "There be a big clearing beyond it, where Bryan did tell me we're to meet after we sup, so the minstrels can practice all they'll do in the market square tomorrow. Mayhap the sheriff will come to see if they be worth the gelt he's paying for them, Bryan said, so they want to perform well."

They walked toward their sleeping place as they talked, making it easy for Jenny to hide her reaction to this second mention of the sheriff in so short a time. If Sir Hugh identified himself as Laird of Thornhill and asked the sheriff to help him take quiet custody of Lord Dunwythie's rebellious ward, she feared he would agree.

It occurred to her then that perhaps it had been no more than Gib's mention of the sheriff's likely presence that had stirred her uneasiness before.

"Some do say t' sheriff may attend this practice tonight," Lucas said as he deftly sorted Hugh's things. "Happen ye should grow a beard like."

"Before the sheriff arrives?"

"Nah then, nae one can grow a beard in an hour. I'm just saying—"

"I ken fine what you're saying. Now hush and let me think. I'll wear the purple cape again and the soft black cap, but I want its plume attached so it will conceal more of one side of my face. It matters not which side."

"Ye've met t' man afore, I'm thinkin'."

"Aye, several times," Hugh admitted. "Not for two or three years, though. One of his minions has collected the Thornhill taxes since my father died."

Lucas dismissed the years and the sheriff's minions with a gesture. "T' minute ye start to sing and the man sees your face, he'll ken fine who ye be."

"I doubt it," Hugh said. "Men see what they expect to see. Maxwell cannot know yet that Lady Easdale left Annan House, so he'll not recognize her in Bonnie Jenny. Nor will he expect to see the Laird of Thornhill in troubadour's clothing."

Lucas shook his head. "Yon troubadour's garb be gey close to what a nobleman wears, m'lord. That purple cloak of yours be pure silk."

"Have faith, Lucas," Hugh said. "I have a plan."

When Jenny joined the others in the clearing after a hasty supper, she was astonished at the number of people who had come. Clearly, news of their arrival had preceded them, because it looked as if most of Dumfries, if not folks from miles around the town, had come to watch them practice.

That was surprising enough. What was more so was the chanting that began midway through the dancers' performance. For a time, she did not catch the words.

When she did, she did not know where to look.

"Bonnie Jenny, Bonnie Jenny," they chanted. "We want Bonnie Jenny."

Repeatedly, their voices gaining strength and volume, they chanted.

Wishing that she could disappear into the ground, she turned abruptly away, only to find Sir Hugh right behind her, smiling.

It was the first time she had seen him smile, and she felt its warmth. She also noted, to her surprise, an element of sympathy in it.

The chanting continued.

Sir Hugh's gaze shifted to a point to her left, behind her.

"What is it?" she asked him.

"The Sheriff of Dumfries has arrived, I believe."

"Aye," she said, eyeing him warily now. "People said he might come."

"Also, the Joculator is trying to get your attention. He looks pleased, lass."

It was also the first time he had called her "lass" without first nearly calling her "my lady." But the sheriff's arrival had not stopped the chanting.

Swallowing, looking straight ahead—at the middle of Sir Hugh's chest—and fighting to retain her composure, she said, "I . . . I'm not sure I can face that."

"Aye, sure, you can," he said. "Just imagine the whole lot of them, sheriff and all, stark naked and standing on their heads."

Her vivid imagination promptly produced such a picture, and a choke of laughter escaped her. Squeezing her eyes shut only made it worse. As most of the chanting voices were male, in her mind's eye, she saw a forest of waving bandy-legs and male appendages.

"Come along," Sir Hugh said, chuckling. "I'll walk with you. I've had an idea for a song that I think might be amusing."

She went willingly, finding comfort in his presence. She was not shy, because her father had been painfully so and she had often had to serve as his spokesman when he had not felt up to speaking for himself. But never before had she had to face an audience filled with such high expectations of her.

Singing at Castle Moss and at Lochmaben had been much like singing at home. Although individuals in an audience might criticize, most sought only a good time. At home, others had also contributed their talents on such occasions, so one had simply done one's best and stepped aside for the next performer.

As they made their way toward the Joculator, who

stood near the audience, Sir Hugh asked her if she knew a song called "Donsie Willie." She nodded, pleased with his choice. Describing a Border romance between an innocent girl and a lad with a reputation for mischief, the song had some twenty verses with distinctive characters all telling their bits of the tale, and was particularly fun to sing.

"If I were to sing the men's verses and you the women's," he said, "I think we'd have something special that we could do whenever we sing together."

"Do you mean to stay for some time then?"

"I did not say that," he said, darting another glance at the sheriff. "Sithee, all these people want you to sing. I just thought it would be easier if we began together."

She nodded as if she understood. But he had said "whenever" they sang together, so she decided he must have reconciled himself to staying in Dumfries for at least a day or two longer.

As they neared the circle cleared for the entertainers, she saw that jugglers had followed the dancers. Although the chanting for her had eased a little, it continued to provide a low, rhythmic background for the performers.

"Ye'll go next, Jenny," the Joculator said.

"She's a bit skittish, sir," Hugh said, putting a light, reassuring hand on her shoulder. "I thought perhaps a comic song that we both know might ease the way."

"Aye, sure," the Joculator said, visibly noting the hand on Jenny's shoulder and giving Hugh a speculative look.

Jenny saw both and felt a stab of guilt, recalling the fib she had told him about Sir Hugh wanting her. Nibbling her lower lip, she avoided Hugh's gaze but did not reject his touch.

Chapter 7—————————————

Hugh could see that the Joculator was still unsure of him but wondered what Jenny was thinking to bring such a look of guilt to her face. He had no time to think about it, though, before the Joculator turned and gestured to a horn player, who instantly produced a fanfare.

Scanning the crowd as the Joculator announced them, Hugh located the sheriff's party by the shire's banner flying above them.

The audience fell silent, their expectation nearly palpable. Hugh had seen such reactions before and the resulting uproar if the performers fell short of expectation. He doubted that would be the case tonight.

The clouds had parted, the half moon gleamed overhead, and torches bathed the central area in soft, orange-gold light.

Noting frowns on a number of faces in the audience when he strode forward first, Hugh bowed deeply to Jenny, careful to keep the plumed side of his face toward the sheriff, and gestured her forward.

Jenny came to him, moving with easy grace and smiling as she curtsied, first to him and then to the audience. She had also noted the sheriff's position, because she looked that way and nodded before she turned back to Hugh. Then she plucked the first notes of their tune and began to sing.

The first verse of the song described a gentle, innocent lassie and her love for Donsie Willie despite his many sins and lack of repentance.

Hugh replied with the second verse in the exaggerated accents and tone of an angry Border father outraged by his daughter's choice and determined to forbid the banns. As he sang, he heard delighted chuckles from the audience.

When Jenny sang the next verse, that of the worried mother, she, too, exaggerated her accent and feelings until, once again, she seemed to lose herself in the music. Back and forth they went, to the increasing delight of their audience.

By the end, when Hugh sang of his joy as a reformed Willie outsmarting the lass's determinedly doubting father, and the father's responses, shifting accents as he did, the audience clearly was finding it hard to suppress laughter long enough to hear the words.

Stepping back at last, he waited for the applause to die before plucking the first notes of the love song he had sung with Jenny at Lochmaben.

She quickly picked up the cue and began to sing the first verse.

Altogether, they sang four songs before the Joculator stepped forward again as the audience cheered wildly.

Tossing three clubs in the air, he quickly set them spinning in rapid rotation.

As cheers faded to expectant silence, Gillygacus hurried in with three even larger clubs of his own, tossing and spinning them just as high and almost as fast.

When the Joculator turned and glowered at him, the wee man stopped dead, clapped a hand to his head with his clubs crashing around him, snatched them up, and ran back the way he had come. As soon as the Joculator turned back, however, Gilly tiptoed out behind him, tossing the big clubs in the air and imitating the Joculator's every move again until the Joculator produced his first dagger.

Then, with a comical look of dismay, Gillygacus dropped his clubs and ran to hide behind Gawkus. When their turn came, they performed their skits and tricks with rapid repartee, much of it having to do with the sheriff, his minions, and the taxes they collected. The fools' wit was sharp, their quips amusing. The audience loved it, and such was their skill that the sheriff laughed as much as anyone did.

Hearing Jenny laugh, Hugh glanced at her and saw that she was as delighted as the audience was. "They are good, aren't they?" he said.

She nodded, shot him a thoughtful look, and then looked away again.

"We should talk," he said for her ears alone.

She nodded but did not look at him.

Hugh looked around. Everyone else seemed to be watching the fools, and he supposed that the other minstrels would watch each turn as critically as the audience did, if not more so.

"They won't need us again," he said. "Let us walk away from here and talk."

She caught her lower lip between her teeth. But she let him lead the way to a fallen log far enough away so that no one would hear them talking.

"We can sit here if you like," he said.

"I think we should at least *look* as if we are watching the others," she said.

"Have you thought more about the wisdom of returning with me to Annan?"

"I have no need to think," she said. "I don't want to go back until I must."

"You have a duty to obey your guardian," he reminded her.

"But you are not he, sir, and I owe you *no* duty."

It had not occurred to Hugh that she would doubt his word that he acted in Dunwythie's stead. Nor, upon reflection, did he think she did. But if she were to claim that he had no authority, he had no way to prove otherwise.

It occurred to him that Sheriff Maxwell would accept his word. But having no desire to reveal himself to the man in troubadour's guise, he rejected that avenue. He did not need anyone's help to deal with one defenseless young female.

She was eyeing him as a puppy in expectation of supper might, so he said bluntly, "You would do better to obey his lordship's wishes. And not just for your own sake. Doubtless you are unaware that some jewelry disappeared when you did."

"Jewelry!" She looked at him indignantly. "When *I* did!"

"Aye," he said, studying her. "Several guests reported pieces missing."

"You think *I* took them?"

"I did not say that."

"You were thinking it!"

"Nay, I was not. But I'd not be amazed to learn that Dunwythie, Phaeline, or both suspect that your Peg may have taken them."

"Peg would *never* do such a thing," Jenny said. She frowned then as if she had had a second thought.

"You sound sure of her but do not look so," he said. "In troth, I do not suspect Peg, but I would like to know what gave you pause just now."

She hesitated, drew a breath, and then said with visible reluctance, "'Twas only that she was ready to leave when I entered my bedchamber and had already laid out my night things. But that was because she wanted to walk with her brother. She'd had no chance to speak much with him earlier, she said. Peg has served me now for months, sir. By my troth, I do not believe she would steal from anyone."

"I think it unlikely, too," he admitted. "The minstrels fell under suspicion at once, of course. But apparently some things disappeared after they had left Annan."

"Well, Peg was with them, so she cannot have taken those jewels either."

"Your saying so may persuade me that she had nowt to do with it. But it is unlikely to satisfy Phaeline or a suspicious sheriff. Recall that as a member of the household, Peg enjoys first-head privileges and therefore would not be searched. If she is to persuade others of her innocence, you must be there to speak for her, lass."

"I will be then, but it cannot matter if I finish my adventure first," she said. "Peg came with me and will return with me. I won't let her suffer for her loyalty."

A short silence fell before he said gently, "You implied earlier today that you had something you wanted to confide to me. Will you tell me what it is, or have I proven myself undeserving of such a confidence?"

Jenny's breath caught in her throat. Having expected him to pursue his own course to the exclusion of all else, she had thought that he would continue to urge her return to Annan House. She had not expected him to invite her confidence.

It was hardly the first time he had surprised her. His singing that very night had amazed her. She had already learned that he had a pleasing voice, speaking or singing. But as he sang the men's parts of the song, he'd altered not only his accent but also his voice and appearance, to become the very characters telling the tale.

In two instances, she had recognized traits of men in the minstrel company. His portrayal of the stern, indignant father displayed much of the Joculator with a touch of Dunwythie thrown in. The result had been so amusing that at times she'd had trouble keeping a steady voice to sing her own verses.

He had inspired her, too, to put more feeling into the women's parts of the story than she might have otherwise. He had also helped her forget herself and the uneasiness she had felt at the prospect of singing to such a large, expectant audience.

And now his willingness to listen to her made it seem wrong not to tell him of her odd feelings, especially in view of the missing jewelry and his mentioning Peg's first-head privileges, which had reminded her of the knacker.

Recalling that he was kin to Archie the Grim settled it. Despite his determination to take her back to Annan House, she instinctively trusted Sir Hugh. It seemed only right to share her feelings, however vague, with him.

Wary of eavesdroppers, she glanced toward the shrubbery behind them. As far as torchlight and moonlight allowed her to see, the shrubbery there was particularly dense. No one else seemed to pay them heed, and his very presence calmed her, encouraging her to speak. Still, she kept silent.

At last, he said, "You will have to answer me one way or another, you know. Have I put myself beyond the pale?"

She did not want him to think she believed him untrustworthy. And he had given her no cause to fear what he might say or do. Although he might easily have gone to the Joculator and told him he represented Dunwythie and had come to fetch his lordship's errant ward home, he had not issued even the mildest threat to do so.

Such a course would have proven almost as embarrassing as the scandal that her uncle feared would have—and potentially as damaging to her reputation. Clearly, Sir Hugh was protecting her name as carefully as he protected Dunwythie's.

She tried to gather these rambling thoughts but could seem only to marvel at his patience. Certain it could not last much longer, she blurted the first words that came to her: "I fear I may have stumbled onto some sort of intrigue."

Even in the dim light, she saw his eyebrows slant

upward and could scarcely blame him. When had *she* decided that her unease had substance?

He said mildly, "What manner of intrigue do you suspect, and who are the intriguers?" Blunt questions to which she had no solid answers.

With an inward sigh, she gathered her thoughts. Then she said, "I don't know why I said that about intrigue, sir. In troth, I can tell you only what happened and hope you can help me explain why it makes me feel as I do. First, I saw a man struck down in the road for no apparent reason."

"What man?"

"A knacker, Parland Dow." She described the event.

"I know Dow," he said. "Someone doubtless tried to rob him."

"They took naught, he said, but mayhap you are right. Next I overheard a spat between a man who had been away overnight and his wife. It was not the spat that struck me but his saying the King may be at Threave for the coronation celebration."

"Aye, that would strike anyone," he said with a smile.

"Aye," she agreed. "Primarily, though . . . I . . . had a gey strange dream."

She thought she heard his teeth grind together, but he said evenly enough, "What sort of a dream?"

The only reason she could recall the details she had pieced together was that they reminded her of the confrontation she and Peg had had with the two men-at-arms at Lochmaben. She did *not* want to describe that to him, so she said, "You know how it is with dreams. They fade quickly and one never remembers all the details."

"Try," he said.

"Cath and her man, Cuddy, were in it." Hastily, she added, "But I do not suspect them of anything, sir. Both of them vanished from the dream rather quickly, although the voice I heard continued to sound like Cuddy's."

"He vanished but his voice went on without him?"

"Nay, he . . . he turned into someone else," she said. "A . . . a man-at-arms at Lochmaben." Without looking at him, she added, "Peg and I had asked him the way to the garderobe."

To her surprise, Hugh smiled. "You should not be dreaming of Englishmen, lass. That is practically treason."

She shook her head, saying, "I don't think the voices sounded English. They just sounded like Borderers. I saw two men in my dream but not together. After that, it sounded as if one man were talking to himself in Cuddy's voice."

"What did he say?"

"He said, 'We pay for what we want and ye'll do what I say.' Then, as if he were irritated with himself, or pretending to be someone else, he said, 'So, I'm just to take ye along to Threave, am I?' You know," she said thoughtfully, "I have not said these things aloud before. They've all run together in my mind. But it was very much as if *two* men were talking, even with the voice sounding always the same."

"Are you sure the voice was Cuddy's?"

"I barely knew anyone in the company then," she reminded him. "I'd heard his voice only once. Sithee, he was the man in the spat with Cath. She thought he'd been seeing too much of a cousin she doesn't like because she thinks he's a bad influence on Cuddy. Sithee, I've seen such encounters amongst our people, and the voice in my dream had the sort of aggrieved tone a man gets at such a time. The tone might simply have reminded me of Cuddy."

"What did your dream character say after the bit about Threave?"

"He said Archie the Grim would ken nowt, nor Old Bleary."

"So he spoke of the King, too."

"Aye, and the other one— Sakes, but I'm sure now there must have been two men talking in that dream. Not that it matters, since it *was* a dream. At all events, the aggrieved one told the other to whisst, and I woke up. I remember wondering if it was *all* a dream. For a moment or two, it was as if one man were still speaking."

" 'Twas a strange thing, to be sure," he said. "But as it was a dream, lass, it may have sprung from no more than comments you'd heard before."

She thought he might be right. She did tend to let her imagination run free, and perhaps that was what she had done. Just being inside Lochmaben could easily have stirred her to imagine an enemy at work. At least Hugh had not rolled his eyes or explained at length that she was just being foolish, as Phaeline so often did.

She said, "There's more, though. I met a juggler and a musician, Jem and Gib, in the woods just a while ago. Gib thought I was Cath and called out to ask if they should try their new skills tonight or wait for larger crowds."

"There is not much in that," Hugh said.

"Nay, but as Jem greeted me, Gib went on to warn him that they must do nowt to imperil the performance at Threave. Then he said the sheriff might come tonight to watch, and Jem told him to whisst. But Gib just complained that Cath had vanished, which made me think of her vanishing from my dream and brought it all back. I did not know then about the missing jewels. But even so . . ." She paused. "Do you see?"

"I see how you have been thinking, but I cannot see how a dream you had at Lochmaben has aught to do with minstrels hoping to perform exceptionally well at Threave. 'Tis likely they don't want to spoil that performance by practicing all their tricks or skits in front of folks likely to spread word of all they do. Sithee, if that happened, it would lessen their impact on the grand occasion."

"I suppose so," she said. "I know there is naught of substance in any of it, but I still think something is not right. It may be the *way* they said things or a certain look they had, or just . . ." She shrugged, frustrated. "I don't know!"

"Then we will continue to ponder," he said. When she looked closely to see if he meant that, he added, "What made you decide to confide in me?"

The image of her father presented itself in her mind and made her smile reminiscently. "I like to talk such things out," she said. "My father said it was the surest way he knew to learn whether to trust one's instincts or not."

"'Tis a good plan, I should think. But—"

"Do you trust *your* instincts, sir?"

"Aye, sure, sometimes," he said. "Not always."

"Well, I am much the same. But I do think I ought to trust this one, even if I do not quite understand it. It feels gey strong, like a warning."

"Then we must see what more we can learn," he said.

"Meantime, your people at Annan House want you home. They have not been unkind to you, have they?"

"Nay," she said. "But they would order my life, and . . ." Trying to think of a tactful way to explain how she felt about Phaeline and Reid—who were his siblings, after all—she spread her hands instead.

"You know you must go back," he said. "In these uncertain times, you should be glad to have a man to help you run your estates and protect you."

She looked straight at him then, no longer caring about his sensibilities. "Would *you* trust Reid to protect me? Would you allow him to run *your* estates?"

"That is different," he said. "I am quite capable of running my own estates and protecting myself."

"Aye, well, so am I," she said.

"Nonsense, a woman cannot do either as well as a man can."

"So you believe *Reid* would do better?"

He hesitated, grimacing.

"Just so," she said. "I had begun to wonder if you knew your brother at all."

"He will learn," he said.

"Then *you*, not I, should be the one to teach him. I do not want him learning on *my* estates by guess and by consequence. I shall suggest, sir, that he apply to you for lessons before he tries taking the reins at Easdale."

He smiled. "That would teach me, would it not?"

"Aye, it would," she said, unable to resist smiling back. Then she added seriously, "I am sorry to be the one to tell you, but your brother is feckless, sir."

"Even so, you have formally betrothed yourself to him and must return."

"You say naught that you've not said already, and naught to persuade me," she said. "The others are finishing up now, I think," she said, turning away.

He caught her by an arm. "Hold there, lass. You would be wiser not to walk away from me until we have finished talking."

"But we *have* finished. You are kin to Archie Douglas, are you not?"

"You know I am."

"Well, you agreed to try to learn more about this odd warning sense I feel, and with Threave popping into everything—"

"Sakes, if they worried about the sheriff, the whole business is more likely to lead to the missing jewels," he said. "That is the only crime we know about."

"But the missing jewels have naught to do with Lochmaben!" she said. "My dream could not have—"

"Lass," he said patiently, "your dream is doubtless just a dream, or mayhap you had noticed things you did not understand whilst traveling with the minstrels, and your dream was how your imagination tried to make sense of them."

"But, if that is so, why would anyone in it declare that Archie the Grim and the King wouldn't ken aught of whatever it is *until afterward*," she demanded.

"Afterward? I don't believe you said that before."

"I only remembered as I was saying it, but I'm sure that is what he said."

"I suppose it is possible that a nearby conversation may have intruded on your dream," he said thoughtfully. "Where were you sleeping?"

"In the corner of the courtyard near the keep entryway.

When I woke, I did see men walking about but no one was near enough for me to have heard them speak." She brought the scene to mind again. "The entryway had that stone archway over it, and it was dark inside. I expect someone might have stood talking there. Anyone doing that would likely be English, though."

"And idle speculation is useless," he said.

"But if somehow they might threaten Archie the Grim, you do have a duty to learn more, do you not? You do serve him. Reid said that you did."

"I won my knighthood from him and owe him fealty, but I no longer serve him in the field. Were Scotland to be attacked, it would be otherwise, of course."

"If *he* is to be attacked, surely that counts as well."

"Aye, sure, it does," he agreed. "But whatever your odd feelings may mean, you have no evidence, and I have committed my service to Dunwythie. I can see you safely home and still ride to Threave in time to warn Archie of possible trouble. That is all it will take, I promise you, to foil any mischief—if mischief even exists."

"My dear sir, I have made it plain that I will not go unless you are willing to snatch me away by force. You would do well to reconcile yourself to that fact. If warning him is all that is necessary, I'd advise you to ride to Threave at once."

He was silent, giving her hope that he was considering her advice.

"Mayhap I should," he said. But to her consternation, the emotion that surged through her was disappointment, not elation.

Ruthlessly concealing it, she said, "An excellent notion, sir. Doubtless you will want to be away early tomorrow morning."

"Doubtless I will," he agreed. "I shall consider it. Now, as it appears that tonight's practice has ended, I'll escort you back to the encampment."

"We have been talking together too long as it is," she countered. "I would be wiser to walk back with Peg. I see her now," she added firmly. "Goodnight, sir."

Again she turned, and again he stopped her. "Peg is walking with her brother and Lucas. No one will think it odd that you walk with me after we have sung love songs to each other. Moreover, the path is uneven. Take my arm, lass."

He had been holding it out to her, and once again, he had succeeded in making her feel small and as if she were behaving in an unseemly manner. He did not say so, but the feeling persisted even after she accepted his arm.

"I did not mean to be rude," she said at last.

"Nay, lass, I'm sure you did not," he said.

His tone was consoling, even sympathetic, so she could not imagine why it stirred only a desire to smack him.

She resisted it but only by pressing her lips firmly together.

~⌐

Hugh felt her hand tighten on his arm and thought he knew what she was thinking. She was a woman who revealed her thoughts in every expression, every line of her body, and in the slightest tone of her voice. He had annoyed her.

The knowledge made him smile, and he was glad she

could not see it. She was staring straight ahead, and although her chin was a little higher than usual, the difference in their heights made it unlikely that she could see his expression without turning her head to look up at him.

The smooth, firm line of her jaw and his certainty that she had her lips pressed tightly together stirred a childish desire to make her smile, even if it took tickling to do it. He stifled the thought, but it soon returned in a teasing speculation about which parts of her curvaceous body might be the most ticklish.

Moonbeams piercing the canopy lit the narrow pathway well enough for him to see even without the ambient glow from the torches behind them in the clearing. They would stay lit until the townsfolk had all gone, after which, someone had told him, the lads watching them would douse them and bring them back to camp.

He did not mean to leave her in Dumfries with the minstrels. Even if he could trust both Peg and Bryan, they could not provide sufficient protection for her. If something was amiss within the company, plot or no plot, she might not be safe.

She remained silent, and he wanted to hear her voice again. He had enjoyed singing with her, especially the comic song. As she sang her replies, her eyes had twinkled, her rosy cheeks had glowed, and he had had trouble concentrating on which one of the four male characters was singing each of his verses.

He could not remember any woman affecting him so since Ella and the bairn had died. But she was nothing like Ella. Indeed, he feared she was as stubborn as he was, and Ella had not had a stubborn bone in her sweet body. She had been all pliable submission, bowing to his every whim and decree. She had never disputed with him but had, in fact, made him feel every inch the lord and master of his home.

Jenny, on the other hand, stirred only the primitive desire in him to master *her*.

But he was a mild-mannered man. It was strange to think how many times of late he had had to remind himself of that fact, and Jenny seemed to make a mockery of those reminders. From the outset of his journey, he had wanted to shake sense into her, to make her mind him, to force her obedience to Dunwythie's authority.

But, so far, she had defeated him at every turn without even raising her voice.

Bad enough that she stirred him to contemplate behavior he thought well outside the scope of his character. Worse for one who knew he was an able leader of men was the fact that his powers of persuasion, long held to be one of his greatest strengths, seemed to have no effect whatsoever on the stubborn lass.

She listened to him. At least, she appeared to listen. But no matter what he said to her, she continued to insist that she preferred to stay with the minstrels.

Such a life could not be comfortable for her; yet she made no complaint. Indeed, she seemed sincerely to be enjoying herself. As to the nonsense about running her own estates and protecting herself, he blamed her father. Clearly, the late laird had been a man of little sense, or he would have married again to provide her with a mother to teach her how to go on in life, and to give him a proper heir.

They were approaching the sleeping area, and he saw

Peg waiting for Jenny. As he glanced down at his silent companion, his earlier thoughts echoed through his mind. He could imagine her derision had she been able to hear them.

All very well for him to talk about her father and his own easy certainty that the late Lord Easdale ought to have remarried. But what about *him*? Despite the urging of his sister and others, including Dunwythie, he had not given remarriage a thought. After all, he reassured himself, he did have a male heir.

He glanced at the lass again, knowing how she would respond to that. Indeed, she *had* responded to it, and he had to admit that she had made an excellent point. He had done naught to teach Reid his responsibilities as heir to Thornhill, and yet he had assured her that Reid would quickly learn to run Easdale.

She looked up and met his gaze, raising her eyebrows. "Is aught amiss, sir?"

"Only that I owe you an apology, lass, if one can apologize for arrogance."

Her eyes twinkled then. "Arrogance, sir? How so?"

"Having acquaintance with your intelligence, minx, I am disinclined to explain what I am sure needs no explanation. However, I promise you that Reid will learn something about estate management before he takes the reins at Easdale."

"Faith, sir, the parson cried our banns in Annan Kirk this morning. Our wedding will take place just over a fortnight from now, yet you still assume *Reid* will take the reins. How do you imagine you can teach him anything about a place you have never seen, let alone do so in so short a time?"

"I cannot, of course. But I can recommend that he seek guidance from his lady wife, and that I certainly will do."

The light faded from her eyes, and her soft lips pressed together again. A moment later, she licked them and said flatly, "You do not know your brother at all, sir, if you think he would ever accept advice from a mere woman."

"I do not think you 'mere' at all, lass."

"Well, Reid does. He has often said so. So, pray, do not try to help me. I do not need your help. I *am* Easdale of Easdale, and so I will remain, Reid or no Reid. If you mean to teach your insufferable brother anything, see if you can teach him *that*."

Hugh struggled for a moment against a base inclination to shake her soundly and order her to heed him. Even as he did, though, he knew she was right again.

Her rank was equal to his, and had anyone suggested that he let someone else run things at Thornhill, he would have reacted more fiercely than she had. Even so, a woman was less able to enforce her commands than a man was, and was thus less able to run a large estate. She would do better with a good man at her side.

She continued to look at him, studying him, as they drew nearer to Peg.

At last, Jenny said, "You don't mean to ride to Threave tomorrow, do you?"

"I don't," he said shortly. "Goodnight to you, lass. Sleep well."

With a nod to Peg, he turned on his heel and strode away into the woods. As he did, he heard a sound that he suspected was a most unladylike snort.

His irritation evaporated, and although there was none but the moon to see it, Hugh grinned.

Chapter 8

Annan House

Where the devil are they then? Tell me that," Reid Douglas demanded of his sister and brother-in-law as they broke their fast that Monday morning. "Just thinking of all those folks in the kirk yester-morn, staring at me as the priest cried the banns . . . All of them were wondering where she was! I tell you, I won't stand for such antics after we're wed."

"No more should you," Phaeline said soothingly. "But you will be her husband then, Reid dearling. She will have to submit to your authority."

"You said she'd do as she was told now," he reminded her.

Fiona, sitting near the end of the table, said musingly, "Jenny is accustomed to running her estates and doing as she pleases. So one does wonder why anyone should think she would submit to Reid's authority when he has never run anything."

"That will do, Fiona," her mother said. "If you cannot remember to wait until someone addresses you before speaking, you will have to leave the table."

"I apologize, madam, but one cannot help wondering about such things."

Reid said, "I think you *wonder* just to see if you can stir mischief, my lass, so take care that you don't find yourself well slapped for such comments."

"I'll thank *you* to remember that she is my daughter, not yours," Phaeline said. "Although he does have cause to be irked with you, Fiona. You will oblige me by remaining silent until you are excused."

"Yes, madam," Fiona said.

"So much for her silence," Reid said grimly.

Mairi said, "I don't mind admitting that I'm growing more anxious about Jenny. She has been gone for two days and three nights, yet she cannot have got far on foot as she was. Should not Sir Hugh have found her by now?"

With an air of relief at this return to the primary topic, Dunwythie said, "First Hugh had to discover which way she went. Although Sadie suspected that Jenny went with the minstrels and Peg's continued absence gives credence to that opinion, Hugh had to be sure. We know only that they intended to go to Dumfries and to Threave. In troth, they may have gone anywhere from here."

"Well, I for one do not mean to sit here awaiting their pleasure," Reid said, getting to his feet. "I warrant *I* can find them easily enough. What that wench wants is beating, and I am sure that as her betrothed husband, I have—"

"Sit down, Reid," Dunwythie said.

"Damnation, sir, she is mine! That you sent Hugh after her is bad enough. But now, when nearly three whole days have passed—"

"I said sit down, sir," Dunwythie snapped. "I can think

of only one reason for Jenny to run from her betrothal feast—that *you* did something to upset her."

"*I*? I did nowt, and well do you know it! I left the table before she did!"

"He was pawing at her throughout the feast, my lord," Fiona said with a grimace. "Poor Jenny kept twitching to keep away from him. Indeed, one time—"

"Fiona, I warned you," Phaeline said angrily. "Leave the table at once, and without another word!"

"One moment," Dunwythie said as Fiona got up. "What did you see, lass?"

"I think she pinched him, sir. At all events, he snatched his hand from under the table and looked as if he wanted to murder her. Mairi and I both saw it."

"Sakes," Reid said, rolling his eyes. "A man has every right to touch his betrothed. And I'd say she has a duty to allow it. In any event, I shall certainly go after her. She deserves—"

"We will not discuss here what she deserves, sir," Dunwythie said. "Nor will you leave this house unless you want to incur my strongest displeasure. You asked for my reasons, so I will tell you that you are too hot-tempered. I cannot trust you to avoid scandal. By my troth, I cannot trust you not to *create* one."

"If there is to be scandal, my lord, it will be of Jenny's making."

"We will not discuss blame here, either," Dunwythie said. "I have said all I mean to say. But as you seem unwilling to hear my words, I shall send an order to the stables that you are not to take out any horse until Jenny returns."

"You cannot do that!"

Dunwythie met Reid's angry gaze with his own cool, steady one.

"Oh, very well, of course you can," Reid snapped. "But you cannot mean what you say, sir. Sakes, what would the stable lads think?"

Silence.

"My lord, please," Phaeline said. "You are upsetting me, and I fear—"

"I am sorry for your upset, my lady. Mayhap you would do better to go upstairs and rest, because I do not mean to let this . . . your brother . . . raise a riot and rumpus that could spread who kens how far? He will give me his word that he will not leave Annan House, or I *will* send that order to the stables."

She looked at Reid. "Please, laddie?"

"Oh, very well," he said, sitting down again. "You have my word."

Fiona, still standing at her place, said sweetly to him, "How wise of you. But one cannot help wondering if, having given your word, you will keep it."

"Fiona!"

"Aye, madam, I'm going," Fiona said, demurely making her curtsy.

Dumfries

"Where be ye a-going, lass?"

Jenny turned to find wee Gilly behind her. "Faith, how do you walk so quietly, and with bells on your cap?" she asked him. "Things crackle under my feet with every step I take."

The little man chuckled. "When ye look as I do, it be safer to walk softly lest ye wake a tiger sleeping under a bush. Sithee, Gawkus isna the only man who has hung me by me coat from a tree branch after I've angered him."

"I didn't know that anyone had done such a thing to you. How dreadful!"

"Aye, 'tis aggravating, to be sure. But ye shouldna be out and about on your ownsome, Mistress Jenny."

"Just Jenny, sir. I'm nobbut plain Jenny."

"Aye, well, dinna be calling me 'sir,' then. Ye'll have all them others a-doing it and making mock o' me when they do. I be Gilly to me friends. But still ye should turn back, Jenny, or find some o' the other lasses to walk wi' ye."

She sighed. "Cath was with me, but she went back. 'Tis such a fine day, I thought I'd walk until I could see the town and mayhap go in and have a look at it."

"Nay, then, ye mustna do that," he said. "Sure, and I've me doots that ye'd do such a thing at home, either, wherever your home may be."

"I expect you are right," she admitted. "I've not spent time near any town or roamed such streets alone. And Dumfries is large."

"Not as large as Edinburgh or Glasgow, though Dumfries be a royal burgh, too," he said. "Still, 'tis a fair-sized place, withal. We could find Gawkus and ask him does he want to go into town with us."

"Are you not sufficient protection for me? I warrant you can handle a dirk as deftly as Gawkus does."

His eyes twinkled. "I can, and all, but walking alone wi' me would only add to your woes. 'Twould doubtless bring trouble down on both of us."

A thought occurred to her. "Could you teach *me* to throw a dirk, Gilly?"

"If your eye be as fine as your voice, I can," he said.

"How can we find out if it is?"

He looked around, then pointed and said with a grin, "See that tree yonder?"

As she nodded, a dagger flew from his other hand, striking the trunk of the tree about five feet above the ground.

"I'll fetch it," she said.

"Nae need," he said, flipping a second one so that he held it by the blade with its hilt toward her. "Take hold o' that and get a feel of it. Dinna cut yourself."

Having watched the Joculator juggle six daggers at once, she had thought they must be light. But the one Gilly handed her had weight to it.

As she hefted it, another appeared in the little man's hand.

"Faith, how many do you carry?"

He laid a finger beside his nose, saying, "Nay, now, that would be telling. Now, hold the dirk on your finger with the blade toward ye, so, till it balances. That's it. Now, hold it there wi' your finger and thumb, step forward so, and fix your eyes on yon dirk stuck in the tree. Dinna take your eyes from it as ye bring your hand back and then forward, so. Look right down your arm to your thumb and the end o' the dirk's handle, then to the tree. Aye, that's it," he said approvingly.

"It feels awkward," she said.

"Aye, it will for a time. Now, do that all again and let fly, so." He threw his, and it stuck beside the first one.

Hers missed the tree.

Disappointed, she said, "Clearly, I lack the eye."

Gilly chuckled. "Nay, then, ye were off by only a foot. The first time I flung one, it stopped flying halfway to the tree. Ye'll do, but ye shifted your gaze to watch the dagger as ye let it fly. Dinna take your eyes off your target."

Three throws later, her dagger hit the tree a few feet below his with a thunk that thrilled her to the bone. "I did it!" she cried.

"Aye, ye did, but ye'll need much more practice afore ye'll hit it every time. And, mind now, ye canna practice in camp, nor yet anywhere too nearby, lest ye unintentionally put an end to some unfortunate soul."

"Intentionally is all right?"

He chuckled again. "Throw again, mistress."

She looked at him.

"Throw it again, Jenny."

With a smile, she did, and it hit the tree again . . . barely . . . catching in the bark on one side, evidently without adequate force to dislodge the bark altogether.

"Good enough," he said, unbuckling the sheath he wore strapped to one thigh. "Fix this belt round your waist," he said. "It should be loose enough so the sheath can slip betwixt folds o' your skirt. Other lasses do as much wi' their eating knives, so it should cause nae great stir. But dinna try to defend yourself with it, because any man wi' the slightest training will be able to take it from ye."

"Then you must next teach me how to keep one from doing that," Jenny said. "I would know how to protect myself."

"I'm thinking we should be getting back," he said. "Ye've much more yet to learn, but I dinna want yon great Hugo looking to skin me for flirting with ye. The man looks as if he'd ken one end of a blade from another better nor most."

Aware that Hugh might well come in search of her if he did not see her with the others when he thought he should, she agreed. But when she realized they'd soon reach the campsite, she said, "I must leave you here, Gilly, for the usual personal reason. But thank you for teaching me. I want to learn all I can of such things."

"Hoots, lass, mayhap ye'll become a fool like us. I warrant ye could add much to our performance by singing whilst ye fling your knives. I ha' nae doots ye'd soon outdo both Gawkus and me."

"Aye, sure," she said, laughing.

He grinned back and hurried away.

Hugh frowned at the long, stout stick of wood he held and then scanned the common area of the encampment again. Still no Jenny. Where the devil was she?

"D'ye mean to hold that stick all day, man, or will ye be turning it into a proper torch for us?"

He smiled ruefully at Gawkus and thought the man looked as if he had been put together from sticks himself. His long thin arms were akimbo, his long-oval head tilted to one side, and his mop of red curls was as wild as Peg's, albeit not as long.

"I'll have this one finished in a twink," Hugh said, noting that others who helped them were also watching him. "Do you really mean to juggle torches?"

"Aye, sure," Gawkus said. "We dinna fling them about inside great halls, because their owners tend to object, but we nearly always do it when we're outside at night, as we will be in Dumfries market square."

"The torches always impress folks," the Joculator said, joining them.

"Gawkus is not the only one who juggles them, then. You do, too?"

"Most of us do any number of things," he said with a smile. "I just do everything that everyone else does, plus a few trifling things of mine own."

"Your skill with the daggers is most impressive," Hugh said.

"Ah, so ye saw that, did ye? I thought ye'd come into Lochmaben afterward, but I expect I miss a number o' things whilst I'm juggling the dirks. It does require at least a prick's worth o' concentration even when one has done it for years."

"I'm sure it does," Hugh said, castigating himself for the slip. He had spoken without thinking, remembering the man's skillful performance at Annan House.

"So where do your wits keep a-wandering, lad?" Gawkus asked. "Not that one has to ask," he added. "She's a bonnie one, I'll grant ye."

Hugh smiled, glad that Gawkus had changed the subject but wishing he had chosen another. Mildly, he said, "We sing well together. Doubtless that is why you suspect me of thinking about her more than perhaps I should."

"Aye, sure, and ye were just looking around for another suitable torch stick, I expect. Sakes, lad, she seems to treat ye kindly enough."

"She does, indeed," the Joculator added. "I've nae doubt ye'll bring her round your thumb yet, if ye exert a wee bit o' patience."

"I wish that were so," Hugh muttered. Then he said frankly, "In troth, it did occur to me that I'd not seen her for some time. And she does tend to wander about without thought o' the dangers one may find in the woods."

"She went off with me wife, Cath," one of the others said.

Hugh recognized the man Cuddy, who played a flute and the pipes. Eyeing him, he wondered what had possessed Jenny to dream about a scrawny middle-aged man with crooked teeth. But he also noted that Cuddy's accent was more akin to the English Borders than the Scottish ones. The accents were much alike though, and Hugh doubted that Jenny's ear was as well tuned to the differences as his was.

As Hugh pondered what the discovery might mean, if anything, the Joculator said. "Aye, Jenny and Cath went off together over an hour ago, but Cath came back shortly afterward. Doubtless, our Jenny went on to the hilltop for a look at the view and lost track of the time."

"I think I'll just take a walk myself then," Hugh said. "I've made at least a dozen torches. With all these others helping, we should have enough for the first performance at least."

"As that first performance is tonight, I hope ye're right," the Joculator said. "We expect a sizable crowd."

"And, with luck, it will rain gelt," Gawkus added with a grin.

Saying he would return long before then, Hugh strode off, wondering if the sheriff would grace that night's performance, too. The thought did not worry him. The sheriff had not recognized the purple-caped troubadour as the Laird of Thornhill, so doubtless he would accept him henceforward as a troubadour.

The encampment was well behind him before he saw Jenny, standing with her back to him, peering into the woods. There seemed to be a small clearing there, with the sun beaming mote-ridden rays down into it.

Whatever she saw fascinated her, because she did not hear his approach.

"What are you doing here?" he asked, meaning to startle her, to remind her how dangerous inattention could be in such a place.

She turned quickly, clearly angry. "You scared them away! Two fawns!"

"Look here," he began, "you have no business—"

"*Don't* try again to tell me my business. I—"

Grabbing her by the upper arms, he gave her a shake that broke off her reply, making her eyes widen and her lips part in shock.

They looked invitingly soft and rosy.

He had intended to tell her just what he thought of her behavior. Instead, without another thought, he pulled her close and kissed her hard.

~⌒~

No one had ever kissed Jenny in such a way in all her life. Her first reaction was stunned disbelief that Hugh had taken such a liberty. But as he pulled her closer, her body began to respond of its own accord to sensations racing through it.

He kissed her hungrily, letting go of her left arm to put his right one around her as his other hand moved to cup the back of her head. Her breasts pressed against him, and the warmth of his body radiated through hers.

A warning flitted through her mind that she ought to feel trapped. Instead, she felt a sense of comfort that she had not felt since before her father's death.

When the pressure of his lips eased against hers, her own moved as if something deep inside her wanted him to go on kissing her. Curiosity, she told herself as her body pressed harder against his. That's all it was.

Then his tongue touched her lips and tried to slip between them. She put a tentative hand to his chest, uncertain whether she wanted him to continue or not.

That light touch was enough.

With a low moan, he straightened and looked at her ruefully.

The woods felt chilly again.

"As you see, the woods can be dangerous to a woman alone," he said. "Especially when she pays more heed to a pair of fawns than to her own safety."

Striving for calm, she said, "I should slap you for taking such a liberty."

"I'd advise against that, although I'll admit I should not have done it. What were you doing here?"

"I *was* watching a pair of fawns," she said.

"Don't try me too far, lass. You've been away more than an hour."

"Mercy, do you keep such a close watch over me?"

"I should," he replied. "I'm sure Dunwythie would expect me to, but I was helping make torches for the performance tonight. Cuddy saw you go, but 'twas the Joculator who knew how much time had passed. He must have been watching you."

Catching movement in the trees behind him, she shifted to see who was coming, but saw only a flash of red-and-black stripes.

"I think he is still watching me," she said. "Or us."

"The devil he is!" He turned. "I don't see anyone."

"I saw red-and-black stripes. He has a robe—"

"Aye, and he was wearing it," he said. "Mayhap I shall have to tell him the truth about you. But I dislike taking anyone here into our confidence, especially if there might any substance to these feelings of yours."

That he might confide in the Joculator reminded her of the fib *she* had told the man. That produced a stab of guilt and made her say hastily, "It may be better if I talk to him. I can tell him I saw him watching us and explain that singing love songs with me stirred you to think I might . . ." She looked down, uncertain just what she could say, then added impulsively, "I can just tell him it won't happen again."

"Aye, that might be best," he said. "And it won't, lass. I'll see to that."

She nodded, hoping the twinge of disappointment that stirred then did not reveal itself in her expression.

"So, what *were* you doing out here for so long?" he asked, stern again.

"I was learning to throw a dirk," she said with a smile, patting the sheathed blade nestled on her hip between two folds of her skirt.

Clapping a strong hand atop of hers, he said curtly, "Give it to me."

Stiffening, angry again, she said with ice in her voice, "Take your hand away, or by heaven I will do you an injury."

Already annoyed with himself for giving way to a foolish impulse and kissing her, Hugh realized he had taken a second misstep. But he had acted from pure instinct when she reached for the weapon.

Certain that she had only meant to show him where she kept the dagger she had supposedly learned to throw, he relaxed his grip but did not let go of her hand.

Gently, he said, "Just as it is unwise to hit someone larger and stronger who might well hit back, lass, it is unwise to issue threats you cannot carry out. Nay, you won't catch me that way," he added, turning slightly when she brought up a knee, so it struck his hard thigh rather than the target she had surely hoped to strike.

"Let go of me," she said, her tone still icy.

"I want to see that knife. You may give it to me properly, or I will take it from you. I can promise you won't like it if I have to do that."

"I could shout for the Joculator."

"Aye, you could," he agreed, holding her gaze.

With a sigh, she said, "Very well, but you may not keep it. It was a gift."

"From whom?" he demanded, hearing an unexpected note of jealousy in his tone and nearly wincing at the sound. Bad enough that he had betrayed Ella's sweet memory by kissing Jenny. What he felt now was surely naught but the childish feeling many men felt at learning that someone for whom they bore responsibility had been doing something unbeknownst to them with another man.

Jenny said calmly, "Wee Gilly gave it to me."

Mentally giving himself a shake, Hugh took his hand from hers and said, "I'm told that both he and Gawkus are highly skilled with knives, albeit not as skilled as the Joculator. Show me what Gilly taught you."

She took the knife carefully from its sheath and found its fulcrum. Then, taking a moment to seek her target, she said, "That tree with the boll on its trunk."

Bringing her arm back, she let fly . . . and missed the tree.

Looking chagrined, she bit her lower lip but started toward the tree.

Hugh stopped her. "I'll fetch it," he said. "Your aim was off and you need to step back a pace or it will strike hilt-first, but you throw better than I had expected."

"I hit my target several times when Gilly was with me," she said.

Without comment, he strode to the dagger, wiped the blade on his buckskins, and returned to her, hefting the weapon as he did. "You were holding the blade too tightly," he said. "And you shifted your gaze to the knife as you let go."

"Gilly warned me to keep my eyes on my target, but I do tend to forget."

"Watch," he said. Throwing, he buried the blade in the center of the boll.

"I'll get it," she said. "It is only fair. You fetched mine."

He did not reply, but he watched with amusement as she tried first just to pull the blade free, then to wriggle it free. He had buried it deep.

When she used both hands and put a foot against the

tree trunk, he nearly laughed, but she managed at last to free the blade.

"Throw again," he said when she returned.

She threw six more times and hit the tree three times.

"Why do you want to learn such a skill?" he asked her.

She glanced at him with a startled look in her eyes, much as her fawns might have looked earlier at the sound of his voice.

Then she said, "I . . . I just like to learn things." She looked away.

Catching her chin between a forefinger and thumb, he made her look at him again. "Don't try to lie to me. You haven't the knack. Now, what made you think such a skill might serve you?"

"I don't know why you think you have any right to ask me such things."

"We have picked that bone clean. Answer me."

⤙⤏

Having little choice, since he still held her chin, Jenny said, "I don't know that I thought of such a skill serving me, exactly, but . . ." She still did not want to tell him about the men who had accosted her and Peg at Lochmaben, so she said, "I just thought I might feel safer if I kept a dirk by me, and learned how to use it."

"A false feeling at best," he said grimly. "But you are equivocating if not lying to me again. If you want to keep that thing, you'd best tell me the truth."

Instead, she wondered if perhaps the Joculator had

known she was lying when she told him that Hugo the troubadour fancied himself in love with her.

"I can be a patient man," he said. "But this is *not* one of those moments."

Damping dry lips with the tip of her tongue, she said, "I saw Gawkus throw one of his knives and pin a man's sleeve to the wall. I thought such a skill might prove useful one day, that's all."

"Just when and where did Gawkus perform this feat?"

"It wasn't a performance . . ." She caught herself, then gave it up. "Two men followed Peg and me upstairs to the garderobe at Lochmaben. They wanted us to go with them to another chamber. I said we had to sing, but they insisted that at least one of us had to comply. Gawkus and Gilly intervened, so it came to naught."

"I see." His tone was grim. "Was one of the men who accosted you the man-at-arms in your dream?"

Warily, she nodded. Standing as near him as she was, only too aware of his height and his strength, she feared the dirk would not aid her in defending herself against any man. Indeed, Gilly had said it would not, and she doubted that she could ever throw it at one. Not that it mattered, since Hugh would likely take it now.

He was still frowning.

She drew a breath, bracing herself for what he would say.

"Very well," he said at last. "You may keep the damned thing. But whilst you remain in this company, I want you to promise you will practice with it each day. I want to know when you do, and if Gilly cannot go with you, I will. It won't hurt for word to spread through the camp that you have some skill with the thing."

"I'll practice," she said, trying to hide her surprise.

"Aye, but attend to me now," he said, catching her chin again to make her look at him. "If anyone does accost you again, use your voice, *not* your dagger. You would do better to unfasten that belt with the sheath and clout the scoundrel with it. Better yet, fling that knife as far from you as you can. Do *not* give anyone else a chance to take it from you. Do you understand me?"

"Aye," she said, feeling those little shivers dance up her spine again.

"We'll go back now," he said and offered an arm.

Tucking her hand in the crook of his elbow, she reflected that although he took liberties with his presumed authority and otherwise, his presence was nonetheless comforting.

"Have you seen the Joculator following you before?" he asked.

"Nay," she said. "He may not have been following us at all. Cath says he always sets his tent at a distance from the rest, so I warrant the man just likes his privacy. Shall we sing the same songs tonight as last night?"

Discussing songs, they strolled amiably back to the encampment. There they found others preparing their midday meal and Jenny hurried to assist them.

She looked back as she joined the women, and watched with mixed feelings as Hugh strode away. One minute she had wanted to slap the man and the next she had invited more kisses. What manner of behavior was that for a betrothed lady?

Chapter 9

Starving, and looking for Lucas Horne, Hugh found him setting up the trestle table where the minstrels would eat their dinner.

The rest of the company found places wherever they might, but Hugh had already learned that the Joculator used mealtimes to discuss new ideas for their acts and preferred not to air these discussions before all and sundry. Hugh counted it as a compliment that the man included him in the group at the table.

Lucas squared the planks on the trestles and nodded at Gerda, who stood by with a cloth, to fling it over the boards. As Lucas helped her straighten it, Hugh pulled up a bench, and Lucas said, "I'll get t' other one. Thank ye, lass," he added. "We'll finish up 'ere, and ye can tell 'em at the fire that we be ready to eat."

"Aye, sure, Lucas," she said with a seductive smile. "I'm hoping ye dinna mean to spend the whole afternoon on chores and such."

"Happen I won't," he said. "Get along wi' ye now."

She went, swinging her hips, and Lucas looked at Hugh. "None of your nash-gab now, sir," he said. "She 'as a tongue hinged like a clapdish, as ye might say, so I were thinkin' it wiser to let 'er talk than to send 'er away, mayhap to make up tales for other ears. Where 'ave ye been keepin' yourself?"

"Here and there," Hugh said, helping him pull up the second bench. "Learn all you can from that lass, or from anyone else who likes to talk. Her ladyship thinks someone here may be brewing mischief against Archie the Grim."

"Be a dangerous business if that be so," Lucas said thoughtfully. "They dinna call the man Grim for nowt."

"No, they don't," Hugh said. "He's a bad man to cross, and would liefer hang an offender than discuss his errors with him. 'Tis how he conquered Galloway when none before him could do it, and how he holds the region now. Still, they do say his tournament will be a grand affair. Even his grace the King may attend."

"Old Bleary? I wish I may see it," Lucas said scornfully. "I hear 'e scarcely gets out of bed on 'is own. And t' furthest I've heard of 'im travelin' be from Stirling to Edinburgh wi' the court, or back again to Stirling."

"That's true enough," Hugh said. "But Archie's tournament is to honor the third anniversary of the Steward's taking the throne, as well as the completion of Threave Castle. So the rumors may be true. The King does like men to honor him."

"Aye, sure," Lucas said. "We'll see then. Did ye want me to do summat?"

"Just to keep your eyes and ears well open. I should also warn you that the lass now carries a dagger."

"That Gerda lass?"

"Ours," Hugh said curtly.

"What be ye about to allow that? A lass wi' a dirk be more likely to cut herself than aught else."

"Wee Gilly has been teaching her to throw it," Hugh said. "She has an eye but needs much more practice before she'll hit anything with regularity. Still, it won't hurt for some of the louts in this company to see her carrying it, and to hear that she knows how to use it."

"Happen she does, but she canna ken *much* about such."

"She has other protectors, though," Hugh said. "I want her to carry it as much to encourage them to keep an eye on her as for any other reason."

"Then we'll be bidin' a wee while longer wi' them 'ere," Lucas said.

"Aye, we will," Hugh said. "At present, she is determined to stay with the minstrels, and I'm thinking we'd meet with stiff resistance if we tried to take her away against her will."

"'Ave ye no got another of your fine plans, then?"

"Not a dependable one," Hugh said. "I've a fancy to persuade the lass without making an enemy of her. We'll soon be kin, after all."

"Aye, that would be why," Lucas said sagely.

⟳

As Jenny helped Peg pile bread in the baskets, she kept an eye on those around them, wondering if any of them was brewing mischief. She wondered, too, if Sir Hugh might be right and the minstrels sought nothing but a fine performance at Threave for the Lord of Galloway and perhaps the King.

Something felt wrong about that, but she could not put her finger on what it was. She had repeated what she could remember to him, but the memory of her dream still seemed more ominous than her description of it to Hugh.

One thing he had said did not feel wrong, and that was his suggestion that perhaps someone's nearby conversation had got mixed into her dream. The words she recalled had seemed clear when she awoke, and despite what she had said about the nature of dreams, the words she remembered had not faded with time.

Seeing Gawkus coming toward the table with Gilly, she smiled. She was sure that neither had been among the men walking about when she awoke. With tall, thin Gawkus looking all joints and bones like a stick puppet, and Gilly so small, she knew she would have recognized either of them, even in the dimly lit courtyard.

The Joculator gestured to her then, motioning her toward the table, where the only obvious space left on either bench was between Sir Hugh and Gilly. The little man waved and patted the space.

"Hugo said ye've been practicing," he said as she lifted her skirt to step over the bench and sit down. "Three times out o' six ye hit your target, he said."

"Aye, but I'd rather have hit it six times."

"Be patient, Jenny. Ye've a keener eye than most."

"Most women?"

"Most anyone,' he said with a chuckle.

Gawkus leaned across the table. "Mind, ye're no to start juggling wi' that blade o' yours, Jenny-lass. We canna stand the competition."

"Attend to me, all o' ye," the Joculator said from the head of the table. "We perform tonight in the market square. We expect a large crowd, and we want them to return often during the next sennight. Be ye all ready to give them a good show?"

"Aye!" they cried as one.

"Good, because I have a notion for our players. 'Tis long since we have performed 'The Troubadour's Wife,' and I'm thinking the folks of Dumfries would enjoy it. We've done 'The Wicked Brother' so often of late that I fear the piece has grown stale. Moreover, it came to me that with our Hugo's canny way of aping accents and the like, we might add summat new to the 'Troubadour.' What say ye?"

The reply was one of general approval except, Jenny noted, for Hugo.

"Faith, sir, I'm no actor," he said.

"Dinna be daft, lad. What d'ye think your mimicry be if not acting? Any troubadour can tell a tale or sing a song, and ye do both well. I warrant that with a mite o' practice, ye'll don the odder characters' skins as if they were your own. Our Gerda ha' played the wife many and many a time, so she can help ye get it right."

Plump Gerda beamed at Hugh, and when Jenny saw the sour expression on his face, she nearly burst out laughing. Leaning near him, she said demurely, "I warrant you will make her a fine husband, sir."

"Do you know this play?" he demanded.

"Nay." She turned to Gilly. "What is the play about?"

"Och, 'tis a silly thing about a troubadour who courts all the ladies he meets, then marries one who likes him, only to rue the day he wedded her. There be many characters but only four players. Gerda and Cath will play the ladies' roles, and Hugo will play Gerda's father and other parts I expect, as well as the Troubadour."

"Mercy, but it sounds complicated," Jenny said, glancing again at Hugh.

Gilly shrugged. "'Tis nobbut prick's worth o' foolishness," he said. "But folks always laugh most heartily. We're going to do 'The Puppet' one night, too, Gawkus and I, most likely on Friday. Ye'll like that fine, I'm thinking."

"I'm sure I will," she said. "You two always make me laugh."

Hugh was more conscious of Jenny beside him than he'd have wanted to admit. As he glanced around the table and at others in the clearing, he saw several men eyeing her and felt a strong temptation to tell them all to look elsewhere.

One in particular scarcely took his gaze off her.

The man stiffened as if he felt Hugh's steady gaze. Meeting it, he flushed and looked away. One down, Hugh thought, then laughed at his own foolishness.

To be sure, it was his duty to protect her, but this . . . He scanned the others again, wondering if the lass was right to suspect trouble brewing. The likelihood was that she had made more of an innocent conversation than she should, seeking an excuse not to go home. He would indulge her another day or so, but then . . .

As his thoughts drifted thus idly, he continued to look for men watching her too closely, until his gaze collided with the Joculator's.

The man seemed to be studying him, and Hugh thought about the play. He did not like the idea of taking on so singular a role. Playing troubadour in a company of real minstrels was strain enough. To play the double role of

a troubadour playing a troubadour would border hazard-
ously on the absurd.

The Joculator summoned the players together directly
after the meal and began to describe the play to them. It
seemed that Hugo was to have no choice.

⁓

Jenny watched for a time as the group at the table discussed the play. But fat Gerda's simpering smiles grew
tedious. So, when she saw some of the children aping the
fools' behavior, she went to watch them instead.

Some of the little ones tumbled and flipped as skill-
fully as Gilly did, and for a while their antics amused her.
But the afternoon crept slowly, and she itched to practice
throwing her dirk. That she had hit her target in only half
of her attempts while Hugh watched was disappointing.
She had wanted to impress him. Somehow, it had mattered more for her to do well while he watched her than
when Gilly had.

Finding Peg busy with her mending and Gilly practicing with Gawkus—and having no desire to sit and chat
with the other women—she was tempted to return to the
hilltop alone. Glancing toward the table, she met Hugh's
gaze. When he frowned as if he knew exactly what she
was thinking, she decided to practice her lute instead.

Fetching it, she sat on a rock where she could see the
children playing and began to play the comic song she
had sung with Hugh the night before.

The memory of that performance made her smile.
His ability to turn himself into another character without

changing anything but his expression, accent, and tone of voice had both astonished and amused her.

Motion at the table diverted her as the players moved to the end of the clearing, where they began to walk through their parts. The Joculator stood a little to one side, watching them. Recalling his promise to let her try her skill on the hurdy-gurdy, she returned her lute to its casing and went to him.

"I warrant ye'll be ready for me to let ye try the *vielle*," he said, smiling.

"Aye, sir, for ye did say we might play it if I stayed with ye long enough."

"So I did. Would ye like to walk with me to my tent? I'll fetch it out and we can sit on the rocks there and try it out."

She agreed and was not surprised when he took the path she had taken that morning. As she had suspected, his tent stood not far from where she and Gilly had thrown their dirks. It was lucky, she thought, that they had faced the other way.

She realized then that Gilly had probably known where the tent was but decided to say nothing about her new skill unless her companion mentioned it. From what she had seen of him, she would not be surprised if he knew all about it.

Heat flooded her cheeks when she remembered that he had seen Hugh kissing her. She was grateful that he said nothing about it as they walked, but she could not help wondering what he had thought about that kiss.

After all, she had sworn to him that she had not encouraged the troubadour. She had said she did not want to encourage any man. And those had been the parts of what she had told him that she had thought were at least true. But no one witnessing that kiss would think she had been reluctant or was just being kind.

Reaching the green tent, set again near a bubbling rill, she waited while the Joculator dove inside and emerged with the five-foot-long *vielle*.

It had a body shaped something like a lute, with a very long neck into which the keys were set, and three strings, two of which ran over its bridge. It also had a small wheel. One person turned the wheel while the other pulled the keys.

He suggested a tune and Jenny agreed. She also agreed that she would pull the keys as he turned the wheel. She had forgotten how slowly one played the *vielle*. After the lively tunes she and Hugh had played, it seemed especially slow.

When they paused to rest, she expected him to comment on her playing, but he said, "You and Hugo make a fine couple." When she looked at him, struggling to think how to reply, he added, ". . . for singing, lass. Your voices blend well together."

Gathering her wits, Jenny thanked him but squirmed again at the fib she had told him about Hugo's supposed interest in her. Having misled him to think Hugo had offered her marriage but that she preferred men of a more delicate manner, she felt her cheeks burn anew at memory of Hugh's anything-but-delicate kiss. Then she wondered if the Joculator might be looking for just such a blushing response. Even if he was, she decided, if he wanted to talk more about Hugo, he would have to say so, and she devoutly hoped he would not.

She was a poor liar at best, having had little practice in

what she was rapidly coming to think was an art form. She would not make matters worse by telling more lies—or by telling him the truth. Instead, she concentrated on the music and on trying to avoid any topic that might lead him to ask questions about Hugh.

As it was, he cut their practice time short. And although she had enjoyed it, she could not imagine that her skill on the *vielle* was such that he would invite her to play it for their Dumfries audience.

He said only, "Thank you, lass. That was a pleasant interlude and brought some pleasant memories. I have a gittern as well, though, that you might prefer."

Taking leave of him, she returned to the clearing to find preparations for supper in hand. Hugh, standing with Lucas Horne, saw her and strode to meet her. To her relief, his expression revealed only curiosity.

"What did the Joculator want? You have been gone for nearly an hour."

She shook her head at him but kept her voice low enough so that only he would hear. " 'Twas not the Joculator who told you so this time. Truly, sir, I am not a dafty or a bairn. If you are going to suggest that I ought not to have walked back here by myself, you would do better to save your breath to cool your porridge."

He smiled. "Porridge? We'll be lucky tonight to get cold beef. In case you've not noticed yet, they have lighted no cook fires. So it will be cold fare only, I fear."

"I know it will, because Peg said they won't risk leaving hot coals here in the woods. I warrant it would take a miracle to set them afire though, as damp as everything is with patches of melting snow still on the ground."

"A good habit is a *habit* only if one maintains it

regardless of the weather," he said. "Do you mean to tell me what you have been doing all this time?"

"I was learning to play the Joculator's *vielle*," she said.

"I have never played one. Is it difficult?"

"One always feels awkward when one is new to an instrument, and the *vielle* does not accommodate itself to lively tunes," she said as they strolled toward the others. "In any event, I'd prefer the lute or a gittern. Should we practice what we're going to sing tonight? I expect we'll have time before we eat."

He said, "We'll sing the songs we sang last night, and I'll tell a tale I've told many times before. So we'd do better to rest whilst we can and then decide by the audience's reaction what else we should do. Gawkus said he and Gilly always add bits on the hop, so folks never know what to expect from them."

"I thought we might be singing more songs with such a large audience."

"The Joculator wants us to add a new thing or two each night, rather than show everything straightaway. His object is to persuade as many as possible from each audience to attend our next evening's performance."

She noted the pronoun but ignored it as bait to which she would be foolish to rise. He might expect to leave the minstrels before the end of the week, but she hoped to remain with them at least long enough to learn just what was going on.

"When will you be doing the play?" she asked.

"We begin tomorrow night, but he suggested that we do just a short version first, mayhap the first act. It shows the troubadour wooing his many ladies whilst the woman he eventually marries plots to snare him. It has more physical humor than lines to learn, so it is simple enough, and I won't have to remember everything the first night. I'm no player, though, so be warned, lass. I want to be away from here before we have to act out the whole play."

"Faith, sir, it cannot be so hard if they think you can do it. And surely you won't leave them without a troubadour for their final performance here. That would be most unkind when they have been so generous to you, and to me. Moreover, you and Gerda make a most charming couple."

"We'll have less of that, if you please," he said with a grimace. "If that woman keeps simpering, and ogling me from under her lashes, I'm likely to upend a pot of water over her head."

"Suggest that to the Joculator," she said. "He prefers comic things to romantic ones, I think. I wonder if he has ever been married. He said the *vielle* belonged to his son, but he has never mentioned a wife to me."

"I didn't know he had a son," Hugh said. "But I'll suggest the pot of water. I'd rather douse Gerda than marry her, even in pretense. I'm sure she's a kind lass, but I think she has much more experience with men than I've had with the lasses."

Remembering that the Joculator had said at least one of the gleewomen invited liberties, she nearly told Hugh as much but decided against it.

The cold supper was soon ready, so they joined the others for a hasty meal, and then packed up the things they would need for their performance. The company took two cartloads to the market square and had things set up there before dark.

As soon as they had people enough to count as an

audience, the jesters began their antics while Cuddy and two other musicians played, and Gerda and Cath sang.

By the time the main performance began, the market square was packed. People perched in trees and on roofs of the buildings that lined the square. Others had brought stools, and still others made places for themselves wherever they could.

The performance was much the same as the previous night's practice, with Jenny singing her first song alone as she had at Lochmaben. Hugh joined in on the second one, and the applause afterward encouraged them to sing two more, including the comic one they had done the night before.

"That was grand, ye two," the Joculator said when they had finished. Clapping Hugh on the back, he said, "Ye've a great talent for mimicry, lad. Just take care ye dinna mimic any o' the nobles we meet, lest one take offense and lop off your head. I'm thinking o' the sheriff especially. Them two fools of ours may rattle his temper yet if they go on as they did last night, so I'm thinking it would be as well if ye'd try soothing him rather than riling him, for all our sakes."

"I don't want to rile anyone," Hugh said, "least of all the sheriff."

He spoke so firmly that Jenny said without thinking, "Do you know him?"

Hugh seemed taken aback by the question but rallied swiftly, saying, "I just dinna want to anger anyone with as much power as *he* wields."

"'Tis as well ye don't," the Joculator said. "Sithee, at Threave, we'll be performing for men with even greater power, and I dinna want any o' my people to suffer for their wit."

He spoke firmly, too, even adamantly.

Jenny looked from one man to the other and doubted that either feared she might do such a thing. She could not imagine herself doing or saying anything to anger the Sheriff of Dumfries or the Lord of Galloway, let alone the King of Scots if he should attend the celebration at Threave.

She turned to watch Gilly and Gawkus, who had returned to the central area to do a turn in which Gilly pretended to be Gawkus's shadow. Whatever the tall man did, the short one imitated, and the pair of them soon had the audience roaring with laughter. She had not seen them do the sketch before, so clearly, Hugh was right and they would do as they pleased and say what they pleased.

She enjoyed their antics, but as she watched them, she was strongly aware of Hugh standing near her. Others in the company milled about as they waited to take their turns in the clearing, but Hugh stayed right beside her.

Tumblers and jugglers dashed in to take the fools' places, and painted clubs and balls flew into the air and from juggler to juggler.

"You did not answer my question," Jenny said quietly to Hugh when she was sure that no one else would hear. "*Do* you know the Sheriff of Dumfries?"

⁓

Hugh had been expecting her to ask the question again, but the Joculator had moved away, and he had no reason to avoid answering now.

"I do know Sheriff Maxwell," he said keeping his voice low. "That is, I have met him and he knows me by name. It has been two or three years since we met."

She nodded thoughtfully. "Do you think he recognized you last night?"

"I took care to give him only glimpses of my face, and the plume waving from my cap should have made it hard for him to get a good look. I don't mind admitting, though, that I was wishing I wore whiteface as the fools do to perform."

She chuckled. "I can just imagine you in an eared cap with its bells tinkling accompaniment to our songs, sir."

He found himself wishing she would laugh more often but quickly reined in his fancies. He would do better to think of a way to persuade her to go home.

Their luck so far had been extraordinary. The company accepted her as simple, bonnie Jenny. But surely, people from Easdale must visit Dumfries. It was just a matter of time before someone from home saw and recognized her.

For that matter, it was only a matter of time before someone in Dumfries recognized him. The Joculator's damnable play would make that even more likely.

Following that thought, Hugh wondered if the Joculator might suspect him of being more than a simple troubadour. The man had given no such indication, but having seen more than one conversation break off at his approach over the past day and a half, Hugh was beginning to suspect the minstrels of playing an even deeper game than he and Jenny were. Whether it involved jewels, Threave Castle, or something else altogether, he had nary a clue.

⁓

Tuesday passed as Monday had, although their performance Tuesday night produced more daring tricks from the tumblers, more audacious songs from the musicians; and the Joculator thrilled them all by juggling torches with his daggers.

Jenny had taught the children a merry round and encouraged the audience to sing it with them. And "The Troubadour's Wife" began with a fanfare of horns and a humorous introduction of the play and the players by the Joculator.

The audience received the opening act with cheers and applause, whereupon the Joculator announced that the play would continue on the morrow.

"Our players will repeat the first act again then, so that any who have not seen it can do so then. So invite your neighbors and friends to join ye," he cried as the fools and gleewomen passed hats and long-handled collection baskets so members of the audience could show their appreciation with their contributions.

As the minstrels gathered their gear, Jenny adjusted the strings of her cloak and stowed her lute in its case, keeping an eye on Gilly and Gawkus, who continued their antics as they cajoled yet more coins from the dispersing townsfolk.

When a hand touched her shoulder, she nearly jumped out of her skin.

"You should not have let me get so near unbeknownst, lass," Hugh said, eyeing her sternly and forgetting for once to keep his voice low. "In a crowd like this one, nearly anything could happen."

"I was woolgathering," she admitted, annoyed with herself. Even so, she did not want him thinking he had any right to scold her. "I doubt that anyone would try to molest me here, amidst so many of our company."

"Don't be daft," he said. "A strong man could easily clap a hand across your mouth and snatch you into the bushes or into the next street without anyone's being the wiser because the crowd would conceal his movements. Sakes, any member of the company could do it by making it seem part of an act."

"Now *you* are being daft," she said. "I need only scre—"

His hand stopped the word and any other sound beyond a squeak as he scooped her into his arms and strode through the crowd, away from the minstrels. She kicked and struggled, but those who saw her only laughed or cheered him on.

To her shock, Hugh nodded and grinned as he carried her into the woods, plunging them into what seemed to be pitch blackness.

There was no moon, and if he followed a path, she could not discern it. But he seemed to know where he was going. As strong as he was, she wondered if he meant to carry her all the way to Annan House.

Hugh strode through the woods with his burden and enjoyed knowing that he had truly startled her for once—and doubtless infuriated her as well. He knew he'd have to take care when he set her down not to let her draw her damnable dagger.

Not that he feared it, but neither did he think it would do her good to learn how little protection it offered her. The confidence that carrying it gave her, aided by her natural habit of command, would serve her well in a crisis—he hoped.

"Don't set up a screech when I set you down," he said. "I know you're angry, and I don't doubt that you have much to say to me. But I have no evil intent other than to prove to you that I mean what I say and know more about danger than you do. Can I trust you to keep a still tongue if I set you down?"

His night vision was excellent, and her face was as expressive as ever. When she nodded, he took his hand from her mouth and set her on her feet, whereupon she raised a swift hand to strike. He had expected it, though, and caught her wrist easily.

When she tried to jerk it free, he held it, saying, "You would do better to control your temper, lass."

"You asked only if you could trust me not to screech," she said.

He grinned. "Aye, that's true. Nevertheless, you should think before you act. My father raised me as a gentleman, and knighthood adds responsibilities of a similar sort. But before you strike anyone, you should consider whether he or she might strike back. And I'll tell you now," he added, still firmly grasping her wrist. "If you try to lay hand to that wee dagger of yours, I'll put you straight across my knee and not spare a thought for your screeching."

"You wouldn't!"

"I think you ken fine that I would," he said. "Moreover, I'll let you tell any tale you like to anyone who tries to come to your aid. Now, will you behave?"

She hesitated, glowering, then looked pointedly at his hand on her wrist.

He relaxed his grip a little but did not let go.

Chapter 10

Jenny continued to glower at Hugh but to no avail. He just held on to her wrist and smiled. Light from the blanket of stars above pierced the canopy, making his strong white teeth glow. Faith, but it was hard to stay angry with the man, even when he had threatened violent retribution for a simple act of self-defense!

His strength was another point of confusion for her. It annoyed her that he was so much stronger than she was. But she had to admit that over the past days his strength had also provided comfort and security. Even when he had snatched her up and proven how easily a man might abduct her from the middle of a crowd of townspeople and protective minstrels, she had not known a jot of fear.

He would not harm her, and the safety she felt in his presence had naught to do with his being the brother of the man to whom she was betrothed. Indeed, the one certainty in her mind now was that marriage to Reid Douglas was going to be an even greater hardship than she had imagined it could be.

Clearly, Hugh did not mean to release her until she promised to behave. Determined not to make him any such promise, she said, "Why *did* you snatch me away like that?"

"I told you why," he said, no longer smiling. "You put too much faith in your own ability to protect yourself. I thought it better that I show you how wrong you were before someone else did and terrified you witless."

"You did not terrify me. You just made me angry."

"If you are expecting an apology, think again."

She grimaced. "We should get back before they come looking for us."

"In a moment," he said, but he released her wrist. "This is a good chance to talk, lass. Have you learned any more yet to lend credence to your suspicions?"

She shook her head. "But I've heard naught to prove the minstrels are planning a surprise for the performance at Threave, as you suggested, either, except perhaps your play. I must say, sir, Gerda suits her role. All that simpering and fluttering of eyelashes seems less ridiculous when it is supposed to be funny."

He chuckled. "I'll admit I'm enjoying the thing. If it weren't for my fear that Sheriff Maxwell or someone else might recognize me, I'd be having a fine time."

"You looked it," she said, and was surprised to hear an edge to her voice.

Evidently, he heard it, too, because he looked more carefully at her. But he said only, "We must both take care whilst we're here. I'd not be amazed if you should meet someone who knows *you*."

"But I have never been to Dumfries before," she said,

suppressing the remains of her sharp reaction to his delight in playing opposite fat Gerda.

He was shaking his head. "'Tis not whether or not you've been here before that endangers you. 'Tis the likelihood that someone else from Easdale may come here and recognize you from home."

She had not considered that, but it could certainly happen.

To avert Hugh's telling her again that she must go back to Annan House, she said, "There must still be much snow in the hills all around Easdale. So I expect folks there will wait a few weeks before venturing forth to any large town."

Nodding but clearly with his mind already on something else, he said, "Have you given more thought to the missing jewels? I had hoped concern for Peg might nudge your memory to recall something useful. As she has first-head privileges at Annan House and might easily have carried a small sack of jewels past the—"

"Good sakes," Jenny said, annoyed with herself. Lest he think she was annoyed with him, she added hastily, "Sithee, sir, the knacker, Parland Dow, also enjoys such privilege. And he left Annan House that night just before we did."

"Even if he did, lass, he is trusted everywhere. You won't persuade me that he is dishonest or that he somehow managed to steal jewels from Dunwythie's guests."

"But recall that I told you someone struck him down. We came upon him straightaway afterward, but the attacker got away. What if someone, knowing that the guards would not search him, slipped the stolen jewels under one of his packs, then clouted him and stole the jewels back?"

"Retrieving such a sack would be risky," he said. "But concealing it might not be. I warrant the stableyard and forecourt were full of activity at the time."

"Aye, with people, horses, and mules milling everywhere," she said. "I recall something else now, too. I saw Cuddy come out of the woods just after . . . Nay then," she amended, frowning as the image came alive. "Men were searching the woods for Dow's attacker by then. Doubtless, Cuddy was just one of them."

"You seemed certain it was Cuddy's voice in your dream," he said. "But you told me you'd heard it only once before then, when Cath scolded him."

"I only heard a bit of that scolding," she explained. "They were just out of sight on the same path. When we met, he directed me to the Joculator's tent. He has a certain musical quality to his voice that makes it particularly memorable."

"I ken fine what you mean," he said. Altering his voice, cocking his head, and plumping out his cheeks, he said, "Aye, sure I'll tell ye, lass. His tent be just yonder."

"That's it exactly," she said with a smile. "I don't know how you do that."

"I've mimicked voices and character traits all my life—and often suffered for it, too, I can tell you," he said, smiling back. "Some are easier than others, though. Higher voices are more difficult, and women's voices nearly impossible."

"You did Gerda's well enough when you mimicked her tonight," she said.

"Aye, well, that was supposed to be comical," he said.

"I doubt I could make anyone think I was Gerda speaking in the dark. It is easier for me to mimic her facial expressions than her voice."

She thought about that. " 'Tis true that one knew you were aping her, and so paid less heed than one would just hearing that voice come out of the darkness."

"Enough about Gerda," he said. "I want you to think now, lass, because what I just did . . . the musical note you heard . . . was little more than the difference between Cuddy's English Borderer's accent and that of a Border Scot."

"Sakes, is he English? Cath did not tell me that."

"Aye, I'm sure of it," he said. "Recall that minstrels travel far and wide, and come from many countries. And, you did have that odd dream at Lochmaben. Rather than talking to himself in it, might Cuddy have been talking to another Englishman?"

"I don't know," she said. "In troth, as time passes, it becomes harder to recall *what* any of it sounded like, but I don't think my dream had aught to do with jewels."

He sighed, and she felt as if she had disappointed him. "I wish I could remember it more clearly," she said. "Or know why I reacted as I did."

His hand grasped her shoulder, giving it a squeeze. "Nay, Jenny, don't apologize. Better to be honest and accuse no one than to make a false accusation."

Until she released her breath, she was unaware of holding it and unaware, too, of how much she had wanted him to understand her feelings. When he slipped an arm around her shoulders, she leaned into him. Then she promptly felt guilty, knowing she was seeking comfort from him when she should not.

As she started to step away, his embrace tightened, and she relaxed again.

"We should go back now," he said, releasing her and urging her forward.

Her emotions in turmoil, she protested. "But we're going the wrong way! I left my lute behind when you snatched me up. Faith, it's not even mine!"

"Lucas will have collected everything," he said. "Even your lute."

"But he didn't see us go. No one paid us any heed."

"I hope you think hard about that, and learn a lesson from it," he said, serious again. "But you may trust Lucas as I do, lass. He does not miss much that concerns me or anyone in whom I take an interest."

"Very well," she said, relaxing. "At least I can see where I'm putting my feet now. I don't know how you knew where you were going before."

"I have good night vision," he said. "And there's plenty of starlight tonight."

As they neared the encampment, Hugh suddenly put out a hand to stop her. "Who's there?" he said quietly.

"It be only me, sir," Bryan said as he stepped from the shrubbery onto the track. "The sheriff's men be searching the camp. I thought ye'd want to know."

⌒

Bryan vanished back into the shrubbery as soon as he had warned them, and they watched the sheriff's men from the woods. But if they turned up anything incriminating, neither Jenny nor Hugh saw any sign of it.

"Do you think they are looking for the missing jewels?" Jenny asked.

"If they are, it means jewelry has gone missing from other houses, too, because your uncle said he would not report the theft at Annan House yet."

When the sheriff's men had gone, Jenny said, "Peg must be gey worried about me by now."

"Nay, then, she won't be," Hugh said. "Lucas will have reassured her."

He proved right about that, but Peg was clearly angry.

As she and Jenny settled at last into their sleeping places, Peg muttered, "A fine thing! Them sheriff's louts pawing through *our* things, saying they be looking for jewels that they *admit* went missing afore this lot ever got to Annan House!"

"Did they?" Jenny said. She dared not tell Peg that jewels were missing from Annan House, too, because to do so would be to risk word of her own knowledge of that fact spreading to the others. Without a way to explain how she knew—

"As if Bryan and them would take aught!" Peg said. "But *ye*, wandering in the woods wi' a man whose own brother ye're betrothed to. Nobbut what Sir Hugh be a fine-looking man and a better one, I'm thinking, than the one you're to marry."

Jenny remained silent, hoping to put Peg on the defensive but knowing, too, that she could say little to defend her own actions with Sir Hugh, either, without revealing more than she wanted Peg to know.

Peg took the hint and said no more, so Jenny counted the few stars she could see through the canopy until she fell asleep.

Having left Jenny with Peg, Hugh had gone in search of Lucas to be sure the sheriff's men suspected nothing and that he had collected everything.

"I did," Lucas assured him. "Once they learned we'd joined these folks at Lochmaben, they took nae interest in our things, any road. Ye were a time though. I canna think what ye were about to abduct that lass as ye did."

"I wanted to teach her a lesson about keeping her eyes open in a crowd," Hugh said. "I don't know that I succeeded. Did you find her lute?"

"I did," Lucas said. "By, though, if ye're thinkin' ye'll sleep now, ye should ken that t' Joculator did say he'd like to see ye afore ye go to bed."

"You do not think perhaps you ought to have told me that straightaway?"

"Nah then, the man's no master of mine, nor yours, come to that. It does 'im nae harm to wait some for ye."

Hugh frowned. Lucas's instincts were sometimes better than his own. "You don't like the man?"

"I dinna dislike 'im," Lucas said thoughtfully. "'Tis just summat and nowt. He smiles much, and sometimes 'e does it in a way to melt lassies' hearts, withal. Other times, he smiles and 'is eyes be like shards of ice. And, times when he smiles, he looks as if he'd weep instead of laughin'. I canna tell which be the man 'imself. And, sithee, I'm thinkin' we ought to ken which one it be."

Hugh nodded but had no other answer. Nor did the Joculator's smile reassure him much when Hugh found him at the trestle table with other men of the company, including Cuddy and the two fools. Everyone looked pleased with himself and with the fact that the sheriff's men had found nothing and had gone.

No one admitted knowing why they had searched the camp, but each man had a mug before him, and a tall pitcher sat near the Joculator's elbow. He picked it up and reached for another mug. Pouring it full of ale, he gave it to Hugh.

"Drink up, lad," he said. "Ye've earned it. They'll be talking o' your fine performance tonight from Dumfries to Kirkcudbright tomorrow. If our audience doesna double itself overnight, I'll be that amazed."

"Thank ye, sir," Hugh said, drinking deeply. The ale was a little sweet for his taste, but he could not deny a strong thirst. Nor did he object when the Joculator topped it off again as Hugh took the seat beside him.

"We'll rehearse again tomorrow after we break our fast," the Joculator said. "D'ye ken your lines yet up through the marriage at the end o' the second act?"

"I think so," Hugh said.

"Aye, well, if it teases ye, Gerda can go over it all with ye afore we begin."

Hugh hoped that would not be necessary. Gerda was beginning to get on his nerves. She simpered and fluttered as much when they weren't acting as when they were, and he was not sure how to discourage her without giving offense.

Later, as he stood to make his way to bed, he realized he must have drunk much more than he had thought. The Joculator had rarely waited for his—or anyone else's— mug to be empty before refilling it, and he had sent one of the lads at least twice to fetch more ale from the barrel.

Hugh decided that he would not be amazed if a number of them missed breakfast.

～

Two voices, nay more than two—mayhap three or four sets of two. He could not remember. In fact, he could not think properly. Thoughts tumbled swiftly one moment and, the next, seemed to plow through muck to form themselves, or whatever it was thoughts did to make themselves known in one's head.

How did thoughts think, anyway?

"Are ye sure?" a voice said close by, startling him a little.

"Aye, o' course," said another. "Ye can see that he's no himself."

That was true. He wasn't, but how did his thoughts know it when he had not? Or were those real voices rather than just louder thoughts in his head?

In either case, how could he be other than himself? Mayhap all his pretending had done it. But if he was no longer himself, then who was he?

The puzzle proved beyond him at that moment to solve.

"Here, lad, sit up now."

He felt himself smiling, although nothing funny had occurred. Then, numbly, he felt pressure on his arms, pushing or pulling him upward.

"Sleeping now," he muttered. He thought he was still smiling, which was odd, because if nowt was funny, he ought to stop.

"Come now, do as ye're bid," the voice said. "Ye'll be glad of it in the end."

"The end of me?" he murmured.

"He looks daft, he does, and sounds it, too," another voice said.

He opened his eyes and saw a face close to his own, a white face.

"Gawkus," he muttered.

The face grinned at him, and the other voice said firmly, "That's it, lad. Now, take this quill and write your name on the paper, just here, carefully—your full name, mind, just as ye always write it . . . that's it, Hugo, and now the rest."

Obediently, he wrote his name. His hand and arm felt as if they floated.

"Good lad," the firm voice said. "Now again, just here."

Again he obeyed, hoping they would then leave him be. He wanted to sleep. Indeed, he thought he was sleeping, but if this was a dream, it was an even odder one than Jenny's had been.

The voices had stopped, and he did not miss them.

⌇

Jenny broke her fast with Peg Wednesday morning and then found her lute and took it to a nearby rock slab, where she could sit and practice her songs for that night's performance. Sometime later, she saw Hugh making his way to the table.

He paid her no heed and seemed to concentrate hard on finding a place to sit, then clapped a hand to his head as he sat. When one of the lads pushed a pitcher of ale toward him, Hugh grabbed it and poured a healthy draught into his mug.

Jenny had lived an isolated life but not so isolated that she did not recognize a man who'd had too much drink the night before. The sight annoyed her. She had thought him an unlikely candidate for heavy drinking. However, Reid drank more than he should, so mayhap Douglas men simply liked their ale and whisky.

Later, though, when she found Gilly and persuaded him to give her another lesson with her dirk, she felt disappointment when Hugh did not follow them.

"Fix your mind on the knife," Gilly said when she had missed the tree for the third time. "It'll do ye nae good if ye dinna concentrate. Throw again."

Biting her lip, aware that her feelings had betrayed her, she retrieved the dirk, put her mind to her throw, and struck the tree trunk dead center.

When she cast Gilly an exultant smile, he nodded, saying, "Throw again."

When she had hit the tree five times in a row, he finally grinned and said, "Ye'll do. But practice often, and recall what I told ye. Dinna think to use yon dirk to defend yourself. Like as no, some villain will just snatch it and use it against ye."

Promising to heed his warning, Jenny thanked him, and they walked back to the encampment to find Gawkus waiting impatiently.

"I've had a notion for tonight," he said to Gilly. "I want to discuss it wi' ye."

Parting from them, Jenny went to prepare for her own performance.

As the Joculator had predicted, their audience was larger, and the minstrels outdid themselves. Tumblers flipped and tumbled over each other, and the dancers danced more wildly, whirling and stomping their feet to the music. The audience began clapping and were still clapping when the jugglers ran in to the center.

All three juggled torches. Then the Joculator joined them, juggling axes with his. People shrieked whenever it looked as if he might drop one.

Gawkus and Gilly began with the jugglers, stood aside while the Joculator did his stint, and then ran back out with ten clubs flying back and forth between them. At the same time, the two carried on a seemingly naïve conversation about taxes and other duties of the sheriff that drew gusts of laughter from their audience but seemed most unlikely, that night, to amuse Sheriff Maxwell.

Fortunately, as Jenny noted to Hugh, the sheriff was not there to hear them.

"Someone is bound to tell Maxwell what they said about him, though," Hugh said. "Those two should take more care to mind their tongues."

"But it is the nature of fools to say what they think," Jenny said.

"A fool who doesn't mind his tongue, lass, is likely to lose his head."

The play came next, so their discussion went no further.

Everyone laughed when Gawkus strolled out to perform the wedding ending the second act. He wore priest's garb and his eared and belled fool's cap, but Jenny stopped watching when the ceremony began. Somehow, Gerda became even more irritating as a bride, managing somehow to simper at Hugh even through her veil.

The Joculator had changed the order of things, so that Jenny's songs with Hugh followed the play, and the change felt odd to her, as if Hugh had left his bride to sing love songs with *her*. When he smiled warmly at her in the midst of her favorite song, she wondered if it felt the same to him.

The audience loved it, though, so she decided that, as usual, the Joculator had known what he was doing.

When the applause began to fade, Gilly stepped forward to announce that they would do the entire play on Thursday night, from beginning to end.

The audience roared its approval.

When Hugh awoke early Thursday morning, the sun was peeking over hills to the east, the day was clear but crisp, and again the feeling of imminent snow touched the air. His persistent grogginess of the day before had vanished, leading him to think he had simply grown too old to enjoy drinking into the night after a busy day.

As to the likelihood of snow, its supposed imminence having misled them now for nearly a sennight, he decided the weather gods were just playing their usual spring pranks on the inhabitants of southwest Scotland.

In the mood for a brisk walk, he went first to the cook fires, where women were taking hot bannocks off flat iron griddles. Taking three bannocks for himself, he accepted generous slices of warmed-over beef to go with them and headed away from the camp, into the woods. A short time later, catching a glimpse of a blue skirt on the path ahead of him, he lengthened his stride.

Minutes later, he realized the woman he followed was Gerda's mother Cath, the eldest of the gleewomen. His spirits sagged, making him laugh at himself.

The reminder that he might spend much of the day practicing the farcical third act of the play with Gerda made him turn back to look for another blue skirt.

Seeing Jenny with Peg near their sleeping place, he strode toward them, saying casually when he reached them, "I'd like a word with ye, Jenny, about the new song we have practiced. Will ye walk with me for a spell?"

"I have not yet broken my fast," she said.

He hefted his bannocks. "I've plenty for two. Come along now, for shortly I'll have to be practicing yon play with that Gerda."

She nodded, spoke quietly to Peg, and then joined him, making no comment as he guided her back to the path he had followed earlier.

"Did you bring your dirk, lass?" he asked then.

"Aye, sure," she said. "Will we have time for me to practice?"

"We will. In troth, I want to spend an hour speaking freely. I dreamed the other night that I'd lost my self to become one of the characters I've pretended to be. That is, I think that was what happened. 'Twas a strange dream, withal. In any event, I want to be myself for a while. Art still enjoying your grand adventure?"

She was silent for a moment, as she looked to the left and right of the path.

"No one else is near," he said. "I saw Cath earlier, but

she returned whilst I was talking to you. So, tell me, have you had enough of this yet?"

"I have not yet learned what I want to know," she said. "I expect this life could grow tedious, though. Also, it will soon be time for planting at home, and I do not know if the steward his lordship installed there knows his business."

"I warrant he does, or Dunwythie would not have put him there."

"I suppose," she said, and they went on talking about crops until they came to the hilltop where she had practiced throwing her dirk before. Finding a flat rock, they ate his bannocks and beef, and then practiced flinging their dirks at deadfalls.

As they walked back in companionable silence, Hugh tried to recall any other time that he had talked as easily about planting and crops with a woman as he had with her. He hoped Reid would appreciate her knowledge, but he had a strong feeling that his brother did not appreciate her at all.

⟡

Jenny had likewise enjoyed their discussion. Hugh clearly cared as much about Thornhill as she did about Easdale, and from what he had said, the size of the two estates was similar. He had also given her some more tips to improve her aim, and had promised to teach her the best way to hone her blade.

When they returned to the encampment, Gerda waved to Hugh.

"Like a wife already," Jenny said with a chuckle.

Hugh shook his head. "That's why *I* mean to stay single."

Still smiling, she watched him go, and then turned her attention to tasks of her own. One of the dancers had offered to help her furbish up her old blue kirtle for the remaining performances in Dumfries, and she wanted to practice some new songs to add to them. They would keep the love song that she and Hugh always sang, but everyone else was adding new things, and she wanted to do likewise.

The evening's performance went well. Some of the tumblers and two of the jugglers appeared in whiteface, wearing colorful caps without ears or bells. In the minstrels' world, Jenny had learned, the latter such trappings were for fools alone.

Gawkus and Gilly jested again about tax collectors and such to the delight of *most* of the audience. However, the sheriff was there with a large party of his own, and Jenny noted that he did not look as amused by their jests as he had before.

When the Joculator had finished his turn, the audience, which always fell silent to watch his juggling and sleight of hand, burst into applause and then fell as quickly silent again when Jenny walked into the clearing alone with her lute.

After the first two songs, she gestured to the children to join her, and they soon had the audience singing along with them. Thus, the mood was merry when the players ran in to begin their play.

The action moved swiftly through the first two acts. Gawkus drew much laughter by playing the priest with a solemnity wholly at odds with his clownish appearance.

At the end of the wedding ceremony, when Gerda grabbed an astonished Hugh by his ears to kiss him soundly on the lips, the audience roared its approval.

The third act paraded the troubadour's lady loves, all played by Gerda. Her costume changes were little more than the addition or deletion of a scarf, hat, apron, or wig. To each of these ladies, Hugh's reaction was the sorrow of love lost. When Gerda returned as herself at the end and led him off with a collar and leash, the audience laughed, hooted, jeered, and otherwise expressed strong appreciation.

As Hugh joined Jenny directly afterward to sing, he murmured, "We'll do the comical song first instead of the love song. In troth, I'd prefer that Maxwell hear only my character voices tonight."

She smiled and nodded as if to the audience and began to pluck the tune on her lute. Hugh let her play it through, joining in with his lute only as she began to sing the first verse.

The evening ended as the previous one had, although the sheriff glowered at the fools when they reappeared to pass baskets as the audience prepared to depart.

But the following night, midway through the second act of the play, it became clear that something was amiss. Gerda played her role and said her lines correctly, but she lacked the spirited attitude she had displayed before.

As Hugh and the other two players argued about the upcoming wedding, one trying to talk him out of such a false step, the other encouraging him to take it, the Joculator approached Jenny and drew her well away from the stage to say, "Ye'll ha' to take Gerda's place for the rest o' the play. The poor lass be puking up her guts behind yon trees and canna finish."

"But I don't *know* the play," Jenny protested. "Surely, Cath—"

"Nay, she'd be too old for it. Ye're of a height wi' Gerda, and ye'll put on a veil and a padded gown, so none will ken any difference till ye take off the veil."

"But I don't know the lines!"

"The priest will tell ye what to say, just as they do in real weddings," he said.

"And for the third act? What then?"

"Why, ye'll take off yon veil and reveal yourself as Bonnie Jenny. Then ye and Hugo can sing that love song ye do so well. Nae one will think aught but that we've changed the ending from farcical to romantic. Trust me, lass, they'll love it."

Jenny did not think that she was going to like it at all. And what Hugh would think, she could not imagine.

Chapter 11 ————————

Apparently the company kept costumes ready for any emergency, because Cath and another woman quickly swathed Jenny in a red dress that added pounds to her figure, and a thick veil that concealed her face. Meantime, Hugh continued to argue with the other players onstage, adding considerably to the audience's delight by playing his own father and arguing with himself.

When Jenny was ready, the Joculator guided her to the stage, and the actor playing the bride's father escorted her to an altar that had appeared as she dressed.

The priest was yet another fool in whiteface, cap, and bells. When Jenny stood before him, he turned to the audience and said in stentorian tones, "Look ye all on these two. If any amongst ye ken just cause or impediment why this marriage should not go forward, speak now or forever keep a still tongue in thy head."

Silence.

"Aye, good then," the priest said. Turning to Hugh, he

said, "Now, lad, d'ye take this lass for your wedded wife, to have and to hold, for fair, for foul, for . . ."

When he finished reciting the familiar phrases, Hugh declared loudly, "I do!"

To Jenny, the fool-priest said, "Lass, will ye have this man for your wedded husband, to be meek and obedient to him in bed and at board from this time forward till death ye depart and if holy kirk will ordain?"

"I will," she murmured.

"Louder, lass," he said in stentorian tones. "They canna hear ye in the back."

"Aye, I do then; I'll tak' *all* o' him," Jenny shouted back, trying to mimic Gerda's accent and manner. The audience responded appreciatively.

She could barely see through the thick veil, but she saw Hugh's quick frown and knew he had just realized she was not Gerda. Whether he knew who had taken Gerda's place or thought she was someone else, she could not tell.

When they had finished reciting the vows, the priest said, "I now pronounce ye man and wife. Will ye kindly sign the marriage lines declaring this union, sir?"

"Aye, sure, I will," Hugh said. Taking the quill the man handed him, he signed with a dramatic flourish.

"There now," the priest said. "If ye'll be so good as to turn and face the congregation, I'll present ye to them as man and wife. 'Tis proper at this point, madam," he added *sotto voce*, "to put back your veil."

Grateful for the cue, Jenny faced the audience and with an exaggerated gesture worthy of Gerda herself, flipped back the veil to reveal her face.

The reaction was a mixture of raucous cheers and laughter that increased greatly when Gerda ran up to the edge of the clearing in a tizzy, fully recovered from her ailment and apparently trying to tear her hair from her scalp.

The Joculator strode forward with two lutes, handing one to Jenny and the other to Hugh.

As Jenny began to pluck the notes of the love song, Hugh quickly picked up the cue. The audience reacted as the Joculator had predicted, and as Jenny and Hugh took their bows afterward, the fools, jugglers, and tumblers ran about, filling their collection baskets and hats with generous offerings from the appreciative crowd.

As Jenny and Hugh walked from the clearing at last, the priest-fool walked up to Hugh, grabbed his hand, and shook it fervently.

"'Twas a great pleasure, sir," he said. "A more entertaining wedding I vow I never have performed. I want to thank you for letting me take part in such an unusual and inspiring event."

Jenny stared at Hugh, who was staring in shock at the man in whiteface.

"See here," Hugh said curtly. "I don't even know you, and this jest has gone far enough. Who the devil are you?"

The man looked from him to Jenny and back again. "Why, who else should I be but Father Donal from the abbey kirk? You sent for me yourself, did you not?"

Jenny swayed as if the ground had heaved beneath her feet. Had it not been for Hugh's firm hand catching her elbow and steadying her, she was sure her knees would have given way.

⌒

As they walked on, Hugh tried to discern the priest's features under their chalk coating. The man's whiteface lacked the details that Gawkus and Gilly added to theirs, such as the teardrops under Gilly's eyes and the tiny hearts under Gawkus's. This man's whiteface lacked all such detail. Only his eyes and mouth showed color.

"I want an explanation," Hugh said. "That wedding cannot have been real."

"But it was," Father Donal assured him. "Your letter spelled out your wishes, sir. And the Bishop of Glasgow, who chanced to be visiting Sweetheart Abbey when your application for a special license arrived, approved it himself."

"Then he must *un*approve it," Hugh said. Glancing at Jenny's face, which was nearly as white as the priest's, he realized that although by rights he ought to be furious, he wanted only to protect her.

"I'm afraid his eminence returned to Glasgow yesterday," the priest said. "In any event, I do not think he *can* annul your marriage, sir. Only the Pope can do that—or mayhap a papal legate when one is at hand. But why would you *want* an annulment after going to such lengths to marry so quickly and so publicly?"

"Because I did no such thing," Hugh told him. As he said the words, he recalled that his odd, ale-induced dream had included the signing of documents. Nevertheless, he said firmly, "I sent you no letter or application, Father. 'Tis you, I fear, who have been fooled. This marriage cannot be valid."

"I brought the application and special license with me, in the event that anyone from the local kirk should desire to see them," the priest said as they drew to a stop. "I also have your letter of instructions. Moreover, earlier, when I asked you to sign the marriage lines, I specifically noted that in doing so you would be declaring yourselves married. That precaution was necessary, of course, as you had requested that your names not be mentioned as you took your vows."

"But surely, the marriage cannot be valid if our names were *not* used."

"On the contrary, sir, your vows themselves were sufficient. Forbye, the declaration by itself satisfies Scottish marriage law. You and this lady are legally wedded and may now enjoy all the rights and privileges of marriage."

Feeling Jenny tremble, Hugh firmed his grip under her elbow to steady her again. As he did, a male voice behind them called out, "Hold there, Sir Hugh! We would congratulate you and your bonnie bride!"

Jenny stiffened and looked at Hugh. He was grimacing, but even as he did, she saw his facial expression alter to a most un-Hughlike look. As he turned to face the shouter, she braced herself and turned with him.

He called out, "Was ye shoutin' at me, sir?"

Recognizing the two men approaching them, Jenny nearly turned to flee.

Sheriff Maxwell held out his hand to Hugh. "Thornhill," he said. "One would never expect to meet you in such circumstances as these. Indeed, sir, I have twice now attended these most amusing performances, and I trow, I never did recognize you. However, my man here knew you straightaway."

To Jenny's amazement and right beside her, Hugh had turned into a wide-eyed bumpkin in nobleman's clothing.

He gazed in astonishment at Maxwell's outstretched hand and then at his minion before saying in the distinctly common phrasing he had used before, "Gor, me lord, I dinna ken neither o' ye. I'd be glad to shake your hand, but I'm thinkin' one o' them fools ha' set ye on to me as a jest."

The sheriff looked dumbfounded, but his minion peered more closely at Hugh and said, "I dinna understand the jest, sir, but I'd ken ye fine anywhere. Sakes, I collected your taxes last year. Ye be Sir Hugh Douglas o' Thornhill."

"Nay, then," Hugh said, passing a hand across his mouth and then grinning.

To Jenny's shock, his grin revealed a number of blackened teeth clearly on the verge of rotting. "Just ye wait till I tell me brothers and all that a sheriff-depute o' Dumfries mistook *me* for a laird!" he exclaimed. "Ay de mi, how they'll hoot, all six o' them. Next, I warrant, ye'll be beggin' me to pay the laird's taxes, withal."

Sheriff Maxwell chuckled and clapped his man on the back. "I told you, you were mistaken, lad. Nobbut what this man's nearly the spit and image of Thornhill."

Hugh leaned closer to him. "Did we look into that, sir, happen we'd find the laird and me be kin. Sithee, I dinna ken *who* me da were. Mayhap this laird and me do be brothers, as ye might say. I dinna look a mite like me own da. And me mam . . . Aye, well, she were a rare lass for the lads, that 'un. Scarce knew where she slept night to night. And I ha' nae doots that some o' her mates was nobles and the like."

"Come along, lad," Maxwell said. "This man is *not* Thornhill."

The younger man nodded. "Aye, he'd never say such a

thing even in jest. Prideful as a cock on his own dunghill, the laird be, like most Douglases. Sorry to ha' troubled ye," he said to Hugh. "You go on about your business now. I expect ye'll soon be bragging that your acting impressed the Sheriff o' Dumfries."

"Aye, sure I will, sir," Hugh assured him.

Watching the two men turn and stride away as she struggled between outrage and laughter, Jenny took a deep breath, becoming aware of Hugh's warm hand at the small of her back as she exhaled. She looked up at him, but he was watching the sheriff and his man as if he thought one of them might look back. Neither one did.

"How could you *say* such a horrid thing about your own mother, and with a priest to witness it?"

His eyes twinkled when he met her gaze, but he looked ruefully at the priest before he said, " 'Twas the first thing I could think to say that might disarm them."

"Good sakes, sir, you should give thanks that a lightning bolt did not strike!"

She would have liked to say more, but the priest *was* still with them.

As they followed others in the company who were leaving the square with the audience, Hugh said, "You kept gey quiet back there, Father."

Eyeing him shrewdly, the priest said, "I don't mind saying, sir, that although I saw you do it several times tonight, during the play and the song you sang with your lady, it astonishes me how much you can alter your features and voice with apparently no effort. You change from one man to another before one's very eyes. I'm wondering who the real person inside your skin may be."

"We can discuss that later if you like," Hugh said. "But

first I mean to find out who played this witless prank on us, and why."

Jenny had been looking around to see who was paying heed to them. Most folks were clearly going home. Aside from the first shout, she doubted that anyone other than the priest had heard what the sheriff and his man had said to Hugh.

She saw the Joculator watching them from the north side of the square, where he stood with a few of the company still packing away gear from the performance.

"Hugo," she said quietly, "I should think the man who arranged for the play would most likely be the one responsible for the whole."

"I agree," he said. "Wait here, if you will, Father. I believe we should speak to him privately first."

"Of course, my lord."

Hugh turned back. "We'll have no 'my lords' if you please. And no 'my ladies' either. We remain just Hugo and Jenny whilst we are with these minstrels."

"As you will, my son," the priest said. "I do recommend, however, that you arrange, both of you, to make proper confessions soon. I will hear them if you like."

Hugh did not reply to that, touching Jenny's shoulder instead to urge her toward the Joculator.

The tall man was still watching them, and although those with him were beginning to depart, he waited for Jenny and Hugh. By the time they reached him, he stood alone.

Jenny saw Lucas Horne with the others heading along the High Street toward the woods and their encampment just as he paused and looked back. She did not see Hugh make any gesture or sign, but Lucas gave a slight nod and walked on.

"I must offer you my congratulations," the Joculator said with a smile to Hugh. "You have wed yourself to a bonnie, charming bride."

"Then you know that the priest and his ceremony were real," Hugh said grimly. "Father Donal tells me he performed the marriage under a special license for which I apparently applied. Mayhap you will explain how you managed that. By sleight of hand? Was it something you put in my ale the other night?"

"I confess that *is* how we got your signature on the letter, the application, and a prepared copy of the marriage lines, but I assure you, we meant well."

"What on earth inspired you to such an outrageous act?" Huge demanded.

"Fellow feeling, I expect," the Joculator said. "The lass here told me how ye'd pursued her—even offered marriage—and that she had rejected ye. One could only admire your persistence, lad. And, withal, one soon noted that she needed a strong protector and did not reject ye as sternly as she told me she did, if she rejected ye at all. As she is apparently without proper kin to look after her, and ye seemed determined to protect her, I thought it only right to aid ye in your purpose."

Listening to him, Jenny felt as if some powerful force had pinned her in place from the moment he said, "The lass here told me . . ." When he paused, leaving her awash with guilt, she could not move or think of a word to say.

She did not have to look at Hugh to know he was furious. His anger radiated toward her, engulfing her so that her usual courage deserted her.

"Perhaps you would care to explain your part in this to me," he said.

It was the last thing she wanted to do.

⁓

Hugh watched Jenny even more narrowly than he had watched the Joculator. He believed the man but could not imagine what would induce a frank lass like Jenny to tell such falsehoods.

When she hesitated, Hugh said sternly, "What exactly did you tell him?"

Visibly swallowing, she faced him then and said, "I told him we had met at Annan House, that you had expressed interest in me and had followed me, but that I had no interest in marrying any man, and had tried to make that plain to you."

"Marrying! What demon possessed you to say such a thing?"

"Mayhap it was just the first thing I could think of to *disarm* you."

Recognizing the echo of his words to her, regarding what he had said about his mother, he gave her a look calculated to make his lack of amusement plain.

Men were dousing torches in the square, but her deep flush was visible even in the diminishing light. She looked from him to the Joculator and back before she said, "Please, Hugo, can we not discuss this privately? I ken fine that you are angry with me, but I'd liefer explain it all only to you."

He hesitated and instantly recalled a few likely details

of her tale that he, too, would rather not reveal to others. So he did not press her.

Turning to the Joculator instead, he said, "I'd also like to know what demon possessed *you* to believe her. I have seen her try merely to equivocate and fail. One can easily read her thoughts in every expression."

"Aye, sure," the Joculator agreed. "I knew she was lying. But I'm seeing now that I mistook which bit was the lie. Sithee, I thought 'twas what she said about her feelings for you. Anyone seeing the pair o' ye together of late would ha' made the same mistake, especially seeing ye kiss, as I did."

"So you did see that," Hugh said with a sigh.

"Aye, but even had I not, ye keep your eyes fixed on her from dawn to dusk, lad, and fidget yourself to flinders when she disappears for longer nor ye think she should. And, whilst she's singing to ye, she looks at ye as if she'd climb right into your arms. What else was any sensible man to think?"

Hugh looked again at Jenny, who was eyeing the Joculator with guilt clearly lacerating her conscience. "I . . . I never meant to make such trouble," she said. "I hope you can forgive me, sir."

The Joculator shook his head. "Sakes, lassie, 'tis m'self ought to be asking ye. I thought from what I'd seen that ye'd both be thanking me. But I'm thinking now I've put me foot right in it. Still and all, if ye want to undo this marriage, it should be no great thing to apply to the Kirk for an annulment. 'Tis no quite the thing, sithee, for a priest to lend himself to a minstrels' play."

"You seem to know much about many things," Hugh

said dryly. "Have you created such ticklish alliances before?"

"Nay, then. I have not. But a man in my position does learn much. Be there aught else ye'd want to discuss wi' me, lad, or shall I bid ye both goodnight?"

"I've nowt more to say to you," Hugh told him. "But I have much more to say to *you*," he added, looking at Jenny.

"Please, sir, Peg will be expecting me. And . . . and the priest is still waiting, and Lucas will be looking for you. We must get back to the encampment."

"There is one thing," the Joculator said to Hugh. "The others know only that ye sought to wed her and that summat had kept ye apart. They think we were all doing ye both a favor. Sithee, we none of us had any intent to do ye a mischief."

Hugh nodded, then watched as the Joculator strode away toward the High Street. Letting him get well ahead, he slipped an arm around Jenny's shoulders, urging her to follow. "Now, lass," he said. "You have some explaining to do."

When she gestured toward the priest, still waiting patiently in the shadows a short distance away, Hugh paused beside him to say, "I expect we will have to sort this out by ourselves, Father, unless you have managed to think of a simple way to undo what was done tonight."

"There *is* nothing simple, my son. Of that I am sure. Until you can arrange an annulment, you are legally married to each other. May I say that you seem to suit each other as a couple much better than many I have united."

"You may say what you like, but we are going to bid you goodnight. I have a few things yet to say to my bride, whether she wants to hear them or not. And she is going to say a few things more to me, as well. Are you not, sweetheart?"

Jenny grimaced.

"Just so," Hugh said. "Goodnight, Father."

As they left the square and walked along the High Street, Jenny braced herself. She knew Hugh was still angry and that he had every right to be.

Remembering the threats Reid had made to her, and the way he had flung himself off when he could not deal with her as he believed he should, she hoped Hugh's temper would not express itself in similar ways.

"We're private enough now," he said. "Tell me."

She could see torches ahead, nearing the path into the woods. But most of the townsfolk had vanished into their own dwellings, so she and Hugh were practically alone on the High Street. The moon was just showing itself in the west. Waxing toward full, it cast its silvery light along the street.

"Well?" he said with a trace of impatience. "Telling me you seized the first thought that came to mind, as I did with the sheriff, won't serve now, lass."

"I know," she said. "I used your words only because I could not tell the truth without revealing more to the Joculator than either of us wants to reveal."

"Nevertheless, you must be honest with me."

"You are going to be angry."

"Sakes, I'm already angry!"

She drew a breath, let it out, and then said, "I told him

you were an unwelcome suitor because I wanted to make it harder for you to take me back. I never thought he'd decide for himself that I *ought* to marry you. Well, who *would* think such a thing? It was an outrageous thing to do."

"It does argue, though, that he still does not recognize us," Hugh said. "I doubt that he would risk such a stunt except in the belief that he was uniting an unprotected maiden to a man who would protect her. I find it troubling, however, that he did not ask why Sheriff Maxwell accosted me. He must have seen that."

"Do you think he heard him call you Sir Hugh?"

"Perhaps," he admitted. "Even if he didn't, there were others about when Maxwell called to me. I think our luck may be running out."

Hastily, she said, "We still do not know what, if anything, threatens Archie the Grim or Threave. Nor have we learned aught of the missing jewels other than that the sheriff apparently did not find them in this camp. We must at least go on with the minstrels to Threave, sir, to warn Archie Douglas."

"There is plenty of time before the anniversary of the King's coronation for me to take you to Annan House and still ride to Threave in time to warn Archie."

"Well, I don't want to fratch with you, especially when you are vexed with me already, but you did ask if I was tired of my adventure. I would not like to live like this forever, but I'm not tired of the minstrels. I'd liefer go on with them than return and wait in disgrace to marry Reid. In troth, I hope waiting for the Pope to annul *our* marriage means I can put off mine to *him* indefinitely."

"There must be other ways to annul this marriage," he said.

"Even so, it will take time," she said. "So there can be no great hurry for us to be going back. By the bye, sir, what *did* you do to your teeth?"

Accepting a brief change of subject, Hugh said, "charcoal," and used a sleeve to wipe the residue off his teeth. "I'd kept some with me to use in just such a case."

As they walked, he could hear others chattering ahead and realized that he would miss the minstrels almost as much as she would.

He had done many things, traveled great distances, and met people of all sorts. But although he had posed as a troubadour before, he had done so only to glean information and not as part of any company. Their way of life differed from any other he had known, and in truth, he rather envied them their freedom.

She was silent, making him wonder what she was thinking and if she worried that he was still angry. In truth, he did not know what he felt.

He had sworn he would never marry again. The pain of losing Ella and her bairn had been too great to risk suffering through it again, ever. The thought that Jenny might suffer the same sort of death was too horrible to contemplate.

As the thought crossed his mind another, much worse one, chased it—that Jenny could suffer the same fate as Ella had. After all, many women did die in childbirth, or from complications afterward. But how much worse it would be if he were not with her then, if she had only the self-serving Reid to look after her!

He put his free hand atop hers in the crook of his arm. She was not wearing gloves, and her hand felt small and warm under his. Her skin was silken, her fingers slim and fragile. His urge to protect her was stronger than ever. That he had other strong urges where she was concerned was a fact, too.

He would not mind taking advantage of those husbandly rights the priest had assured him were his. But getting the annulment would be more difficult if he did.

When he sighed, she looked up.

"What are we going to do?" she asked. "About this marriage, I mean."

"We should be able to get it annulled easily enough in time. The priest said we can, and he does not know about Reid. I'm nearly sure that a prior betrothal is always grounds for annulment."

"Then what about those rights and privileges he mentioned?"

"Sakes, I'm not going to take advantage of them, if that's what you're thinking," he said, wishing more than ever that he could.

"Oh."

Was it his imagination, or had there been a touch of disappointment in that single word? Calling himself a witless fool, he fell silent again.

The silence lasted only until they entered the encampment, when raucous cheers erupted all around them.

The Joculator stepped forward, hoisting a pitcher and two mugs. "My finest claret to toast your wedding," he

said. "And ye'll see yonder that the lads ha' refitted your
tent for ye, Hugo, so ye can sleep wi' your lady tonight."

"Aye, and we all promise to ignore your moans o' pas-
sion," shouted some wag from the crowd, sounding much
like Gilly.

"Oh, no," Jenny murmured.

Hugh saw to his chagrin that every member of the company was happily waiting to celebrate with them. "Sakes,
lass," he muttered. "We'll have to go along or tell them all
the truth and disappoint them. Which shall it be?"

Although the thought of spending the night alone in a tent
with Hugh shook Jenny, the thought of having to confess
to them all that she had lied horrified her. It was true that
the Joculator had arranged their marriage, but she harbored a fear that her fib had run through the whole camp.
Even if it had not, people would want to know, in detail,
why their leader had thought the wedding was such a fine
idea.

Even Peg and Bryan, although they knew her real identity and Hugh's, looked utterly delighted. "I'd hate to spoil
everyone's pleasure by refusing to sleep with you," Jenny
murmured back to Hugh. "But if we sleep together, won't
that—"

"That's all we'll do, I swear," he said in the same tone.
"I'll have Lucas make up two pallets in the tent. He'll say
nowt to anyone else."

"I suppose that may serve," she said. She had been
about to point out that if they spent the night together,
everyone would assume that they had coupled. But her

choice remained the same. And, in truth, the thought of sleeping beside him stirred so many thoughts and feelings that she could not think straight.

For the next half hour, she stayed close to him and drank claret from his mug. She knew she had talked to people, thanked them for their kindness, but she could not remember what, exactly, she had said to anyone. And when Hugh took her to his tent at last, urged on by cheers and rowdy comments, her knees quaked and her skin felt numb.

"I'm going to sleep in my kirtle and shift," she muttered.

"Aye, that's a good notion," he muttered back, his voice sounding hoarse. Snatching up a tallow candle in a dish, he turned away rather abruptly to look over the sleeping arrangements as if to see if Lucas had followed his instructions.

Although there were indeed two separate pallets, with separate blankets, Jenny thought they were too close together. Evidently, Hugh thought so, too, because he tried to shift them farther apart, but there was not enough room.

Peg brought water but left straightaway, leaving Jenny alone with him.

Hugh handed the candle to Lucas, saying, "See that no one gets up to any mischief tonight. I'd liefer not have to knock heads together."

"Aye, sure," Lucas said. His lips twitched, and he turned away as quickly as Hugh had earlier. Seconds later, they were alone in the dark.

After they got into their beds, Jenny lay stiffly and

sensed that Hugh did likewise. But after a time, exhaustion claimed her, and she slept.

When she awoke, gray dawn light peeked in around the tent flap and Hugh lay just as he had the night before. The only difference was that she had evidently grown chilly, because she was snuggled closely against him.

"Good sakes, I'm sorry!" she murmured, wriggling back to her own place.

"Don't apologize," he said. "I'd have spent the night reflecting on certain rights and privileges even if you hadn't made it impossible to avoid such thinking. But although my thoughts dwelt on the rights husbands think most about on their wedding night, one right did occur to me that I'm afraid you will dislike."

"If you *think* I'll dislike it, I *know* I will," she said, sitting upright and facing him, prepared to do battle. "What is it?"

"A husband's right to command obedience," he replied. "We will leave for Annan House today, Jenny, and I *don't* want to hear any argument."

Chapter 12

Hugh had indeed scarcely slept, other than to doze from time to time, and had wakened well before Jenny had, when her warm body had snuggled against his. His had leapt in welcome of her presence as he wakened, and he had lain stiffly, quietly, since then, not wanting to awaken her. But he ached to hold her.

Although he told himself he would ache to hold any comely lass, he knew it was untrue. None had stirred him since Ella's death, although he had met many in the meantime. He had believed no woman would ever stir him again. But Jenny did.

He eyed her now, glowering at him, and had to struggle not to smile.

He did not expect her to submit to his decision without argument. But after days of feeling helpless to do anything but keep an eye on her, he now had a legal right to enforce his authority—and he would.

Continuing to glower, she said, "Do you really think you can *make* me go if I don't want to?"

"Aye, I can," he said. "I could toss you over my shoulder and carry you to your horse, and not one man here would interfere."

"They would if I asked them to."

"Lass, like it or not, these people contrived to make me your husband and they accept me as such. But you do have a choice. You can obey me in this or you can reveal your identity, and mine, and admit to everyone here that you have deceived them from the outset. When you tell them that you lied to the Joculator about my being your suitor, how do you think they will react?"

She sighed. "You know how. You also know how *I* feel about it. I behaved badly, stupidly. But I lied only to him. He must have told someone else, because they all seem to think that you care for me. If only everyone had detested you—"

She broke off, grimacing. "That was a horrid thing to say. I never meant them to dislike you. I just wanted to make it harder for you to take me back by force."

"I couldn't have done that in any event," he said. "Dunwythie asked me to fetch you but gave me no written authority to do so. That I might need such a thing occurred to neither of us, because he wanted no scandal."

"I'm glad he gave you no authority," she said, putting her hands to her flushed cheeks. "Just think if you'd had a document to show to the Joculator! You'd have taken me straightaway. How embarrassing! Of course, if you had, I'd never have told him that fib, and—"

"I doubt if any document would have persuaded the Joculator to let me take you against your will," Hugh said. "Minstrel companies, being itinerant by nature, rarely expect the law to treat them fairly, so they look after their own, and you became an accepted member of this company overnight. I knew from the start that they would take your part against me, especially the Joculator. Having no family of his own, other than this company, the chances of his siding with your uncle—"

"He did have a son," Jenny reminded him. "Recall that the *vielle* belonged to him, but he died years ago. Cath said the anniversary of his death is near, which is why the Joculator spends so much time alone and sets his tent apart from the others."

"What happened to his wife?"

"I don't think he ever married. But that is naught to do with us, sir. I still think we must go to Threave to warn Archie that he may have trouble brewing!"

Hugh shook his head. "I'll see that he learns of your suspicion."

"Faith, you still don't believe there *is* any plot threatening him," she said more sharply than she had yet spoken to him.

"Whether I believe it or not, I will see that Archie hears of your concerns," he said, careful to keep his voice even and not reveal a hint of his own increasing suspicion that something was at least amiss. "He is my kinsman and I served him loyally for years. I would not keep any such possibility from him."

"Still, you do not attach much importance to warning him, or you would set off straightaway and just leave me here. I would be perfectly safe."

"I also have a duty to Dunwythie," he reminded her. When she opened her mouth to go on arguing, he added curtly, "Think, lass. If I were to ride off to Threave, leaving you with this company, what do you think would happen if you are right and some plot does exist? What would the plotters think?"

She frowned. "You need not say you are riding to Threave."

"Sakes, I told everyone at the outset that I was going there," he said. "'Tis why they've let me travel with them."

"Even so—"

"Don't you see, if someone *is* plotting mischief and has reason to think you might suspect as much, *you* might be in danger *here*. In any event, you will go back to Annan House so his lordship can begin to undo this marriage of ours and set things right. Betrothals are complex matters, and the Kirk takes a dim view of treating them lightly, let alone of ignoring one and marrying someone else."

"But I didn't do that!"

"You know that, and I know that. But yon priest has a copy of our marriage lines, which he will duly record in the parish book at Sweetheart Abbey. You heard him say he must follow his rules, and we must follow the Kirk's laws to undo what he did. Until then . . ."

"But you said the minstrels don't care about laws, so what makes you so sure they won't support me if I say I want to stay with them?"

Exerting himself to find patience, he said, "We have already plucked that crow. The plain fact is that a husband has absolute right to command his wife, and every man and woman here knows that."

She met his gaze for a long moment and then sighed, pushed aside the covers, and said, "Where did I put my shoes?"

"Yonder," he said, pointing to the shadows at the foot of her pallet.

She nodded, stretched to retrieve them, and put them on. "If you will permit me to go outside, sir, I must . . ." She bit her lip. When he nodded his understanding, she stood, pushed aside the tent flap, and stepped out.

Finding his boots, Hugh pulled them on, wishing he could think clearly. His body still ached for hers, as if it called him a fool for honoring his promise to her.

It had been all he could do to pretend that he was unaffected by having her so close to him. The temptation to grab her and stop her arguments with kisses and caresses had been almost more than he could withstand.

⁓

Jenny hurried into the woods, found a place to see to her immediate need, and then, hoping Hugh would not look for her right away, went to find Peg.

The erstwhile maidservant was talking with Gawkus near one of the cook fires, but seeing Jenny, she broke off her conversation and hurried to meet her.

"I didna think ye'd be up so early," she said.

"Sir Hugh means to take me back," Jenny said. "However, I do not want to go. He thinks our marriage is not legal, sithee, because of my betrothal to his brother. So, he means to hand me back to my uncle to sort things out."

"Sakes, mistress, I thought ye'd be gey pleased to marry Sir Hugh. The two o' ye seem to like each other, and more. Sakes, when ye sing to him—"

"That was an act, Peg, like everything else!" Ignoring the silent protest that arose within her at the words, Jenny added fiercely, "I don't *want* to go back!"

Peg frowned. "I dinna blame ye for that, mistress, especially if they can still make ye marry that Reid Douglas. Sakes, me own cousin were overnight with a man—and him another cousin—'cause his mam died whilst she were a-staying wi' them. He arranged to send her home the very next morning, but the man she were betrothed to demanded she be examined to make sure her cousin hadna taken her maidenhead—aggrieved as the poor man were, and all!"

"Examined?"

"Aye, sure, d'ye ken nowt o' such?

When Jenny shook her head, Peg said, "Me cousin told me half the women in the village came to watch when the midwife felt to see did she still have her virtue intact. She'll never forgive her man for demanding such a thing o' her."

A shiver shot up Jenny's spine. Would Reid demand such an examination? The image Peg's words had stirred in her mind made her skin crawl.

"I can't go back," she said firmly.

"Aye, but ye must, mistress. A woman must do as her husband bids her."

Jenny ground her teeth together to keep from shrieking that *she* need not do so. But she knew that arguing the point with Peg would be useless.

Looking around, she saw that Hugh had come out of their tent and was talking with several other men near the second fire.

He caught her gaze briefly but made no move toward her. Nor did he motion her to join him.

Taking it to mean he would not try to order her about yet, and seeing that Gilly had joined Gawkus where Peg had left the latter, she strolled toward them, trying to think how to put her case to them.

They both smiled at her approach. But she noted, too, that they looked as one toward Hugh.

"Good morrow," she said, drawing their attention back to her. "I hope you have some time for us to practice after breakfast, Gilly. I want to show you how much better my aim is with my dirk."

"Aye, sure, Jenny," Gilly said. "That is, if your man approves it. Husbands, sithee, can be prickly creatures."

"Oh, Hugo will not mind," she said.

Gawkus frowned. "Sakes, lass," he said. "The man has watched over ye like a wolf wi' one cub since he came here. And Gilly may be small, but he's aye another man for all that."

Feeling heat flood her cheeks, Jenny said, "Even so, Hugo knows that Gilly has been teaching me. He won't object to another lesson."

"Will he not?" Gilly asked with a slight movement of his head.

Following the motion, expecting to see Hugh striding toward them, she saw instead with a sinking sensation that Lucas had begun to take down their tents.

"He has already taken out the pallets, lass. For all that your Hugo said he meant to ride with us to Threave, I'm thinking he has taken another notion into his head now. He were none so pleased as we thought he'd be by yon wedding."

"Sakes, do you think he is leaving me?"

"Nay, then," Gawkus said. "The man doesna breathe wha' would be such a dunder-pate as that. He wants ye to himself now, is all."

That thought shot new sensations through her. She was sure Hugh could make her do almost anything if he set his mind to it, and instead of infuriating her, the knowledge intensified the unfamiliar feelings and made her feel hot all over.

"Ye're blushing, lassie," Gilly said with a knowing smile. "I'll just go ask him does he want me to go on teach—"

"Nay, then, don't," she said, flustered but determined not to give Hugh a chance to tell Gilly he was taking her home. "I'll . . . I'll ask him myself."

"Aye, that would be better," the little man agreed.

Certain now that with Peg, Gilly, and Gawkus reacting as they had to her marriage, she could count on no one else—least of all the Joculator—to side with her, Jenny felt more irritated than ever with Hugh.

She equaled him in rank. In fact, for all she knew of Thornhill, her estates might be larger and more valuable than his were. Yet, because of her foolish lie and the contrivance of her supposed friends, Hugh was now her husband and could command her to do whatever it occurred to him to command.

"It is not fair," she muttered.

"What's that, Jenny-lass?" Gawkus asked gently.

Still watching Hugh as Gerda swayed up to him, doubtless with eyelashes aflutter, Jenny had forgotten about the two men who stood with her.

Glancing up at Gawkus, she wished she had kept a guard on her tongue. But knowing she owed him an explanation, she decided on the truth and said ruefully, "I don't want him to take me away from here."

"Then ye've only to tell him so," Gawkus recommended.

"I did."

"I see." He exchanged a look with Gilly, then looked

soberly back at her. "Did we do ye a disservice, Jenny-lass? We none of us meant to do that."

Gilly, too, looked upset.

Jenny could not let her two friends think they had betrayed her, not when the whole thing was her own fault. "Nay," she said gently. "'Twas no disservice. I . . . I am just not accustomed to submitting to any man since my father died."

"Aye, we did think ye must lack a father, as sure o' yourself as ye be," Gawkus said. "I warrant ye've nae brothers either."

She shook her head, realizing she could not continue a discussion of her family without revealing the truth or trying to lie again, and she did not want to do either one. If she had her way, she would never lie again, to anyone.

"Yon Hugo still be a-staring at us," Gilly said. "I think ye should go now and put the man's mind to rest afore he comes over here and puts *us* to rest."

Jenny looked at Hugh and saw that Gerda still chatted with him. Even so, he was watching *her*, and Gilly was right. Hugh looked grim.

Wary of stirring his temper further, she said, "I had better go."

⁓

"So I were just a-thinking that mayhap we should practice yon scene again lest we forget our lines," Gerda said.

Gerda had been batting her eyelashes at Hugh as if she were trying to fling them off her eyelids. Twice now, she had touched his arm as if she sensed that he was trying to ignore her. Glancing away, he saw Jenny walking toward them.

When Gerda put a hand on his forearm and left it there, he reluctantly wrenched his gaze from Jenny to look at the plumper lass, wishing he could think of something to say that would discourage Gerda's flirting without giving offense.

He had not decided what he would say to the others in the company, but he would have to think of something soon. Lucas had packed the sumpter baskets and nearly had the tent down. Although he had acted quietly, someone would demand an explanation soon. The minstrels would not pack up for at least two more days.

Bustling up to them, Cath said, "Gerda, if ye're going to break your fast, ye'd best get to it. Hugo doesna want to hear your blandishments today. The man just married, love, so leave him be—at least till his passions cool some."

Hugh met Cath's laughing eyes and smiled. "Such cooling may take time," he said, knowing that would be true, annulment or no annulment.

"Aye, sure," Cath said. "But everyone forgets these first days soon enough. I see that your man be a-packing your things. D'ye mean to be away, then?"

"I expect ye'll understand how it is," he said. "I followed me lass for so long and came so near giving up thinking I might win her that I want her to m'self now for a time. Will the others think the worse o' me for that?"

"Nay then," she said, casting a teasing glance at her daughter. "What I'm thinking is that only one person will grieve your loss, Hugo, and that be our Gerda. Lanky Gawkus can take your place in yon play, for if Gilly plays the priest, 'twill be even funnier. And," she added with a sour look, "Cuddy's cousin Drogo be going to Threave with us, so he can take your place wi' the singing."

Seeing Jenny pause nearby, Hugh motioned her close and put an arm around her. "I was just telling Cath and Gerda that we mean to leave, lass. I think now that I ought to have told the Joculator first, though. We had better go do that now."

He saw her glance at Gerda, her expression revealing little. She held out a hand to Cath then, saying, "Thank you, and you, too, Gerda, for making me feel so welcome here. I shall miss you both. Indeed, I will miss everyone here."

Cath opened her arms, and Jenny walked into them. With tears in her eyes, she hugged the older woman hard. Then, turning to Gerda, she opened her own arms.

Grinning, Gerda hugged her. "I willna say ye're the better woman for him, Jen," she said. "But ye do sing well. So, if he casts ye off, come and find us."

With a watery chuckle, Jenny said, "I will, and gladly. Thank you!"

As they walked away, Hugh said, "You have a good heart, lass."

She did not answer, and he knew she was still fighting tears.

⁓

Jenny would not have wanted to admit that, briefly, she had felt more like scratching out Gerda's eyes than hugging her. Why that impulse had leapt into being she could not have said. It had formed when she saw Gerda rest her hand on Hugh's arm and had swiftly ballooned to near fury. Surely, she was not jealous!

Neither did she want to admit that she had made herself hug Gerda only because she had hugged Cath and did not want to give Gerda cause to speak against her. It had seemed right to do it, so she had simply followed an instinct that had served her well in the past. Now, she was glad she had.

Walking to find the Joculator, she waited for Hugh to speak.

"Looks like snow," he said at last, frowning at the sky.

"As it has every day for a sennight," she reminded him.

"Those clouds in the west are blacker though, and 'tis growing colder."

He was right, but normally in March, the nearer one came to the end, the milder the weather. Moreover, they had not had a heavy snowstorm in weeks.

She was more concerned about what they would say to the Joculator and what he would say to them. They found him at his tent.

He had heard them coming and came out to meet them. Looking from one to the other, he said, "So ye're leaving us. I trust there be nae ill will betwixt us."

"None, sir," Hugh said. "Though I do mean to take my lass away from here. I hope you have no objection."

"Nay, how should I? I'm thinking I dinna ken the whole tale yet, but mayhap someday ye'll see fit to tell me."

Jenny stiffened, not daring to look at either man now that she knew how easily each could read her expressions. To ease her tension, she drew a breath and concentrated on doing it slowly and exhaling just as slowly.

As she did, Hugh was saying, "Mayhap we will have

more to discuss another time, sir. In any event, I am grateful to you and the others for welcoming us both as you did. 'Twas kind of you, and generous. We wish you well at Threave."

"Aye, but ye'll be there, too, will ye not, Hugo lad—bound as ye be to perform for the Lord o' Galloway?"

Hugh nodded. "I will. But my lass will not. I mean to take her home first."

"A good notion," the Joculator said. "Doubtless, ye'll be leaving her in safe hands. Your parents, belike."

"I promise you, she will be safe," Hugh said. "Come now, Jenny. I want to be away as soon as we can."

"'Tis a black day for traveling," the Joculator said.

"Aye, but we'll be safe," Hugh said.

"Will ye be taking that Peg wi' ye, too?"

"That must be up to Peg," Hugh said.

Jenny, to her shock, having focused her thoughts on her unsuccessful search for someone to support her in her determination *not* to leave, had failed to spare a single thought to warning Peg that *she* needed to pack.

～～

Hugh waited until they were away from the Joculator before he said, "You looked a little stunned when he mentioned Peg. Did you not tell her we are going?"

Jenny shook her head.

"What did you say to her then, when you talked to her?" he asked.

When Jenny shut her eyes, he almost smiled, guessing at once what had happened. How the lass had ever dared trying to prevaricate, he could not imagine.

The silence lengthened until he said gently, "I must suppose that Gawkus and Gilly likewise proved unhelpful."

She opened her eyes at that, glared at him, and turned away. Had he not caught her by a shoulder to stop her, she would surely have stormed off.

"Nay, nay," he said with a chuckle. "Only think what a figure you'll make if you stride back into camp with your nose in the air and your eyes flashing. If you don't trip over your own feet, you will certainly stir amusement in all who see you."

She whirled back, arms akimbo, and her chin still high—if only because she had to look up to scowl at him. "Does it give you such pleasure then that my friends feel helpless to aid me?"

"Not pleasure, no," he said. "But it is good to see you facing the truth and accepting it for once. That is, if you *have* accepted it. I am not sure yet that you have. Shall we go together and tell Peg, or shall I tell Lucas to do it?"

"She may be better pleased if Lucas tells her," Jenny said. "She likes him, I think, so she will doubtless be as wax in his hands."

But they saw Peg before they saw Lucas, and her reaction was unexpected.

"Ye're returning to *Annan* House? I was sure ye'd be going straight to Thornhill with . . . wi' him," she added, glancing at Hugh and then around as if she were uncertain what to call him as they were still with the minstrels. Then, in a harsh whisper, she said, "Mistress, I dare not go back there."

"Don't be foolish, Peg," Jenny said. "I will protect you."

"How can ye? I work for his lordship, aye, *and* for her ladyship. And if ye think she'll keep me on after this, ye canna know her. Ye did say I could work for ye at Thorn-hill, sir, and I might ha' done that, although it be far from Annan and I'd liefer stay here. Sithee, Cath says I'm good wi' a needle, and I'd be wi' our Bryan."

"Would you not rather be with Lucas?" Jenny asked.

Peg looked astonished. "That one? Nay, I would *not*! I'll help ye pack, mistress, but unless Sir Hugh— Ay de mi . . . unless Hugo says I must, I'd liefer stay."

Hugh frowned. "My lass should have a woman with her, Peg."

"She has her husband and his man. Surely, she'll be safe wi' the pair o' ye."

"I cannot command you to go," he admitted.

"Sakes, sir, I'm thinking ye're daft to be going your-self. Look at that sky!"

Obediently looking, Hugh saw that although blue spaces still showed among the clouds, the clouds them-selves were even blacker than before, and lower. Wind stirred leaves on the trees, but in the woods, it was hard to judge its strength.

Jenny looked hopeful. "Mayhap we should wait a day or two," she said. "They do need you for the play."

"Nay, they do not," he told her firmly. "Nor do they need you. This storm will pass just as the others all have. You'll see."

She sighed. "I am sure you are right, sir. You do have the most annoying habit of nearly always being so."

Hugh chuckled, but for once, he was wrong.

Chapter 13

They had been traveling a couple of hours when the snow began. At first, it was just a few gentle flakes, but when Jenny saw Hugh exchange a look with Lucas, she knew that both men believed it would grow worse.

They kept on, but she could tell they were looking for shelter. At one point, they paused to consider a cottage on a hill with smoke curling from its chimney.

Lucas said, "Happen there'd be some soul there to give us shelter, sir."

"Aye, but I'd liefer not draw unnecessary attention to ourselves. Annan lies only fifteen miles southeast of Dumfries. We should be able to cover that distance before nightfall, but we must find a place to wait out this storm. It won't be the first time we've provided our own shelter in such a case, Lucas."

"Nay, sir, it will not. There be one or two villages ahead, too. Happen w—"

"There will be woodland before we reach the next village," Hugh interjected. "I'd prefer that we keep to ourselves to avoid any comment. If her ladyship had a female companion, no one would pay us heed. But, as it is, unless we make a point of my being her husband . . . well, I'd prefer that we name no names. That would be gey difficult anywhere we might request shelter. As we get closer to Annan, we also risk the possibility that someone may recognize her."

Lucas nodded, but the snow fell harder, and Jenny saw Hugh look skyward more often as they rode. It had grown much colder, too.

By the time they reached the woods he had mentioned, the horses' pace had slowed to a walk. Jenny's teeth were chattering, and it was hard to discern the road.

In the woods, it was easier, because the trees were mostly beeches, creating a high, dense canopy. It thinned over the roadway but so far had allowed snow to fall only in sporadic patches to the ground. They rode nearly to the woods' eastern edge before Hugh turned off the road into a small clearing under the canopy.

"We'll stop here and make a fire," he said, glancing at Jenny.

She tried to smile, but her lips felt numb.

Grimacing as he dismounted, he strode to lift her down, saying as he did, "Your lips are blue, lass. With that thick, hooded cloak of yours, I thought you were warm enough. You should have said something."

"I did not realize how cold I was," she said as he set her on her feet. They felt as numb as her hands and lips, and when she tried to walk, she stumbled.

Muttering an oath, he scooped her into his arms and shouted at Lucas to fetch blankets from the sumpter and to get the tent set up and a fire going.

"Her ladyship is frozen to the bone," he added. "Just fling over what I can use to warm her whilst you see to the tent and the fire. Has the snow soaked through your cloak?" he demanded brusquely of Jenny.

"Nay, not yet," she said.

"For a sensible woman, you're as daft as a bairn sometimes," he retorted. "You must have known your hands were cold. And don't try telling me they aren't."

"I don't know how cold they are. I can't feel them," she said.

Grimly, he said, "I'm going to put you on your feet again. I'll hold on to you when I do, but I want you to move them about whilst I rub your hands. It will hurt, but that's to the good. And it serves you right for not paying better heed in such weather. Sithee, your hands and feet will freeze first, lass. When Lucas gets the pallets down and the blankets on them, he and I will gather more wood for the fire. But in the meantime we must do all we can to warm you."

He had spoken the truth. Her feet hurt when she moved them, and when he told her to stamp them on the ground, she said irritably, "I can't. It hurts too much. Surely, it cannot be a good thing to do."

"Do as I tell you," he snapped, grabbing her shoulders and giving her a shake before going back to rubbing her hands.

She would have liked to stomp on his feet but knew it would hurt. Also, she saw that Lucas had the tent up already and was throwing the pallets into it.

"Ye can bring her now, sir," he said. "By, but t' lass looks perishin' starved! Tha should hutch up with 'er for a time. I'll get the fire going straightaway."

"I'm not even hungry yet," Jenny protested.

"He doesn't mean that you look hungry," Hugh said. "In Yorkshire, 'starved' means freezing cold, and hutching up is one way for me to warm you until he gets the fire going. So, get yourself moving."

As Hugh gestured to the tent, she said, "Won't all the wood here be wet?"

"Only on the outside, and it is dryer under the trees than out in the open," he said. "That's why we stopped here. Now, cease your fretting, and get into that tent."

She wished he would carry her. He was strong and able, and the tent, though only a short distance away, seemed too distant for her aching feet.

"Go," he snapped.

She went. Each step shot pins and needles through her feet, but her legs were no longer numb and would, she hoped, soon feel normal again.

When she ducked into the tent, Hugh followed her, ordering her to lie on the pallets, which Lucas had stacked one atop the other.

"I'll cover you," he said. "You'll be warm again in no time."

"I should take off my cloak," she said.

"Aye, give it to me. I'll shake it out and lay it on top. It still has your body heat and will help warm the blankets."

She lay down and let him pull off her boots and pile blankets on her, but still she shivered. The blankets felt cold, her feet icy, and her teeth chattered again.

"Damnation," he swore, staring at her. "Lucas was right."

Laying his cloak atop hers and pulling off his boots, he

slipped into the bed beside her, pulling her close. "This is what he meant when he told me to hutch up with you, although he meant skin-to-skin, like rabbits. Try to relax now," he added. "Slip your feet between my legs and press as close to me as you can."

She had stiffened as he got into the bed, but the warmth emanating from him was irresistible, and when he slid an arm around her, she snuggled closer. His breeks felt damp through her stockings, but even damp they felt toasty warm.

As his warmth penetrated, she did begin to relax. Then he shifted position, and her head came to rest on his shoulder with her cheek against his hard chest.

A short time later, he said quietly, "Better?"

"Aye," she murmured. "I'm nearly warm again. Should you not help Lucas?"

"I'll go presently. He doesn't need me yet, but I think we may be here for a while. We may have to build a stronger shelter."

"How?"

"We'll make one from branches, so when the snow in the canopy begins sifting or clumping down on us, as it will, it won't smash the tents or melt through."

"We're using two tents then?"

"Aye, Lucas does have his own, after all. You and I will share this one."

"Won't he get cold, all on his own?" she asked, noting with a sense of gratitude and other less identifiable feelings that he had not suggested that he and Lucas sleep together and let her have a tent to herself.

"Not unless it gets much colder than it has been. If it does, he'll come in here with us. It will be a tight fit, but we'll stay warm. I don't expect this storm to last long enough or grow cold enough to warrant that, but we'll do what we must."

"Are you still angry with me?" she asked abruptly.

"Nay, lass. I wasn't angry before."

"You sounded angry."

"I warrant I did. I was worried that you'd done yourself an injury through being too prideful to ask us to stop and let you get warm."

She thought about that. "I suppose I did fear you'd think me a nuisance," she admitted. "I also thought that you and Lucas must be as cold as I was."

"Next time, don't think about anyone's needs but your own."

"No one has ever told me *that* before," she said with a chuckle. "From birth, I've been told that I must always think of others first, especially our people."

She could not see his face without shifting her position, but she heard amusement in his voice as he said, "I've heard those words many times myself. But my advice now is a matter of survival, Jenny. You won't be of any use to your people if you freeze to death because you were too prideful to ask for help."

"Aye," she said. "Although I don't know how much use I'm going to be to them now, anyway. Your brother will take over."

He was silent for a time before he said, "Reid will need your guidance. You will remain Easdale of Easdale, after all."

"Aye, but in name only. Phaeline and his lordship said that after we marry, I must leave the management to Reid. He said the same. In fact," she added, "I doubt that he will *allow* me to guide him. He told me he looks forward to schooling *me*."

His arm tightened, pulling her closer.

"I think he looks forward eagerly to that," she said. "Were you eager to school your wife, sir—your first one?"

His arm twitched again. "I'd rather not talk about Ella," he said quietly.

"I know what you mean," she said, nodding. "I don't like talking about my father either, particularly with people who did not know him well."

"Like Phaeline and your uncle?"

"Aye. Phaeline no sooner mentioned him than she said he was a fool not to have married again. She said my uncle had been wiser, because he'd provided Mairi with a mother and himself with a woman who will give him a proper male heir."

"Something Phaeline has yet to do," he murmured.

"Aye, but they are certain that this one will be a boy," Jenny said, keeping her doubts about that to herself. "In troth, for Mairi's sake, I hope it is."

"Mairi's sake? I should think she would prefer to remain her father's heiress. Why do you think it better for her if Phaeline bears a son?"

"Because, as it is, Mairi has no suitors. Young men want to know what they are getting when they wed. If my uncle were to acknowledge her as his heiress, she would have suitors aplenty. But whilst Phaeline remains able to produce a son, my uncle neither acknowledges Mairi nor provides her with a proper tocher. So no suitor can be sure that she is *worth* marrying."

"I see," he said. "I must agree that knowing one's birthright does make one's responsibilities clear."

"If you had only a daughter, would you teach her or keep hoping for a son?"

"I did have a daughter," he said. "Now Reid is my heir, and I realized not long ago that I've done nowt to make his future responsibilities clear to him."

"But you can still marry properly and have more children, sir. You could easily produce a better heir than Reid."

"You are very blunt, madam. Does it not occur to you that you will also benefit when Reid inherits my estates, as he will be your husband by then?"

"Nay, I did not think of that, nor would I. But I meant no offense, sir. You may be responsible in some way for how Reid has turned out, but changing him now would be gey hard. My father, on the other hand, was a shy man who had no interest in remarrying. He was content with his daughter. He taught me all he knew about our estates, and I know he expected to have a say in my marriage, but I wish he had told me more about what to expect."

"I warrant it would have been as he commanded, whilst he lived," Hugh said. "It would certainly have been easier for you if he had. You must miss him sorely."

"As sorely as you miss your wife and daughter," she said. "Sithee, I could ask him anything, and he would answer my questions. But I did not know I would need answers to questions that it never occurred to me to ask."

"You may ask me, if you like," he said.

"Just what do you suppose your brother would say if I were to tell him I had sought your advice and your answer disagreed with what he had decided to do?"

When he did not reply, she turned toward him, raising herself on an elbow to look at him. "I did not put that well, but you must know what I meant."

"Aye," he said. "And you are right. Reid would be angry."

She was quiet as a question she was burning to ask him repeated itself over and over again in her mind until she said, "Things are going to be difficult when we reach Annan House, are they not?"

"Aye, a little," he said. "But I doubt that Phaeline will rip up at you too much whilst I am at hand, if that is what concerns you."

"What about your brother?"

After another silence, he said, "I cannot speak for Reid."

"Peg said he would demand an examination," Jenny said, blurting it out before she lost her nerve. "Do you understand what that means?"

"Aye," he said, his voice sounding harsh again.

"Well, that would be *very* difficult."

"It is not unusual for a man to demand such a test before his marriage if his bride has not been closely guarded until then. You should have thought of that before you ran away."

"How could I think about something I did not know could happen? My father never told me about such examinations. He assumed I would be under his eye until I married, so it never occurred to him that I might need to know such a thing."

Lucas called, "Sir, the fire be a-going, and I've cut some long branches, so we can begin our shelters if ye'd like."

"I must go, but you'll be warm enough now, I wager," Hugh said, carefully pushing the blankets off himself and tucking them close to her as he got up.

"Aye," she murmured, watching as he pulled on his boots and went outside in only a leather jack and breeks, leaving his heavy cloak atop hers.

It occurred to her that since they would seek an annulment, for her to lie with him was improper under any circumstance. Even so, it had seemed natural to let him hold her, and a blessing to share his warmth.

In truth, although Hugh had often annoyed and exasperated her, something deep inside thrilled at the thought of having him even briefly as her husband. She respected him, and she could talk with him. He understood what it was to manage large estates and bear responsibility for others' lives. He did not regard his estates or hers as mere sources of income. Reid, she suspected, saw Easdale that way and spared not one thought for her or for her people.

She lay a few minutes longer in the warm bed. But now that she was warm, she decided she ought to be up and doing things, helping to keep the fire going if nothing else, while the men dealt with their shelters.

Accordingly, she got up, pulled on her boots, and smoothed the covers on the pallet with Hugh's cloak atop them. Reassuring herself that the inside of her cloak was dry, she put it on, put up the hood, and went outside. She was surprised to see that although the patches of snow were deeper, much of the ground was still clear.

The men were piling branches near the tent, and she saw another pile beside Lucas's tent. Lucas had cut firewood, so she went to see if the fire needed tending.

It burned merrily, and Lucas had lashed a spit together,

ready to put over the flames later. Hugh glanced at her but said nothing about her having come outside. He and Lucas were already arranging the cut branches around and over Hugh's tent. It seemed to take only minutes and doing Lucas's took less time.

The two men disappeared into the woods then, returning a short while later with a brace of rabbits. They skinned them, and Lucas fixed them on the spit. Then he stood the spit over the fire.

"Where did you put the food we brought?" Jenny asked him, knowing the women had given them a bag of food before they left.

"'Tis in t' sumpter basket, m'lady," Lucas said, pointing. "We thought we'd liefer 'ave hot food as well, just now."

"Those rabbits already smell delicious," she said as she went to find the sack.

It contained crusty rolls and apples, as well as cold sliced beef. Knowing the men would be hungry and that they would have little use for the food after they reached Annan House, she took it all to a flat rock near the fire.

"We'll have a feast for our midday meal," she said.

"Walk with me for a time first, lass," Hugh said. "I want to see how much snow is flying beyond these woods, and we should come to the end of them a short way from here. We'll have a look whilst Lucas minds the rabbits."

She went willingly. Walking would keep her warm.

"Will the minstrels be building shelters, too?" she asked him.

He shrugged. "'Tis more likely that their resourceful leader has arranged for them to move into the town hall.

I'm hoping this storm will be of short duration, though, so we won't have to stay overnight."

She had mixed emotions about that, but when they reached the edge of the woods, the snow seemed to be falling heavily. She saw no sign of the road other than an area that appeared consistently flatter than the surrounding countryside.

"Is it safe to try following a road we can hardly see?" she asked him.

"We'll wait until it is safe enough. I want to walk a little farther, though. I can't see much to the west from here, and since the storm is moving eastward . . ."

"I'm coming with you," she said when he paused.

"Aye, sure," he agreed, offering an arm.

Clutching it, she stomped through the snow with him, noting how feathery light it was, and dryer than earlier snows had been. It was already inches deep.

She folded her hands together over his arm, to take advantage of its warmth.

"Cold again?" he asked.

"Not yet," she said. "You're warm enough for two."

He chuckled, and she smiled at the sound. She liked his voice, but even more did she enjoy his laughter. He laughed at the same things she did, and she felt more comfortable with him than she had thought she could feel with anyone.

They walked eastward for a time before he turned and skeptically eyed the dark, forbidding western sky.

"It is going to last a while," Jenny said.

"Aye, a few hours," he said. "We may still have time to reach Annan before nightfall, even so. But I think Lucas and I should cut more firewood."

They returned to find the rabbits ready to take off the spit, and when they had eaten, Hugh told Jenny to go back inside the tent while they cut wood.

The fire was not large, but they had pitched their tents and built their shelters to face it, so she could leave the flap open, snuggle in the blankets, and still watch the men at work. Hugh had not yet put his cloak back on, but when she returned to the tent, Lucas asked her to pass it out to him so he could dry it before the fire.

He had contrived a clever rack for the purpose, and the area where he had built the fire remained relatively dry, the snow piling for the most part in the treetops. She remembered that one reason for the cavelike branch shelters was to protect them if a heavy pile of snow should suddenly fall through the branches overhead.

An hour later, Hugh came to tell her that although the snowfall had eased, it still snowed, so he had decided they would wait at least an hour more to be sure it would not grow worse.

An hour after that, he said it looked as if it might clear before nightfall but not soon enough to travel safely.

Jenny received the news calmly. She was in no hurry.

～⌒

Hugh watched Jenny, not having to ask what she was thinking. He knew she hated the thought of going back, but he had to take her. He had given his word.

When he and Lucas had cut enough wood, Hugh left him to watch the fire and ducked back inside the tent to see how she was doing.

She smiled when he asked. "It is gey cozy in here now," she said.

"Aye, well, I think the snow will ease again soon," he said. The truth was he was enjoying himself. He always did when he pitted himself against nature or any other foe. For that matter, he had enjoyed playing troubadour with the minstrels. But he was not looking forward to returning her to Dunwythie, let alone to Reid.

Nonetheless, he reminded himself firmly, he had a duty to keep his word.

"I was thinking," he said as Jenny scooted over to make room for him on the pallet. "When we get to Annan House, they will have much to say to you—to both of us, come to that. I have no doubt they expected me to return you within a day or two at most—certainly not to take ten days."

"Aye, for they would expect you to act swiftly," she agreed. "You have a reputation for getting things done competently, I know."

"Do you?"

"Aye, sure; Phaeline told me." Her cheeks flushed then, as she looked away.

"What else did Phaeline say about me?"

Jenny nibbled her lower lip and then grinned at him. "She said that when you make up your mind, you won't change it. You fold your arms and pretend to listen, but one's arguments have no more effect on you than drops of water on a stone."

"*That* is an absurdity, as I hope I need not tell you."

"Sakes, sir, I don't think it an absurdity. You made up your mind to fetch me, and you've not turned from that course. Phaeline also said," she added hastily, "that one cannot push you to do aught you do not want to do, that even if one were to light a fire between your toes, you would stick to your purpose. She said, too, that you'd pay less heed to your pain than to whether one had built the fire properly."

His lips twitched, but he said, "I trust you do not believe all Phaeline says."

"No, sir, I do not. In troth, I have wondered . . ." She hesitated.

"Wondered what?"

"'Tis naught, and I should say no more, for I'm sure I am thinking wishful thoughts. I should be kinder, but I do wish you would not take me back there."

"I must," he said gently. "I promised Dunwythie, just as you promised to marry Reid. We must both honor our promises."

"Well, I wish I did *not* have to marry Reid," she said fiercely.

"But you agreed to become betrothed to him, and betrothal is more than a promise," he said. "'Tis a complex, legal agreement involving land issues and other matters that can require long negotiation before the settlements are completed."

"Well, I don't like him any better as my betrothed than I did before."

"If you disliked him so, why did you agree to marry him?" he demanded.

"They gave me no choice!"

"Don't be daft. You had only to refuse to sign the marriage settlements."

With a bewildered look, she said, "But I didn't. I have

never signed any document having aught to do with my marriage to Reid Douglas."

Hugh clamped his lips together, stopping the angry words that threatened to spill from his tongue.

———

When Hugh looked furious but said nothing, Jenny stared at him. "Why do you not speak? Do you think I am lying again? I swear I am not."

He shook his head. Then, as if he thought a headshake had not been enough, he muttered, "I ken fine that you are not lying, lass. I must think on this, and if we are going to spend the night here, we must have more hot food."

With that, he got up and left the tent. Jenny stared after him, her own temper igniting at such treatment. If he were not so big . . . If Lucas were not also out there . . .

Then, despite her anger, she smiled. The image of herself running after Hugh, shaking him, and forcing him to speak his thoughts to her was too absurd to sustain.

Still, she wanted to know what she had said to make him so angry, and the only way she could imagine doing that was to ask him. So she pushed off the blankets, put her boots and cloak on again, and went after him.

She found him skinning rabbits with Lucas.

"Mercy, but you caught those quickly," she said to Hugh.

His lips twitched, but he said only, "Lucas set the traps before and had just collected these two."

"Fine work, Lucas," she said with a smile. "Doubtless, you have caught more by now. Mayhap you should go and see."

He glanced up at her, then looked at Hugh.

"Go, Lucas," Jenny said firmly. "I would have a word with Sir Hugh."

"Stay, Lucas," Hugh said. "We have nowt to discuss, lass. I told you to stay inside where you will keep warm."

"Did you, sir? I did not hear you say any such thing. I heard naught and saw only your back as you left. If you want Lucas to hear what I will say to you, he must of course stay. However, I should think—"

"I'm goin'," Lucas said, standing and setting aside his rabbit, neatly skinned.

"Nay, then, you'll not," Hugh said curtly. "You will—"

"Master Hugh, I 'ave stuck by ye through many a good day and many a bad 'un, but ye'll 'ave to deal with your own sorrows now. They be none of my making, nor nowt to do with me. Shout when ye want me, mistress."

With that, he strode off into the woods.

If Jenny was astonished, Hugh was more so.

"By heaven," he exclaimed, "I'll have something to say to that—"

"You already have much to say that you do *not* say, sir," Jenny said crisply. "But Lucas is *not* the one who put you in such a temper."

"Jenny, wait now, lass—"

"What concerns me is what *I* must have said to put you in such a fury. I had been thinking how easily I could talk with you. Then, with a single statement, I got a look as near rage as I have seen on any man's face before you walked off without explanation. That will not do, sir. You would not tolerate it had I done it, nor will I tolerate such treatment from you. If I said aught that I should not have said, pray—"

"Sakes, lass, I'm not angry with you!"

"Then who or what has put you out so?"

He grimaced. "It is not so easy to explain," he said, clearly making an effort to speak quietly. Glancing in the direction Lucas had taken, he sighed.

"It cannot have been Lucas," she said.

"Whisst now," he said. "I wish you would go back inside that tent."

"I warrant you do, but unless you mean to pick me up and carry me there, you will *not* get your wish. So, talk to me, Hugo," she added softly. "Explain."

It was the first time she had called him Hugo in private, but it felt comfortable to do so, and right.

"I should not discuss the matter with you at all, let alone explain why I feel as I do," he said. "It is wrong to meddle in another man's affairs."

She frowned, thinking back to what she had said before he stalked out. "'Tis the marriage settlements, then. That I did not sign any made you angry. Moreover, you had just said that I should *not* have signed them if I did not want to marry Reid."

"Let be, lass. Do as I bid you now, and get back inside."

"Nay, then, I won't."

When he moved to stand, she said, "Stay where you are, sir. You cannot come the husband over me only to force my *obedience*. You say you will not meddle in another man's affairs. But whose business is it if not mine and my husband's?"

Chapter 14

Relaxing, Hugh shook his head at Jenny, but her argument impressed him.

Although she was naïve in some ways, her habit of command was clear. He had not seen her reveal it so deliberately before, but he had a sense now of having committed a wrong for which he ought hastily to apologize.

He suppressed the impulse, saying instead, "Jenny, I cannot expect you to understand my dilemma. Still, I hope you will believe that I've been wrestling with my conscience since I left the tent. Sithee, lass, you are Dunwythie's ward, you are under age, and I gave the man my word that I would find you and restore you to him. Moreover, *because* you are his ward, he does have certain rights. And, as he has been managing your affairs, this tangle we're in is his business."

"I do not see that such details have aught to do with the matter at hand, sir. You are legally my husband, are you not?"

"Aye, for the nonce, but—"

"Never mind the nonce, Hugo. If you are legally my husband, then you replace my guardian, do you not? A woman cannot have both, can she?"

"In certain circumstances, such as when the husband is also a minor—"

"Good sakes, but you put me out of patience, sir. You are *not* a minor. At present, you are my husband, however little you like it and for whatever time you remain so. *As* my husband, you have a duty to protect me, do you not?"

"I do," he said, his voice gentler, his expression softening.

"Then I ask you, what would you, as my lord husband, say to me and to my uncle about my *not* having signed those marriage settlements?"

He hesitated, although he knew exactly what he'd like to say to Dunwythie for treating her so badly.

"Tell me, sir, or by heaven, I shall begin to throw things!"

Her hands were on her hips, her beautiful golden eyes flashed, and both dimples showed, deep and enticing.

He stood up. "Jenny, love," he said, "if you *ever* throw anything at me, I'll put you across my knee and see that you don't so much as think of doing so again."

She stared at him, clearly surprised, as the endearment echoed back to him.

"Jenny, I should not—"

"Tell me what you would say, Hugo," she said softly, standing her ground.

"I don't know," he admitted. "You say I should simply act as your husband, but it is not simple at all. You know it is not. We do not even know if ours is a legal marriage, but whether it is or not, we've agreed that it must be annulled. Dunwythie will then resume his position as your guardian until you marry Reid."

"But if I have signed nothing—"

"You are still betrothed, lass, and that betrothal still predates our marriage, so your uncle has the right to annul it. Moreover, I doubt that Phaeline will allow him to do aught else. Or Reid, come to that. As your betrothed, he also has rights."

"Do I have none?"

"Aye, you do," he said, resting his hands gently on her shoulders and looking into her eyes. "Did they truly say nowt to you about any settlements?"

"Phaeline said only that after I was married, Reid would take over the management of my estates. She said that that is a husband's right."

"In most instances, it is," he said. "But you are a baroness in your *own* right, and although you are still legally a minor, any sensible magistrate would consider you old enough to know your own mind, not just now but also when your father died. Even without such a decision, your uncle had a duty to explain *any* agreement he made on your behalf. That would include anything having to do with your estates, and certainly any marriage settlements. Not only must you understand them, but you must swear an oath that you do, before witnesses, when you sign them."

"But I didn't do any of that! I never even saw them. I do know that my father said I would remain Easdale of Easdale after I married, but Reid certainly did not understand that. He said *he* would become Easdale of Easdale."

"Did he?" Hugh frowned.

"I expect he just did not understand about the title," she said.

"Or they inserted some such agreement into the settlements."

"Mercy, can they do that?"

"They can put anything they like into them. That is why the law requires them to explain the settlements to you and you to agree to them by signing them. I think we will have more to discuss with your uncle now than just your . . . your adventure."

She drew a deep breath and let it out. "By heaven, sir, if you will stand by me, I begin to look forward to that discussion."

His hands were still on her shoulders. He gave them a squeeze, wishing he dared do more to comfort her, and said, "I'll stand by you, Jenny. Now, will you shout for Lucas, or shall I?"

After they ate their supper, Jenny walked again with Hugh to the edge of the woods and saw that the snow had stopped. The air was still, the only sound the distant tinkling of a rill. A lone star shone briefly before a cloud concealed it.

"Do you think it will snow more tonight?" she asked.

"I shall no longer predict the weather," he said. "It does feel warmer than it did last night, however. It may rain tomorrow, but I doubt it will snow."

They turned back, and she thought how comfortable it was. Despite her words earlier, she had no wish to return to Annan House and Reid Douglas.

When they reached their little camp, she saw Lucas eyeing them warily, as if to judge whether one or the other was likely to show temper again.

Hugh said, "Go to bed, lass. We'll see to the fire, and then we'll sleep, too."

"How early must we leave?"

"Not early," he said. "We'll let it warm a bit first if it has a mind to."

She nodded, understanding that he did not want to make it obvious to everyone at Annan House, by arriving too early in the day, that they had spent the night together on the road.

Without snow, on such a good road, travelers could easily manage the fifteen miles from Dumfrics to Annan in four or five hours. Even with the snow, it would take only two hours from where they were to reach Annan House—three at most.

After washing her face in the icy water of the rill, and brushing her teeth with a handy twig, Jenny pulled the two pallets apart as they had been in Dumfries, sought her own, and snuggled under her share of the blankets. She was still awake and not nearly warm enough yet when Hugh came in.

"I don't seem to have enough blankets," she said.

"We'll share them all then," he said evenly.

"Would you mind if I got close to you again for a while?"

"Nay, lass. As you said, we're husband and wife to-night, whatever the future holds for us."

She was soon warm but made no effort to move away and wondered if she should feel guilty for staying where she was.

"What do you suppose God thinks about this tangle?" she murmured.

To her surprise, he chuckled, then laughed out loud. When he could speak, he said, "Only He can know that, but I warrant He must have a sense of humor."

Content with that answer, she soon slept, only to waken some hours later aware that she must have tangled herself in her kirtle. The skirt had crept up around her hips, and she felt an odd bunch of material or something under her left breast. There was also more weight than usual on her bottom.

Coming more clearly to her senses, she realized that she had turned onto her stomach in such a way that Hugh's left hand cupped her breast and his right cupped a bare bottom cheek. Smiling contentedly, she relaxed.

"Art awake, lass?"

Hugh had wakened some time before, noted their positions, and told himself he should not risk waking her by moving. The memory of that thought made him smile when she stiffened and wakened anyway. Remembering certain dreams he had had, he hoped this was not just another one.

Her breast fit his hand perfectly. So did her bum cheek, come to that.

He wanted to see if their mates would fit as perfectly. In truth, he wanted to explore her whole, fascinating body from top to toe.

He wondered with a grin what God would think about that!

She had not answered him, making him wonder if she worried that he would take his hands away if she did. He hoped that was what she was thinking. No God with any kindness in Him would continually put a man in such a position unless He expected the man to take advantage of his opportunities.

"Jenny," he whispered, "I know you're awake."

"I think I'm too sleepy to move," she murmured. "I'm nice and warm."

"Aye, you are," he agreed. "But a healthy man has limited command over his urges and instincts, lass."

"What if they examined me and found me no longer a virgin?"

His breath stopped in his lungs. When he could breathe again, he said, "I think you know that my brother is more interested in your estates than in your maidenhead, but he could make life very hard for you. Consummating our marriage would also make an annulment more difficult to get, I'm sure."

"Then I wish you would ravish me," she muttered. "By my troth, sir, I'd rather have your hands on me than your brother's, or some horrid midwife's."

"Ah, lassie, you tempt me sorely."

"Submit to the temptation, my lord. It will do us both good." She turned over then, and the hand on her bottom cheek was suddenly at the fork of her legs.

Gently, he shifted it upward to her smooth, bare belly.

"Would you not like to straighten your clothing, Jenny? You cannot be comfortable with it as tangled as it is."

"I'm not, so help me pull off this kirtle," she said. When he hesitated, she added with a sigh, "I don't blame you for finding it easy to resist my charms, sir. I've had this dress on now for two days without even taking it off to air it out."

"I only wish it were that easy to resist you," he said, not moving.

She sighed again. "Your odious brother could not keep his hands off me, and I've heard that a woman's first night can be painful. 'Tis likely he will enjoy making it so. His attentions would prove the easier to bear if—"

"Stop it, Jenny! I don't want to hear about Reid or first nights."

"No more do I," she agreed. "I don't know why I said that. Perhaps I hoped you might teach me what to expect, but prithee, do not take your hand away. I like the feel of it against my skin."

"You would be more comfortable in just your shift if it will keep you warm," he said, wondering if he was being more foolish than Gilly and Gawkus together.

"*You* keep me warm enough," she said.

He had taken off his breeks and jack, and was sleeping in his shirt and netherstocks. Swearing to himself that he would take nothing more off, whatever the temptation, he helped her doff her kirtle. He realized only when his hand met a bare breast that she had managed to push off her shift with the gown.

"You, my lass, are not to be trusted," he said severely.

"Nay, for I fear I am a wicked, wanton woman," she said. "But you are my husband. It is only right for you to teach me. What does a good husband do first?"

His dreams had predicted nothing like this.

Her skin was so soft and smooth that he feared his calloused hands would hurt her, but she did not seem to mind his stroking her.

"Do husbands not talk whilst they are seeing to their wives?"

"Some do," he said, shifting onto his side. "Others find better uses for their wives' mouths, and their own," he added, capturing her mouth with his.

Her lips were full and soft, and he took time to savor their softness. The danger in what they were doing only excited him more. She was forbidden fruit in one way, but legally, she was *his* fruit to peel, taste, and enjoy as he pleased.

The paradox teased and taunted him. His baser self urged him to take her swiftly, to claim her utterly as it was his right to do. His nobler self—by far the lesser entity in the battle now raging within him—urged caution, reminded him of promises and honor, and recommended instant cessation of all illicit activity.

"Just a taste," he murmured, and his baser urges danced within.

"What did you say?" she asked.

"Shhh," he whispered, capturing her mouth again. His hands busied themselves, stroking as much of her as he could easily reach, albeit staying away from the area his hand had found when she turned over.

"I want to touch you," she whispered.

His cock, already alert, stiffened and pulsed eagerly.

"Nay," he groaned. "We dare not."

His baser self ached for her to plead with him, to unlace his shirt and netherstocks. It urged him to tease her more, to make her ache as he did.

He shifted his mouth to her nearest nipple and licked it.

She moaned and arced beneath him. He reached for the other breast, teasing the nipple there with his thumb as he taunted the nearer one with his lips and tongue.

One of her hands clutched his hair. The other reached under his shirttail and found his belly. His cock pulsed harder, as if stretching toward her hand.

"Take me," she muttered. "I don't want Reid to be first."

The pulsing below stopped abruptly. She could not have reminded him more sharply of what he was doing to his own brother had she slapped him.

Drawing a long breath, he eased himself away from her.

"I'm sorry, lass, but we must not do this," he said. "I wish we could. I do not blame myself for our marriage, but I would always blame myself if we were to continue now. You are too innocent. You do not know what the consequences could be—lifelong consequences for you, and that even if we did not beget a child."

He heard her breath catch and knew the possibility had not occurred to her.

Then, as he eased farther away, she sat up and said, "Phaeline was right; you do not change." And with that, she turned her back on him and curled into a tight ball, clutching blankets around her.

He wanted to comfort her but could think of nothing to say that would not make things worse. Softly, he said, "I do not want to hurt you, Jenny, but I fear that I have. Still, it would hurt you more did I not put a stop to it."

Receiving no reply, he lay back and tried to sleep.

⌒

The journey to Annan House seemed too swift to Jenny. Hugh, having snapped twice at Lucas as they packed up, had fallen silent once they were on the road. Lucas remained silent, too, more doleful than ever. But riding between them, lost in her own thoughts, Jenny felt as if the miles simply sped by.

She could not stop thinking about her interlude with Hugh in the middle of the night. She had only to close her eyes and she could feel his big hands on her—hard, possessive hands—or his lips devouring her. Her body tingled more with each new thought until she felt hot all over again.

Each time she glanced at him, though, he looked the same, grim and unapproachable. He had set a fast pace after wrapping the horses' hooves in burlap to keep them from slipping if they struck ice on the road.

Before fording the river Annan, he stopped long enough to unwrap their hooves, then dried them again after the crossing and put on dry wrappings. Half an hour later, they passed through the gates of Annan House into the cobbled forecourt.

Gathering her dignity, Jenny waited for Hugh to lift her down.

As he dismounted, the front door opened and Dunwythie, his wife, and his two daughters hurried down the steps to meet them. They were crossing the courtyard when Reid appeared in the open doorway behind them.

Jenny sighed. To say that Reid looked angry was not enough. He looked ready to murder someone. "Me, most likely," she murmured.

"Don't look at him," Hugh advised, startling her. He'd dismounted and come up behind her while she watched the others, and was waiting to help her dismount.

His warm hands caught her at the waist, and she rested her hands on his shoulders. As he lifted her down, she smiled uncertainly at him.

"You have not said a word to me since we left the woods," she said. "Why offer me advice now?"

"'Tis good advice, lass, useful at *all* times," he said. "Never let the villains know they can disconcert you. Put your wee chin in the air now. Just think of all the things you'd like to say to me."

Her chin went up until she looked him in the eyes.

"That's it," he said. "You'll do."

Hoping she could believe him, she turned toward the house and right into Mairi's arms.

"I'm so glad he found you!" Mairi exclaimed, hugging her hard.

"Me, too," Fiona said. "But why did you run away, Jenny?"

"That will do, my dears," Phaeline said sternly. "You have greeted your cousin Janet and may talk more with her later. But first your lord father has much to say to her, and she will not thank you for your presence. Go back inside now."

Jenny watched them go back up the steps and inside past the scowling Reid, feeling as if the only family members she cared about were basely deserting her.

Hugh said quietly as he shook hands with Dunwythie, "I warrant the fewer people present for our conversation the better, sir. I'd like to speak with you privately first, if I may."

"Don't be absurd, Hugh," Phaeline said. "Reid has a right to hear anything you will say about Janet's misbehavior, as do I. I have stood as a mother to her these past eight months, have I not? We will adjourn to my solar at once."

"She might like to refresh herself first," Hugh said evenly as they walked toward the steps, where Reid still awaited them.

"Aye, my love," Dunwythie said to Phaeline. "'Tis only—"

"Her needs can await our pleasure, my lord. We have waited here without one word of her for nearly a fortnight. Poor Reid has been most impatient."

"Then I'm glad you managed to keep him here," Hugh said as they began to mount the steps. "You did want her return accomplished quietly, after all."

He was watching Jenny as she warily eyed Reid. Phaeline's attitude, Reid's visible fury, and now Dunwythie's silence made Hugh certain the lass would not prevail against them all by herself. He was glad he was there.

"Where the devil have you been?" Reid demanded angrily, reaching for her when she was still a step below him.

"Doucely, lad, doucely," Hugh said, putting a hand out to intervene. "You will get more answers to civil questions than to rants. And, prithee, do not carry on so before the servants. I have been at pains, after all, to manage this quietly."

"Where is Peg?" Phaeline asked tersely.

"She decided to stay where she is," Hugh replied.

"But she is my servant! She had no right to make such a decision."

"Sakes, woman, she is not your slave," he retorted. "She is with her brother and quite safe, not that you inquired about her safety."

Reid looked from one to the other. "With her brother? The juggler?"

"Enough," Hugh said sternly. "You may ask all your questions when we are in the solar with the door shut."

"Aye, that would be best, lad," Dunwythie said to Reid.

"Well, don't, *any* of you, think you can keep me out," Reid said belligerently.

Hugh heard Jenny say quietly to her uncle, "Truly, my lord, it *would* be better if we could talk to you privately first."

Dunwythie looked at her, then at Phaeline.

Before Phaeline could intervene, as Hugh was sure she would, he said quietly to Jenny, "Reid and Phaeline do have a right to hear your tale, lass."

She gave him a fierce look, but he met it squarely and with a touch of warning in his expression. "Remember what I told you," he said.

"Just what *did* you tell her?" Reid demanded.

"That she deserves to hear all you would say to her," Hugh replied, holding Jenny's gaze. When her fierce look faded, he knew she would hold her tongue unless Reid's ranting became more than she could bear.

Relaxing, Hugh shut the door and suggested that everyone find a seat.

Before they had done so, Reid said in the same belligerent tone as before, "If Peg is with her brother, she and Jenny must have left here with the minstrels."

"Aye, that's right," Hugh said equably.

Rounding on Jenny, Reid said, "By God, would you make a fool of me? Leaving our betrothal feast to run off with a lot of common minstrels!"

"Hardly common," Jenny said. "They are highly skilled."

"Do you ever hear such impudence, sir?" Reid demanded of Dunwythie. "By heaven, she wants a good thrashing for this trick of hers, and I shall see that—"

"You scarcely have the right yet to beat her," Hugh said, striving to sound matter-of-fact. "You are not yet married to the lass."

"Sakes, but she must be punished! Who knows what she got up to in such company? If you followed them, why did it take you so long to fetch her back?"

"Because it did," Hugh said.

"Damnation!" Reid exclaimed, flinging out his hands and turning away, only to turn angrily back again. "What am I to think when you say only that to me? I have the *right* to know every detail—and, by God. I *will* hear them!"

"The details are unimportant now that she is safely home again," Hugh replied calmly. "She can tell you all about her adventure later if she chooses."

Glowering at him, Reid said, "So, that is the tack you mean to take, is it? You have made up your mind and will say nowt more on the subject. But, she *will* tell me everything and I'll want a trustworthy woman to examine her before *I* will touch her. Sakes, but God alone knows whose brat she may be carrying!"

This last suggestion brought Jenny indignantly upright, but Hugh threw her such a fierce look that she sat back again without speaking.

Satisfied, Hugh said softly, "I can vouch for her innocence if you insist."

"Sakes, you weren't with her the whole time!"

"Nay, but others were, women and men. They would all vouch for her from first day to last. However, you must do as you will. Perhaps you have decided that you don't want to marry her after all."

Pausing to stare at Hugh, Reid gave a petulant shrug and said, "Oh, I don't mind marrying her. I just want to know that when she produces a child, it's mine."

"It occurs to me," Hugh said thoughtfully, "that I ken nowt of your marriage settlements. I presume they are all they should be."

"Aye, of course they are," Reid said, glancing at Phaeline. "Dunwythie and Phaeline saw to everything."

She said, "I cannot think why they should concern you, my dear Hugh."

"Why, how can they not when I am head of the family? It is no less than my duty to look them over. Just think what folks would say of me if aught went awry."

"There is no need to look at them, I assure you," Phaeline said firmly.

Dunwythie, looking surprised, said, "Bless us, my dear! Hugh has every right to see them. As head of your family, he is responsible for Reid's well-being."

"Pish-tush," she snapped. "When has Hugh ever cared for that?"

"Can you lay your hand on them now, sir?" Hugh asked Dunwythie.

"Aye, sure," Dunwythie said, getting up. "I'll just fetch them, shall I?"

"Perhaps you could send someone else," Hugh suggested. "In troth, I do not want to stay longer than necessary. I have information that I must present to Archie

Douglas's attention as soon as possible. My intention was to deliver her ladyship to you and then take my leave."

He took care not to look at Jenny.

Dunwythie said amiably, "Aye, sure, I'll just step out and ask one of the lads to fetch those documents."

⁓

Phaeline glowered at Hugh, but he did not speak, and she apparently could think of naught to the purpose to say to him. The blessed silence made Jenny decide that, for once, Hugh's family reputation for obstinacy was serving a good turn.

Even Reid was silent.

When Dunwythie returned, Hugh said, "I did ask her ladyship about those settlements, my lord. She seems unable to recall anything about them."

Dunwythie shrugged. "There was no need to discuss them with her. Sakes, but a lass can know nowt of such matters."

Jenny stiffened again but, encountering another look, held her tongue.

With a slight smile, Hugh said, "You must know that the late Lord Easdale taught her all he knew about managing their estates. And since she is now Baroness Easdale in her own right, she is surely capable of understanding anything to do with her property. Moreover, she has the legal right to know exactly what arrangements you have made on her behalf and with regard to that property. In troth, if I do not mistake the law in such matters, she is *required* to sign any settlements."

"I signed for her," Dunwythie said. "As I doubt she can even read them—"

"My father taught me to read," Jenny said indignantly, not caring this time if Hugh did shoot a warning look at her.

But he said only, "There, you see, sir. Legally, you cannot sign for someone who is herself capable of understanding your negotiations and signing the related documents. No magistrate would uphold your signature if she challenged it."

"But he is her guardian!" Reid exclaimed. "He has every authority over her."

"Unless her father named him steward of her lands as well as guardian of her person, you are mistaken. Well, my lord?"

"He named me her guardian," Dunwythie said. "One presumed, since she is a mere female, and so young . . ." He spread his hands.

"You assumed incorrectly and should, if I may say so, have inquired into the rights of it long before the betrothal ceremony."

"Aye, well, we can set it all to rights," Dunwythie said as the door opened and a manservant entered. "Here are the documents now. She can just sign them, and all will be in order."

As Jenny opened her mouth, Hugh said hastily, "Tell me this, Dunwythie. What arrangement did you agree to for the Easdale estates?"

"Why the usual one, to be sure," he said.

"Usual, sir? How would you *know* what is usual? How often have you negotiated for a baroness in her own right?"

Lord Dunwythie looked at his wife.

Phaeline said, "Naturally, Hugh, the management of her estates will be in Reid's hands. That is as you would wish it to be, I am sure."

"Even if that were true," he said, "you cannot make such an arrangement without her consent, not when her ladyship holds the barony in her own right. Only she can release that right to someone else."

Dunwythie, Jenny thought, looked honestly surprised.

So, in his own way, did Reid.

Hugh said, "I'll just glance over those documents for myself now, shall I?"

Chapter 15

Tense silence engulfed the room as Hugh took the documents and began to read. Jenny noted that Reid was frowning thoughtfully as he looked at Phaeline again, but Phaeline's expression was indecipherable. Dunwythie watched Hugh.

He read fast, and Jenny could judge nothing by his expression. She did think, when he set aside the first page, that his movements lacked their usual lithe grace.

She was wishing she could know what he was reading when he glanced at her and reached for the sheet of vellum he had put aside.

Without comment, he handed it to her and went back to his reading.

Seeing Phaeline's lips press tightly together, Jenny did not look at Reid. Determined to conceal any reaction she might have, she began to read.

By the end of the page, she knew why no one had discussed the settlements with her. Knowing she could not trust herself to speak without losing control, she suppressed her anger, set the sheet aside, and accepted the second one from Hugh.

Reminding herself again of his advice not to let them see that they had disconcerted her—surely, such advice applied to fury even more than to disconcertion—she kept her mind focused on the words.

It occurred to her abruptly that as Hugh was Reid's brother, and Phaeline's, family duty might stir him to approve their acquisition of the Easdale estates, and the barony title, as well. He was, after all, head of their family.

Deciding she had no need to read more, she looked at him.

He was still reading. When she saw a muscle twitch in his jaw, she inhaled deeply and relaxed, not realizing until then that she had been holding her breath.

He lowered the pages he still held and looked at Dunwythie.

"I will be civil enough to accept your word that you thought you were acting in her ladyship's best interest," Hugh said. "However, we will have to renegotiate these settlements, and she will take her full part in that discussion."

Looking bewildered, her uncle said, "Surely not the whole thing! Which particular agreements concern you, Sir Hugh?"

Impatiently, Hugh said, "Guardian or not, Dunwythie, you do not have any right to sign away her estates, let alone to sign away her inherited title."

Jenny detected a hard edge to his impatience. Looking at Phaeline and Reid, she knew that Phaeline at least had also recognized it and knew Hugh was angry.

He went on, "Imagine, sir, if some well-meaning but

ignorant person were to do this to the lady Mairi after you died. Would *you* want that to happen?"

"Sakes, I should hope that her guardian would choose her husband carefully and then do exactly as I did." Dunwythie said. "I selected Reid because I could be sure of advising him and keeping an eye on things. Mairi will likewise need good counsel. She has no knowledge whatsoever of how to manage my estates!"

"Then it is your duty to teach her," Hugh said.

"That is quite unnecessary," Phaeline said testily. "Janet's father never remarried or had a son, but my lord husband will soon have a proper male heir, God willing. You speak most prematurely of training Mairi for the position, sir."

"Do I? Mairi is eighteen and still has no brother. She deserves the same careful training that Jenny received from *her* father, training that Jenny must have described to you both. I'd wager the late Lord Easdale mentioned that training in his will, too. He seems to have thought of most things she might need to protect her."

For the first time, Lord Dunwythie looked flustered. "I own, I did not read the entire will. Once I saw that I was to be her guardian . . ." He spread his hands.

"You assumed you'd take full control. Do you have a fair copy of his will?"

"Aye, sure," Dunwythie said. "I expect you'll want to see that, too, now."

As Hugh nodded, Phaeline said testily, "That, too, is unnecessary. Look here, Hugh. You take too much upon yourself."

"Peace, my love," Dunwythie said gently. "You upset yourself to no purpose. Hugh is right about the will. Mayhap he is also right about teaching Mairi. It can do no harm, after all, and may even help her find a husband."

"'Tis only practical to teach her," Hugh said. "We all know how abruptly an unexpected death can change the lives of everyone it touches. Indeed, sir, you should teach both of your daughters. Thanks to years of strife and battle here in the Borders, *many* of our women have inherited titles in their own right. And, despite the present truce, such strife could reoccur at any time. Therefore—"

"I see what it is," Reid snapped. "You're afraid that I'll own more land than you do, *and* an older barony. That would give me precedence, and you have always resented me! You and Father just wanted to rid yourselves of me. Only Phaeline—"

"That will do," Hugh interjected in a tone that brooked no argument.

"But no woman can manage estates as well as a man can," Phaeline put in swiftly. "You must know that, Hugh. In troth, you should *support* Reid's claim."

"You astonish me, Phaeline. I'd expect you of all people to agree that a well-trained woman must be a better manager than an untrained man. Has anyone trained Reid, or is his sex alone enough recommendation for the task, in your opinion?"

"If anyone *should* have trained him, it is *you!*" Phaeline said waspishly.

"I should have, aye. But Thornhill is not on the moon, and having accepted your insistence that you knew what was best for him, I left him to you. Moreover, as far as I can tell, he has shown small interest in learning anything."

Jenny, seeing Reid grimace, wondered if he would

speak for himself or if Phaeline would defend him again, but both remained silent.

"Just so," Hugh said. Hefting the pages he held, he added, "If any or all of the three of you thought you could simply seize these estates, you would soon have learned your error. Not only does Jenny know that a husband cannot take her title against her will, but the law would be wholly on her side if she had to fight these settlements. They are worthless. You must tear them up and negotiate new ones."

"Then that is what we will do," Phaeline said, nodding reassuringly at Reid.

"No, we won't," Jenny said, standing. "I won't sign anything of the sort. As every one of you has known from the outset, I do *not* want to marry Reid Douglas."

"We'll see about that," Reid snapped. "You are promised to me in the sight of God, and I *will* hold you to that promise."

Hugh said gently, "You might succeed, too, were there no just impediment to such a union. However, much as you will dislike hearing it, I'm afraid there is one."

"What the devil are you nattering about now?" Reid demanded.

"Why, only that Jenny is already married," Hugh told him. "To me."

~~~

In the uproar that followed, Hugh's temper—which had fought for release from the moment they had entered the solar—rapidly subsided. The sight of his sister, Reid, and Dunwythie all bursting into speech at once was amusing enough to ease his fury with all three, albeit not enough to obliterate it.

He made out only a few phrases here and there, but Phaeline and Reid seemed to accuse him of betraying the Douglas family and Dunwythie of betraying his own. Dunwythie, oblivious to the other two, kept repeating demands for an explanation.

In the midst of it, Jenny stood still, looking cool and aloof, as if she were a visiting dignitary and a cluster of local children had suddenly begun to quarrel. It had, she might as well have said, nothing to do with her.

To Hugh, she looked like an island of tranquility in the midst of a storm, although he had no doubt that under that cool façade, she was seething.

Nothing she had said to him suggested that she harbored affection for any of the three, but she had to feel Dunwythie's betrayal especially. As her guardian—faith, as her uncle by marriage—he owed her his honest duty. But whether through ineptitude or his unfortunate habit of bowing to his wife's every whim and fancy in a natural, masculine desire for peace, he had let Jenny down badly.

Reid's voice suddenly soared above the others as he whirled toward Hugh. "I knew you would try to ruin everything for me! Damn you, Hugh Douglas!"

"Peace, lad," Hugh said, bracing himself hopefully. "None of this was my doing." He nearly added that it was none of Jenny's either, but honesty forbade that, since her abrupt departure from Annan House had begun it all.

In any event, Reid did not give him time to speak, shouting, "*Not* your doing? How can that be if you have married the curst woman?"

"Mind your tongue, for I want to hear no more of

that," Hugh said curtly. "My following her to the min-strels' camp created a misunderstanding. Believing I was a suitor and that she liked me and needed a protector, they arranged a play about a marriage in which we believed we played roles. The priest, however, was real."

Reid sputtered, "But . . . but so what if he was?"

"It means the ceremony was likewise real, and a priest lacks authority to undo a marriage. Nevertheless, you will have no difficulty getting it annulled, my lord," he said to Dunwythie. "Their prior betrothal will ease the way. The process will take time, of course, but 'tis time you will doubtless devote to sorting out things here. In any event, as I said, I must go to Threave. It is at best a two-day jour-ney from here, and there is some urgency."

"If there is urgency, lad, you may want to travel faster," Dunwythie said. "I can arrange for you to take a ship from Annan to Kirkcudbright if you like. From there, I believe, it is but a few miles or so to Threave."

"If you have men's business to discuss now, I doubt anyone can think it concerns Janet," Phaeline said. "And, as you will remain here whilst we arrange your annul-ment, Janet, you may retire now to your bedchamber. When you are ready to apologize properly for your rash behavior, you may do so. Until then—"

"No," Jenny said flatly.

"No? By heaven, whilst you are under this roof, you will do as you are—"

"No, Phaeline, I will not. I am going to Threave with Sir Hugh."

Hugh was still considering Dunwythie's offer of a ship and had paid little heed to the exchange, but at these words, he looked at Jenny.

"Now, lass," he said firmly, "we've already decided that you'll stay here."

"*We* did not," she retorted. "*You* declared that I would, but that was before I understood all that has taken place here. You *are* still my husband, are you not?"

"Aye, legally, I am," he admitted.

"Then, until the annulment my place is with you. After all, it is your duty to protect me, and they have proven beyond doubt that I cannot trust them."

As Hugh tried to think of something sensible to say that would refute her logic, Reid said, "Faith, she's probably already slept with *him*!"

"Nay, lad, that is not—"

"Aye, sure," Jenny declared roundly. "I *have* slept with him."

"Now, see here," Hugh exclaimed. "She does not know what she is—"

"I knew it!" Reid exclaimed. "By heaven, you *do* want thrashing, and I—"

"Enough!" Hugh roared, stepping between them as the thought of Reid touching Jenny snapped the tenuous hold he had on his temper. "By God, Jenny is right. I *am* her husband, and as far as I'm concerned, the only way we'll see *any* annulment is if Jenny wants one. Until that day, she *is* my wife and will remain so!"

~⌒◠

Jenny swayed dizzily. Such an impulsive speech was the last thing she had expected to hear from Hugh. She had hoped only that he would agree to take her to Threave, because she wanted less than ever to stay at Annan House.

Phaeline and Reid would both exert themselves to make her miserable. And although Mairi and Fiona would be kind to her, it would not be enough.

But to stay married to Hugh . . . she had to think about that.

He was watching her now, narrowly, as if he would judge her reaction. Well, she would recall his good advice yet again and reveal her feelings to no one.

Accordingly, she turned to Dunwythie and said matter-of-factly, "How soon can a ship set sail from Annan Harbor, my lord?"

"Sakes, lassie, we must talk about this," he said, glancing at the others.

"How soon, sir?" Jenny repeated.

Looking at Hugh and finding no support there, he said, "'Tis best just now if ye leave on a morning tide. Sithee, Kirkcudbright lies some fifty miles from here. But whilst that would mean two long days' travel on horseback, or longer if snow flies again, 'tis nobbut a half day's journey by galley if ye go with the ebbing tide."

"Then we can leave tomorrow morning, sir," she said to Hugh.

"We'll see what his lordship learns of ships in the harbor first," Hugh said.

"Very well, then I shall see to my packing. I do not mean to visit the Lord of Galloway with only this kirtle, two shifts, one pair of boots, and a cloak." Curtsying to Dunwythie, she added, "Pray, grant me leave to go to my chamber, my lord."

"Aye, to be sure, lass. But ye shouldna go like this. 'Tis as if ye were running away again, and I cannot believe we've been so unkind to ye as to make ye do that."

"I'll talk with her, my lord," Hugh said. "But you should ask your conscience if it was kindness to negotiate those marriage settlements without consulting her about them or referring to the late Lord Easdale's will for his direction."

"Aye, lad, I ought to have read the will. And I'll grant ye, the lass did say summat about his teaching her. But she's still just a lass for all that. Still, ye were right to say I should teach mine own lassies summat about managing my estates."

"An excellent notion," Hugh said, but he was watching Jenny.

"I'll leave you now," she said. With another brief curtsy, she left the room and hurried upstairs, hoping Phaeline would not follow her.

Reaching her own bedchamber, she found Mairi and Fiona inside, waiting.

"We knew she'd send you here as soon as they stopped scolding," Fiona said.

"I'm leaving with Sir Hugh," Jenny told them as she shut the door. "Prithee, do not try to dissuade me, either of you. Do you ken aught of marriage settlements?"

Both Mairi and Fiona shook their heads.

"Apparently, Phaeline and my uncle contrived things so Reid would take over my estates and title, but Sir Hugh said they broke the law. As he and I are married—"

"Married!" they exclaimed in unison.

Jenny explained, adding, "So I'm going with Hugh. I expect we truly are married now, for they all say they will seek an annulment. But I can *not* stay here."

"Did you really sleep with him?" Fiona demanded. "What was it like?"

Jenny chuckled. "I did *sleep* with him, but not as you mean or as Reid thinks, because Hugh did not want to make getting an annulment more difficult or to get me with child. But after the wedding, the others prepared his tent for us, and I did not want to tell them what a coil they had made for us. Nor did I want to make Hugh tell them, especially as it was my own lie that began it all."

"Was Hugh furious?" Fiona asked. "My mother has spoken often of his fearsome temper. *Is* it fearsome?"

"I do not find it so, although he did say things I'd liefer not have heard. I had not seen him truly furious until today. But I could tell he was angry as he read my marriage settlements, and he grew angrier yet when Reid said I must be punished."

"Reid does have a right to be angry with you," Mairi said reasonably.

"Aye, perhaps, but when he demanded punishment, Hugh declared that as far as *he* is concerned, we are married and will stay married unless I will it otherwise."

"But you do will it otherwise, don't you?" Fiona said. "You cannot want Sir Hugh for a husband. Why, you said as much, yourself, the night you left."

Jenny hesitated. "I don't know what I want anymore," she said. "But I am leaving with Hugh in the morning. So, if you two mean to stay here and talk, you must help with my packing and tell me all that happened whilst I was away. Did they find any of the missing jewelry."

"How do you know any jewelry was missing?" Fiona asked.

"Hugh told me, of course, when he found me. Was much taken?"

"Aye, a good many pieces," Mairi said. "But a traveler

found nearly all of them not far from our gate, so it must have been someone playing a prank. Phaeline was furious that she and Father had to return the missing pieces. She said it made it look as if someone here had taken them, whilst she is sure the minstrels did."

"Except they couldn't have taken *all* of it," Fiona said. "Recall that things were taken after they had gone, including Mam's pearls."

Jenny said, "I just don't think minstrels would steal from houses where they perform. If people even suspected they might, they would not let them into ordinary houses, let alone into places like Lochmaben and Threave."

"Lochmaben!" Fiona exclaimed. "Sakes, everyone there is English!"

"Aye, but I sang there," Jenny said. "As for the minstrels' honesty, the Sheriff of Dumfries invited them to perform in the market square there."

Recalling that the sheriff's men had searched all the tents in the Dumfries encampment for missing jewels, she tried to fit a simple prank at Annan House with that knowledge. They had found nothing, though. She needed to think more.

However, Mairi and Fiona demanded then that she tell them the whole tale of her adventures, so she did her best to comply. But she left out her suspicions of intrigue brewing and other, more private things.

Supper was a tense meal, made tolerable only by Hugh's presence and that of Fiona and Mairi. When Jenny finished eating, she had no desire to linger at the table or to join Phaeline in her solar with the others, so she excused herself, saying she was tired from all her travels and wanted to sleep.

No one tried to dissuade her, but alone in her bedchamber, she felt unusually lonely and uncertain of herself. Remembering that Peg had suspected Phaeline was not pregnant at all, Jenny sent a gillie to find Phaeline's maidservant, Sadie.

When the girl came to her, Jenny said, "I'm leaving early in the morning for Kirkcudbright, Sadie. Prithee, help me fold these dresses into yon sumpter basket."

"Och, aye, I did hear that, me lady. We'd nae suspicion that ye'd marry Sir Hugh. 'Twere a rare stunner, that, as we thought ye was to marry his brother!"

"It was a surprise to me, too," Jenny said with a smile, watching as Sadie deftly folded one of her gowns. "How well you do that! I vow, I tried three times to make it fit without crushing it."

"Aye, well, I do ha' to look after her ladyship's things, don't I? And her being that particular, I can tell ye."

"How does she fare?" Jenny asked. "Peg said she feared something may have gone amiss."

Sadie's eyes flew wide, and she stared as if she did not know what to say.

"What is it, Sadie? Should I not have asked after her?"

"I'd liefer ye didna ask *me*, me lady. I shouldna say nowt."

"I see," Jenny said. Peg had been right then. "Did she find her missing pearls?"

"Nay, not her, although Lady Johnstone did find *her* necklace. And them other pieces that went missing, they all turned up, too. I did think I'd found three o' the lady Phaeline's pearls, but she said they was old ones from summat else and she were missing her whole string. Faith, though, she slapped me so me ears rang."

"Oh, Sadie, no," Jenny said sympathetically.

"Aye, *and* she thinks someone in the castle took them. I feared she meant me, but I'd never take nowt that wasna mine. We none of us would, Lady Jenny . . . Sakes"—she threw up her hands—"what do I call ye now? I'm thinking I should call ye Lady Douglas or Lady Thornhill, but I dinna ken which."

"Neither," Jenny said with a chuckle. "I am still properly Lady Easdale, Sadie, but I shan't mind a bit if you go on calling me Lady Jenny."

She wondered what Hugh would think of that, but as he had made the point himself, he would surely understand that she retained her title. Just thinking of him made her wish he were there so she could talk to him. Doubtless, a wife had the right to summon her husband to her. She wondered if Hugh would come if she did.

⁓

Still at the high table, Hugh was longing for his bed. He was not particularly sleepy, but he was tired of listening to Dunwythie.

He had long since acquitted his lordship of evil intent, because it was plain that he was just a man who preferred peace to the sort of discomfort Phaeline could create for him if he displeased her. The woman had only to moan and put a hand on her belly for the poor hen-hearted man to leap up and do her bidding.

Hugh could understand Dunwythie's longing for a son. Most men wanted sons. But to wait fifteen years and do nothing in the meantime to secure the well-being of his estates and his people was dangerously irresponsible.

Realizing that he had done much the same by failing to insist that Reid learn to run Thornhill, he could say no more to Dunwythie on that subject. Mayhap the man would teach his daughters what they needed to know. Mairi, at least, seemed capable and would doubtless learn quickly. The mischievous Fiona was another matter, but might well improve with age.

As soon as he could decently excuse himself after supper, he went to his bedchamber. There, he found Lucas tidying the room and sorting his clothing. A large tub full of steaming water sat beside the small fireplace.

"That tub looks inviting," Hugh said, beginning to strip off his jacket.

"I did 'ear we'd be going to Kirkcudbright by galley, so I knew ye'd be glad of a bath. I'm thinking though that ye mightn't want to take all your gear."

"You were right about the bath but wrong about the gear," Hugh said as he unlaced his shirt. "We'll take it all. I mean to return straight to Thornhill from Kirkcudbright. I have already been away from the place too long."

"Aye, sir, and my lady?"

"So you've heard about that, too, have you?"

Kneeling to pull off Hugh's boots, Lucas said casually, "Being as I were present for the wedding, as ye might say . . ."

"Don't play the fool with me. I know you've learned she is to go with us and doubtless that I have declared she'll remain my wife unless she wills it otherwise."

"Aye, sure, and wise I thought ye, too, sir—although

I ken fine that ye'd sworn ye'd never marry again," he added gently.

"Too late to think about that now," Hugh said. "Just see to it that our horses get safely back to Thornhill and our baggage gets aboard the right galley. Oh, and you'd better see if her ladyship has orders for you, as well."

"What about a maid for her ladyship, sir? Happen she'll want one."

"Go and ask her as soon as we have finished washing my hair," Hugh advised, wondering what Jenny would think of his sending Lucas to her.

When the man had gone, Hugh finished his bath and dried his hair by the fire. Although it was early for bed, he decided he could use a good night's sleep.

He had scarcely settled in, however, when a rap on his door roused him.

Certain that it must be Lucas returning with men to carry away the tub, he growled, "Come in then!"

But when the door opened, Jenny stood on the threshold with a candle in her hand, her unplaited hair hanging in soft waves to her hips. "Oh," she said. "I did not think . . . That is I thought you would still be up. I . . . I should not have come."

Hugh sat up, recalled his nudity, and forced calm into his voice as he said, "I can pull my breeks back on and be up again in a trice, lass. Don't run away."

In truth, one part of him was already up. It had leapt to attention the moment he saw her. She turned her back, making him fear she would leave, so he grabbed his breeks and yanked them on, imperiling the most wakeful part of him as he jerked the lacing tight.

"Come in, Jenny," he said as he tied off the laces. "What

is it, lass? I sent Lucas to you. Did you forget something you wanted to tell him?"

"Nay, he went off to get his supper. But my room is cold and lonely, and I knew you must still be angry with me, so I thought . . . I guess I want to apologize."

Since she still stood on the threshold, he went to her and urged her inside with a hand to a shoulder, nudging the door shut behind them with his foot.

She wore only a loose lavender robe and slippers, and she smelled of roses, his favorite perfume. It was the first time he had seen her hair unplaited. It hung in long waves, and where his hand still touched her, it felt silky soft and a bit damp.

"You washed your hair," he said.

"I washed all of me," she said. Then, catching sight of the water-filled tub, she added, "You must have, too. It smells of musk and cloves in here."

Unnaturally aware of his hand on her right shoulder, he warned himself that he ought not to be touching her at all before he sorted out why she had come. But when she turned toward him and stood there, looking trustfully up at him, he could not resist putting his other hand lightly on her left shoulder.

The lavender robe was soft, and her eyes, reflecting the light of her candle, looked more golden than ever.

He took the candle from her, set it on a nearby stand, and put his hand back on her shoulder. "Now," he said, "why did you come to me?"

"I told you, I should apolo—"

"Lass, when I am angry, you won't just suspect it. You will know it."

"But you were," she insisted.

"Aye, but not with you. I should have said when I'm angry with *you*, you will know it. I am not one who conceals true anger when I feel it."

"You were hiding it today. I could tell."

"Could you? I was angry that they had treated you so unfairly. I saw your father's will, and it makes his wishes clear. If Dunwythie read only far enough to learn he'd named him your guardian, I suspect he wanted to know no more, lest it make difficulties for him. That amounts to cowardice and did make me angry, but I hid it for the same reason I warned you not to display your feelings to them."

"So as not to give them the satisfaction of knowing they had angered us."

"Aye, and you did well, lass. But I was talking of more personal things a moment ago. You need not hide your anger with me—if ever I should stir it," he added with a teasing smile. Then, more seriously, he said, "You should also know that I don't always manage to control mine. Sometimes, it just leaps before I can."

"Phaeline said you have a fearsome temper."

"Aye, well, she should know. She has stirred it more than once."

"Is that why you told me not to throw things?"

"Aye, and you should take that warning to heart," he said. "But now that we have established that I'm *not* angry with you, is there aught else you want to say?"

"I expect Lucas told you that I don't need a maidservant to go with us."

"Not yet; I thought you were he coming back for the tub. Art sure you don't want someone? There are unlikely to be other women aboard the ship."

"I don't have my own servants here from Easdale," she said. "And I don't want anyone from Annan House."

"Then you need not have anyone. Anything else?"

She hesitated, then looked him in the eye. "Phaeline told me that you swore you would never marry again, and today you declared me your wife because they made you angry. I . . . I just wanted to talk to you . . . to . . . But now I don't know what to say. That is, I don't know what you really want from me. Will you tell me?"

His fingers gripped her shoulders tighter. He had not been sure either at the time. But looking into her golden eyes, feeling her tremble as she waited for him to speak, and feeling his cock vote its prick's worth, he knew exactly what he wanted.

"I rarely say aught that I don't mean, Jenny, especially when I'm angry. I meant what I said to them. As far as I am concerned, we are husband and wife and will remain so unless you choose otherwise. Twice now, you have demanded that I act as your husband. Mayhap you should consider that demand more carefully."

"And mayhap the third time will make it so," she said. Then, with a hesitant smile, she added, "May I sleep here with you tonight?"

"I cannot think of anything I'd like better," he said. "But you should know that if you do, I will act the husband in every way, lass, from now on."

"Sakes, I already told them that you had," she said. "Shall I undress?"

"Nay, I want to undress you. Then, if you are very good—and very quick—perhaps I will let you undress me."

Chapter 16 ——————————

Jenny thought she had sounded sure of herself when she asked if she should undress, and she stood silently now, hoping she looked as if this sort of thing were easy for her. But as Hugh reached for the sash of her robe, the back of his hand brushed the tip of her left breast, making her gasp.

His lips twitched as if he would smile, but he did not. If he had spoken the truth in saying he would show his feelings openly to her, his only intent now was to undress her. She trembled again, hoping he did not expect her to help.

The sash was swiftly gone, and he pushed her robe wider, revealing the narrow silk ribbons of her shift. A gentle tug, and the ribbons parted. The gathered top of her shift opened wide.

He put his hands on her shoulders again but only to push the fabric of both garments away as if they were one. Easing them off her shoulders and down her arms, he bared her torso and paused, caressing her breasts with his gaze and making her tingle warmly inside, as if he had touched them. Then he did, with both hands, and her robe abandoned her shift and slid to the floor.

⁓

She was so soft, and when she gasped again, her breasts swelled to fit his palms. Hugh wanted to strip her where she stood and explore every silken inch of her with his hands and lips. However, being bare-chested himself and feeling the chill despite the flickering little fire on the hearth, he knew she would soon feel it, too, if she was not freezing already.

He was hungry for her though, and not ready yet to take her to his bed. He wanted to enjoy her for a while first, right where they were, and reveal some of the delights of her own body to her.

Briefly and with unexpectedly little emotion, his memory served up an image of his first time with Ella. How frightened she had been! So young, and tearful. He had been young, too, but sensible enough even in youth to know that moving slowly was good, and that being gentle was paramount.

He liked to savor his sexual experiences. But in truth, it had been long since one had meant anything to him other than the fulfillment of a basic instinct.

Jenny was not tearful or scared. He did not know what she thought, but he sensed that she was curious and receptive to whatever he might do. That thought stiffened his ever-interested cock until it pressed hard against the lacing of his breeks and began to throb and ache. He hoped it would wait upon his pleasure, and hers.

He thumbed a nipple, watching her eyes and her always-expressive face. She had been watching him soberly as he bared her breasts and studied them. But from the moment he'd touched their softness and she had gasped, she had looked only wide-eyed and perhaps a little wary. Her breathing was shallow and quick.

Easing her closer until they were breast to chest, he stroked her back and gently pushed her shift lower until it caught at the swell of her hips. Leaving it there, he shifted one hand to a bum cheek, gently squeezing it, certain that the skin there would be as softly silken as it was everywhere else, even softer than the fine cambric shift that still concealed her nether parts from him.

With his free hand, he cupped her chin and tilted it up so he could claim her soft lips. Tasting them lightly, he pressed harder on her bottom, forcing her hips against his so she would feel what awaited her there.

When she moaned, he moved his hand from her chin to cup the back of her head, kissing her more hungrily, sucking and tasting her lips, then parting them easily with his tongue and thrusting inside to explore the interior of her mouth.

He paid no heed to her hands until they slipped around to the small of his back and her right one dipped lower to squeeze his left buttock. Then, groaning, he ground himself hard against her, aching so much for her that he could not think.

⌒

Awed by the sensations that swept through her when he touched her breasts and squeezed her buttock, Jenny had shut her eyes, put her hands to his bare waist, and then daringly squeezed his backside.

She had hoped to make him moan a little as she had.

She had not expected him to react with such strength. Seconds later, when he swept her off her feet and headed for the bed, her breath caught in her throat again.

Laying her down, he wasted no time in removing the rest of her clothing. Nor did he waste time with his own or ask for her help. She was not sure if what she had done was a good thing or a bad thing, but she did not care.

She was far more interested in what he would do next.

He did take a moment to straighten the covers before he climbed in with her, but he did not lie back and hold her as he had before. Instead, he leaned over her on one elbow, capturing her mouth again and stroking her breasts with his free hand, teasing her nipples and stroking lower until his hand cupped her at the fork of her legs. Leaning closer then, as if he thought he might have to hold her in place, he pressed a finger inside her, stroking her as he did, nearly to her undoing.

She arched hard against him, gasped, and cried out.

When she could speak, she gasped, "What . . . what are you doing?"

Close to her ear, he murmured soothingly, "I have not much control left, Jenny-love, and I wanted to make you ready for me. But you are hot and ready now, I think. I'd just like to stretch you a little."

To her own surprise, she chuckled low in her throat. "Good sakes," she said. "I thought you were examining me."

"I am, but only because I mean to examine every inch

of you. You're a beautiful woman, lass. Touching you is like stroking fine, warm silk."

She wanted to tell him all she was feeling, but she could not find the words. She could only let her body tell him with its movements and moans how much she enjoyed what he was doing to her.

When he shifted his weight, she knew what was coming and welcomed it. He had teased her to a hunger she had never known, one that only satisfaction could fulfill. When he pressed himself inside her, gently at first and then harder, hurting her and stirring an ache she was sure she would never forget, she moaned louder and pressed closer to him, hoping to ease the aching.

He thrust harder then and faster until at last he must have worn himself out, because he collapsed atop her, panting, and stayed so until his breathing eased.

Then he raised himself up on his elbows and smiled ruefully at her.

"I enjoyed that, lass. I hope I didn't hurt you too much."

"Nay," she said, deciding it was not too much and if she told him it hurt, he might not want to do it again. She would endure it whenever he liked as long as he could reproduce the other, much more wonderful feelings he had stirred first.

⁓

Hugh woke early at the sound of the latch. Seeing Lucas, he put a finger to his lips, waited until the man had nodded, set down the lighted cresset he held, and vanished.

Then Hugh gently tried to wake Jenny, who was sprawled on her stomach between him and the wall.

She did not stir.

Sometime during the night, she had thrust a knee into his ribs, where he was sure he would have a bruise, but she had not stirred then even when he shifted her knee to a safer position and snuggled her closer to him.

They definitely needed a bigger bed.

Picking up a strand of her hair, he tickled her nose with its ends. Her nose twitched, but she did not waken. Delighting in the faces she made, he did it again.

"Stop that," she muttered.

He did it again, and at last, she opened her eyes. They widened, and he knew she had only then remembered where she was and how she had come to be there.

"Good morning," he said, bending to kiss her nose.

She turned onto her back, stretching from head to toe like a kitten as she did. When she smiled at him, her dimples danced and he kissed them, too. Then he found her mouth, and for a time after that, he forgot they had a boat to catch.

When he had sated his hunger for her, he remembered the boat and said, "Get up now, lass, and quickly. You've caused me to waste too much time as it is. Make haste, or that boat will leave without us."

"But I'm not the one who—"

"Aye, well, you're too bonnie and you tempt me too sorely. Now, up! I'm going to shout for Lucas and you will want to be dressed before he comes in."

"You made me feel wonderful," she said, languorously stretching again. "It scarcely hurt at all this time."

"I thought you said it didn't hurt last night," he said, pulling on his breeks.

"Aye, well, it did," she said. "But not today."

She got up then and moved past him, bending to pick her shift up off the floor. As she did, he smacked her on her bare backside.

"Ow!" she exclaimed, rubbing the place. "Why did you do that?"

"Because you lied to me," he said. "Don't do it again."

"Do I get to smack *you* if you lie to *me*?"

"Aye, you may," he said. "Now get dressed."

She stuck out her tongue at him and then moved hastily to obey.

Hugh shook his head at her but could not suppress a smile.

⌒

The sky was still a blanket of stars when the galley's crew rowed from Annan's port with the outgoing tide into Solway Firth. There they shipped their oars and put up the sail. The galley made good speed sailing with the tide as it ebbed from the Firth toward the Irish Sea.

Jenny had never been on a boat of any size before, or on water in the dark, and she reveled in the experience. She loved the taste and smell of the salty air, and the sight of gulls dipping and whirling in search of fish as soon as it was light.

When the sun peeked over the eastern horizon revealing a cloudless sky, Hugh declared that he wanted to stretch his legs and talk to the captain about what to expect when they reached Kirkcudbright.

"You stay here with Lucas, lass," he said. "I shan't be long."

The bench near the stern was hard, but Jenny was glad to sit with Lucas.

"Thank you for seeing to my baggage this morning," she said.

"'Twas nowt, m'lady," he said.

"Well, it is not nowt to me," she said. "Had you not brought me my cloak before we left, I doubt I'd have thought about it until we reached the forecourt."

He shot her a twinkling look from under his eyebrows. "Happen ye had other matters on your mind, mistress. Times, t' laird do be a handful."

She chuckled, remembering the smack on her backside and wondering if Lucas might have been outside the door by then. She had certainly yelped.

"You have been with the laird a long time, I expect."

"Aye, nigh onto eight years now."

"Only eight? I thought you must have been with him since he was a boy."

"Nay, then, no so long as that."

"Where did you meet him?"

He glanced toward the sea. Then, licking his lips, he looked at her and said, "I dinna talk about it much, but bein' as ye're one of t' family now, I expect he'll tell ye 'imself—although I dinna doubt he'll tell *his* tale and leave out t' best bits."

"Sakes, do you mean he might *lie* to me?" she asked hopefully, recalling that smack yet again, and his promise afterward.

"Nay, then, not to say lie," Lucas said. "He'd just clean it up, like."

"Tell me *your* tale then."

"Aye, well, we met in Yorkshire—in t' city of York, that was."

"But Yorkshire is in England. What were you both doing there?"

"Me? I were born there. T' laird were just a-visitin', as ye might say."

Enviously, she said, "I expect he has traveled many places, has he not?"

"Aye, so have we both," Lucas said. "Even into France once."

"Was he serving Archie the Grim then?"

"Happen ye might say he were, in a way."

"Sakes, was he spying on the English *and* the French?"

"Nah then, not if ye mean were 'e listenin' at doors and such," Lucas said with a hasty glance in the direction Hugh had taken. Relaxing again, he added, "He were just a-jawin' wi' folks about summat and nowt, like."

"As ye might say," Jenny said with a grin.

The twinkle glinted again in his eyes. "Aye, and what 'e learned in t' city of York, amongst other bits, were that they was a-meanin' to hang me."

"Who was?"

"Sithee, 'twas t' York magistrate, withal."

"So what did Sir Hugh do?"

"They'd built t' gallows in Whip-ma-Whop-ma Gate, which is how they call t' street with t' whipping post and such. And he were a-singin' to t' crowd gathered there, playin' troubadour as he did wi' ye. They was a-leadin' me to t' rope when up 'e strolled with 'is lute and said 'e wanted a good look at such a gallous ruffian."

She chuckled. "I can imagine it. Doubtless, he used someone else's voice."

"Aye, sure. Then, as t' crowd jeered some clumsy jugglers on their boards near t' gallows, he fetched one of me keepers a clout with 'is fist, made t'other one's brains rattle with t' first one's club, and never took even a scratch on 'is lute. Next thing I knew, 'e cut me bindings with a wee dirk from 'is boot and were a-runnin' me through snickets and ginnels of which even I 'ad nae ken, though I'd grown up there. Afore I could catch me breath, we was horsed outside t' wall farthest from Whip-ma-Whop-ma Gate and a-ridin' for t' coast."

Fascinated, she said, "What are snickets and ginnels?"

"Passageways," he said. "Sithee, t' streets in York be called gates, and they be narrow and crowded, so t' local folk 'ave their own ways between 'em of which visitors 'ave nae ken. Ye open a wee door, and a snicket or ginnel wends between garden walls or buildings to t' next gate. Them what was a-seekin' me didna ken where we'd gone. They sent word to the city gates, which they call bars, but we'd changed our look by then and walked out with a flock of shepherds what had drove their sheep to fleshers in t' Shambles."

"Shambles?"

"Aye, fleshers' row, as ye might say, where they butcher kine and the like."

Jenny sighed again. Crossing her arms over her breasts and leaning back against the gunwale, she said, "Men always get to do the best sort of traveling and have all the most exciting adventures."

"Sakes, mistress, ye could've 'ad my part of *that* adventure and a sight more for the askin'! I didna ken t' laird then, but I knew I owed 'im me life."

"Why were they going to hang you, Lucas? And why did he save you?"

"T' hangin' were over one wee sheep, as ye—" Catching her eye, he grinned and went on. "The savin' were because he thought I might ken summat useful to 'im or to Sir Archibald Douglas."

"And did you?"

"Summat or nowt, I canna say, for I dinna ken. He asked me all manner of questions though, and I've served 'im ever since. He's got me into some proper scrapes, I can tell ye, but so far, bless 'im, he's always hauled me out of them, too."

"And, to think, he looked so stern and upright when I first saw him."

"Aye, sure, that'd be t' laird. He could stare t' devil out of 'ell without breakin' a sweat, as ye m—" Breaking off, he added with a chuckle, "Ye'll do, mistress, ye'll do. Happen ye'll be the perfect match for 'im."

⁓

Hugh, walking toward them, saw Jenny eyeing him askance and wondered what he had done to annoy her. When he asked her, she just shook her head, but Lucas was smiling.

He shot a shrewd look at his man. "Have you been telling tales, Lucas?"

"By, sir, she asked how we met. I couldna tell her we never did, could I?"

"Don't listen to him, lass. He's got a keen imagination, does Lucas."

She gave him a straight look and said, "Do you mean

to say I should not believe what he tells me, sir? Is Lucas not trustworthy?"

"I did not say that," Hugh said. Then, "Why do you look so disappointed?"

Her smile was a teasing mixture of mystery and mischief that made him wish he could pick her up and take her straight to bed. As the thought crossed his mind, he remembered their exchange in his bedchamber when he had given her permission to smack him if he ever lied to her.

He returned her smile then but said only, "If you get sleepy, lassie, tell me. The captain said he has blankets and pillows if you want them."

"Nay, I don't want to miss any of this," she said, indicating the Firth and its forbidding shoreline in one sweeping gesture. I'm glad the day is clear. Is that a castle in the distance ahead of us?"

"Aye, Caerlaverock, or what's left of it. It belongs to the Maxwells, and they did the damage themselves to keep the English from occupying it again. Lord Maxwell wants to rebuild it, but he'll get little help whilst we still have English occupying Lochmaben."

She asked many more questions, clearly enjoying the journey. She did not seem to mind a bit when he served her a meager dinner of rolls, beef, apples, and ale from a basket that Lucas had ordered packed before they left Annan House.

When the oarsmen finally rowed them into Kirkcudbright Bay on the turning tide, she seemed fascinated by everything she saw, eyeing the high cliffs to the west and east, and listening intently to all he could tell her about the place.

When their boat dropped anchor in what seemed to

be the middle of the bay, the captain made his way back to Hugh, saying, "The tide has turned, sir. So we'll bide here an hour or so until the water is high enough to let us clear the sand bar west of St. Mary's Isle in the river channel. Beyond that bar, a vessel our size has draft shallow enough to go upriver for miles."

"You will dock at Kirkcudbright, will you not?"

"Aye, we'll beach her on the sand. They've a fine shelf beach for our boat."

When he left them, Hugh explained to Jenny that St. Mary's Isle was the narrow, densely wooded peninsula jutting into the bay just ahead of them.

"It looks as if it sits in a sea of sand and mud," she said.

"Aye, the tides leave it so when they run out, but the incoming tide will soon surround it with water. It will rise to cover most of yonder cliffs as well," he said.

"Where is the town?"

"Ahead about four miles," he said. "You'll see the kirk tower first, and other towers to the left of it. Those belong to Castle Mains, where I hope to find Archie."

"I thought we'd find him at Threave."

"We may yet, but if we're lucky, we'll find him here. Castle Mains has been the seat of the Lords of Galloway for a century or two, and 'tis where Archie stays when he is here. Threave is eight or ten miles up the river Dee from here. We'll borrow horses at Castle Mains if we have to go on."

"I *want* to go to Threave, sir," Jenny said. "I want to know what happens."

"We'll see," he said. But he hoped to keep his word to warn Archie and be on his way again. They would soon be harvesting the early crops at Thornhill, and although his steward was competent, Hugh wanted to show Jenny his home.

⁓

Jenny was annoyed to know that Threave was still a considerable distance away and that they might find Douglas in Kirkcudbright. Not only did she want to see the castle that Archie the Grim had built as a symbol of Douglas power but she also wanted to see Gilly, Gawkus, Peg, Cath, and the others.

She was less eager to see the Joculator, because he would doubtless learn that she had deceived him more than he knew. But, having survived the confrontation at Annan House, which she had dreaded more, she felt less anxiety about telling the Joculator the truth about herself. And she did want to thank him again for accepting her into his company when he had thought she was just a kinswoman of Peg's.

She hoped to watch the oarsmen row their galley onto the beach as the captain had said they would, but they arrived first at Castle Mains. Located on a promontory that jutted into the river just ahead of them, it clearly guarded the inner harbor, the town of Kirkcudbright, and the navigable portion of the river beyond it.

The massive stronghold stood right at the river's edge, so its stone walls, ominous and battlemented, loomed high above the galley. Not until they rounded the promontory did Jenny see the tall gatehouse, flanked by two buttressed towers.

When the galley, oars up, docked neatly alongside a

long wharf that led to the gate, Hugh helped her disembark. Then he helped Lucas with their baggage, while she watched a party of armed men stride toward them from the gates.

Hugh put a hand on her shoulder a few moments later, startling her, but his touch had the same effect it always did, sensuous and invigorating, as if he filled her from within, lending her strength and confidence.

His left arm slid around her shoulders as he extended his right to the leader of the approaching men. "Well met, Tam Inglis!" he said. "I trow you'll let us in."

"Aye, sure, my lord, and glad we be to see ye." He glanced curiously at Jenny and then peered at Lucas. "Be that yon dafty Lucas Horne?"

"The same," Hugh said with a grin. "And this is my lady wife, Tam."

"Lady Thornhill, it be a pleasure to welcome ye to Castle Mains."

"Thank you," she said with a smile. "But, properly, I am Lady Easdale."

"Aye, sure, me lady," the man said with an uncertain glance at Hugh, whose arm had stiffened where it stretched across her shoulders. "I ken fine that Himself will be sorry he were no here to welcome ye personally."

Still smiling but well aware of Hugh's reaction, Jenny said to Tam, "I expect his lordship must already be at Threave."

"Nay, Himself were meeting some o' his visitors at Morton Castle for a day's hunting. But he means to return on Wednesday to greet folks who come by sea. Your galley captain may want to take his boat upriver, me lord, for the laird means to have a water tournament wi' jousting from galleys. I mean to see that, I can tell ye. But come ye in now. Me lads will help daft Lucas see to stowing your gear."

"Mind your long tongue, ye gaumless gawk," Lucas said with a snort. "If ye be in charge of these fine lads 'ere, happen ye should set them a better example."

Tam Inglis chuckled, clapped Lucas on the back, and shook hands again with Hugh. Then, giving rapid orders to his men, he escorted Hugh and Jenny to the gate.

"Ye'll take your usual chambers, sir. I've nae doots the steward were meaning to assign them otherwise, but he'll ken fine that Himself ha' decreed they be yours whenever ye've a mind to use them. Ye'll have a window, me lady, looking across the river into Borgue with its grand forest and the Firth beyond it. Sakes, on a fine day, I warrant ye might see to the Irish Sea from up there."

Inside the wall, they crossed a graveled courtyard to a massive round keep rising at least five stories from the court to its crenellated ramparts.

Jenny looked around in awe. The place teemed with men-at-arms, but she and Hugh crossed the yard quickly in the captain's wake and entered the keep by way of a timber stair that led to its second-level entrance.

Inside, they crossed a winding stairway in the thickness of the wall, then went up a single stone step into the great hall.

"Is Lady Archibald here?" Hugh asked.

"Nay, sir, she's a-visiting kinsmen, but Himself means to bring her back wi' him, and I'm thinking she'll be gey pleased to see ye married."

Tam left them in the hands of Archie's steward, who

informed them that they would be serving supper in an hour and took them straight up to their chambers.

"This castle is as big as Lochmaben," Jenny said when they were alone and she discovered that they had a tiny sitting room and a large bedchamber.

"And we have a proper-sized bed," Hugh said.

Knowing she was blushing, she said quickly, "But Lucas will be coming—and others, too—with our baggage."

"Mayhap that is why we have two rooms, Lady Easdale."

Her blushes forgotten, she eyed him warily. "I am still Easdale of Easdale, sir. Our marriage did not alter that. Are you vexed?"

"I just wish we had talked about it first," he said. "You are Janet Douglas now, after all, but 'tis my own fault that we have not discussed your title."

Shaking her head at him, but feeling as if she ought to have raised the subject after Sadie had wondered what to call her—and just as aware that she did not want to argue with him—she went to the tall, narrow window and looked out.

Most of the snow had melted, and the land across the river was green and heavily forested. There were rolling hills in the distance and she could see other, higher, snow-capped ones to the north. To the south, she could indeed see the Firth.

"Do you think we can really see the Irish Sea from here?" she asked.

"Nay," he said from right behind her. He put a hand lightly on her shoulder and turned her to face him, his touch having its usual effect.

"Kiss me, lass," he said quietly, lowering his mouth

AMANDA SCOTT

toward hers. Hesitating before his lips touched hers, he added, "I shall have to accustom myself to the fact that your rank matches my own, but it may take some time."

Without awaiting a reply, he kissed her, and she responded instantly.

Lucas interrupted them with the luggage before things had gone far, and Hugh cursed him, but his man only grinned and said he'd hurry the other lads along.

As soon as they left, Hugh barred the door and took Jenny to bed.

They made it to supper with time to spare and found other guests, also awaiting Archie's return. But none tempted them to linger, and there was a full moon.

The next two days passed too quickly to suit Jenny or Hugh, because they were able to spend them together. Hugh talked much of Thornhill, and Jenny knew he longed to get home. She said nothing about Easdale, wondering when it would occur to him that they had negotiated no marriage settlements between them.

Archie arrived as promised late Thursday afternoon with his lady wife and a party of men-at-arms, having sent his hunting guests on to Threave.

He soon sent a message to Hugh, informing him that he and Jenny were to take supper at the high table. Before suppertime, however, more guests arrived, including Lord Dunwythie, his wife Phaeline, his two daughters, and Reid Douglas.

Chapter 17

Hugh and Jenny discovered the new arrivals when they entered the upper hall for supper. Reid looked uncertain, Phaeline angry, and Dunwythie rueful.

Shaking hands with Dunwythie, Hugh said, "You surprise us, sir. You should have told me you were coming. We might have traveled together."

"Och, lad, by my troth, I didna ken we *were* coming. Then, too, we make a large party by ourselves for a galley. I did hope to attend the celebration at Threave, m'self. But sithee, I'd meant to ride there, and young Reid here was still making up his mind whether to come with me. Then our Jenny ran away, and when you returned with her at last, the news of your marriage unsettled us all. By my troth," he added, lowering his voice, "I fear it nearly caused my lady to lose her bairn."

"How dreadful," Hugh said. Wondering why Jenny, beside him, did not respond, too, he glanced at her as he added, "It surprises me even more then that Phaeline has

come with you, sir. Surely, she ought to be at home, resting in bed."

"She frets too much so," Dunwythie said.

"But such a journey—"

"Nay, she likes sailing and kens fine that she can also
take a boat from here to Threave," he said. "She would
upset herself more were she to stay home."

Hugh glanced at Phaeline, talking with Joanna Douglas and looking perfectly stout. Finding Dunwythie's
explanation implausible, he wondered what had really
prompted his sister to undertake the journey. She had
displayed little interest in Threave or Archie Douglas, although he was as much her kinsman as Hugh's.

He noted, too, that Reid stayed close to her, as did
Mairi and Fiona. Neither had yet greeted Jenny, making
him certain that Phaeline had forbidden them to.

Hugh had nothing he wanted to say to any of them.
But evidently, Phaeline desired to speak with him, for she
approached him alone just as Archie entered and began
wending his way to the high table. He took his time, pausing to shake hands and talk with some of his guests.

"I see you arrived safely, Hugh," Phaeline said, watching as Jenny slipped away to greet Mairi and Fiona. "Because of your odd burst of temper the other day, I must
assure myself that your sense of rectitude and hope for an
annulment have prevailed. Pray, tell me that you've had
the good sense not to couple yet with Janet."

"She is my wife, Phaeline. I declared as much before
we left Annan House."

"Then you *have* taken her. That will make things more
tedious, I expect, but I believe we can still get your marriage annulled. I must say, I am grieved that you would so

unashamedly try to rob your own brother of his intended wife."

"Go back to your husband, Phaeline, before I tell you what I think of what you and Reid—aye, and Dunwythie, too—tried to do to Jenny. If you truly mean to seek an annulment, I would also recommend that you consider well what others will think of such a foolish action against the head of your own family."

"Pish-tush," she said. "The fact is that Reid and Janet *are* betrothed, my dear Hugh. And a prior betrothal, as you said yourself, is grounds to annul any marriage. Moreover, my lord tells me the Bishop of Glasgow will take the mass on Sunday. Doubtless, he will take a dim view of any priest acting in a minstrel play. He has the power to grant your annulment, and we mean to ask him to do so."

Since the Bishop of Glasgow was the very man who had approved the special license for which Hugh had supposedly applied, he was afraid Phaeline might be right. He realized, too, in that moment, that he would fight buckle and thong to keep Jenny as his own. Reid clearly wanted only her wealth, her title, and sufficient power to force her to do his bidding. Hugh wanted Jenny for herself.

To be sure, they would fratch some, because he wanted her as his wife and she was determined to remain and act as a baroness in her own right.

But she would learn, he thought.

And, doubtless, so would he.

Having moved to stand with Mairi and Fiona while Phaeline talked with Hugh, Jenny kept an eye on him as she exchanged greetings with her cousins.

"Is it not astonishing?" Fiona demanded. "Who would have thought they'd bring *me* to Galloway? One wonders particularly why Uncle Reid wanted to come," she added with a mischievous look at Jenny.

"Hush, Fee," Mairi said quietly. "Your voice is too loud."

"What if people do hear me? I did wonder, that's all."

Jenny wondered, too, but seeing Hugh gesture to her as Phaeline left him, she excused herself, saying, "We are to sit at the high table, so I must go. I'll talk more with you later this evening or when we all ride to Threave tomorrow."

"Oh, we are not riding," Fiona said. "Phaeline said *we* are to go in a boat."

Jenny nodded, smiling, but her attention had already fixed on Hugh.

He was annoyed. His expression looked as placid as usual, but she knew he was angry and wondered *how* she could tell.

When she reached him, he smiled and offered his arm. Curious though she was, she resisted asking him at once about his conversation with Phaeline.

Resting a hand lightly on his forearm, she went with him to the dais and saw with relief that he relaxed as he greeted Archie Douglas.

Tall, lanky, and broad-shouldered with dark, eaglelike features, Archie grinned back at Hugh and clapped him on the shoulder. Then he took Jenny's hand as she curtsied to him, and said, "We are pleased to greet you, Lady Easdale, and to extend our felicitations on your marriage."

"Thank you, my lord," she said, then curtsied again as he presented his lady wife, Joanna.

Indicating that Jenny was to sit beside Joanna, Archie moved to his place with Hugh beside him, and Jenny knew she would hear none of their conversation.

The hall was too noisy. Musicians in the gallery played music she could barely hear, and Archie had provided no other entertainment. Service was swift, too, making it clear to her that he did not intend his guests to linger over their supper.

Joanna leaned nearer to Jenny and said, "My ladies and I, and some others, will depart early in the morning, my dear. Do you come with us in the boats?"

"Sir Hugh said we would borrow horses and ride to Threave, madam," Jenny said. "But, pray, do call me Jenny."

"Most ladies prefer the boats, Jenny. Are you sure that you want to ride such a distance? To be sure, the boats will take longer, rowing against the current as they do. But 'tis a pleasant journey, and we will stop on the way to eat our midday meal."

"Doubtless the riders will stop, too, madam," Jenny said smiling. "If it will not offend you, I should prefer to ride with my lord husband."

"I do not take offense so easily, and of course you would prefer it, as newly married as you are. I am still stunned at our Hugh's taking another wife! Sithee, we were certain he would hold by his word and never remarry. But what extraordinary dimples you have, my dear. I vow, they must be an inch deep, both of them!"

They chatted amiably as they ate, and Jenny was careful to talk with the lady on her left, too. But it was not long before Archie said to Joanna, "We will leave now, my love. Hugh wants a private word with me, and doubtless others will, too."

Obediently, Joanna stood, and everyone else did likewise. Many would stay after their host and hostess left the hall, but Jenny would not be one. As Joanna turned to leave, Jenny stepped aside for her and thus nearer to Douglas.

"Pray, my lord," she said quietly, "I do not know if Sir Hugh mentioned that I would also like to speak with you . . ."

Archie looked surprised but said politely, "Nay, my lady, he did not. Nor do I think it suitable for a woman to take part in men's conversation." Motioning for the lady who had sat at Jenny's left hand to follow Joanna, he turned to Hugh. "What say you, lad? Did you expect your lady to take part in our talk?"

"I did not," Hugh said, giving Jenny a stern look.

She ignored it, saying to Archie, "With respect, my lord, what Sir Hugh is about to discuss with you is a matter that I brought to his attention. I heard things said, and experienced other things, that he did not. Nor, I fear, does he view the matter as seriously as I do. I would ask, therefore, that you hear me as well."

Archie looked at Hugh and back at Jenny.

Hugh said firmly, "Madam, I will tell him all we know. There is no need—"

To her surprise, and clearly to Hugh's, Archie cut him off with a chuckle and said, "Bless us, lass, I think you'll lead our Hugh a dance. But I like you. So you may come

with us now and keep an eye on him if you want to be sure
he tells the whole tale. I own that betwixt the two of you,
you have piqued my curiosity."

Jenny took care not to let Hugh catch her eye as they
followed their host to a private chamber.

Archie shut the door himself and gestured toward two
back-stools near a large table. As they sat, he took the
chair behind the table and nodded to Hugh.

"Let's hear it, lad."

Hugh began to explain Jenny's concern that certain in-
cidents and associations might suggest mischief-makers
plotting to disturb the royal celebration at Threave. He
no sooner mentioned the minstrels, however, than Archie
stopped him.

"Hold there, lad. I may, from experience, imagine how
you came to get yourself mixed up with such a tribe. But
I cannot imagine how your lady could do so. Begin at the
beginning now, and don't be leaving things out." With a
roguish look at Jenny, he said, "I begin to see why you
were fretting, lass."

Heat flooded her cheeks, and although she managed
to smile, she could feel Hugh's increasing displeasure.
She had known he'd have to include the minstrels in his
explanation, but it had not occurred to her until that moment that the most likely reason he had wanted to talk to
Archie without her was that he had meant to omit mentioning her altogether. Now, though, she was sure he had
meant to do just that.

She knew, too, although he had not said a word to her
or done aught else to reveal it, that he was angry with
her—even more so than she had guessed before.

Nevertheless, obedient to Archie's command, he described

the betrothal feast, its aftermath, the attack on the knacker, and their suspicion that someone might have exploited his first-head privilege to smuggle jewels out of Annan House.

"I should perhaps describe the Joculator," Hugh said just as Jenny was about to mention that someone had returned the Annan House jewels.

"The Joculator?" Archie said.

"Their leader," Hugh explained. They all call him so. As I recall, a joculator is proficient in most if not all of the minstrel arts. He has many talents, including juggling, acting the fool, deftness in training animals—and legerdemain."

"Sleight of hand?" Archie said. "A good way to steal jewels, I should think."

"Aye, and I must say, although I like these minstrels exceedingly, sir, and believe they are as honest as any, I did wonder about that."

"It is not just about the jewels, though," Jenny said, deciding it was not the time to mention that the theft at Annan House might have been a prank. "For one thing," she went on, "the sheriff's men searched the camp at Dumfries and found no sign of them. But something is amiss. People talking together break off when they see one watching, and twice I have heard mention of Threave Castle spoken in such a way as to sound ominous. One of those times was at Lochmaben Castle."

"Lass," Hugh said sternly, "you heard that voice in a dream."

"Aye, sure," she admitted, this time avoiding Archie's gaze *and* Hugh's. But she added nonetheless firmly, "I am sure now, however, that not all of it was a dream, sir."

Meeting Archie's gaze then, she said, "I continued to hear at least one voice after I had wakened, my lord. It was the same voice that had said, 'So, I'm just to take ye along to Threave, am I?' The one arguing with that one had said, 'We pay well for what we want,' and something about a chance to get inside the castle."

"I own, I don't much like the sound of that," Archie said.

Jenny waited for Hugh to protest, but although he opened his mouth as if he would, he shut it again and was silent.

"Is that the sum of it?" Archie asked him.

"Aye, it is," Hugh said evenly. "It is not much, I'm afraid."

"Even so," Archie said, "it does sound as if something is in the wind, and I cannot have upset at Threave when the purpose of this tournament is to show off the new seat of Douglas power and honor his grace's third year on the throne. *Any* trouble could undermine the peace we have now in Galloway, and in the Borders."

"Only if they succeed, my lord," Jenny said. "Mayhap we can learn—"

"We have done our part by warning his lordship," Hugh interjected then. "He is entirely capable of handling it now without our help."

"Now, now, lad," Archie said. "When has a man ever had too many eyes and ears? I'm thinking that since your lady has shown us that she can use her wits, she may be the very one to identify them. I would have her at hand."

Hugh nodded. "Then it must be as you will, my lord."

"Aye, sure, but take that dour look off your face.

Doubtless, you're thinking of your crops. But your people have managed without you before, and they will now."

"They will, indeed, sir," Hugh said, standing.

Archie shook hands with him again. " 'Tis good to have you here, Hugh, and I felicitate you on your choice of a lady. You've done well, lad. We'll not wait for the boats in the morning but will ride out after we break our fast."

"Aye, sir, thank you."

Archie grinned at Jenny. "If you need a champion later, my lady, you may call on me. I warrant I can still show even our Hugh here a trick or two."

"You are kind, my lord," Jenny said. "But I fight my own battles."

"Come along then," Hugh said, grasping her arm. "We'll see how you do."

The last thing Jenny saw as Hugh whisked her out the door was Archie's grin.

Hugh said not a word until they reached their bedchamber. But then, finding Lucas putting out their night things, he ordered the man out without explanation and barely waited for the door to shut behind him before he said, "We have to get some things straight between us, madam wife."

"Aye, sir, I think we do," she said, stepping a little away from him.

"First of all, when I said I would be your husband in every way, I was including the part of the wedding service that binds you to obey me."

"I know."

"Well, you have a mighty poor way of showing that you know it. It would serve you right if I ordered you to stay here whilst I go on to Threave with Archie."

"Aye, doubtless it would."

"If you think to get round me by agreeing with everything I say, you will miss your mark," he said curtly.

"At least Archie Douglas knew to call me Lady Easdale."

"Because Tam Inglis, his captain of the guard, made sure you wouldn't be *correcting* Archie," he said savagely. "Look here, lass. Although you equal me in rank, if you try to tell me your father would have expected you to behave as if your husband does not exist, whoever he *might* have been, I say you are—"

"He would not expect that," Jenny interjected.

"Don't interrupt!" Hugh snapped. "Our duties as husband and wife demand that I protect you and you obey me. You will remain Easdale of Easdale, but you are nonetheless my wife, and I will expect you to behave like it, not like some contrary vixen who takes her own road regardless of what I say. Even where Easdale is concerned, your father would expect your husband—especially one with my experience—to advise and guide you. In some instances, you may even have to accept the fact that I can legally enforce your obedience to my will."

"Aye, sir," she said meekly.

Catching her by the shoulders, he gave her a shake. "Do not think to cozen me with this show of submissiveness, Jenny, for I don't believe a word of it. How you dared to twist that dream of yours into such a tale for him about sneaking spies into Threave and paying well for what was wanted—"

"The words just came out like that, but those things *were* in my dream, sir."

"You are willful and stubborn, and you think you can look after yourself, but you can't! And if anything should happen to you—" He stopped, realizing he was losing control of himself, albeit not necessarily of his temper.

She put a gentle hand on his cheek. "Take me to bed, Hugo. I know you worry, and I know why you do. But nothing bad will happen to me whilst I'm here with you tonight, and I promise, I'll be as obedient as you please."

"Ah, Jenny, 'tis an irresistible offer, but we will renew this discussion later. Don't think we will not."

She smiled, and he shook his head at her, but he took her to bed and held her to her promise. However, when she slept, he remained wakeful, thinking of how he felt about her and wondering what he would do if he lost her, as he had lost Ella.

No matter what else he tried to think about then, his thoughts kept flying back to the horrible image of riding home to learn that Ella was dead. At last, he got up and put on breeks, shirt, jack, and boots to walk about and refresh his knowledge of Castle Mains, hoping its memories would banish the one that haunted him.

In the hall, some of the male guests still remained, dicing or playing other games. Not in the mood for camaraderie or to talk with Reid, who was one of them, he continued through the hall as if he had a goal in mind, and out into the courtyard.

It was cold there under a clear sky and a high, brilliant, still nearly full moon. But the chill was more than his jack alone could offset, so he took himself back inside and began to climb the stairway to his chambers.

He reached the landing, then knew no more until he wakened, crumpled on the hard stone steps with an aching head and Lucas bending over him, speaking his name in urgent tones.

"Thank t' Fates, ye're no dead yet," the man said as Hugh opened his eyes. "I thought this time ye'd done it. What did she clout ye with, any road?"

"*She*! You're as daft as Tam Inglis says you are if you think—"

"Och, I didna think nowt of the sort," Lucas said, stepping adroitly out of reach. "I just wanted to see did ye keep all your senses, laird. Your sweet wee lady couldna reach high enough to fetch ye such a clout."

"Could she not? I am sure you wrong her," Hugh said. "But she would not, nor had she reason."

"Then she didna lock ye out, either?"

"Nay, she did not. She was sleeping soundly when I left, but I could not get to sleep. I kept thinking about . . . about things I should no longer think about."

"Aye, sure," Lucas said wisely. "We'll just be gettin' ye to bed then. I did fear ye'd slozzled a mite over t' limit, ye ken, but I couldna smell whisky nor wine on your breath. Then I felt yon great lump on your head, so—"

"Lucas, stow your gab," Hugh said. "Help me to my feet."

"Aye, sir, and then I'll help ye to your bed."

"Nay, you will not."

"Hush now, ye'll wake your lady."

Hugh gave up and let Lucas have his way.

Jenny heard them shuffle into the room but, hearing no voices, felt quickly for Hugh in the bed. Just as she realized he was not there, she heard Lucas mutter, "Dinna try to 'elp yourself, laird. I'll get them clothes off ye and fetch ye a cold cloth for that lump on your head."

"Lump!" She sat up, clutching covers to her breast. "Light a candle, Lucas. I'm awake. What happened?"

"Nowt," Hugh said. "Go back to sleep, lass."

"Don't be daft," she snapped. "There are still embers on the hearth, Lucas. Light something. I want to see him."

"Unless you have more clothes on than you had when I left, you'd best be covered to the neck, lady wife," Hugh said. "We still have things to settle between us, so now is not the time to vex me further."

"Aye, sir, I'm covered. What happened? And don't say 'nowt' again unless you want to find out how much temper your lady wife has. If you've a lump on your head, 'nowt' was clearly a lie, so don't make me get up to shake the truth out of you."

Lucas had moved from Hugh to kneel by the hearth, and he stood with a lighted candle in time for Jenny to see Hugh's quick grin turn to a wince.

"Good sakes, the pair of you ought to be flayed," she said, starting to put a leg out when she saw that Lucas was also smiling.

"Nay," Hugh snapped. "We'll tell you what happened, but stay where you are. I'll be with you in a trice if Lucas can find a dish to set that damned candle in."

"Aye, sure, blame me," Lucas said. "Behear the man! Nae doots, I saved 'is life, but t' fact that he 'as displeased your ladyship be on *my* head."

"Saved his life!"

"Lucas, if you don't want to feel my fist on your jaw, you'll cease your gabbing," Hugh said. "You're giving me a headache."

"'Tis me that's givin' 'im an 'eadache, aye, as if nae one clouted 'im."

"Someone struck you?"

"Aye, but that's all," Hugh said. "I'm not dead, so hush, the pair of you."

"Happen, savin' 'is life again puts us even, but I've lost count," Lucas said thoughtfully. "Some devil's limb clouted 'im, but I'd seen t' laird a-strollin' through t' hall and up t' stairs. Thinkin' he'd 'ad more than he ought to drink and might need 'elp with his disrobin', I followed 'im. By, when I heard 'im fall—"

"We don't need to hear what you thought then," Hugh interjected. "Cease your gab now, and get these clothes off me. Then you may take yourself to bed."

"Nah then, I'm a-doin' it," Lucas said, hastening to help Hugh undress.

As he was leaving, Hugh said quietly. "I do thank you, Lucas."

"'Tis nae more than ye'd do for me, laird, and *have* done, as ye might say. Dinna let him take that cold cloth off his head till the ache eases, me lady."

"Good night, Lucas," Hugh said firmly.

The door shut, and Jenny smiled. "He loves you, you know. Who do you think hit you?"

"That loving scoundrel who just left suggested it might have been you."

She laughed then. "Earlier, perhaps, but not after . . . Why did you leave?"

"I couldn't sleep, and I was afraid I'd wake you."

"I think you're not telling me the whole truth," she said.

"Nay, but I'm not lying, so don't smack me. I can't take another hit tonight."

"Too many tormenting thoughts?"

"Aye, a few."

"I know how they go," she said. "Most begin with 'what if?' or 'if only.'"

"Aye." He reached for her and drew her close. "Sleep, lassie. Tomorrow will be a long day."

"How does your head feel now?"

"Don't ask."

She did not ask again, but she could not help wondering who had anything to gain by attacking Hugh. The only person she could imagine who might think he had was Reid, and she doubted that Reid had the courage to act on the thought.

That left a castle full of mostly unknown persons with, as far as she knew, not one member of the minstrel company among them.

~

Hugh woke to gray light through the tall, narrow window. As it faced west, he could not tell if the grayness was dawn twilight or sunlight obscured by clouds.

His head ached, but the ache was dull. Lucas had assured him the night before that his assailant had not broken it, and the dullness of the pain reinforced that fact. But it was going to be a long day.

Jenny slept soundly beside him on her stomach as she

had the past three mornings. At least, this bed was large enough, so she had not kicked or kneed him.

Waking her at last but with the same difficulty he had had every morning, he recalled how quickly she had wakened the night before and wondered if she had had some sixth sense that there was trouble. If that were the case, perhaps the reason she slept so soundly otherwise was that he was with her. The thought was a comfortable one for him, but he smiled as he imagined what she would think about it.

Despite his headache, he'd have welcomed a brief interlude with her. But since Archie wanted to be away early, he did not suggest it. In any event, the long, narrow-eyed look Jenny gave him as she climbed out of bed suggested that she would have been too concerned about his aching head to enjoy it.

He noted the same appraising look many times during the morning. He saw it as they broke their fast and in the courtyard as they mounted their horses. He saw it so often as they rode alongside the river Dee that when their large party stopped to eat the dinner packed for them at Castle Mains, he took her firmly aside.

"See here, lass," he said. "I am not made of glass. My head aches and I'm tired because I did not sleep well. But I won't fall off my horse or die in the saddle before we reach Threave. My temper is a mite uncertain, though, so let be."

"Aye, sure," she said, dimpling. "I must be acting like a mother cat with one kit, but I did not realize I was vexing you. Sakes, but it would vex me, too!"

He nodded, satisfied that she would keep her word. It occurred to him then that she often agreed with him.

Although he had learned that he could make her angry, she was ever quick to agree with his rebukes. Then experience reminded him that she was nonetheless capable of doing exactly as she pleased afterward.

Recalling that his sister Phaeline had often accused him of doing the same thing—listening, agreeing, and then doing whatever *he* had decided to do—he found himself for once agreeing with Phaeline. It was a damned annoying habit!

As they rode, he watched the other riders, wondering which, if any of them, had struck him. He had no memory of the event other than that he had been walking up the spiral stairway . . . until Lucas had spoken his name.

Hugh was no stranger to violence. No knight of the Scottish realm was a stranger to violence, death, or destruction. He had cultivated an inbred sense of self-preservation that had served him well in battle and tournament, and had seen him safely through his extensive travels and a few very dangerous adventures.

Yet he had sensed no danger beforehand, had heard no sound of warning or marked anyone who seemed to take particular note of his presence. Such details, he decided, strongly indicated someone with experience to match his own.

That eliminated Reid as a suspect, although Hugh had never seriously considered him. Doubtless, Jenny suspected Reid though, and perhaps Lucas did.

Reid and Dunwythie had both chosen to ride to Threave, leaving the Dunwythie ladies to travel by boat with Joanna Douglas.

Noting that Reid seemed friendly with several other men, none of whom Hugh recognized, he was conscious of another stirring of guilt. Since Ella's death, thanks to his grief or a disinclination to associate closely with the rest of his family, he had ignored his duty to the lad. To be sure, he had also been busy with Thornhill and lingering obligations to Archie. But those were just excuses.

He was still considering the wide demands of duty when they topped a rise and the massive, square, battlemented splendor of Threave loomed into view.

Inside a high, nearly finished curtain wall with watchtowers at all four angles, and rising magnificently above a surrounding flat, watery landscape, the immense symbol of Douglas power dominated an islet formed and protected by the river. All around it, colorful pavilions and tents of visitors decorated the driest patches of ground much as wildflowers might adorn other fields.

Threave's forbidding majesty silenced the party as its members drew rein.

If Archie intended to awe the residents of Galloway and all forthcoming visitors, Hugh thought he would succeed beyond his dreams.

Chapter 18

Jenny saw the man as they were fording the river Dee—alongside an observably temporary, narrow timber foot-bridge—to Threave's islet.

At first, she thought only that the man looked vaguely familiar and wondered if he might be someone she had met at Easdale before her father died.

She and Hugh were entering the ford as the group she had noticed emerged onto the islet, so the man who had drawn her attention provided only his profile.

He looked every inch a nobleman, elegant of garb and arrogant of demeanor. He had one of those faces that look much the same from middle age to later years, but she judged him to be some years older than Hugh, yet younger than Dunwythie.

Reid rode behind the man but urged his mount up alongside the other's as their horses stepped onto the islet. Jenny realized then that she had seen the nobleman with Reid earlier, in the hall at Castle Mains.

She glanced at Hugh. If Reid knew the man, perhaps he did as well.

Hugh was looking straight ahead, minding his horse, a nervous animal that, even after a tediously slow eight-mile ride, still tended to start or rear at perceived obstacles or enemies. Hugh managed him deftly enough but without his usual look of being at one with the animal. She knew he was tired, but after his earlier rebuke, she would not ask him if his head still ached. However . . .

"Sir, do you know that man with whom your brother is riding?"

He began to shake his head but visibly thought better of it. "Nay, lass," he said then. "Why do you ask?"

"I feel as if I should know him, but I cannot place him."

"Aye, well, doubtless you saw him at Castle Mains. Or do you imagine he may be one of the villains we seek?"

"I don't know who he may be," she said. "I did see him with Reid at Castle Mains, but something else about him is tugging at my memory. I warrant it will come to me later."

"Well, do not waken me with it in the middle of the night," he said with a slight smile. "Archie still seems to think I'm going to enter the tourney."

"You cannot mean to joust!"

"Nay, not to joust, Jenny. One pays a fee to enter a tournament and may joust if challenged. But few enter merely to joust one against another. There will be large parties of men competing, party against party. Whether I participate is something I must decide before this evening. But I am not daft, lass, nor am I in practice for tilting or running at a quintain."

"I do not know precisely what those things mean," she admitted. "I have never watched a tournament."

"Tilting is riding a horse full speed down a course, holding a lance that one is to put through a small ring dangling from a spring at about the level of the rider's eyebrows. Jousting is horseman against horseman with lances, spears, or swords, and a quintain is a man-shaped target that one hits horsed or afoot and which *can* hit back. But you will see it all, and I'll explain anything you do not understand."

With that, she had to be content. She hoped, though, that enough men would take part in the events to make it unnecessary for Hugh to do so.

They dismounted in the bailey and followed Archie up a steep timber stairway to the entry of the huge keep and, from there, into its great hall.

"The kitchen lies beyond that wall at the far end," he said. "Storage cellars, dungeons, and a well lie beneath it, and the main stairway ascends through the west-corner angle wall. The garderobe tower in the south angle serves every level."

"Can you house everyone who will come here?" Jenny asked.

"Bless me, my lady, most will set up their own tents and pavilions, just as they do for any tournament. Many have already done so, as doubtless you saw. Those who hang their helmets and arms on the front of their tents show they mean to compete. We've already laid out courses for the contests, and we'll soon be moving the boats anchored or beached in our harbor upriver, so we can set up our water quintain where spectators will have a good view of the water contests."

"How many boats will compete?" Hugh asked.

"Two only at a time, and each with no more than eight oars," Archie said. "Small boats don't need as much room to move about as large ones do, but they'll still give us good sport. We'll set the quintain post in the midst of the channel. I saw such a contest on the Firth once. That was grand, although with the tide running as fast as it did then, that contest was more dangerous than ours will be.

"As to your quarters, Lady Easdale," he went on with a smile, "as my kinsmen, you and Hugh will stay here in the keep. If you find aught that stirs your displeasure or concern, tell me straightaway. I want my guests to be comfortable."

She smiled and assured him that she would, but as she had little knowledge of fortresses, she doubted she would offer criticism of his. Kind though he had been, criticizing someone called Archie the Grim seemed unwise.

Glancing again at Hugh, she wondered if he had found opportunity yet to mention the knot on his head to Archie. The thought had only to express itself, however, for her to realize that she knew the answer.

Hugh had *not* sought such an opportunity, nor would he thank her for mentioning his injury to anyone—or the attack that he had suffered, come to that.

She thought she was coming to know her husband.

⌒

Hugh was tired, and his head ached. He would have liked to go straight to bed and sleep, but a man could not do that in the middle of an afternoon.

What he ought to be doing was to refresh himself and

change from his riding attire into clothing more appropriate for supper in the hall. Or, in view of Archie's expectation that he would take part in a tourney, he should walk or ride out to survey the competition that had already arrived.

By the time a minion showed them to their chamber on the fourth level, his head was pounding. Lucas followed them with lads carrying their baggage, and as the latter scurried to and fro, stowing things under Lucas's direction, Hugh felt an impatient, uncharacteristic urge to order them all to get out and leave him in peace.

Meeting Jenny's shrewd gaze, he held his tongue and walked to the window instead to look out to the northwest. There, pavilions and tents covered the higher west bank of the Dee even more densely than they covered the soggier east bank. He had not seen them all before, because the castle's bulk had concealed them. But he knew they would fill every field before the tournament began the next day.

"I'm going out to walk about," he said, turning from the window. "I should see who is here and mayhap talk more to Archie about the tournament."

"An excellent idea, sir," Jenny said, smiling. "I can go downstairs and seek out other ladies who are here. I saw none in the hall as we crossed it, but they must be somewhere. The steward will know, or I can find Joanna and—"

"Nay, lass, you ought not to wander anywhere at Threave. There will be few women here today—few altogether, come to that, compared with the number of lusty men. You will stay here where you can bar the door and keep safe."

"But there is naught to do here," she protested. "I did pack things to occupy my hands or idle hours. But I thought we would be busy seeking mischief-makers. Surely, it would be better for me to mix with people, to look for—"

"Jenny, you will obey me," he said firmly. "If there is mischief afoot as you suspect, it must include the minstrels. But they do not even seem to have arrived yet. They are not camped in the bailey as they were at Lochmaben—"

"At Castle Moss we did *not* camp inside the wall," she said. "We camped in the woods just as we did near Dumfries. And we did see nearby woodlands as we approached this castle. You could take me to see—"

"Not now, and I forbid you to ride out alone—or walk out, come to that."

She glanced at Lucas, still busy with his helpers, and held her tongue. But Hugh knew she had dismissed the danger and doubted he could trust her to stay put.

Tempted to extract a promise from her that she would obey him, he turned to Lucas instead. "When you have finished here," he said, "I want you to keep an eye on this door to see that no one disturbs her ladyship."

"Aye, sir," Lucas said, casting a doubtful look at Jenny.

Hugh turned back to her, determined to make her understand. But, to his surprise, she was smiling, showing her entrancing dimples.

"You mean to protect me, my lord," she said, putting a gentle hand to his cheek and looking into his eyes. "I am grateful for your concern. But do you think Lucas will be sufficient protection? He *is* capable, but *you* are so much more so . . ."

She paused suggestively. And despite his headache and a nagging sense of weariness, part of him began expressing a concern for her that he could not ignore.

"Lucas, collect your lads and leave us," he said hoarsely.

Lucas went, shooing his minions ahead.

⁓

Still smiling, Jenny watched Hugh warily, wondering if he had seen through her tactics to avoid certain boredom, and uncertain how he would react if he had.

He grasped the hand she held against his cheek and shifted it to his chest as he drew her closer and murmured, "Wouldst keep your husband close, lass? Take care, lest men begin to say I let my lady wife beguile me from my duty."

"You owe duty to your wife, too, sir," she said, tilting her face up invitingly.

"Aye, sure," he said, kissing her and letting her draw him toward the bed.

Even so, she saw him wince as he lowered his head to kiss her. "Shall I undress you?" she asked, careful to hide her concern.

"I cannot stay long, Jenny," he warned her. "We'll do this quickly."

"If we must," she murmured, reaching for the lacing of his breeks with one hand as she stroked his chest and belly with the other.

Despite his warning, it was easy enough to keep him from acting too hastily. She had quickly discerned what he liked, and she encouraged him to savor his pleasure, doing more than usual to stimulate him so he would not have to exert himself until the climax. But when that moment began to approach, she let him take over, submitting to his every wish and whim as she was sure he would say the best wives always did. The end justified her efforts.

Hugh collapsed atop her. Eyes closed and gasping, he lay there, spent.

Jenny did not move or speak. Neither did he.

He began gently to snore.

Jenny lay still until his snores quieted to deep, regular breathing. Then, slowly, carefully, she eased herself from under him and slipped out of the bed.

Tidying herself and seeking a robe for modesty's sake, she found her old blue kirtle first, having at the last minute stuffed it into a basket in case she might need it. Flinging it over her head, she laced its bodice shut and quickly plaited her hair. Then she opened the door with caution, expecting to find Lucas on the landing.

She wanted him to find Peg, so Peg could help her dress for supper. But the landing was empty, and no more than two hours remained before they would eat.

Lucas would return eventually, but as Jenny had told him she had no need of a maid, she doubted he would come soon enough to fetch Peg from wherever the minstrels had camped. However, to dress suitably for sitting at the high table with the lady Joanna, Jenny definitely required the services of a good tiring maid.

Glancing back at Hugh and deciding with satisfaction that he ought to sleep at least until she returned, she shut the door as quietly as she had opened it. Then she hurried down the stairs, hoping to meet Lucas coming up.

Rounding the turn onto the next landing, she nearly collided with Fiona.

"What are you doing here?" Jenny demanded.

Fiona's chin lifted defiantly. "I suppose I may go where I choose without you to tell me I cannot."

Jenny raised her eyebrows. "You are fourteen years old and know better than to wander about by yourself. I hope you have not been getting into mischief."

"I have not," Fiona retorted. "In troth, I have just come away from my mother and father and was about to return to the wee cell I share with Mairi."

"Were you?" Jenny asked dryly.

Coloring up to her ears, Fiona failed to meet her gaze.

"Never mind that now," Jenny said bracingly. "As it happens, I must go outside the wall. I was just wondering how to manage it on my own."

"Oh, may we? I own, I did want to look at all the tents. They are so—"

"We are *not* going to look at tents," Jenny said sternly. "I must find Peg."

"Peg? Sakes, is she here?"

"Aye, sure, with the minstrels. She stayed with her brother."

"Then, by all means, let us find her."

Jenny was not sure it would be so easy, and as they crossed the courtyard toward the great gate, she saw at once that it would not be.

Tam Inglis, the guard captain that she and Hugh had met on their arrival at Castle Mains, stood near the gate with a number of other men-at-arms.

Collecting her wits, she said, "Fiona, do not say a word or give any sign that what I say to the captain of the guard is aught save the truth." Receiving a nod in reply, Jenny strode confidently to Tam Inglis and said, "I hope you remember me, for I must find my tiring woman. She stopped to visit her brother, who is a juggler with the minstrels, and has stayed too long. I mean to fetch her myself."

"I do ken who ye be, my lady, but I fear I canna allow two young females to leave the castle alone," Tam said with what she decided was wholly spurious regret.

"Nay, of course you cannot," she said. "That is why I came to you, rather than trying to find my husband in the hall or elsewhere. I hoped that someone on the gate would have the authority to assign a pair of men-at-arms to show us the way. Can *you* do that, Tam Inglis? Without calling undue attention to my rank?"

"Aye, sure," he said with a nod and a look of relief that made Jenny reassess her earlier judgment. Motioning to two stout men-at-arms standing nearby, he gave the order, and Jenny and Fiona soon found themselves outside the gate and crossing the timber bridge from the castle islet to the east bank of the river.

"Would you really have sought Sir Hugh in the hall?" Fiona murmured softly as they followed their escort.

"Hugh is . . . is not available just now, so I am glad you could come with me," Jenny said. "I am to sit at the high table, so I *must* have a maid."

"Aye, well, I hope you will tell my mother as much if she looks for me, or if Mairi does," Fiona said frankly.

Jenny smiled at her. "Where *were* you going?"

Fiona shrugged. "I wanted to look around, that's all. My mother has scarcely let me stir from her side since we left Annan. I am not accustomed to such restraint, and I have never seen such a place. Why are all those tents set up across the river?"

Jenny explained, feeling rather puffed up in her knowledge. "Archie and Hugh say there will be twice as many tomorrow."

As they crossed a long, muddy field, Jenny saw that the whole area around the castle was already growing crowded. Fires already burned and she could smell the aromas of supper in the making. At one point, looking back, she thought she saw Reid Douglas. A trio of men-at-arms passed then, and when they had gone, she did not see him and decided she had been mistaken.

Many folks were erecting tents and pavilions, and she saw a line of men in jacks-o'-plate and helmets taking turns running with a lance at a post bearing the figure of a man with a sword. A lancer ran at the target with his weapon at the ready, and struck the figure on its shoulder.

The figure whipped around and the wooden sword in its hand smacked the runner so hard on his back that he fell flat in the mud as his lance went flying.

Fiona chuckled. "I warrant he feels a bit of a fool."

The two men escorting them apparently overheard her, for one said, "That 'un would be disqualified in a tourney or joust."

The two knew just where the minstrels had camped and found them easily.

As they neared the camp, it occurred to Jenny that if she were not careful, their reception could stir the very scandal she and Hugh—and Dunwythie—hoped to avoid. Archie knew the whole tale, but he would not thank them if her sojourn with the minstrel company became the primary topic of conversation during his royal celebration. Just thinking about what Reid might contribute made her wince.

As she wore her blue kirtle and had her hair in plaits, the minstrels would recognize her as their Bonnie Jenny. But what could she say about Fiona, who wore a simple but nonetheless elegant gown? And what about their escort?

Dealing with the latter problem first, Jenny said to the men, "I warrant the minstrels would prefer not to have armed men in their camp, so prithee wait for us at the edge of the camp whilst we fetch my tiring woman."

"Aye, sure, m'lady," the older of the two said genially.

"Come along, Fee," she said, catching Fiona's arm. "We must hurry."

As they entered the clearing, a shout went up: "Bonnie Jenny! It be Bonnie Jenny back again!"

"Is that what they call you?" Fiona demanded as a number of persons rushed toward them from several directions.

"Aye," Jenny responded before they engulfed her. Hugging first one then another, she tried to introduce the most important ones to Fiona. "This is Gawkus, and Gilly, and this is Gerda," she added as she hugged that young woman. And . . ."

Her voice failed when she looked up from the hug into the stern gaze of the Joculator. Swiftly, she curtsied and said, "Good day to you, sir."

"You should *not* be here on your own," he said. "Where is Hugo?"

"In the castle," Jenny said, realizing that she lacked the nerve, facing his stern demeanor, to embellish further. The thought crossed her mind then that when Hugh learned what she had done, he would take an even dimmer view of it.

"I see that he did provide you with an escort," the Joculator said, nodding toward the two men at the edge of the clearing. With a slight smile, he added, "One must suppose that Hugo has decided *against* seeking an annulment."

"I came seeking Peg," Jenny said, wishing he would not look so forbidding and hoping he would not ask *why* she wanted Peg. She could not lie to him again.

Flicking a glance at Fiona, he gave Jenny a long look that she managed to meet directly if not with confidence. Then, to her relief, he nodded and said, "Peg is at Cath's tent, stitching things with Cath and some others. Yonder." He pointed.

Motioning the two men-at-arms to stay where they were, Jenny hurried with Fiona along the barely visible track he had indicated.

"Faith, he seems nearly as ferocious as my mother says Sir Hugh can be," Fiona said. "Why did he call him Hugo?"

"Some people do," Jenny said. "I do, myself, from time to time." Then, flinging aside her dignity at the sight of Cath's tent just ahead, she called, "Peg!"

By the time they reached it, Peg was outside, her arms wide. "Sakes, mistress, where did ye spring from?" Glancing warily at Fiona, she added, "Ye canna ha' come back to us!"

"Only for a moment, Peg. I must get back inside the castle as quickly as possible, because Sir Hugh does not know where I am. But I need you. I brought no tiring woman with me, and we are to sit at the high table tonight."

"Did ye bring proper clothing this time, at least?"

"Aye, sure, I did, but I cannot get into it all by myself, and I'd liefer not have to depend on my husband."

"Ye'll be keeping him then?"

"I expect so," Jenny said, smiling.

Peg grinned. "It be a good match we made for ye, if I do say so m'self."

"Will you come now?"

"Aye, sure," Peg said. "I must just pack a wee sack for m'self first, if I may. I've some things the others gave me, and I'd like to ha' summat else to wear if I'm to stay in the castle with ye. How long will ye need me?"

"As long as you can stay," Jenny said frankly. "Sir Hugh means to go straight to Thornhill from here, so if you would like to come with us . . ."

Peg nodded. "Aye, I'd fain do that. I like the folks here, and Cath and Cuddy ha' been teaching me sleight o' hand, wi' scarves and such. But I'd forgotten what it be like to live wi' Bryan. I vow, mistress, I canna talk to any man for more than a wee minute without having to endure me brother's scolds afterward."

"We must hurry," Jenny said. She was growing more nervous each minute and more worried about the scolding she might have to endure, herself.

Cath had come outside, so Jenny gave her a hug, glibly introduced Fiona as her cousin, and told Cath they would look forward to seeing more of her before the tournament was over.

"Faith, I hope ye mean to sing with us," Cath said. "It hasna been the same without ye, lass. Nor can Cuddy's cousin Drogo sing like Hugo can."

"Cath," Jenny said, "Hugo told me Cuddy is English. Is that so?"

"Aye," Cath said. "He were born across the line. But he's lived here longer."

"Is Drogo English, too?"

"Aye, may the devil fly away wi' the man! I canna talk about him. He's never around when ye want him, only when ye don't."

"Sithee, we're going to slip off now, Cath," Peg said. "Jenny and Hugo be staying inside yon castle, so I'll be a-helping her there. We'll see ye anon though."

Jenny, Fiona, and Peg returned to where Jenny had left her escort as quickly as they could without being rude to any of the folks who wanted to welcome her. But when they reached the edge of the woods, the two men-at-arms were not there.

Seeing Cuddy practicing his flute under a tree near the place she had left their escort, Jenny asked if he had seen where the two men went.

"Aye, sure," he said. "Another o' their sort did come and fetch them away. He said they needed all their men on the field to keep order, because the lads practicing for Saturday be a-breaking up now to ha' their supper. And all o' them ha' weapons."

Jenny frowned, wondering if she ought to ask two of the minstrels to escort them back. She did not want to ask Cuddy. Deciding then that such an escort would likely draw more attention than she wanted at the castle gate, she hesitated.

"What is it?" Fiona asked her.

"Perhaps we ought to have men with us as we cross that field again."

"Sakes, there are three of us," Fiona said. "With so many people around, no one would dare to interfere with us."

Peg agreed with her, and Jenny did, too, albeit without saying so, because she knew that Hugh would vehemently *dis*agree.

Remembering how easily he had carried her away in the crowd at Dumfries market square, she hoped she was not making another mistake.

Still, Fiona was right. There *were* three of them.

Hugh awoke from deep sleep to the sound of a fierce if low-voiced debate between two men outside his door.

Recognizing Lucas's muttering, he began to sit, only to wince at the pounding in his head and lie back again. He waited briefly for Jenny to intervene, realized that she was not in the room, sat up too fast, and roared, "Lucas!"

The door opened, and Lucas put his head in. "Nah then, sir, I been a-warnin' t' lad to cease 'is yammerin', but he—"

Reid, failing to push past Lucas, said urgently from behind him, "Hugh, I *must* see you!"

"One moment," Hugh said. Then, to Lucas, "Where is her ladyship?"

Lucas looked swiftly around the chamber. "By, I thought she were *with* ye!"

"I am *trying* to tell you where she is," Reid said.

"Come in then," Hugh said. "You, too, Lucas, and shut that door."

With a wary look at Hugh, Lucas made way for Reid and shut the door.

Forgetting his aching head, Hugh focused on his brother. "Now, what do you want to tell me?"

"I saw Jenny go outside the gate with Fiona," Reid said. "Look, Hugh, I—"

"How the devil did they get outside?" Hugh demanded as he shoved aside the blankets. Grabbing his netherstocks and breeks, he began to pull them on.

Reid said, "They stopped at the gate. Jenny must have persuaded the guard captain there to provide them with an escort."

"There now, ye see," Lucas muttered. "Her ladyship be nae such a fool as—"

"You be silent," Hugh said. "I'll have something to say to you later. Did you see where they headed, Reid?"

As Lucas moved swiftly to get Hugh's shirt and jack for him, and Hugh tugged on his boots, Reid said, "They went across the fields and into the woods beyond. Hugh, the whole area is alive with men-at-arms practicing for the tourneys. Jenny and Fiona should *never*—"

"How far did you follow them?" Hugh demanded, accepting his dirk from Lucas and shoving it into a boot.

"To the woods," Reid said. "I think they went into the minstrel camp. But that's not all. I think Jenny must have dismissed her escort there."

Hugh frowned. "Did you *see* her dismiss them?"

"Nay, but I did see the two men that the guard captain had provided for them walking back to the castle."

"Let's go," Hugh said, snatching up his sword and sword belt as he headed for the door.

Reid and Lucas hurried after him.

The field was much more crowded than it had been a half hour earlier, and thinking she caught a glimpse of Reid again, Jenny grabbed Fiona by an arm and pulled her off at an angle. She did not want to run into him.

Peg scrambled to follow them, catching up as Jenny was explaining to Fiona why she had grabbed her.

Fiona laughed, saying, "It is just good you took hold of my arm, because when you pulled, I nearly slipped in this horrid mud. My shoes are ruined in any event, so I can just imagine what my lady mother will say."

They walked on but it was slow going. The cook fires and enticing aromas of hot food had apparently drawn people from across the river, as well.

Jenny was growing more concerned about what Hugh would say. The crowd was nearly all male, and the men nearest them seemed closer than they needed to be. At least she could see the castle and know she was going the right way.

Turning to make sure Peg had not fallen behind, Jenny saw a man right behind the maidservant reach out for her in a purposeful, ominous way.

"Peg, look out!" Jenny shouted.

As she did, she heard a man behind her yell, "Beware yonder, lads. Let be!"

"Sorry, lass," the one who had reached for Peg muttered as he stepped quickly past them. "I didna mean to startle ye."

Peg stared at him.

Jenny could not see the man's face, because he wore a helmet as most of the men on the field did, and kept his head down. As he hurried off, others followed him, considerably thinning the crowd that had seemed to close in around them.

"Mercy," Fiona exclaimed. "What was *that* about? Were they *trying* to frighten us?"

"I dinna ken," Peg said. "Ay de mi, though, look yonder, mistress."

Turning, Jenny had a clear view of an angry Hugh striding toward them.

Chapter 19 ———————————

Hugh did not realize how terrified he was for Jenny until relief flooded through him when he saw her emerge from the crowd ahead. Then anger surged, and he quickened his pace toward her, his two satellites hurrying in his wake.

He paid no heed to the crowd on the field, no heed to Fiona or Peg. He had eyes only for his disobedient wife. That she had dared to sneak out and—

She smiled, lifted her skirt a little higher, and ran toward him, heedless of the mucky ground. "I am so glad to see you," she said as soon as she was near enough not to shout. "Someone called our escort away. Then a man tried—"

"Enough, lass," he said, becoming aware again of the teeming throng on the field and unable to tell how far her words might carry. "We'll talk more inside."

Putting an arm around her and thus unable to resist giving her a little hug, he said for her ears alone, "I doubt you will want to hear all I have to say to you."

"I am sure I won't," she agreed, looking up at him.

"But it can be no worse than what I have already said to myself."

"Sakes, Hugh, I hope you mean to do more than just *talk* to her?" Reid said. "If she were my wife, as she may still be—"

"Nah then, cease thy daftish jubber," Lucas muttered. "Tha art worse nor a clackin' hen!"

"Lucas," Hugh said warningly, although he'd have said much the same.

"T' silly gobbins be a-jubberin' that he'd leather her ladyship! But he's no—"

"Enough," Hugh said, quelling him with a look and putting a hand under Jenny's elbow as they led the others onto the narrow timber bridge. Looking back, he saw Lucas gesture to Peg and Fiona to go ahead of him and Reid.

Just then, Jenny raised her voice to say, "Reid, I saw your friend."

"Which friend?"

Noting wariness in his response, Hugh's interest quickened and he kept silent.

"The man you rode with for a time on the way here," Jenny replied. "The two of you forded the river to Threave's islet together."

"How can he concern you?"

"I thought he looked familiar and wondered where I'd met him," she said.

Hugh said to Reid, "I recall the man she means. Who is he, lad?"

Reid said dismissively, "Just a chap I know."

"Then you know his name," Hugh said, keeping tight rein on his patience.

"Sir Alard Bowyer," Reid said. "He's a knight from Roxburgh, I think. I met him at our feast, so I warrant he's a friend of Dunwythie's."

"I've never heard of anyone called Bowyer," Fiona said. "But I do not know *many* of my father's friends. Also, I did not see him riding with you, Uncle Reid."

"How could you?" he said testily. "You traveled to Threave by boat."

They were nearing the gate, and Hugh saw Jenny look back and put a finger to her lips. An acknowledging nod told him Fiona understood and would keep silent.

Catching Tam Inglis's eye as they passed through the gate, Hugh motioned the guard captain over and said, "My lady tells me you recalled the escort you'd sent with her, Tam. That crowd out yonder nearly swallowed her up as she and these other two lasses were returning."

Tam's face paled. "I vow, Sir Hugh, I never recalled those men. I saw they'd returned, but I'd stepped away, so I assumed your lady had returned with them."

"Where are they now?" Hugh asked.

"Yonder," Tam said. He sent a lad to fetch them, and the two men came running. "Why did you two return without her ladyship?" Tam demanded.

"Why, her brother told us we'd no longer be needed, sir," one said, glancing anxiously at his companion for corroboration.

"Aye, sir, that be the truth," the second man agreed.

Hearing a muttered epithet from Reid, Hugh said, "Her ladyship has no brother. What did this fellow look like?"

The spokesman of the two frowned thoughtfully, looked Hugh up and down, and said, "He'd be a nobleman an inch or so shorter than what ye are, me lord. He's none so broad across the shoulders but muscular withal. I'd warrant he'd be one taking part in the tourneys, and mayhap some o' his lads wi' him."

"He was with a party of men, then?"

"Aye, we saw four others awaiting him whilst he spoke to us, mayhap more."

"Are you sure he was a nobleman?"

"Seemed like," the second man said. "He wore a short blue-velvet cloak, a cap wi' a fine plume, and leather boots that looked costly despite being all mucky."

Thanking the guardsmen, wondering what sort of nobleman would play such a trick but unwilling to discuss it there, Hugh urged his party toward the keep.

When they were beyond earshot of the guards, Jenny said, "Prithee, sir, I'd like Reid and Peg to discuss the incident with us after we see Fiona to her chamber."

Hugh looked at her, wondering what she was up to now and meaning to tell her in no uncertain terms that he and she would talk first, privately. But she gazed back at him, her expression so speaking that he glanced involuntarily at Reid.

His brother looked stunned, his face drained of color.

"You'll come with us then, lad," Hugh said to him. "You, too, Peg."

Surprising him, Reid said, "Aye, I think I must."

Peg said nothing.

Neither did Lucas, but Lucas would follow them with or without an invitation.

As they crossed the great hall toward the stairway, Jenny glanced at Peg. But Peg's brow was furrowed and she stared at the floor, apparently lost in thought.

Hugh's hand remained firm on Jenny's elbow until they reached the spiral stairway, when he urged her and Fiona to precede him. She was conscious of his presence behind her all the way upstairs but for once drew little comfort from it.

She could not blame him for being angry with her. She knew he fumed as much because she had left him sleeping while she went to the minstrel camp as from any fear that she might have met with danger.

He was unlikely to accept her need to find Peg as an excuse. Moreover, she admitted to herself that fortuitously meeting Fiona and her own impatience to *see* Peg and the others, rather than any need, had spurred her outside to the camp.

She was glad on two counts that he was letting Reid and Peg come with them. Not only did she hope they could help her explain what she suspected had happened but their presence might also shield her for a time from his anger.

That she and Hugh were again to take supper at the high table should shield her for an hour or two, as well. But she would have to face him alone eventually. And heaven knew what he would do or say then.

They came to Fiona and Mairi's chamber, one landing before their own, then went on as soon as Fiona had stepped inside. Peg, Reid, and Lucas followed them.

At their own landing, Hugh reached past Jenny to push open the door and entered ahead of her to hold it. When they were all inside, he shut it with a snap.

Jenny realized she was holding her breath, waiting for him to speak. Forcing herself to breathe slowly and deeply to calm her nerves, she wondered if he was doing likewise as he stood silently and looked at each of them in turn.

When his gaze met hers, he said, "Well, lass, what have you to say?"

She looked at Reid and said, "I mentioned your friend earlier because I thought the description the guardsmen gave us . . ." She paused, hoping Reid would feel obliged to supply the rest himself. But he just looked steadily back at her until she added, "I think the man you call Sir Alard Bowyer sent them away."

"I *call* him! Sakes, do you think that is not his name?"

Hugh said grimly, "Does the description fit him, Reid?"

"Aye, it does," Reid said. "Just as it fits half the other noblemen here."

"Then, why did you say you thought you should come up here when Jenny asked for you do so?"

"Because I'd feared . . ." He paused then until Jenny wondered why Hugh just seemed to hold his gaze and did not urge him to get on with it. But at last, Reid said, "He does fit their description. At least, he is wearing a short blue cloak, a plumed cap, and Spanish leather boots. So I did think I should tell you more about him."

"I think you must," Hugh agreed.

"At our feast, he introduced himself by asking me what I thought of the minstrels. He was looking to hire some to entertain at his place and had not done so before. I said I thought they were some of the best I'd seen. Then he wondered if I'd heard of a rash of thefts occurring at other houses where minstrels had performed."

"Thefts, eh?" Hugh said. "That *is* interesting."

"Aye, but I hadn't heard of any thefts then, and he did not suggest that the minstrels at our feast were responsible. In fact, he said he knew nowt of them. I knew little myself, but I said I'd heard that such folk were usually honest."

Jenny said, "When you left the table at the feast, you said you had to talk with a chap. Was that when you met Sir Alard Bowyer?"

He gave her a look. "I said that because I was tired of sitting there, ignored by the lass I was supposed to be marrying. I did meet him soon after that, though."

"Did he ask you anything else?" Jenny asked.

"Only if we'd taken precautions. I told him that Dunwythie, being a cautious man, had given orders to search anyone lacking first-head privileges or personally unknown to our guards. Bowyer agreed such precaution was wise and might avert trouble. That is all I knew of him till I met him again at Castle Mains."

~⁀⊃

Hugh thought he had heard more than enough about Bowyer until Reid added, "I did think it odd when he turned up at Castle Mains."

"Why?" Hugh asked.

"I don't know," Reid said. Faced with Hugh's skepticism, he added with a grimace, "It just seemed odd that he would be so delighted to see me on such a brief acquaintance, especially as I knew I'd been gey drunk when we met. But the reason I knew I must talk to you now is that I was sure Jenny had seen me with him."

"She said she had," Hugh reminded him.

Jenny said, "I think he means today, sir, out in that field."

"Is that it?" he asked Reid.

"Aye, I saw him at the same time I saw Jenny, before I came looking for you. But I swear I thought nowt of his being there until those guardsmen described the clothes he was wearing. If he told them he was her brother to deprive her of their protection . . . But why he would, I swear to you, Hugh, I cannot imagine."

Hugh saw Jenny catch her lower lip between her teeth and give Peg a long look. And Peg, who had remained silently thoughtful for some time, looked even more so as she met Jenny's gaze.

"I wondered why anyone would send that escort away," he said.

"Aye, but there's more," Reid said. "When you and I were looking for her, and that crowd around her suddenly thinned so we could see her, I saw him. He was hurrying away from her with a number of others."

Hugh said, "Did you see him, Jenny?"

"Nay, but . . ." Looking as she did at Peg then, and back at Reid, she might as well have voiced aloud her desire to speak privately with Hugh.

He said, "Reid, you and I must talk more later. We all need to change for supper, and I have much yet to say to these two. But you and I will put our heads together on this. Whatever comes of it, I thank you for coming to fetch me."

Reid glanced at Jenny as if he would say more but left without doing so.

"D'ye want me to go, too, mistress?" Lucas asked with unnatural diffidence when the door had shut with Reid on the other side of it.

Jenny hesitated, glancing at Peg. Hugh was about to tell Lucas they could do without him when she said, "Nay, Lucas. I doubt I'll keep many secrets from you."

"*Is* it a secret, lass?" Hugh asked.

"I doubt I'll keep any at all from you, sir," she said with a little smile. "If I'm right, I have already told you about the incident in question, but I'd liefer not tell Reid." She turned to Peg. "What *did* you see after that man grabbed you out there?"

"Grabbed!" Hugh exclaimed.

Without taking her eyes from Peg, Jenny held up a hand to him. "What, Peg?"

"It wasna so much seeing, mistress," Peg said. " 'Twas hearing his voice first and seeing his face after."

"Ah," Jenny said. "I, too, heard a familiar voice but did not believe my ears."

"Nay, for what would one o' *them* be a-doing here?"

"Who?" Hugh demanded.

Peg looked at Jenny. "Did ye tell him about them, mistress?"

"Aye," Jenny said. "So tell us who you saw today."

" 'Twas one o' them English from Lochmaben, me lord. The ones . . ." Again she looked to Jenny for reassurance.

Hugh said, "The men who accosted the two of you by the garderobe?"

"Aye," Peg said, looking relieved that he did know.

"The one who grabbed me today were one o' them for sure."

"And the man calling himself Bowyer is the other one," Jenny said. "His face has been teasing me since I first saw him with Reid. But at Lochmaben he was just another man-at-arms, one who did not talk much. And although I fear you will say I am still dreaming, I think his may be one of the voices in my dream."

Hugh said, "Have you heard his voice since, to compare?"

"I don't know, but just before the man who grabbed Peg spoke to her, I heard a similar voice yell, 'Beware ahead, lads, let be!' Reid said he saw Bowyer rush away from there, so he may be the one who shouted. You did suggest that the voices in my dream may have been English, sir, like Cuddy's. What's more, Cath said Cuddy's cousin Drogo is here somewhere, and he is also English."

Peg said, "But why would that Bowyer warn anyone that Sir Hugh were coming? Them English canna ken that ye be married to him."

"You forget, Peg, that Lochmaben is where Hugo and I first sang together," Jenny said. "The way we sang the love song was one of the reasons you and the others thought we'd make a good match. Moreover, I am wearing the same kirtle I wore then, and Sir Hugh is wearing breeks and a jack-o'-plate that any Borderer might, with no sign of his rank. He needed only look as if he took interest in us to scare them away, particularly if they harbored ill intent toward us."

Peg raised her eyebrows at that. "He did look right fierce, mistress."

"Bowyer also knows Reid, and he was with me," Hugh

reminded them, knowing how fierce he must have looked even before he had seen Jenny. "If they are up to mischief here, they doubtless recognized you two from Lochmaben and tried to grab you to keep you from identifying them as English men-at-arms."

Jenny explained her suspicion to Peg that someone was plotting mischief or worse against Archie the Grim. "I did not tell you before, because I could not explain why I felt as I did, and I could not chance spreading such a rumor."

"And ye ken fine I'd likely ha' told Bryan," Peg said. "If that Drogo be involved in summat that's wrong, Cath willna be surprised. But Cuddy?"

"That is another odd thing," Jenny said to Hugh. "Although the two men who escorted us to the minstrels' camp said the one who had sent them away told them he was my brother, Cuddy told us that another *guards*man had come to say they were needed on the field because the men at practice would be stopping soon for dinner and were all armed. They did stop to eat, sir. So who lied?"

"Cuddy," he said without hesitation. "The two guardsmen had no cause to lie and reason to think the truth might help them avoid their captain's wrath, and mine. I'd guess Cuddy heard what Bowyer said—if it was Bowyer—and doubting you had any brothers here, altered his description and tale to something you would believe."

That statement reminded him that he still wanted to know why the devil she had not asked a couple of stout lads from the camp to see them back safely.

"Nah then, if ye want any supper, sir, ye'll 'ave to stop maulin' this about till later," Lucas said with a shrewd look as he moved to one of the kists containing Hugh's things. "And ye'll 'ave to bestir yourself, Peg-lass, or our mistress will look a proper sloven at t' table. Ye'll find a screen ye can drag out for 'er by t' window."

~⁓

Jenny looked at Hugh and saw his chiseled features form an expression of uncharacteristic indecision. She knew he itched to scold her, but she doubted he would do so while Peg and Lucas were there unless he meant to scold Peg, too.

It occurred to her only then that he might have words for Lucas, too, for leaving the landing after Hugh had told him to stay there. But although he had told Reid he had much to say to her and to Peg, she could not imagine what Peg might have done to incur his displeasure.

Therefore, she was not surprised when he murmured agreement with Lucas and told him to bestir himself as well. After that, they all hurried.

While Peg got the screen and set it up, Jenny slipped her dirk and its belt and sheath from one of her kists and concealed it by wrapping it in a fresh shift. Behind the screen, she grinned when Peg's eyes widened as she uncovered the weapon.

Peg only shook her head and helped Jenny dress. But when Jenny told her she would wear only a lacy veil and pin up her plaits beneath it, at her nape, Hugh said firmly from the other side of the screen, "Wear a proper caul as well, lass. I'll not tell you to pluck out your eyebrows or shave your forehead, because I like your own look better. But recall that the minstrels will perform tonight. I'd liefer none recognize you at the high table."

Jenny opened her mouth to protest, but Peg spoke first.

"How can they not, sir?" she asked. "They'll see *Hugo* on the dais, and ye'll no be wearing breeks and a jack there. Ye'll look much as ye do in your troubadour's garb, and ye canna pretend to be any man save yourself at high table. Also, for all that *she'll* be on the ladies' side, them in the company will be amazed to see *ye* there, and they'll ha' only to look to guess who ye be with. A caul doesna change her *that* much."

Jenny had given thought to the Englishmen again. "I'll wear the caul, Peg," she said calmly. "It will not fool the minstrels, but it *might* keep Bowyer and his men from recognizing me if they are also in the hall."

"It may at that," Lucas said wisely with a look at Hugh. "Men see what they expect to see, aye, laird?"

"They do," Hugh said. "Do you mean to stand holding my doublet all evening or may I put it on?"

"Nah then, hold your whist. I'm movin' as quick as a man can. How many d'ye think yon English be? Could they seize this great castle from within?"

"Their number is something we'd be wise to discover," Hugh said. "But I doubt they can seize the castle. Most of those banners outside are as familiar to me as the people flying them are. And most of them are strong Douglas allies."

"They clearly are not *all* Scots," Jenny said. "And if his grace is coming—"

"Nay, then, he is not," Lucas said. "I did ask, sithee, and they say his grace the King sent his thanks for the honor but excused hisself from the occasion."

"'Tis just as well," Hugh said. "I doubt Archie expected him to attend, for he has not mentioned it. He was bound to invite him to celebrate the anniversary of his own coronation, but the Kirk will offer masses in his honor all over Scotland."

Emerging from behind the screen, Jenny said thought-fully, "If his grace is not coming and the English cannot seize this castle, why *are* they here?"

"I suspect the commander at Lochmaben has simply sent a few of his lads to take a close look at Threave's defenses," he said.

"But someone told me, when we were there, that the Annandale men kept the English pent up in Lochmaben," Jenny countered.

"Aye, sure," he said. "They keep them from sending out parties to harass the surrounding countryside. But it can be no great feat for a few determined men to slip out now and again. 'Tis dangerous business, to be sure, but danger is rarely a deterrent when a commander demands information."

She knew he spoke from experience, but she did not see how an English plan to have a look at Threave—even to send spies there—explained the feelings she had had while she traveled with the minstrels. Nor did it explain the attack on the knacker or the missing jewelry.

That last thought reminded her that Bowyer had been at Annan House, and Cuddy's cousin had been there, too, for Cath had told her so. She turned to tell Hugh. But they had no more time for talk, because he was opening the door and murmuring last-minute orders to Lucas. She'd just have to keep her eyes open.

⁓

Having decided to watch Cuddy and to keep an eye out for Bowyer and his henchmen, Hugh had asked Lucas to do likewise. Believing the Englishmen could hardly present themselves as close friends of Archie's, Hugh expected them to take their meals outside the castle gates. He said so when Jenny asked him as they left their chamber if he would tell Archie the English were so near at hand.

"I'll tell him," Hugh said. "But I warrant it won't trouble him. I expect he'll say their presence just proves that his tournament is serving its purpose, which is to show off the strength of Threave. But that's enough about all that for now, lass. We'll talk more later, when we're alone."

He saw her nibble her lip and knew she had taken his last words as a warning and not just a promise. So be it, he thought.

She wore a gown of soft, rose-colored, branched velvet with elaborate—and enticing—gold front lacing. Over it, she wore a long particolored and embroidered mantle of lavender and pale green silk, held at her shoulders by clasps at each end of a narrow jeweled band. Her caul and the long veil at its back were lavender.

The din of conversation in the hall made Hugh's head begin to ache again. The noise was so loud he could barely hear the musicians in the minstrel gallery.

He and Jenny no sooner reached the dais than blaring horns announced the entry of carvers and their carts of beef and venison. Hastily escorting Jenny to her place near the end of the ladies' side, he found his next to the last one of the men's.

He had known he would not sit near Archie, because the gathering at Threave included many nobles of higher rank than himself, not least of whom was the gray-haired Bishop of Glasgow, sitting at Archie's right. Casting a glance in that direction, Hugh looked next for Dunwythie, then for his family and Reid, wondering as he did if Phaeline might yet manage to secure an annulment.

He let himself hope that the distance between him and Jenny would prevent anyone from linking them, but it also made it nearly impossible for him to keep an eye on her. Having given Lucas orders to keep *his* eyes open and to get Peg to help him, Hugh hoped he had done enough.

He knew he was not thinking as clearly or as quickly as usual. He knew, too, that he had been glib in answering Jenny's question about the English presence at Threave. He tried now to imagine why that should seem important.

⁓

Jenny, sitting between two much older ladies who apparently knew each other, offered to change her seat with the one who sat at the end of the table as soon as the bishop had spoken the grace before meat. Responding politely to the woman's gratitude, she turned her attention to the minstrels and to the pompous ritual accompanying meals served to the Lord of Galloway and his guests.

Service was quick on the dais. And once the carvers had finished and the meat platters at the high table were full, other carts moved toward the long trestle tables standing perpendicular to the dais, and serving continued. As it did, jugglers ran into the U-shaped space formed by the dais and the four tables flanking it, two to a side.

As Jenny ate, she watched the entertainment idly until she realized that Cuddy was not with the musicians in the gallery. He strolled along the aisles between the trestle tables with Cath, Gerda, and Gib the gittern player instead, all smiling and chatting with folks as the jugglers performed nearby.

When the jugglers ran off, Gawkus and Gilly ran in. Smiling at their antics, Jenny looked for Cuddy and saw him palm a brooch or pin from a lady's coif. His victim, laughing at the fools, started when he touched her shoulder. As she turned, Cuddy seemed to pull her jewel from the ear of the gentleman sitting next to her.

People nearby smiled, then returned their attention to the fools.

When Cath produced a scarf from thin air and handed it to another gentleman, Jenny watched more closely. They had not engaged in sleight of hand during the fools' turn at Castle Moss, Lochmaben, or in Dumfries market square. Could those be the skills, she wondered, to which Gib had referred when, thinking she was Cath, he'd shouted to know if they should try them on the crowd that night or wait for a larger audience? She wished she could discuss *that* question with Hugh.

A gillie whisked by close behind her, startling her. As she turned to watch, he vanished through the archway to a service stair near her end of the dais. Her gaze collided with Peg's when the latter peeped in from the landing.

Glancing around to make sure the two ladies to her right were still engaged in their conversation, Jenny got up and slipped out through the archway.

"What are you doing here, Peg?" she demanded. "Is aught amiss?"

"Ay de mi, but that Lucas will snatch me baldheaded," Peg said. "He said I weren't to let ye see me. But how I'm to keep me eyes on ye without looking, I canna say, and nor can he, I'll wager. Be Bryan and them out there now?"

"Nay, Gilly and Gawkus are. But Cath, Cuddy, Gib, and Gerda are performing sleight of hand, too, strolling behind people at the tables."

"May I look?"

"We'd be wiser to find another archway to look through," Jenny said. "I do think Cuddy's up to something though, and mayhap Cath and the others are, too."

"I dinna like to think they'd be doing aught that's bad," Peg said.

Jenny agreed, but her concern for them only strengthened her curiosity. "Do you know how to get to the main stairway from here?"

"Aye, sure," Peg said. "But ought we—"

"We'll say we're visiting the garderobe if anyone asks," Jenny said. "I just want to see what they are doing, and you said they were teaching you, so mayhap you'll see more than I will. They always fool me."

Peg led the way upstairs to the next landing, through an antechamber there, and onto a gallery that led to the main stairway. Hurrying down, they reached the great-hall entrance. A number of people stood watching the fools just inside the entry arch, and Jenny and Peg were able to slip in among them unchallenged.

Peg watched for only a few moments before she grabbed Jenny's arm and urged her toward the exit. On the landing, she murmured, "They be taking two items for every one they return. What d'ye think they'll be doing wi' the rest?"

"I don't know," Jenny said. "But we must tell Sir Hugh. If we return to the dais, I can ask one of the gillies there to take a message to him." She could also, she hoped, return to her own seat before Hugh realized she had been gone.

Reversing their route, they hurried upstairs and along the gallery to the anteroom. As Jenny entered, she heard a muffled squeak from Peg.

Turning, she found Bowyer right behind her. "So we were right," he said. "Now, what was a fine lady like you doing at Lochmaben with common minstrels?"

The man who had tried to grab Peg earlier—and had been with Bowyer when the two accosted them at Lochmaben—stood behind him with a hand clapped over Peg's mouth and his other arm tight around her waist. "Up or down?" he muttered.

"Up," Bowyer said, grabbing Jenny. "Fewer servants are likely to be on these stairs. We'll stow them in one of those wee rooms we found below the ramparts."

Peg struggled to free herself and managed to cry out before the man clapped his hand over her mouth again. But she fought so hard that they ended up with him holding her face down across a knee as he tried to right himself. Slapping her hard, he managed then to gag her before he picked her up again to carry her.

Bowyer was still holding Jenny tightly by an arm, and when she tried to jerk loose, he showed her a dagger. "I'd not want to mar that lovely face or put an end to ye, lass, but I'll not hesitate if I must. We want only to put ye somewhere safe where ye'll not interfere with our plans tonight. Mayhap ye can even help us see our plans through. Go quietly up the stairs, and we'll stay friendly-like."

She obeyed, hoping to find a better chance for escape. Peg was quiet, so all Jenny heard was the sound of the men's footsteps until a familiar voice said, "Nah then, where d'ye think ye be a-takin' them lasses, ye gallous knaves?"

Bowyer's henchman turned without hesitation and, hitching Peg higher in his arms, kicked Lucas down the stairs. Then, hurrying upstairs without meeting anyone else, the two men deposited Jenny and Peg in a dark, cell-like room under the ramparts—gagged, sitting on a hard timber floor, and bound to wooden posts.

Chapter 20

Hugh had finished eating and was wondering how much more entertainment his aching head could stand when it came to him that the reason he had suggested for the English presence at Threave did not explain enough.

Thanks to his years of mimicry, he had an excellent memory for dialogue and, particularly now, for things that Jenny had said to him.

Despite his pounding head, he summoned up her description of her meeting in the woods their first day in Dumfries, with the lads who had mistaken her for Cath. One had said somebody wanted nothing to get in the way of their performance at Threave. So perhaps this performance was important in itself. Jenny had, he decided, been right to suggest to Archie as she had that there had been too much talk of Threave. If the minstrels had helped mischief-makers get inside the castle, perhaps they had helped the same mischief-makers get into Annan House and other places.

Believing that Cuddy's lying to Jenny about the man

who had dismissed her escort that afternoon proved that Cuddy was involved, Hugh looked for him now.

The dancers were performing, but he soon saw Cuddy, Cath, and some others strolling about, engaging in acts of legerdemain to the amusement of watchers and victims alike. He had seen several of minstrels perform magic tricks, especially the Joculator. But he had never seen them do so while others performed.

Seeing that now stirred a new train of thought.

Archie's guests included not only the Bishop of Glasgow but also many of the wealthiest, most powerful lords in southwest Scotland and the Borders. If thievery was taking place right under Archie's nose, it would be more than an embarrassment.

How powerful would folks think the Lord of Galloway, after all, if he could not keep his guests' belongings safe in his strongest—supposedly impregnable—fortress? And who in the area could gain most by undermining Archie's power and influence?

Deciding the sooner he talked to Jenny again the better, Hugh stood and turned toward the ladies' end to fetch her, only to see that her place was empty.

Muttering a curse, he strode to Archie instead, waited impatiently for a pause in his discussion with the bishop, and then said, "If I may interrupt you, my lord, I would ask leave to look into a certain matter."

Archie raised his eyebrows as he met Hugh's gaze, then glanced out at the minstrels before he said, "I've lads watching them, Hugh. Two stand right behind us."

"Aye, sir, but you should know that men from Lochmaben are here to view your tournament or even to take part. At least one of them previously gained access to other noble houses, so I'd like to see if I can spot him inside the castle."

"If he *has* got in," Archie said, "I hope he takes a good look and goes back to tell his comrades-in-arms that Threave will defy their strongest attempt to seize it."

"Doubtless he will," Hugh said. "But I'm thinking he may make mischief here first. I must also seek my lady wife. She has been away overlong."

"Sakes, don't tell me the lass has run off again!"

Hugh smiled. "Nay, my lord, I'll find her easily enough."

"Before you go, I must make you known to his eminence, the Bishop of Glasgow," Archie said with a wicked twinkle in his eyes. "My lord, this is Douglas of Thornhill. I believe you recently provided him with a special license to marry."

"Aye, sure, I approved it," the gray-haired bishop said in a gravelly voice. "I am pleased to make your acquaintance, Sir Hugh, although I own to some distress at learning that your lady's family seeks an annulment."

"Mayhap they do, but we do not," Hugh replied bluntly.

"Ah, but if a prior betrothal *does* exist—"

"Forgive me, my lord, but that betrothal was improper—unlawful, too. My lady is a baroness in her own right, capable of reading, understanding, and signing any marriage settlement. Yet they said nowt to her about her own and insisted she betroth herself to my brother without telling her they had granted him title to her barony, although she had steadfastly said she did not want him. If the Kirk requires evidence, I will supply it. In the meantime, if you will forgive me, I must find her."

With a nod to the bishop and one to Archie, and his concern mounting with every minute that Jenny failed to return, Hugh went without further ado to find her, only to meet a battered-looking and angry Lucas first.

"Laird, t' blighted English 'ave took your lady—aye, *and* that Peg lass, too," Lucas said. "They kicked me down t' stairs, and though I'm no dead yet, I'd me doots whether I could best 'em on me own. So I came to fetch ye to do it."

"Show me where this happened," Hugh ordered, trying to ignore the chill that shot up his spine at the thought of Jenny in any man's hands but his own.

———

Gagged and alone with Peg in the small, dark chamber, Jenny struggled to loosen her bonds until Peg said quietly, "I'll be wi' ye in a trice, mistress."

Astonished, Jenny was more so when she felt Peg feeling for her gag and tugging its knot. "How did you get free?" she demanded when she could speak.

"Aye, well, ye ken how Cath and them ha' been teaching me their magic tricks," Peg said, as she touched the rope binding Jenny to the post. "'Tis how I could see what Cuddy were doing below, and how I slipped this dirk out o' yon English ill-doer's boot when he dropped me over his knee."

"But how did he not feel you take it or see the blade in your hand?"

"I pinched him with one hand as I slipped his dirk into a fold o' me skirt wi' the other. Then, after they brought us here, I slid m'self low on me post as he wrapped the rope round me, wi' me arms at me sides, so I could get at the hilt when they left us. This blade be gey sharp, mistress," she added. "So keep still now."

"You did well," Jenny said. "I just hope they did not lock the door."

When she was free of the post—one of several supporting shelves along the wall—she stood and lifted her skirt to take her own dirk from its sheath. Recalling that Hugh and Gilly had warned her against using it to defend herself, she clutched it tightly anyway, telling herself that as she and Peg were now both armed, they should manage to make it safely back to the hall.

Feeling her way to the door, she put a hand on the latch and held her breath as she silently lifted it. Then, slowly, gently, she pushed the door ajar and sent up a prayer of thanks when it met no resistance. Inching the opening wider, she peeked out. Moonlight from a high window revealed that the chamber beyond was empty.

Moving as silently as before, she led the way toward the stairway until shadowy movement on the landing stopped her in her tracks. Gesturing to Peg, she eased close to the wall, hoping that whoever had moved would not look back.

Nearly certain from the shape that the man ahead of them was Bowyer, she reminded herself that his chief henchman might be just a short distance away.

As she crept closer, she saw the figure move furtively off the landing, down the stairway. Motioning again to Peg, Jenny followed.

Hugh led the way swiftly to the service stairs and up them. When they reached the next level, he glanced back to mutter, "Art armed, Lucas?"

"I've me dirk, 'aven't I? And nae one inside has a sword, I'm thinkin', save the guardsmen. They went higher nor this, laird," he added. "I did 'ear that much."

Hugh hurried onward as silently as was commensurate with speed. He heard nothing above him but rounded a curve to meet a booted foot thrusting hard at his head. Ducking to his right, he avoided the direct kick but took the brunt of it on his left shoulder. It knocked him off balance and back against the wall.

The advantage lay, as it nearly always did in a confrontation on the wedge-shaped steps of a spiral stairway, with the man coming down. The one going up had to hug his right-hand wall to maintain his footing. Unless he was left-handed, that necessity impeded his weapon hand, while the man coming down enjoyed the better footing near the wall to his left with his weapon in his free hand.

Hugh's attacker did not wait for him to regain his balance but flung himself at him with dagger in hand. Hugh deftly parried the blade with his left forearm, but with his right arm pinned between his body and the wall, his own dirk was useless.

Below him on the stairs, Lucas could not aid him and was in imminent danger of being knocked downstairs a second time. As Hugh's assailant moved to strike again, a second dirk flew from above and struck hilt-first against the man's right temple, hard enough to knock his head into the wall with an audible crack.

His weapon fell from his grasp, and he lurched heavily against Hugh.

Hugh grabbed him and made sure Lucas had snatched up the attacker's dirk before looking up to see Jenny a few steps above, watching them.

"That's the one who calls himself Bowyer," she said calmly. "Did I kill him?"

"Nay, lass, you just clouted him a good one. The wall did the rest. I think the best thing for us to do now is to make a gift of him to Archie. You come along, too, Peg," he added, seeing her anxious face appear around the curve above Jenny.

"His chief henchman is here somewhere, too," Jenny said. "It was he who kicked Lucas down the stairs when he tried to prevent them from taking us."

"Tell me what else they did," Hugh said grimly.

Hastily Jenny explained, assuring Hugh that neither she nor Peg had suffered any more than a loss of dignity from their capture and brief confinement.

"We will discuss your part in all this later," he said, still grim. "Have you any idea where the other chap may have gone?"

"When they caught us, we were coming to tell you that we'd seen Cuddy and Cath lifting more items with their sleight of hand than they returned to their victims," Jenny said. "Bowyer and his man caught us minutes afterward, so they must have seen us and realized what *we* had seen. That can only mean they knew what Cuddy and Cath were doing, sir, but I don't know how they *could* know."

"Cuddy will tell us," Hugh said in such a way that she

did not question it. "This chap seems to be awake now," he added. "So mayhap he will talk, too."

Bowyer glowered at him but said nothing.

Meekly, Jenny said, "I expect I should return to my place at the high table."

"You and Peg will stay with me," Hugh said. "I don't want *you* out of my sight again until we have solved this puzzle."

"D'ye really mean to give that ill-doin' lout to his lordship *now*?" Peg asked.

"Archie's men are watching the minstrels," Hugh said. "Two stand just at the rear of the dais, so we can give him to them to hold until we find his friend."

"You'd do better to let us go," Bowyer muttered as Hugh pulled him upright. "I doubt Archie Douglas wants to stir trouble now with England by holding us."

"That is not my decision to make," Hugh told him. "Make sure he does not have more weapons on him, Lucas. And you two," he added with a stern look at Jenny and Peg, "had better keep well behind us and out of his reach."

He fixed that stern look on Jenny alone then, as if to add that she had better stay out of *his* reach, too. But as he turned to push Bowyer into Lucas's waiting grasp, she stepped down close behind him and put a hand gently to his cheek.

The jolt through Hugh's body from her touch nearly undid him. Turning to face her, he drew her closer and looked into her beautiful face.

"Ah, Jenny-love, I don't know what I'm going to do with you."

Her eyes twinkled. "You'll think of something, sir."

Smiling then, he said, "Aye, sweetheart, I will."

Then, giving her a quick hug, he turned to follow Lucas and their captive downstairs to the dais landing. As they neared it, Lucas stopped and put up a hand.

Hugh had realized at nearly the same moment that the hall was unnaturally silent. Slipping past Lucas and Bowyer, he saw that the Joculator stood just below the dais in his long red-and-black surcoat, juggling scythes. He turned this way and that, silently inviting every man and woman in his audience to watch closely.

"Do you see Cuddy and Cath?" Jenny whispered from above Hugh.

He caught sight of them just as Cuddy, taking advantage of the audience's rapt attention on the Joculator, slipped something into his baggy doublet. Then, turning away from Cath, he strolled toward the back of the hall.

For once, the man carried no instrument, but Hugh saw him nod to someone ahead of him in a group crowded near the hall entrance.

A man wearing breeks and a leather jack emerged from that little crowd.

The Joculator produced a lighted torch just then, tossed it to join the scythes, and then turned to look straight at Hugh.

Bowyer drew in a breath, but Hugh clapped a hand hard across the man's mouth, stifling any outcry before he could make it.

Without missing toss or catch, the Joculator gave a slight nod.

Just then, behind him, Gawkus and Gilly flitted across the open space and others of the company, including Cath and Gerda, moved toward Cuddy and the other man, surrounding them as Cuddy clapped the leather-clad man on the back.

The Joculator whirled, and his long cloak swirled. Scythes and torch, the latter still alight, dropped neatly into the agile hands.

Dropping the scythes at his feet, the Joculator passed a hand over the torch.

The flame went out, but as he silently faced the dais, a scuffle erupted at the back of the hall, drawing everyone else's attention.

Archie roared, "What the devil is the row back there?"

A man-at-arms shouted back, "We've got a sack o' jewels here, m'lord!"

"Bring it here to me, one of you."

"Sakes, m'lord, this chap's got several sacks on 'im! In troth, these two—"

"Bring those men forward, too," Archie bellowed.

Men-at-arms escorted Cuddy and his friend to the foot of the dais.

"That's Bowyer's henchman," Jenny hissed from behind Hugh.

"With respect, my lord," Hugh said, motioning to the armed men behind Archie and taking Bowyer onto the dais. "I have one more who belongs with them."

At a nod from Archie, the men-at-arms took Bowyer in charge.

"Put him with the others," Archie ordered. "Which of you would speak?"

"An it please ye, my lord, I will," Cuddy said, stepping forward a pace.

Archie nodded.

"Though I think o' m'self now as a Scot, my lord, this man here be me gallous cousin Drogo from England," Cuddy said, gesturing toward Bowyer's henchman. "He serves at Lochmaben wi' that 'un what our Hugo caught, who likes to pose as a nobleman. The two o' them said they'd kill me, me wife and daughter, and anyone else wha' got in their way, did we no collect jewels for them tonight. They did capture our Bonnie Jenny, too, and said they'd kill her, as well," he added.

"If I ask them who they are and what they are doing here, will they tell me the same?" Archie said, "Or will they say you are lying and are as guilty as they are?"

"By your leave, my lord," the Joculator said in a quiet but nonetheless carrying voice, "I would speak for this man."

"Aye, sure," Archie said. "I expect you will tell me that no member of your company or any other minstrel would ever even consider stealing from my guests."

"By my troth, my lord—"

"By the Rood," Archie snapped back. "Your word means little more than the word of your man there or those chappies beside him. Why should I believe *you*?"

"Because I am more at fault than my man is," the Joculator said. "The original idea was mine own."

⌒

Jenny clapped a hand over her mouth and moved onto the dais to stand by Hugh, so she could watch the Joculator more closely.

The silence that had greeted his statement began to fill with restless whispers and movement until Archie said curtly, "Explain yourself, sirrah."

"Aye, sure, my lord, for I did begin it all," the Joculator said, meeting Archie's stern gaze. "I believe that a man must take responsibility for his actions—any man, commoner or lord o' the land."

"I expect you mean something by that statement," Archie said.

"Only that I am much to blame for what happened here tonight—as ye are, my lord. Actions have consequences, and an action of yours some years ago led me and my company here tonight—aye, and these English villains, too."

"Do you dare tell me that *I* am responsible?"

"Ye are, my lord, but only in part. Seven years ago, soon after ye'd imposed your rule on Galloway, ye held a feast at Castle Mains and hired minstrels to amuse your guests. One of those minstrels was a young fool whose comments on the harshness of your rule offended ye. For that offense, ye sentenced him to death." He paused. "That lad, sir, was my son."

A collective gasp greeted the declaration.

"Now, see here," Archie began. "I never—"

The Joculator interrupted, saying, "These may be my last words, my lord, so I would finish if ye'll permit me." Without awaiting that permission, he said, "Unlike more experienced fools, the lad had failed to learn that the trick is not to lie or to overstate a powerful man's faults for humor's sake but always to speak truth to such men. The greater trick is to make them laugh when one does it. My son thought it enough to make *others* laugh or merely to stun them to silence. Because he was not clever enough to speak as a fool, my lord, he was much a fool to speak so to ye."

"He was, aye," Archie agreed, although Jenny noted that his voice was less harsh than usual. "But he did not deserve to die, nor did I order his death," he added. "I recall that lad, sithee, and I did order him out of the castle for his insults, because although I knew it snowed, I did not know how heavily. Castle Mains lies less than a mile from Kirkcudbright, where I knew he'd find shelter. You won't care that I was horrified to learn of his death, but by my troth, sir, that is true."

"I do care, my lord," the Joculator said quietly.

"'Twas dreadful, and tragic," Archie said, speaking directly to him as if no one else were there. "My men found him on the sands the next morning when the tide was out. We did give him a Christian burial, but that is not enough, I know."

"Not enough to bring him back, certainly," the Joculator agreed. "But that *is* something I did not know, my lord, and it is something of a comfort to learn. I had feared wolves might have got him, or that the sea had swept him away."

"My lord, may I speak?" Tam Inglis said from the back of the hall.

When Archie nodded, Tam stepped forward and said to the Joculator, "I were newly captain o' the guard at Castle Mains then, sir, and I sent me own lads out when I saw how the snow had thickened, to see if they could find him. When they found nae sign o' him, we decided he'd made it safe to the town. It appalled us all to find the poor lad on the sand next morning. He must ha' missed his step and fallen into the water from the wharf or walkway. It be sma' comfort, sir, but cold as that water were, he'd no ha' suffered long."

The Joculator nodded. "I thank ye for telling me that." Turning back to Archie, he said, "Doubtless, ye wonder how my friend Cuddy here comes into it."

"I do."

"My original plan was to seek vengeance by revealing that even the Lord of Galloway is not omnipotent. But, contrary to what some might think, particularly now, we minstrels are by necessity an honest lot. We do not steal, nor did we intend to steal from ye or your guests. My plan, which emerged out of a dangerous mixture of grief and fury, was to show just how easily we *might* have done so, by doubling the number of items we lifted and returning only half during the performance here. The rest we would have returned at some point afterward."

"By my troth, sir, you may be as big a fool as your son to tell me so."

"Ye may be right, my lord, but I found when we tried it out in a great house that I cared less for vengeance than for the honor of my people. I decided then against proceeding with that plan. However, Cuddy had foolishly revealed it to his cousin Drogo, a musician who sometimes traveled with us. I learned from sheriff's men who recently searched our camp in Dumfries that they suspected we had stolen jewelry from other houses where we had performed. We'd taken naught, my lord, but Drogo had performed with us at each of those houses."

"I warrant he would deny having aught to do with thievery," Archie said.

"I took nowt," Drogo said gruffly.

"Learning of those thefts," the Joculator continued, "I confronted Cuddy and learned that these two Englishmen were forcing him to proceed with our erstwhile plan here at Threave. They threatened him and his family, as you heard, on orders from their commander at Lochmaben, and were determined the mischief should be theft pure and simple, my lord. And that all blame should fall to our company."

"Nevertheless," Archie said, frowning, "you've as good as admitted that your people took the things. And though they may have done so under duress . . ."

"We can discuss at a more auspicious time whether I did admit any such thing, my lord," the Joculator said. "But I suspect the evidence will show that only these two Englishmen have kept anything taken from your guests tonight. I can confidently say that neither Cuddy nor *any* of my people holds stolen property."

"That would surprise me," Archie admitted, looking to Tam Inglis. "What say you, Tam? Did your guardsmen not find such things on this Cuddy chap here?"

"Nay, my lord, only on that one who stepped out to meet him, and *he* had much. In troth, sir, 'twas the minstrels that caught him. That Cuddy just walked up, clapped him on the back, and the others surrounded them. They must ha' seen him lifting summat and moved to stop him afore he could get away with it."

"Here now," Drogo exclaimed. " 'Twas nowt o' the sort! They must ha' slipped them things into me clothes!"

Ignoring him, the Joculator pointed to Bowyer and said, "If your men search him, I suspect they will find that he is also carrying stolen property, my lord. I saw him here in the hall earlier, but I believe he has been in

Sir Hugh Douglas's custody or that of your guardsmen for some time since then."

"Search him," Archie ordered.

The two men-at-arms who had taken Bowyer to join the others proceeded to search him despite his protests, until one produced a pouch from Bowyer's fashionably baggy sleeve.

"Here now, that's my purse!" Bowyer exclaimed.

At Archie's nod, the guard opened the pouch, revealing no coins but a gold collar studded with colorful gems and two pairs of earrings set with others.

Seeing them, Jenny bit back a smile, wondering how the minstrels had managed that bit of legerdemain. Knowing their skills, she had no doubt that one of them had contrived earlier to slip the pouch into Bowyer's clothing, thus casting the blame for the thefts right back where it belonged. She dared not look at Hugh, knowing he would suspect the same and fearing that Archie might, too.

"Throw that pair in the dungeon," Archie said, indicating Drogo and Bowyer. "I'll deal with them anon. Then see that every piece of jewelry they took gets back to its owner. As for you, sir," he added with a sardonic look at the Joculator. "I'm thinking that you're a clever chap *and* a brave one. 'Tis plain, too, that you are far more skilled than most at the arts and tricks of your craft."

Jenny held her breath, fearing Archie *did* suspect they had planted the jewels.

"However," he went on as Bowyer and his man left the hall with their escort, "I have no doubt that, instead of taking vengeance this night as you might have, you have done me a signal service and thus have put me further in your debt."

The Joculator stood silently, neither agreeing nor disagreeing.

"I'd have been in a quandary what to do with those two," Archie went on. "Whilst I'm strongly inclined to hang them for their mischief here, I don't want to create trouble with England by doing so. Moreover, I had hoped they would take word of Threave's strength back to Lochmaben to discourage the rest of that lot from more mischief. Thanks to your cleverness, I can now simply return them to their commander. The man lacks both a charitable nature and a sense of humor, and will be gey displeased that they failed to carry out his orders."

Smiling in a way that sent a chill up Jenny's spine, he added, "I'm sure I can trust him to punish them for me. Meantime, we'll keep them quietly below, and I hope you and your people will continue to entertain us throughout the tournament."

"It will be our honor, my lord," the Joculator said.

"But no more legerdemain involving my guests," Archie said sternly.

The Joculator bowed, murmuring, "As ye wish, my lord."

Tam Inglis approached the dais then. "Beg pardon, m'lord, but we've returned all the jewels save this gold bangle and these pearl ear-bobs, which were in this wee pouch stuck in that villain Drogo's right boot. D'ye think they'd be his?"

"I do not," Archie said. "Likely someone will claim them, so I'll keep them. I do want to continue our conversation, as you suggested earlier," he said to the Joculator. "But, prithee, for now tell your people we would enjoy more music."

The Joculator looked thoughtfully from Jenny to Hugh, whereupon Hugh left the dais and approached him.

Jenny thought she knew what the Joculator wanted them to do, and having no idea how Hugh would react to a request that they sing together, she was half relieved and half disappointed when the Joculator nodded to Cuddy, then turned and motioned to Gawkus and Gilly.

Gilly, on stilts, immediately stepped into the open space, guiding a stiff-jointed Gawkus on strings as if he were a puppet. Their audience burst into laughter, which increased as Gawkus pranced stiffly about in apparent response to his master.

As they performed, the musicians began to play in the gallery, and Hugh and the Joculator stepped onto the dais. Without a word to Jenny, they went next to Archie and Hugh bent to talk to him.

When Archie nodded, Hugh returned to Jenny, saying, "I want you to go upstairs now, lass, whilst I talk briefly with the Joculator. I have questions that still require answers. I know that you do, too," he added swiftly as she was about to protest. "But I ask you to trust me in this and go now if Peg and Lucas are still outside that archway. If they are not, I'll summon an escort for you."

"I see Peg now," she said. "So I'll go, Hugo, but prithee, don't be long."

He gripped her upper arm and looked deeply into her eyes. "I won't be long, sweetheart. We still have things to discuss between us, after all."

He turned away as her heart gave a flutter. His look had been most intent, and she knew she had displeased him. By rights, she ought to be dreading the forthcoming discussion, but she felt no dread at all.

Hoping he would make her excuses to Joanna, she hurried to join Peg and Lucas, telling them as she did that Hugh had said they were all to go upstairs. She said no more until they had reached the chamber she and Hugh shared.

"I mean to retire now," she said to Lucas at the door.

"Aye, sure, m'lady. I'll just set 'ere on the landing and wait for t' laird."

Aside from pale ambient moonlight through the unshuttered window, the room was dark. As Peg moved to stir embers on the hearth to life and light a taper, Jenny watched her shadowy figure silently. Not until she had set the lighted taper upright in its dish did Jenny say quietly, "Did you see the items Tam Inglis showed us at the end, Peg—the gold bracelet and pearl earrings that no one claimed?"

Deep color flooded Peg's face, but she said, "Aye, I saw them. And what I'm to do about them now, mistress, I dinna ken."

Knowing Peg had learned some legerdemain, Jenny had suspected something of the sort but felt nonetheless dismayed. "Whose things are they?" she demanded.

"Cath's."

"You took jewelry from Cath?"

"Aye, sure," Peg said. "I told ye how she and them had been teaching me their tricks. When I were wi' her today, afore ye came, I lifted them things. Then, as excited as I were to see ye when ye arrived, I forgot I still had them."

"Surely, you could have given them back tonight."

"Nay, then, how could I? We was hurrying to get ye ready. Then Sir Hugh told Lucas to keep his eyes open, and Lucas told me to keep me eye on ye. I couldna go near Cath. It were just as well later that I *did* have that wee pouch, too."

"So you did put it in Drogo's boot!"

"Aye," Peg said. "To do summat like taking his dirk, ye ha' to put summat in its place, or he'd soon feel the lack o' his weapon in his boot. I still had the wee pouch up me sleeve, so it were easy enough to slip it in as I slipped the dirk out."

"But how could you have forgotten something that was in your sleeve?"

"Sakes, mistress, them things was light, nobbut brass, beads, and string. Cath wears dunamany o' them brace-lets, and I just slipped one off whilst I were helping her change her dress afore ye came. The ear-bobs, being on strings, was gey easy, too, and I keep a pouch up me sleeve most times, so I won't lose aught I take. We all practice so, to see if we can take from each other without getting caught."

"Well, if you're going to serve me at Thornhill, you'd best not do it anymore," Jenny said with a chuckle. "I doubt Sir Hugh would approve."

Chapter 21

Peg grimaced. "I do ken the difference between stealing and legerdemain, m'lady. What I dinna ken is how to get Cath's things back to her now that his lordship has them."

"As they are only trifles, I think we'll just tell her what you did," Jenny said. "After everything else that has happened, I doubt that Cath will weep for their loss. Now, fetch out a robe for me. I mean to wait until Sir Hugh returns to get in bed."

Peg gave her a sympathetic look, quickly found her most becoming robe, and helped her change. As the maidservant put away the things Jenny had worn to supper, Jenny listened intently for Hugh's step on the stairs.

In the private chamber to which he had taken the Joculator, Hugh said, "I'm very sorry about your son, sir. But I want to encourage you to be frank in answering Archie's questions when you talk. He is *not* a man with whom it is safe to trifle."

The Joculator said, "I am a wise fool, not a daft one, Hugo. And I care about my people as much as or more than you care about yours or her ladyship about hers."

"Sakes, have you known all along who we are?"

"Nay, not until tonight," he replied with a slight, rather enigmatic smile. "I didna realize who our Jenny was until I recognized ye, which I did when I saw ye on the dais here, having seen ye on one before, at Annan House. I didna ken at the time who ye were, though. Had I known, as I do now, that ye were her betrothed's elder brother, mayhap we'd not ha' done what we did. But believing ye were a fine troubadour who loved so bonnie a lass, and that she cared for ye, it would ha' shamed us not to do all we could to see ye safely wed. I'm right sorry, though, if we created a muddle for ye, as I fear we did."

"I'll not complain about that now," Hugh said. "I would like you to answer a couple of lingering questions though, if you will oblige me."

"If I can, I will," he agreed.

"First, as to exactly what happened tonight . . ." Hugh began.

After hearing the Joculator out and agreeing that Archie would be satisfied with his explanation, even amused by it, Hugh lingered only long enough to bid him goodnight before hurrying upstairs to his own bedchamber.

Finding Lucas on the landing, he ordered him to bed. "I'll see to myself tonight," he added. "But wake us early, for I want to be away as soon as may be."

"Away, sir?"

"Aye, we're for Thornhill, Lucas. I'm taking my lady home, so sleep fast." Opening the door, he stepped into the chamber, where he saw Peg sitting quietly by the fire and Jenny on the bed. "Goodnight, Peg," he said pointedly.

"Goodnight, sir," she said, bobbing a hasty curtsy and scurrying out.

He waited until she had shut the door and then went to Jenny.

She stood to face him as he neared the bed. "Did he explain it all?"

"Aye, most of it," Hugh said. "Enough to satisfy Archie, at all events. Did you realize that the minstrels had set Bowyer and his man up to look like thieves?"

"I was sure of it when they found those jewels on Drogo," she said.

"I, too," Hugh said. "I suspect hearing how they did it will amuse Archie."

Jenny looked at his chest and said, "I doubt that anything I might say in my defense will amuse you, sir. But I expect you want explanations from me, as well."

"Look at me," he said. When she did, he pulled her close, put his arms around her, and muttered hoarsely, "I've wanted to hold you since you touched my cheek on the stairs, Jenny-love. If you ever give me such a fright again, I swear I'll—"

"Kiss me, Hugo," she said, her warm breath tickling his chin.

He obeyed without comment, holding her tightly and thus able to let go of all lingering remnants of the tension his earlier fears for her safety had built in him.

Plunging his tongue into her mouth, he ravaged its interior, and when she responded eagerly, he relaxed his embrace and began to let his hands enjoy the softness of her silken robe and her curvaceous body beneath it.

Before long, though, his own body began making demands of him that urged him to a faster pace. Stripping the robe from her to discover that she wore no shift underneath it, he laid her on the bed and began to strip himself of his clothing.

But his disobedient wife did not stay where he had put her. Instead, she popped up again and slid from the bed to assist him. Unlacing his nether hose, her fingers alone nearly undid him. Grabbing her hand, he held it while he unlaced himself. "Now you may pull them off, sweetheart," he said.

"Yes, my lord," she replied, peeping up at him through her lashes.

Encouraged, he exerted patience while she tugged and finally managed to get them off him. Then, pulling her up again, he unlaced his shirt and ducked so she could pull it off over his head. Catching her up in his arms again, he threw back the covers, put her into bed, and followed her. When she turned to him, he pinned her beneath him, kissing her again, forcing himself to move more slowly than instinct demanded, moving his lips over her body to her breasts and belly, then lower.

When he came to the fork of her legs and touched her there with his lips and then his tongue, she gasped.

"Do you like that?" he murmured.

"Aye, but—"

"Then enjoy it, sweetheart, as I mean to do."

"Yes, my lord," she said, relaxing.

He teased her and enticed her until she was moaning and then crying out for him, and then he took her strongly, letting instinct take over, his passions soaring with his possession of her and his overwhelming awareness of the great good fortune he had had in finding his bonnie Jenny.

Delighting in all the sensations Hugh stirred in her, Jenny soared with him, higher and higher, the sensations intensifying until she was sure she could bear no more. But they continued to grow stronger until they finally peaked in one that pulsed through her long after Hugh let himself collapse atop her.

"Ah, sweetheart," he said when he could speak again, "I never knew what love could be before I found you."

"I love you, too," she murmured as she eased out from under him. "Does this mean you are no longer furious with me?"

He sighed and kissed her neck, sending new thrills through a body she had thought must be exhausted. "I warned you that I have a temper," he said. "I warrant you'll see more of it in the years we have ahead of us, but I have also come to see that although you can be impulsive, you are sensible and smart."

"And I was right to suspect a plot against Archie," she said.

"You were," he said, as he pulled the covers up over them. Drawing her closer until she put her head on his shoulder, he added, "You did do a few things you'd be wise not to do again, but I'll not belabor that fact."

Believing almost any reply she might make to that

statement would be unwise, she said, "Did he chance to explain the jewels taken from Annan House?"

"Aye, mostly. He blamed all the thefts on the two Englishmen, but he did not quite persuade me that they deserve all the blame. For example, he was a bit glib about Cuddy's actions. He admitted that Cuddy *retrieved* the jewels stolen from Annan House, but that would suggest he struck down the knacker Parland Dow."

"But how would he know Dow had the jewels?" Jenny asked.

"Apparently, Cuddy told the Joculator that *Drogo* saw the guards searching nearly everyone who left and slipped the jewels under one of Dow's sumpter packs because *Bowyer* had told him that Dow had first-head privileges."

"Good sakes," Jenny said. "And Reid told Bowyer about that!"

"Aye," Hugh agreed. "I'm thinking that Reid needs to join Archie's service for a time if only to develop better sense than to repeat such stuff to strangers. In any event, the Joculator passed rather swiftly over how Cuddy could have known about Drogo, Bowyer, and the sumpter packs had he not been party to it all."

"I expect he was," Jenny said, snuggling closer. "I think Cuddy was the traveler who returned the jewels, too. When I met him with Cath the next morning, she was scolding, saying she had fidgeted all night, wondering where he'd gone."

"As I said, lass, the Joculator explained only most of it. He's gey shrewd, and shows himself and his fellow minstrels in the best light whenever he can."

"Will you really make Reid join Archie's service?"

"I'll strongly recommend it," Hugh said. "I doubt if he

knew what Phaeline and your uncle did with those settlements. He seemed stunned when I confronted them, and
his attitude was gey different at Threave. Knowing Phaeline, I'd wager she kept him in the dark and just promised
that you'd bring him wealth and a title."

"Does Phaeline tell actual lies, Hugo?"

It was a moment before he said, "I don't know about
now. She did lie when we were children if she thought she
could get away with it. Why do you ask?"

"Because I think she is lying about being pregnant,"
Jenny said. "Peg and Sadie think so, and they are in a
position to know. Also, there is the matter of her pearls.
They never turned up, but Sadie said she found three
pearls on the floor. Phaeline slapped her when she asked
if they were not part of the missing string."

"I see, but now that you've mentioned her pearls, was
there not something else that went missing then?" he
asked.

"Lady Johnstone's necklace, but she found it herself
where she had left it."

"Well, I think we'll let Phaeline worry about her own
lies, sweetheart. We're going to leave for Thornhill in the
morning."

"But I've never seen a tournament. And you promised
to explain it all to me."

"My head still aches," he said. "If I stay—"

"Do you really expect me to believe, sir, after all that
has happened today, that you would let a headache prevent you from attending a tournament?"

"Recall that Archie expected me to take part in it."

"Then tell *him* you have a headache."

"I want you all to myself for a time, Jenny-love," he said quietly.

"Aye, that *is* a better reason," she agreed. "Moreover, we have not yet signed our own marriage settlements. But mayhap we do not need any."

"We must draw something up to protect our estates," he said. "But we will talk it all out first, and agree, before we sign anything."

"And you won't issue orders to me anymore?"

He was silent.

"Just as I thought," she said, nestling closer to him.

"I'll agree not to issue orders if you will agree to obey when I ask you to."

She was silent.

"Just as *I* thought," he said, leaning up on an elbow to look down at her. "How, by the way, did that wee pouch of jewelry end up in that villain's boot?"

Jenny told him, and when he chuckled, she reached to touch his face.

"Do you know what it does to me when you touch me like that?"

"Aye," she said with a smile, stroking his cheek. Then she shifted her hand lower—to his chest, to his belly, then lower yet.

"Kiss me there," he murmured.

"Yes, my lord," she said meekly, and bent to the task.

"Now, take me in your mouth, Jenny-love."

"Yes, my lord." And she did.

"By the Rood," he said, "this promises well for an excellent future."

And it did.

Dear Reader,

I hope you enjoyed the tale of Bonnie Jenny. For those who like to know who was real and who was not, Jenny, Hugh, and Reid are fictional kinsmen of the real Dunwythie family of Annandale, which included Lord Dunwythie, Phaeline, Mairi, and Fiona. Sheriff Maxwell was also real. And, of course, Archie the Grim was Lord of Galloway and later became third Earl of Douglas.

The English continued to occupy Lochmaben Castle for another ten years before Archie the Grim collected a formidable force and finally drove them out of Annandale. During their long occupation, despite the efforts of Annandale's residents, they wasted much of the land and destroyed surrounding forests.

Female minstrels were common from ancient days, particularly as gleemaidens, musicians, and dancers.

Employing minstrels as spies dates back to the Saxons and to early Danish gleemen that followed armies in time of war and had access to both camps. King Alfred once assumed the character of a gleeman to enter a Danish camp, where he "made such observations as were of infinite service." Others repeated this stratagem with equal success from that time forward.

For those interested in old coinage, the silver groat Sir Hugh won from Lucas was worth four pence. Scottish pennies were silver until the eighteenth century and were called sterlings. In 1357, Scotland struck its first gold coin, the noble. It was worth half a merk (or mark), which equaled two-thirds of a pound of sterlings. So, if you've ever wondered where the British term "pound sterling" comes from . . .

Special licenses were obtainable from the Church by the early fourteenth century—for people who had lots of money or influence. Then, as now, such licenses allowed a couple to be married anywhere, at any time, without the formality of announcing it beforehand.

The correct spelling of Annan (river and town) long before 1374 and for many years afterward was "Annand," from the French family that settled there. I chose to spell it the modern way to avoid confusion.

Devorgilla's bridge had nine arches in 1374. It now has only six.

Once again I am indebted to friend Donal MacRae for his invaluable assistance—this time, even more than usual, because Donal discovered the basis for this and the two forthcoming books in the trilogy in a sixteenth-century manuscript detailing events of fourteenth-century Galloway and Dumfriesshire.

My primary sources for Douglas history include *A History of the House of Douglas,* Vol. I, by the Right Hon. Sir Herbert Maxwell (London, 1902) and *The Black Douglases* by Michael Brown (Scotland, 1998).

Sources for the minstrels include *Sports and Pastimes of the People of England* by Joseph Strutt (London, 1903) and *Fools and Jesters of the English Court* by John Southworth (Gloucestershire, 1998).

As always, I'd like to thank my wonderful agents, Lucy Childs and Aaron Priest, my terrific editor Frances Jalet-Miller, master copyeditor Sean Devlin, Art Director

Diane Luger, Senior Editor and Editorial Director Amy Pierpont, Vice President and Editor in Chief, Beth de Guzman, and everyone else at Hachette Book Group's Grand Central Publishing who contributed to making this book what it is.

If you enjoyed *Tamed by a Laird*, please look for its sequel, *Seduced by a Rogue,* at your favorite bookstore in January 2010. In the meantime, *Suas Alba!*

Sincerely,

Amanda Scott

http://home.att.net/~amandascott

Don't miss Amanda Scott's
next captivating
Scottish romance!

Please turn this page for a
preview of her next novel

Seduced by a Rogue

Available in mass market
January 2010.

Chapter 1

Annandale, Southwestern Scotland, 1375

What if Dunwythie has *not* gone away?" Will Jardine asked, peering through newly green foliage toward the large green field that surrounding shrubbery and trees sheltered from winds blowing off Solway Firth. "What if he catches us here?"

"He won't," twenty-five-year-old Robert Maxwell, Laird of Trailinghail, said impatiently as they dismounted in the dense woodland. The large, well-tended field was Rob's first objective on that chilly spring morning, but he had others as well, because Dunwythie's lands sprawled at least four square miles, from the river Annan just west of them to Dryfe Water in the east. And much of it was rich land for crops.

"I told you," Rob said. "My lads saw his lordship ride off northward along the river earlier this morning." Sternly controlling a temper reactive to even mild opposition, he looped his reins around a handy branch as he added, "He will be away at least until midday, Will. Moreover, we have every right to be here."

The younger man's eyebrows shot upward. "Have we now?" he said dryly. "Most Annandale folk would dispute that statement, including me own da, were ye daft enough to put these impertinent demands o' your brother's to *him*."

"Need I remind you that my brother Alex is the sheriff, just as our father and grandfather were before him?" Rob said gruffly, scanning the field and noting with satisfaction that a dozen or so workers were busy there, hoeing and pulling weeds. "Sheriffs have duties, my lad, just as every landowner does."

"They do, aye," Will agreed. "However, folks dinna call your brother Sheriff o' Dumfries*shire* but only Sheriff o' Dumfries. They ha' good cause for that, too, as nae one here in Annandale answers to him."

"A sheriff, by the very definition of his position, commands the *whole* shire."

"Aye, sure," Will said, grinning. "Ye tell Dunwythie that, me lad. But dinna be trying it on me. The trouble between ye Maxwells and his lordship—aye, and wi' many another laird, too—has nowt to do wi' taxes and all to do wi' who wields the most power hereabouts, yon Sheriff o' Dumfries or a laird whose ancestors have owned Annandale land for centuries. That, as ye ken fine, be the nub o' the matter."

Unable to deny that statement, Rob kept silent, taking care not to trample any tender young shoots as they crossed the field toward the workers. It would not do to give the defiant Dunwythie good cause for further complaint.

"By God's troth," Will exclaimed moments later. "Will ye look at that now? What d'ye think can ha' brought the two o' *them* here?"

Rob had been watching where he put his feet as he led

the way between two rows of young plants. But at these words, he looked up and followed Will's gaze.

Emerging from woods to the north onto what he now discerned to be a narrow path down the center of the field were two females on horseback.

Although the two were at least a quarter mile away, their gowns, fur-lined cloaks, and simple white veils proclaimed them noblewomen, and their figures and supple dexterity with their mounts declared them youthful. One was so fair that her hair looked almost white, the other dark-haired, and both wore their long tresses in simple plaits. They were looking toward the field men, and Rob was certain that neither had yet realized that he and Will—in their plain breeks, jacks, and boots—were not simply two more of them.

Lingering wispy skirts of early-morning fog still drifted low near the river Annan as it roared along a mile or so downhill to Rob's left, and puffy white clouds floated overhead but did little to block the sunlight. It glistened on the still-dewy green field, and as the two riders drew nearer, it gilded the fair one's plaits.

"I'm glad I came with ye," Will murmured with a wicked gleam in his eyes.

"They are noblewomen, you young ruffian."

"Ay de mi, what noblewomen would be riding out and about by themselves like those two are?"

"Dunwythie's daughters would certainly do so on their father's land, a mile from his castle, amidst his own loyal workmen," Rob said. "Behave yourself."

"Hoots, I've nae wish to frighten them," Will retorted, chuckling.

Rob grimaced, knowing his friend's reputation with

women. Glancing back at the two riders, he saw that the fair one was frowning.

Clearly, she had realized that they were intruders.

"We'll go to meet them," he told Will. "And you *will* behave."

"Aye, sure. I'll be nobbut gey charming to such young beauties."

Rob sighed and altered his course to meet the two, hoping he could avoid trouble with Will. The Jardines being the Maxwells' only allies in Annandale, he could not afford to anger Jardine's eldest and best-favored son. But neither would he allow Will to make free and easy with Dunwythie's daughters.

⌒

"Who are they?" the lady Fiona Dunwythie asked, pushing a dark curl away from one long-lashed blue eye to tuck it back under her veil.

"I don't know them," nineteen-year-old Mairi Dunwythie replied. Wishing, not for the first time, that she knew more about the people living in this part of Annandale, near her father's largest estate, she added, "They stride toward us like men who know their worth."

"Then where are their horses?" Fiona demanded. "Men who know their worth rarely walk far."

"I suppose they left them in the woods," Mairi said. "Mayhap they just want to ask how they can safely cross our land without damaging the young barley."

"If they came through those woods, they'll have come from the south," Fiona said thoughtfully. "I wonder if they are Jardines."

The possibility that the two strangers might be members of that obstreperous family had already crossed Mairi's mind. But, although she had been born at Dunwythie Hall, she knew few of their neighbors by sight. Her mother had died at Mairi's birth, and her father's second wife, on learning of nearly continuous warfare between the Jardines south of them and the Johnstones to the north, had demanded that her lord husband remove at once to the house at Annan that had been part of her marriage tocher, or dowry.

At the time, the lady Phaeline had been pregnant with Fiona, so her lord had readily complied. Thus Fiona had been born at Annan House, at the mouth of the river for which Annandale was named, and Mairi had lived there from the age of four with only infrequent visits upriver to Dunwythie Hall.

Nevertheless, she knew enough to realize that if the two men were Jardines, her father would expect her to welcome them, albeit with no more than cool civility.

Discerning eagerness in the way Fiona now sat her pony, Mairi said in her usual quiet way, "Prithee, dearling, do not be making much of these men. If they *are* Jardines, our lord father would not want us to encourage more such visits."

Tossing her head, Fiona said, "Certes, Father would not want us to be discourteous either, and they are both *very* handsome men."

Mairi had noted that fact as well. Although they did not look as if they were kin to each other, both were large, dark-haired men with well-formed features. The one in the lead was narrow through hips and waist, had powerful-looking thighs and shoulders, and sat taller than his companion. He also looked five or six years older and displayed a demeanor that suggested he was accustomed to doing as he pleased.

His leather breeks and boots had been worn often enough to mold themselves snugly to his body, but the shirt that showed beneath his dark green jack was snowy white, and as they drew nearer, she noted that his boots were of expensive tanned leather, not rawhide. He also wore a fan brooch of three short reddish-brown feathers pinned with a small but brightly sparkling emerald in the soft folds of his hat.

The younger man had gleaming black hair, a lankier body, and looked about Mairi's own age. He was looking at Fiona, and Mairi did not like the expression in his eyes, thinking it resembled that of a hawk eyeing a tasty-looking rabbit.

Fiona, clearly oblivious to the predatory look, was smiling flirtatiously enough to make her sister want to scold her for it. But Mairi held her tongue and shifted her gaze back to the two visitors, almost near enough now to converse.

"Well met, my ladies," the younger one said carelessly. "But what are two such lovely lasses doing, riding amongst these rough field men?"

Stiffening but without looking away, Mairi put a hand out to silence Fiona and noted, as she did, that at the same time, the other man clamped a hand to the brash one's shoulder. Her own gesture failed in its aim, however, for Fiona said pertly to the younger one, "But who are *you*, sir, to address us so discourteously? And *what* are you doing in our field?"

"Pray, forgive him, my lady," the taller man said, looking at Mairi with eyes so clear and pale a blue that she could almost see her reflection in them. His voice was deep and of a nature to send strange sensations through her body, as if its gentle vibrations touched nerve endings all through her.

"In troth," he added, still looking into her eyes, "I must beg you to forgive us both. I am Robert Maxwell, and this unmannerly cub is Will Jardine of Applegarth. I believe you must be Lord Dunwythie's daughters, are you not?"

Mairi nodded, putting a light hand on Fiona's arm as she did, in the hope that actually touching her outspoken sister would silence her, for a time at least, and with a second, more likely hope that the fieldworkers would intervene if either of the two visitors became difficult. For a wonder, Fiona kept silent, mayhap feeling as captivated by the man's low, purring voice as Mairi did.

Robert Maxwell said nothing further though, and Mairi realized that despite the unusual circumstances and what surely must seem to him to be scant protection for two young women, he expected her to speak to him. Gathering her wits, she said, "You must know that you are on my father's land, sir. Have you good cause to be?"

"I have excellent cause, my lady. I am Sheriff Alexander Maxwell's brother, and I am here today as his sheriff-substitute."

"To what purpose, sir?" Mairi asked, although she thought she could guess.

"Why, merely to determine the exact amount your lord father owes the Crown in taxes this year," he said. "Sithee, one determines the figure by the number of people on the estate as well as its exact size and crop yield."

Mairi knew that. Her father had been teaching her— and Fiona, too—as much as he could about running his estates, in the event that his lady wife should fail to give him a son to inherit them. Phaeline had been pregnant numerous times in their sixteen-year marriage, but so far she had produced only Fiona. Dunwythie had long agreed with his lady that in due time God would grant them a son. But, at last, urged by Phaeline's own brother, his lordship had decided to teach his daughters what they would need to know if one of them should inherit his estates.

To that end, he had brought them to Dunwythie Hall a sennight before to observe the progress of his early plant- ings, the estate's crops being a primary source of his lord- ship's wealth in an area where few men had any wealth at all.

Despite her recently acquired knowledge, Mairi was reluctant to cross words with the sheriff's brother. Just meeting that magnetic gaze of his made her feel precari- ously vulnerable, as if without effort he had melted her customary defenses.

As Mairi sought words to explain that the two men must await her father's return and deal directly with his lordship, without offending Robert Maxwell or rendering herself more vulnerable yet, Fiona said, "Surely, the two of you should not be prowling about here for *any* reason without my lord father's permission."

"Did ye no hear him, lass?" William Jardine said, leer- ing. "He acts for the sheriff. And the sheriff, as even such a pretty lass must know, has vast powers."

Tossing her head again but managing, Mairi noted, to flutter her eyelashes at the same time, Fiona said, "Even so, William Jardine, that does not explain what right *you* have to trespass on our land."

"Why, I go where I please, lassie! And I'm thinking

that I may soon give your wee, beauteous self gey good cause to ken me fine."

"Enough, Will," his companion said as he continued to meet Mairi's steady gaze but with a rueful look now in his distractingly clear eyes.

Despite her strong certainty that he would soon clash with her father, Mairi's heart beat faster and heat from deep within warmed her cheeks.

Then the man smiled, revealing strong, even, white teeth. His eyes twinkled, too, as if he sensed the inexplicable attraction to him that she felt. Was he as arrogant and sure of himself, then, as his friend Will Jardine?

As he noted her slowly reddening cheeks and a certain quizzical look in her gray eyes, Rob was conscious of an immediate, unusually strong awareness of an emotion that he could not readily identify.

She looked small and fragile as she sat there on her pony, and so extraordinarily fair that the light dusting of freckles across her nose and cheeks seemed out of place, as if she had been more often in the sun than usual. But as he gazed into her eyes, he sensed serenity and an inner strength that warned him to tread lightly and made him glad he had made an effort to silence the impudent Will.

She seemed strangely familiar. He felt as if he knew exactly how she would move, what she might say next, and as if he recognized the soft, throaty nature of her voice and even the confident way she held her reins in her smoothly gloved hands.

It was almost as if he had thought of her often before,

despite never having met her. As he stood thus transfixed, he realized abruptly that he was smiling. In fact, he was grinning like a fool, as if he were delighted to be meeting her at last.

Such a notion being plain daft, he tried to dismiss it and noted only then that her light blushes had deepened to painful-looking red and spread right to the roots of her hair. He had stared her ladyship right out of countenance!

Aware that reason might now exist, other than his command, for Will's continued silence, Rob avoided looking at him and strove to keep his voice steady as he said, "In my concern for the lad's rudeness, my lady, I fear I have forgotten the path our conversation had taken. Mayhap you can aid me."

"You were attempting to explain how one determines what taxes a man owes," she said quietly. "You are kind to do so, but as we are only women"—he noted that the younger lass shot her an astonished look—"you would be much wiser and doubtless accomplish more by explaining yourself to our lord father, sir."

He would speak to Dunwythie later, but for now he smiled at her again, ignoring instinct that warned him he might be making a mistake to press her. "Surely your father has mentioned the size of this estate," he said matter-of-factly. "Most men talk often of such things."

"Not to their womenfolk, sir. In troth, I doubt you would take my word for its size if I *could* tell you. My father will be away until this afternoon, but doubtless he will tell you all you want to know when he returns. Come now, dearling," she said with a glance at her sister and a nudge of her heel and twitch of her rein for her mount. "It is time we returned to the Hall."

Rob did not try to persuade her to linger but watched the two of them until they vanished into the woods.

"Sakes, my lad, ha' ye lost your wits? Ye stared at yon lass like right dafty."

"Unless you want me to teach you some manners, Will Jardine, you'll keep a still tongue in your head until you can say something worth hearing," Rob growled.

"Och, aye, I'm mute," Will said hastily, his eyes on Rob's hands.

Realizing that one of them had formed itself into a tight fist, Rob drew a breath, let it out slowly, and relaxed his hand.

"Aye, that's gey better, that is," Will said with audible relief. "What do we do now?"

"We look at the other fields, of course," Rob said, fighting a strong urge to glance again at the place where the women had disappeared into the woods.

What on earth was amiss with him, he wondered, that he could allow one young female to affect him so? One thing was certain, though. He must put the lass well out of his mind. To react in any other way, especially in view of Dunwythie's defiance of the sheriff's earlier demands, could lead only to trouble.

⸺◦

"I do *not* think we ought to have left without telling our men to see those two off our property," Fiona said abruptly.

Grateful that her sister had at least waited until they were well beyond earshot of their disturbing visitors,

Mairi forced the powerful image of the truly disturbing one from her mind as she eyed Fiona gravely.

When the image threatened to return, Mairi said quickly and more firmly than she had intended, "You flirted dreadfully with Jardine, Fiona. Do not think I missed that. You know Father does not want us to have aught to do with that family."

"Pish tush," Fiona said without a hint of remorse. "I do not understand how anyone can imagine that such a handsome, charming gentleman can be other than a friend to us."

"He may be handsome, but he was not charming," Mairi countered. "He was cheeky and disrespectful, and he behaved as if he thought he had every right to treat you so. Truly, dearest, you should never respond as you did to such behavior."

"Well, you are a fine one to speak, after blushing as you did at every word Robert Maxwell said to you."

"I did no such thing," Mairi said, devoutly hoping that she spoke the truth. She could not deny that she had responded in a most unusual way to the man. Even now, his powerful image intruded. Remembering his apparent inability to recall his own words to her, she nearly smiled. But catching Fiona's shrewd gaze on her, she added, "If I did, I will not do so again. The Maxwells and Jardines are no friends of ours, Fiona. That is what we must both remember."

"I think we should make them our friends," Fiona said tartly. "Surely, making friends is better than remaining enemies."

"It is not so much a matter of being enemies," Mairi reminded her. "Prithee, recall what our father told us, that the difficulties have accrued over many years' time, from the days of Annandale's own Robert the Bruce when the Maxwells and Jardines sided with his greatest enemy and that of the rest of us here in Annandale."

"Pooh," Fiona said. "That's just history and too long ago to matter to anyone. This is now, Mairi, and Will Jardine is one of the handsomest men I have ever seen. In troth, you have gone so long without an offer from a single eligible suitor that I should think you'd welcome the attentions of a man like Robert Maxwell. To be sure, he is old . . . at least five-and-twenty . . . and not nearly as fine-looking a man as Will Jardine, but you are only six years younger, and he *is* handsome. Moreover, you cannot deny that he intrigued you . . . in some way, at least."

Mairi could not deny that she had felt a strong attraction to the man, so she did not try. Instead, repressively, she said, "Robert Maxwell's brother is the man so clearly abusing the power of his office in his attempt to extort money from the lairds of Annandale. We are well outside his Dumfries jurisdiction, Fiona. And as your handsome friend Jardine is clearly abetting them, we have naught to discuss."

Fiona gave her a speaking look but said nothing further.

Sakes, Mairi thought as the image of Robert Maxwell filled her mind again, but the man had been much too sure of himself in a place he had no right to be.

Even so, Dunwythie would certainly send him on his way, and after he did, she would never clap eyes on Maxwell again. That thought, although it failed to cheer her, told her she was quite right in deciding to forget him.